Tainted

Monica Shantel

tainted

monica shantel

Tainted

ISBN 978-1-960696-04-5 (Paperback) ISBN 978-1-960696-05-2 (Hardcover)

Book Cover by Monica Shantel

Illustrations by Monica Shantel

First Edition

To the women who were told it was their fault for being a victim.
And to all the men who listened to us when we needed them to.

8/7/23

Mya Simons

8/9/23
"Eli Kay"

8/13/23
"Cliff Scene"

001 Sunday, August 25th

Blood tainted the white of my dress as my screams echoed into the sky. As I lifted my eyes to meet the face behind the murder, almond-colored eyes burned into my soul.

"Mya?" a female asked.

I came out of my head and glanced at my hands, loosening the tight grip on my other wrist. It left behind nail imprints. "I'm sorry."

"You all right?"

"I'm fine," I whispered.

These scenes came unannounced and yet they felt too real. I could decipher dreams from reality, but this was a gray area. These glimpses could be from anywhere and a small part of me gnawed at the idea that it could be a memory my brain attempted to bury for good. For now, I called them nightmares.

"Your eyes are doing that weird thing again. They're turning almost white," she said.

They'd been doing it a lot lately. I wasn't sure why, but Juliet made it clear it creeped her the hell out.

"I'm *fine*," I repeated.

Juliet looked my way and gave me a reassuring smile. Her boyfriend was holding her in his lap. He'd always be able to capture her attention so easily.

All of her features lit up as if she didn't have a care in the world. With him present, she never did. Although she cared too much when I crushed on a guy because she would make it her priority to find out what was wrong with him. She wanted to protect me before I got my heart ripped apart. I must not have cared the same way for letting her date Cole for so long.

They were looking my way, staring a little too intently. I assumed they were giving me a look that they had wanted to be alone for more private matters. With that knowledge, I stood up. "I guess I will go off somewhere on my own." I needed an excuse to escape. "I'll be around, Jules." I gave her a nod before slipping on my shoes and heading out. The fresh air would give me time to think.

As I walked towards the shopping center, I scanned the area and my eyes landed on someone who popped. He stood among the crowd, yet his eyes were glued to me. Did he know me?

I hurried into a shop, losing him as soon as I had found him. I wasn't intending to buy much of anything at all, but it gave me an excuse to get out of the apartment.

A pair of eyes watched me from somewhere, and when I turned my head to find where they were, I came up empty. I wasn't crazy. Something in my gut told me that someone took an interest in me. *Too* much of an interest—the kind that ended in bloodshed.

"Excuse me—" I turned back to whoever wanted my attention, ready to lay it on them. However, she was just a woman asking me to move. She backed away, saying, "I'm sorry. I didn't mean to frighten you. I just wanted to grab something off the shelf behind you."

I scooted out of her way. "That's my fault. Sorry." I'd been on edge lately after *his* death, and I wasn't about to drop this bomb on a stranger.

She grabbed the item off the shelf and put it in her basket. She had to be around my age. She looked young, yet her face told me she had seen a lot of things in her day. She left without another word. Maybe my eyes freaked her out.

I shook my head and finished my shopping.

I left the store and yet still couldn't manage to shake off the feeling of someone following me. I walked down the street, stopping in my tracks at the sight of the same guy from earlier. *What was he doing?*

Part of me wanted to confront him but I knew that wasn't a good idea. I could be making it worse for myself if I angered him.

"Walk with me," the girl said beside me. I was startled by her sudden presence, but I trusted her more than the guy. She hadn't been the one stalking me after all.

Taking her advice, we left the shopping center and walked away. "Who was that guy? He was creeping me out," I said.

She shrugged her shoulders, but something told me she knew more than she was letting on. "I saw a woman who needed an easy escape."

While I wanted to say something I'd regret, I knew she was just trying to keep me out of trouble. I couldn't fault her for that. I'd always wished to be noticed but never the way that *man* was noticing me.

"I'm going to ask you to avoid that man, whatever you do. I have a job to complete here, and when that is done, I'll be taking a ride wherever it calls me," she said. "Just don't let him near you."

"What do you do?" I asked.

She gave me a look, one that had curiosity killing the cat. "I just help people." That was the end of that interview.

When I met her gaze, I noticed the confidence. She was radiating with courage that I wished I had. As much as I wanted to make friends, she made it clear she wasn't going to be around for much longer.

"Take care of yourself, okay?" She looked over at me. "There are bad people in this world who want to hurt you. I don't want to see you end up as their victim." Joys of being a woman, I supposed.

I pulled my bag closer to my body. "I'll do my best."

She spun on her heel and disappeared around a building.

Tomorrow, classes would begin. I'd begin my senior year, and everything would fall out of place all over again.

The weather was calm, the wind barely bringing in a breeze. The sky was blue without a cloud in sight. Plenty of people, including I, were walking in shorts and a tank top.

I sat down on a bench near the school building, sticking my earbuds in my ears. Someday I would live in *my own* apartment. I would have a room to hide in when mating season was passing through.

Eventually, it would be the time of year for every couple to get down and dirty. Something about the fall and winter got people into the mood more often than any other season. Most babies were born in July through October. I hoped Juliet wouldn't be one to end up in that situation with Cole.

Everyone seemed so happy, oblivious to all the evil going

on in the world around them.

It was natural for humans to focus on their own happiness while someone was screaming for help just a quarter of a mile away. I was one of those selfish humans.

I brushed my fingers through my hair and reapplied my red lipstick. The bolder, the better. They went well with my black hair and brought out the brown in my eyes.

A strong gust of wind sent my hair flying in my face, strands getting stuck to my lips. "Damn." I pulled them free, fixing the mess on my head.

When I scanned the area, I took notice of all the other people whose hair should have been whipping around from the wind. Why was it just me?

I checked the weather app to see the speed of the wind today, and it was barely 1mph. Where had the wind come from? Had someone been messing with me?

Laughing, I dismissed the idea.

No, of course not. Ghosts *didn't* exist.

But still, it came with no explanation. While it was interesting to think about, it wasn't something worth wasting my time on. I had better things to do, like focus on my next design. I was thinking of maybe going with an outfit that said hello to autumn. I changed my designs with the seasons, and that inspired me more.

In the distance, I saw the same man who'd been following me since the shopping center. Could I call the police and get a restraining order?

I couldn't sit around, knowing someone was stalking me. This put me in danger.

I dialed a non-emergency number, unsure if 9-1-1 was even appropriate for this. "Hi, yes, I'm calling to report...a stalker? Sorry. This man keeps following me around. I don't know who he is but it's scaring me and for all I know, he could be waiting to kill me." When I looked up to mention what he looked like, he was gone. "Oh, well, he, uh... He has dark hair and...a small tan." That was as far as my memory went.

Standing from my seat, I turned to go back to the apartment. "I'll have to take a picture of him the next time I see him. I'll let you know." I looked down at my phone as I pressed the end-call button.

Another person ran into me and my phone flew to the ground. Before I had a chance to dive for my phone, the asshole wrapped his fingers around my wrist and shoved me against the wall, covering my mouth. "Don't make a sound if you want to live."

Don't fight back? Don't defend myself?

I pushed him off me and started yelling out for my safety, but as I did, a few men stopped in front of the alleyway. "What's going on here?" one asked while stepping forward. "Scaring young women, are we?" He tilted his head as if the man beside me was a child being scolded for lying.

"Leave now, or you'll highly regret it," the man next to me said. His British accent stood out to me. We didn't get many people around here who were from the UK and hearing an accent in person was a whole other experience. It sounded out of place.

I lifted my eyes to meet the man who'd threatened me and thrown me against the wall. I wasn't blind to his appearance. He'd had God on his side when this man was created. Dark skin-tone, a curly mess of black hair on his head. Tall. The attractive ones were always the *deadliest.*

The men came charging and I jumped out of the way. Pressing my chest against the wall, I looked back to make sure nobody was coming straight for me.

My attacker took on the men alone, throwing the first one to the ground. The second came and he elbowed him in the face before sending a kick to the gut. The man flew against the wall but appeared unfazed as he wiped a stream of blood from his mouth. "That's how we play, huh?"

As he took a second chance at throwing the attacker to the ground, the attacker grabbed him by the hair and slammed him—back first—into the pavement. A groan escaped. Then his head was ripped off his body as if no amount of effort had been needed.

Gasping, I slid along the wall, out of their way and headed for the end of the alley, hoping to make it to the street where someone could see me.

Thumps, grunts, and screams spilled from the alley behind me. I turned back to see the amount of blood splattered across the walls and pooling on the cement. My attacker hadn't been just a criminal out to harm me. He was out for blood, and he'd manage to paint the alley with the blood of my saviors all on his own.

He was a murderer. Serial killer. I'd be next if I didn't run now.

He didn't look my way as he headed in the other direction, and I began to do the same. I was safe. *For now.*

When I turned my head to watch him walk away, he glanced back at me as well. The color of his eyes stood out, causing me to almost lose my footing. They were the exact color I'd seen earlier today in that nightmare of mine. I could never forget those *eyes.*

002 Monday, August 26th

Yesterday had been a shitshow and I was determined to make sure life didn't throw knives my way today, too. However it worked, I'd manifest a better day into existence.

Today was going to be a *good* first day.

All I had to go off of was the fresh haircut with my new bangs, but it was enough to give me confidence. Or it should have been enough...

After Owen's tragic accident, that was.

The first day in my class was long, but when it ended, I ran errands. I got home close to the midafternoon, but as I pulled into the apartment complex, I saw some asshole parked in my spot. Did this guy not realize that it was given to the person who paid rent in my apartment?

I parked in an uncovered spot a few spaces down, then walked over to the one in my spot. I pulled a pen and piece of paper from my bag, writing a note to the guy. Then, I placed it under his wiper blade. "This better get through to you," I mumbled.

"Get through to who?"

I glance to my right to see the man who must have owned this nice car. I looked away as soon as he saw me staring, lifting his eyebrow in question. He was the same man I'd run into yesterday, the one with the brown eyes.

Talk about small world.

I made the mistake of taking another peek at him to see if he was still looking at me. His brown eyes pierced my own, making mine widen as I looked down again. I let my hair fall around my face so it could hide the redness now heating my cheeks. Was this not what I wanted? He was out here so I could tell him to move, and yet I wasn't so sure I wanted him to know I existed. He was the one from the horrid dreams. More importantly, I'd watched him murder a group of guys.

It'd be easy to blame my shyness on the death of my last boyfriend, but that would be too easy.

This man wore black slacks with dress shoes, a buttoned plaid, and a blazer over it. He was dressed for a date, and I hoped she knew he killed for fun. Did he come from a wealthy family name? If so, it made sense. He gave off the vibe that he was the entitled murderer.

I didn't have any more time to finish my thoughts as he cleared his throat, revealing his thick accent by saying, "To avoid confusion, I live here. I'm not a visitor if that's what you were hoping for." I glanced at him to notice he wasn't looking in my direction. He was facing his car instead.

I snorted at his words and looked forward. Of course I'd assumed he didn't live here, because no man who did would park in someone else's spot. He had to have his own.

A small part of me still wanted to pick apart his words and argue with him anyway. The closer he got, the more noticeable his height became. He didn't get the short end of the stick.

He stepped forward and grabbed my note, glancing at it. "This is your spot? I've never seen you park in it." He stood with a casual and laid-back demeanor. He didn't have a care in the world, especially if he was parking wherever he pleased. His arms were crossed but not folded across each other. He had one on top of the other, both hands holding either side of his biceps.

"I've parked here plenty of times before. I have no idea why you assume nobody parked here. Even if so, you said you live here. You were assigned a spot and my spot is not it. This number is on our lease."

He shrugged and got in his car, rolling his windows down. "Could have fooled me."

I cleared my throat. "This is my spot. I'm letting you know now. I shouldn't see your car in it again."

"Get out of my way," he said, shifting into drive. "I have somewhere to be."

"Don't park here again." I crossed my arms, stepping out of his way. "Please."

The guy chuckled. "Well, since you used the magic word..." He pulled out and disappeared around the corner.

"Jerk," I mumbled. It came as no surprise that the man who was unable to park where he was assigned had no manners. He was an asshole. The psychology behind what made people give into the darkness was fascinating by all means. I wasn't about to chase him down for an answer, however.

So instead, I moved my car back into my spot.

I decided not to give him any more of my time as I made my way to the lockers and grabbed my mail. I hummed to myself as another girl passed me. She seemed familiar, but I couldn't be sure. I mean, everyone here seemed familiar, right? We all lived in the same apartment complex.

Shaking my head, I faced forward and made it back to my apartment.

Juliet wasn't home at the moment. I used that alone time to shower, then I decided to work on a few of my designs. "Damnit." I had left my notebook in my car. Taking my keys, I ran out to my car and scowled at the sight of a car pulling up in the spot beside me.

He was already back.

What really bothered me was him. He sat in his expensive car as if he owned this building, his arrogance radiating like the sun. Nothing would please me more than to crush his ego and show him who he was really dealing with. It was one thing to say I never parked in my spot but telling me to get out of the way without so much as a *please* or *thank you* in his words was another ballgame.

The look on his face at my arrival told me he wasn't happy about seeing me again. I crossed my arms as I leaned against my car. "Care to tell me why the hell you had to be so rude? No please? Thank you? You don't just get to tell someone to get out of the way, especially when you steal their spot." I wanted to add on: *and when you almost attack them at the end of the night.* But that would be too bold. Suicidal, even.

He finally gave me the appropriate reaction by looking at me. I deserved attention when I was talking to someone. There was one thing I hated, one thing that was my pet peeve. I hated people who ignored me when I was taking the time to waste my words on them. "You were too bloody slow. Maybe next time you shouldn't stand there like a stump."

This guy really got on my nerves. "Oh, so is asking someone to please move not allowed? I wasn't aware that it was banned from our vocabulary."

He formed a small smirk. "I only use my manners when I need to, and you are definitely not someone who scares me. I shouldn't have to ask you to do something you should already know how to do. Especially when I was giving you your spot back." He turned his attention back to his car and locked it.

I couldn't believe he was acting all high and mighty. The good-looking ones had the biggest egos. My hand was begging me to slap him right here and now, but it wasn't the right call. I wasn't afraid of him either.

I tried my best to ignore his irritable presence, but he made it so difficult when he went out of his way to not use basic human decency. It was like he did this on purpose and enjoyed getting a thrill out of pissing people off.

"You're an asshole, you know that?" I studied his reaction and came up with nothing. He was a master of disguising his real emotions.

A master who'd been *unreasonably* attractive.

I felt ashamed for even thinking such thoughts, and it made it much worse that his attractiveness painted him as a man with morals—given the freshly ironed dress pants paired with the white shirt. However, he was not that by any means.

Why couldn't his appearance match his personality?

He chuckled and shrugged his shoulders. "Did I ever claim I wasn't?"

His snarky remarks were what made him that much worse. An asshole who was perfectly fine with being one was the worst of them all. He would never change.

I shifted my gaze as an idea popped in my head. "You don't have much going for you and it'll be that much easier to pull you apart and study every piece inside. You might be an asshole, but I'm also a bitch." *Lies.* But I couldn't let him believe that.

Something about him sparked confidence in me I'd always been afraid to expose. Had he caused this, or was it something else? I had no idea how to explain it, but it was as if it were my *innate* desire to never give this guy my weakness, and I didn't even know his name.

Pushing off my door, I went back to my apartment. I assumed Juliet was going to visit Cole, for which I was grateful. I put my notebook down, breaking a pencil in the process. "Aghhh, I hate him! Why does he have to be such an asshole?"

I kicked off my heels and they landed at the foot of my bed as I fell onto it. I never wanted to see his face or hear his voice again. As I lifted my feet onto my bed, I scowled at nothing. "England, you're barking up the wrong tree and now this cat is about to let out her claws."

The day passed by agonizingly slow, and once night fell, I figured it was safe for me to go grab a few more things from my car. He couldn't be out there for a third time.

Just to be safe, I checked out the bedroom window but I didn't see him, so I went outside and started rummaging through the things in my car. Even with the light on, it was hard to see down on the floor in front of the back seats.

After finding what I needed, I stood and turned around as a soft cooing echoed in the trees. Could it be an owl? I'd only ever seen one in my life and it had been just a baby, but maybe I could find this one.

I followed the sidewalk and passed the entry to my front door. Instead, I went around the back way and looked up in the trees, searching.

Hoot. Hoot.

My eyes landed on a white owl and immediately I became mesmerized by its feathers. Was it normal for a white owl to be in this part of Arizona? It didn't seem likely. Had it gotten lost?

Footsteps echoed and I assumed it was another tenant coming home. Many people walked around here at night, and many worked late. At least that's what I told myself to keep from running into my *dark* home.

"Did you lose your family? Do you have a family? Do you need help getting home?" I asked the owl. It cooed as if responding, but of course I couldn't understand it. I stuck my arm out to see if it would come down, but the owl didn't move.

I wasn't an expert but I was certain white owls lived in areas where snow existed mostly year-round, and Arizona saw hardly any snow, if any, at all. It was too odd.

Too *spooky.*

"I'll leave you alone. But promise me you'll make it home safe. I don't want to find an owl who died of heat stroke tomorrow morning. Is that fair?" I hugged myself. The owl cooed once more.

As I walked towards him, the sound of glass shattering against cement filled the area around me. I spun around as fast as I could, but a rock that had been half buried in the ground laid behind me and caught my toe. Down I went into the grass, down into the empty pond of rocks, smacking my head against one. Things blurred out of focus. I couldn't quite grasp reality anymore, but I was more worried that the owl had led me to this. I didn't know how else to fight whoever wanted me dead. I couldn't will myself to move.

Twigs snapped and leaves crunched beneath my bare feet.

Everything around me was one giant blur as I sped up my pace, my feet pounding against the ground. My toes caught on a root a little far stretched, sending me to the dirt. Something hard hit my head—or my head hit something hard. The lightbulb of the world had been turned off and everything went pitch black.

A figure appeared above my head, saying words that came out muffled. They seemed frustrated as they bent down, waving a hand in front of my face. I could only blink. My brain didn't respond to movement.

I could barely make out what they said, "You're clumsy as fuck."

Lightness overtook my body as they scooped me up into their arms. Their chest wasn't curved—no boobs, telling me it was a male picking me up. He carried me as if I weighed nothing.

I was brought to a room, and from there he helped me. I wasn't allowed to sleep, which only made my situation worse. I wanted nothing more than to close my eyes and allow the black night to take me under its *wing*. For just a split second, I thought maybe they'd done it on purpose, but I knew I was simply crazy. Right?

Trying to focus became impossible, and so I allowed my brain to form whatever image it deemed fit. I just hadn't expected to see the same white owl perched on the tree outside the window. Its eyes reflected the color of almonds, and then it swooped down out of sight.

003 Tuesday, August 27th

It was sometime in the morning when I was able to focus, and when my senses weren't failing me anymore. I glanced at the clock and it read 4:32 AM.

The throbbing in my head was subsiding but the ice pack was still softening the blow. I assumed for the split second I was fully alert that I was in my own room. But I wasn't.

"You seem to be aware of your surroundings," I heard the voice behind me. I turned my head, instantly recognizing him. His English accent wasn't that hard to miss.

I narrowed my eyes. "Why the hell am I here?"

"Oh, you mean you don't remember falling outside and getting a concussion? You're lucky it wasn't worse. No blood, nothing else." He looked irritated by my existence, and it made me want to bite his head right off.

I glanced down at my attire, turning deep red when I realized what I had on were tiny pajama shorts and a basic T-shirt. Why was I embarrassed?

"I should probably get back to my apartment," I told him as I stood from his bed. I was a little surprised by how fast he blocked my way. I wasn't back to reality all the way, so I excused it as a hallucination. "Is there a reason you won't let me get away from you? You hate me, so now I'm simply confused." I folded my arms across my chest. My shirt tightened against me and as soon as I shifted my arms, my nipples became obvious.

Every inch of my body refused to move, and his eyes were getting an all-access pass to seeing the cat declawed. I begged my muscles to comply, to do anything to make him look away but my brain couldn't seem to comprehend.

He reached out and grabbed a blanket before straightening his posture. "I think you dropped this." He lifted the blanket behind me, stretching it out to full size and wrapping it around my shoulders. He had long legs, but his arms were not quite there, and he had to decrease a lot of space between us to get the cloth around me.

He pulled the blanket tight, folding it in on itself. "You should be more careful." Was he talking about my nipples or falling outside?

Nothing came to mind—my brain a vacant wasteland.

With our bodies practically squished together, I saw his height compared to mine. I was a whole head shorter than him. "You're not allowed to be alone. You still have a concussion and it's best if you don't go to your place, where your roommate is probably still sleeping. If you sleep, that only makes your situation far worse. I'm the only one capable of watching you," he said.

Maybe he's using that excuse because he secretly wants to be around you.

Was his hate just an act to hide that he had something for me? Was *my* hate just an act to hide my attraction to him?

Absolutely not. He'd killed people. He shoved me against

a wall.

Even if it was, that didn't make it okay. Girls grew up being taught that boys were rude because they liked us, as if conditioning us to believe we didn't deserve to be treated any better. I was a grown woman now, and I wasn't falling for the act.

However, I knew that wasn't the case. This man could never see me in such a way, and after the first impression he gave me, I didn't want to see him in such a way either.

I let out a sigh, knowing that he still had a point, and I wasn't going to win this. "What am I supposed to wear? These pajamas aren't going to suffice." He reached for something off his nightstand and handed it to me. I looked down, taking them into my own hands. They were my clothes, the one's I'd been wearing before I fell.

"I figured you'd be more comfortable in a T-shirt over a bra with a tightly fitted shirt."

Ripping the clothes from him, I scowled. "And you thought it was okay to change me?"

With a shrug, he said, "I didn't look. I'm an arsehole, not a pervert."

I didn't entirely believe him but it was his word that I asked for, so I'd have to take it regardless and hope he was telling the truth.

"Well, you need to go outside if I'm going to change." I gestured to the door.

He rolled his eyes in annoyance. "I just saw your nipples."

We both knew he was right. He had seen me. Still, I didn't consent entirely. "Do you want to see me naked?"

He opened his mouth to respond but he shook his head, dismissing the idea. He left his own room to give me a chance to get dressed.

I removed the blanket and changed my clothes quickly. They were a pair of black shorts paired with a white button-up.

I took a look around the small dorm before he decided to *grace* me with his presence. It wasn't what I had expected, and I wondered if he had any interests or hobbies. There were some pictures upon the white walls, pictures that were random and of no real connection to him. He liked only a few colors, such as black, white, gray, and some red. He didn't want to express himself much here. I found it quite peculiar.

He walked back in without any warning. I gave him a glare to which he ignored. "All right, there has to be some way to keep you awake for a few more hours until classes start." He looked around his room, almost as if he was just now noticing how boring and barren it was. Was it a lack of expression, or was he actually this dull and empty?

"I think something we could start off with to pass time is having you tell me why you're so bitter." Knowing he wouldn't answer, I came up with a new idea that he was sure to agree to. "Better yet, we could play twenty questions." I stood still, arms hanging at my sides. I could see hesitancy in his eyes before he agreed. I continued, "all right, so from my understanding, we each ask each other a total of ten questions." I dismissed anything else using my hand. "I've never actually been properly introduced to this game, so let's just go with that." I wanted to know *a little* about him.

His murderous tendencies. His lack of respect for women. His lack of respect for other tenants. And most definitely his massive ego that should have been kicked down a few notches.

"First question, what is your name?" I stared him in the

eyes.

He didn't move a muscle. "Eli Kay. What's yours?"

I had *expected* him to ask for mine. "Mya Simons. Why are you so rude to me?"

He shrugged like it wasn't anything serious. "You call people you don't know assholes and then block them when they try to return your parking space. You have no manners, Miss Simons. Why do you think it's okay to do that to a stranger?"

I felt a tinge of frustration. "The proper response would have been letting me know you're gonna move. Instead, you were trying so hard to keep a feud. Is an apology what you want to hear, Mr. Kay?" I was going to play this game right back.

He smirked just a tad. "Well, I won't be one to tell a fib and I do enjoy hearing you admit you're wrong. What is the excuse you want to hear from me?"

I thought for a moment before giving my final answer, "That it was a mistake and you're sorry for parking in my spot. Why don't you have a roommate?"

"Because I don't like people very much. I can't stand them, and a roommate isn't the best option for me. Why are you upset that I don't like you?" He lifted that perfect eyebrow of his, *still* smirking.

I couldn't hide the embarrassment in my cheeks if I tried. "I don't care. I just don't want to spend the rest of my year under someone who hates me over something so petty. Why did you help me by the pond if you don't like me?"

"Under? That is quite a view you've got. I'm not heartless, Simons. I won't just let you pass out and go into a coma; even I have to help those I'm not fond of. How do you honestly feel about the situation—in a way that it makes you angry that I was your hero, or you getting butterflies—you tell me?" His gaze never strayed from mine.

I swallowed, knowing I *had* to be honest. "It honestly confuses me. Why were you passing by at the time I fell?" What I *really* wanted to ask.

He glanced away for the first time since the questions began. "I was out late. I'm a night owl which leads to late night walks. I heard the glass shatter, and then I found you in the pond." His nose seemed to twitch as he answered the question. I was seeing right through his excuse.

Had Eli been behind the glass? If so, it was his fault, and now I had to wonder if it was done on purpose.

The bell rang as class started, and here I was once again. We spent the morning finishing questions, and it was just a simple game to get basic information from him. I had mainly used it to figure out what his problem with me was.

Well, now I knew.

I wondered if maybe this meant we could be friends, but I silently laughed to myself as I knew that was not at all what would happen. I didn't think we could ever be friends. I hated him too much, and I didn't need to make a habit of befriending killers.

While scribbling notes from the whiteboard before the professor cleared it, something strange wafted in my direction. The smell of wet dog. Once I'd caught it, the odor dissipated as if it had never been there in the first place. Maybe I *imagined* it.

The day went on as if nothing else mattered. After I was certain that Eli had gone to his apartment, I went to mine. Eli and I hadn't spoken a word since I left his place this morning. I thought it was better that way.

I was far too tired to begin to have a normal conversation with anyone.

I took off my clothes and switched them out for my silk pajamas. I laid back down and got comfortable in the blankets. I was ready to be swept away by dreams after spending the last thirty hours awake.

The door swung open and in walked my best friend who was singing at the top of her lungs. *So much for getting extra sleep.* She was beyond happy today and I assumed it had to do with Cole.

"What the hell is up with you?" I asked.

"What's up with me? I just got a call back from the job interview. They want to hire me." She squealed and sat onto my bed. This got a groan from me.

"That's good. I'm glad. Hey, uh, Jules, can..." I shooed her. She stood from my bed, giving me a look. I knew that look. She was trying to guilt-trip me. It wasn't happening today. I was running on no sleep. I was no longer Mya. "I haven't slept in thirty hours. I'm going to bed early today. I need it." I turned my body away from her as I snuggled into the blankets.

Only a few pieces of furniture stood in my room. My bed, a desk littered with some makeup, many sketches, and sewing supplies, and a TV stand. I didn't use it all the much these days.

I found it was easy to keep little belongings when you didn't know where life would take you. After losing Owen and growing up wondering if my father would ever come home to love me, I was more focused on relationships rather than too much stuff.

"Why haven't you slept?" The question I didn't want to hear came from her lips.

Letting out a sigh, I turned over. "I slipped outside last night and had to stay up all night due to a concussion." I told Juliet everything so I saw no point in keeping this from her.

"How did you keep yourself awake?" More questions.

"I didn't." Eli had made sure that I didn't die and while it would appear as sweet, it was anything but. It was a night I wouldn't forget and that was only because he saw me at my most vulnerable. Exactly what I didn't want.

A pencil hit the side of my face. "Who did?"

I looked over at her and gave her a look. "Hit me with a pencil again and I will snap your favorite pen," I threatened in a playful way. "His name is Eli, but don't be fooled. I hate him."

She leaned against her pillows. "Why is that?"

"He's the upstairs neighbor." Surely she heard him dropping heavy objects in the middle of the night and early morning.

I shook my head as I began to drift off.

"I didn't realize we had an upstairs neighbor. I never see him, and he's so quiet. Hardly noticed he's there." She laughed a bit.

My eyes gave out. "He's definitely there all right." My consciousness was quick to follow.

I stood in a dark forest, only able to make out the outlines of trees. It was dead silent, but it didn't seem to scare me. I was unable to move, my feet completely stuck to the ground.

Lips brushed my ear and whispered soft words. I couldn't make them out, but it sent many shivers and chills down my spine. Goosebumps covered every inch of my skin and the hairs on my neck stood on end.

Arms wrapped around my waist and I turned around in one movement, pushing something into their chest. The wooden stake didn't budge but the blood from his chest seeped out with ease. The coolness of his body stopped the sweat that had been seeping from my skin due to the rush.

The warm blood trailed down his shirt, soaking it in a dark crimson liquid. I didn't know who this stranger was, yet I was craving the satisfaction of watching him bleed. It made no sense to me yet every second he died a little more, exhilaration poured into me.

He used his two fingers to tilt my chin back as his lips danced across the front of my neck. Something in my gut screamed danger and I grasped that fear by throwing him off of me. He fell back, wiping away my scent from his mouth, fangs glistening in the moonlight. I had no control over anything.

My eyes narrowed and he hissed, losing all of his strength. The heartbeat inside me raced as his life drained. I thirsted for blood, but my hunger wasn't the same as his. This stemmed from wanting to watch him bleed out until he became nothing.

The words that left my mouth were laced with venom, "Every last one of your kind will beg for mercy as I shove my stake through their heart, but I will never give any of them the satisfaction."

004 Wednesday, August 28th

Shooting up from my bed, I grabbed my chest. The direction of that nightmare had me worried for a moment, making me question my own sanity. There were many times I never took my dreams too seriously but when my dreams got to a certain point of intensity, I had to decipher it. I had been known for having dreams that came to life and I feared this one would be one of those nightmares.

"Tell me that wasn't a nightmare," Juliet mumbled from the doorway.

"Go back to sleep. I'll be fine." I stood from my bed and walked to my bathroom.

She started to follow me. "But you won't be. You never are. You get really weird when you have bad dreams."

A piece of me snapped on a whim. "It's not your damn problem. Go back to bed." I closed the door before she could say more. I hadn't intended for those words to come out in such a harsh tone.

However, a small voice inside my head reminded me of something. *Don't trust anyone.* It wouldn't have sparked any curiosity if I had known that voice, but I couldn't pinpoint its source. It was that of a woman, but it sounded nothing like my mother's.

I washed my face. Gripping the sides of the sink, I stared at my reflection. "What the hell was that? What did that mean?"

She didn't respond. It was typical. She loved to play the quiet game.

"I will figure it out." I straightened my posture. "You can't keep your secrets forever, Mya."

As I turned, I stopped dead in my tracks. She was still facing me, no longer mirroring my actions. "Watch your back. Don't trust *anyone*."

There were those words again.

I immediately walked out of the back door to get a breath of fresh air.

"Mya?" someone called out.

Spinning to face them, I stumbled into Eli. "What the eff are you doing on my patio?" I crossed my arms to hide the fear once present in my eyes. Sure, my patio had been an open-floor plan for the entire complex to just walk through as they pleased, but I wanted to question him anyway.

My favorite pastime, clearly.

"I'm an insomniac, remember? I take lots of late-night walks, and I heard your voice. Are you talking to yourself? Do you need me to call for help?" He gave me a look of concern, but I read him better than that. He was making *fun* of me.

This was what Juliet was referring to when she meant I got weird with my nightmares. She had them, too, and everyone did. But there was a feeling I could never shake off when they haunted me.

"It's nothing, really." *Lies.* It was everything. I was standing outside at 2 AM after talking to my reflection as if she were my enemy. She was. She knew what the nightmares meant and refused to spill.

"Was it a bad dream? I know that some bad dreams can be so terrifying, so you prove to yourself it was just in your head." He searched my face for answers. Clues.

My guard had been up high, but his probing sucked out all of my strength. He saw inside my soul.

He stepped forward. "Do you want to talk about it?"

Talk about it. That was the last thing I wanted to do but my mind nudged me. Without my walls, I was just a mushy brain without the skull that kept it protected from *harm.* "It's a stupid dream."

He took another step. "I won't laugh."

Was that a promise? With him, I could never tell. Yet, I let my insides pour out. "I killed someone but...it wasn't that simple. I watched him die. Stealing his last breath made me feel alive in a way I've never felt before."

The same way you did when you killed those men.

Had he been influencing me somehow?

Animosity flashed in his eyes as he shifted his weight. "And what is it that you're afraid of?"

I wasn't sure how to answer the question. Why would he ask me that? Could he not guess that it was the fact that I murdered someone in my dream and enjoyed watching them suffer? The way the stake twisted into his heart filled me with serenity. The sight of his blood had me craving for more. The need to kill was so embedded in my memory that I couldn't forget it. I wanted to feel that high for real.

Juliet could call me crazy all she wanted. She wouldn't be able to stop whatever monster was hatching within me.

This piece of me didn't just fertilize inside me. It had been there my whole life, and maybe planted by the father who abandoned me. The egg had cracked. Wickedness was dripping out like acid, burning its path and leaving behind permanent damage that nobody could repair.

"Mya?" He lifted his eyebrows and waved his hand in front of my face to capture my attention. What would I say?

The words pieced themselves together as if making the puzzle a whole picture. They revealed to me sentences that could suffice as a real answer. "Everything, Eli. I'm afraid of the monster buried inside me, just waiting to be unleashed. I may never find anything more addicting than the taste of *murder.*"

It felt really awkward when Eli and I passed each other in the parking lot, him on his way out as I pulled into the spot. I'd had nightmares before, but I'd never confided in people the way I did in Eli. Even Juliet had no idea what I dreamt about. Awkwardness hung heavy in the air and I could only question why Eli wasn't teasing me about it.

It was a good thing we couldn't read minds.

I shivered and swallowed, barely glancing at Eli. For once, he wasn't looking back at me. I was thankful for that. I studied his appearance for a moment, taking it in. As much as I wished to pinpoint who I killed, there was no face I could picture. My mind wouldn't clarify the image.

I noticed his posture before anything else. In the past, he would straighten his back. Today, his shoulders slouched. Was it because of my nightmare?

The AC rattled as the system sputtered. My hand

instinctively covered my mouth and nose as a horrid smell threatened my nostrils. Cat piss saturated the air like cigarettes to clothes. "Damn, that smell," I muttered.

Facing forward, I turned my car off.

As soon as his window went up, Eli was out of his spot and exiting the lot. He was gone in the blink of the eye with the lingering of a revving engine left in his wake, and the scent had left right with him.

Maybe I'd said the wrong thing, but how could he have heard me? I stopped in my tracks at the sight of familiar brown hair. "Juliet!" I nearly jumped out of my seat at her sudden appearance. She stood at the door of my car with her arms dangling.

When I got out of the car, she led us into our apartment, closing the door. "Your mom was getting worried."

"When isn't she?" I laughed as I dropped my bag on my bed.

She leaned against the wall. "She also wants me to ask if you've met anyone, since you never talk to her about it and apparently I'd know the answer."

I stopped what I was doing, which was removing my shoes, to face her. Now wasn't the time to mention Eli. "Have I had sex? No." I lifted an eyebrow. "That's what she wants to hear, right?"

She glanced at the bra on her side. She was the farthest from clean. "What she wants to hear is if you're...being safe." She laughed a little. "She is so paranoid about becoming a grandma. But I reminded her that you are as single as a pringle."

"Then she can call me herself. I'm not going to tell my best friend that I'm not sexually active at the moment, but if I choose to do so, nobody will be hearing about it. I know how to be safe, too." I threw my shoe on the floor. "Changing the subject, I have a ton of homework."

"Ditch it." A sly smile raised on her lips.

I gasped. "What? You want me to rebel? I am paying to get this homework." My brows furrowed. "On second thought, let's go." I put on a different pair of shoes and we left the campus.

We went to the movies and picked out a horror movie. Throughout the movie, Juliet would repeat the lines from the screen in a loud voice. I was the one who threw my popcorn bucket up to make a mess on the people in front of us. Needless to say, we were kicked out pretty fast.

"That was a dumb movie anyway." I threw away the empty container.

She draped an arm around my shoulders. "Got any parties? I'll join you."

"There are always parties." I let out another laugh. "I can hook you up. We can go find one tonight." After the lack of sleep plaguing me as of lately, I needed a good escape.

Juliet and I found a good party within thirty minutes. They weren't hard to come by in a college setting.

Popping off the bottle cap, I took a big gulp of beer. The pumping of the music had me swaying my body to the beat. Altering my mind to be anywhere but the nightmare was freeing. I felt *normal.*

Throwing an arm in the air, I twisted my hips as I made my way to the center of the crowd. Thick sweat hung in the air but the utter bliss I was put under clouded all judgment. I couldn't ask for anything better.

When my bottle was empty, I set it on a table at the edge of the crowd. I twisted my body some more as I moved my head side to side with my hands above my head.

The scent of rain drifted in the air and I turned, seeing a figure flicker in my view long enough for me to recognize him. No. It wasn't Owen. Turning away, I swallowed and blamed it all on the alcohol.

He was dead and buried—and he'd stay that way.

I caught a glimpse of Juliet from afar, but she was preoccupied with some fight. Just as I put another beer to my lips, it was ripped from me. An English accent whispered against my ear. "You might want to take your thirsty arse home now, Love."

Spinning on my heels, I pulled one off and threw it at him as he attempted to duck. "You... You might want to take your ass home before I..." I was out of threats. Shit.

"Hard way it is." He wrapped his arms around my thighs and lifted me off the carpet. "Mya, you need sleep." He carried me out of the house.

I was quick to hit my hands against his back. "I do not need to be told what to do by a man! I am an independent woman, dammit!" I whipped my hair from my face and my breath got caught in my throat. The man from the shopping center stood at the end of the street, watching my every move. "Maybe sleep is good." I nodded my head.

When we got back to his place, he laid me in his bed. "We have to stop ending up like this." He sat on the bed as he shook his head.

Laying on my back, I groaned. "You need to stop stalking me."

The first laugh erupted from his throat. "I wouldn't have to stalk you if you could keep yourself safe." I knew it was just a joke, but I took offense.

I threw my arm over, hitting him. "I can, dickhead."

He grabbed a blanket from the top of the closet, placing

it over me. "I'll believe it when I see it." A small smile had now formed on his lips. It never occurred to me until now that I'd never seen him smile before.

"And what were you doing at that party, hm?"

"I caught word of an enemy, went to scope them out to try and figure out their plan to hope to save myself from harm. Nothing important."

Tempted to ask what that meant, he grinned wider as if saying it was a joke.

However, a small part of me wondered if it was really a joke at all.

I kicked my leg until my heel flew across the room, smacking into the wall. "Also, why did you smell like cat piss in the parking lot earlier today?"

The amused expression dropped like a dead fly. "Go to sleep, Mya."

"What? That's it? You're not going to retort with: *why do you smell like cat piss every day?* You're a mystery." I closed my eyes as exhaustion settled in my bones.

He let out a sigh. "I'm quite aware."

"Where's Juliet?" I smacked my forehead. "You forgot Juliet. I can't leave my best friend behind. Damnit, Kay!"

Eli leaned back against the wall. "I'm sure she's fine. She was interested in someone when I left."

"Who?" I opened my eyes to look at him.

He chuckled. "Oh, you didn't notice? I'd expect you to keep your eye out more." He shook his head. "The guy she was fighting with. The sexual tension was thick, Mya."

"She better listen to my mom's advice and be safe." I closed my eyes again. "Otherwise, I'm going to have a talk with her." Yet at that moment, it never occurred to me that Juliet was dating Cole.

"I'll make sure she's okay. Just get some sleep. The alcohol in your system smells putrid." He gave me a small smirk before I closed my eyes one last time.

The darkness swept me under the rug with the rest of its victims.

Snap—the sound of a twig breaking in two.

My head turned in every direction while I kept my eyes peeled for danger. I could sense it from a mile away. "Come out, coward," I spat.

The scent of wet dog got stronger. Seconds following, a large wolf bared its teeth while its claws dug into my shoulders. My back was pressed against the uneven forest floor, but my smirk stayed put. "What's the matter, mutt? Can't handle fighting a girl?"

I kicked my foot into its stomach, throwing it against a tree. I heard the spine crack, and the wolf whimpered, now paralyzed with fear.

Before I could approach its limp body, I was pinned to a tree, bark digging into my chest. A laugh escaped my lips. "You came for your friend?"

"We are not friends," the faceless man hissed. He flipped me around until I could see his face. There was nothing in particular that made it recognizable until I saw his eyes. Almond-colored.

His features settled into their position and everything became clear. "Eli," I seethed as a boiling rage pumped my heart.

For the split second he was caught off guard, I kneed him where it mattered the most. He let go of me to hold his balls while groaning in pain. "Mya..."

"I don't play nice, Kay," I whispered in his ear as I had bent over to his level.

His fingers threaded through my hair and he pulled my head down. "Neither do I, Simons." As he straightened himself, he pulled me against his body, but it only inspired hatred. He was attempting to seduce me into submission before he made me his prey.

"There's just one flaw in your plan," I whispered against his lips.

He pulled his hand from my hair and used four fingers to trace along my neck. "What's that?" His thumb was placed against my pulse.

"I'm not attracted to men who can't get it up." I swiped my leg and knocked him off his feet, onto the floor. I pulled a pure silver blade from my belt. "Come and get me, leech."

His eyes darkened as he stood to his feet. Cracking his knuckles and neck, he chuckled. "Oh, Love, we surely can get it up."

The ground opened up and swallowed me whole, sucking me to the bottom. Eli followed me in, pushing his foot against my neck. "Maybe I can redirect your blood flow to make your death quicker. Wouldn't that be nice of me?"

I grabbed his foot, twisting his ankle. He collapsed as his hands balled into fists, knuckles painted white. "I guess I should make you suffer, huh?" he asked with a mischievous smile.

"That would be the plan." I rolled over and jumped to my feet. "We both crave bloodshed, and I will smear your blood proudly for my ancestors to see." I brought my left leg up and kicked him in the face, knocking him to the floor.

He grabbed a thread from his pants, pulling it around my ankle and squeezing. The color drained until purple soaked into my foot. "Without blood flow, your limbs don't properly work," he pulled my foot from under me. All that was left in my toes was a cold yet numbing sensation.

He crawled on top, pressing his hands against my throat.

I clawed at his wrists, drawing blood from his veins. The blood wasn't his. It was the blood of his victims coursing through.

My lungs began to burn due to the lack of oxygen. My eyes wanted to roll back but just before I could take pleasure at the end of the suffering, he let go.

Air rushed back as I coughed and choked. He leaned down and moved some hair away from my ear. "That's only a taste of what I'm capable of. Threaten any of us again and you will beg for mercy. You will be begging me to kill you."

Fear blended perfectly with the hatred in my system. Nothing would please me more than to see Eli's blood on my hands. It would be my top priority, and no number of threats could stop what had always been set to happen. I was not going to let them down.

Every last immortal creature would be torn apart for humans to see, their humiliation in the hands of us. What Eli didn't know was the strength growing within. What he witnessed was just a taste of what I was capable of.

005 Thursday, August 29th

Eli lifted an eyebrow in surprise. "So, why do you want to play Truth or Dare again? We're not exactly *best friends.*" Eli gestured between us both.

What he didn't know would hurt him, and that was my intention. I'd failed to save Owen, and make my father stay, but maybe by catching a killer could I then get a little bit of my sanity back. I'd do some justice where it needed to be.

"Because it's another game that allows us to get to know each other. We could invite Juliet. Do you have a reason to say no?" I raised my eyebrow in question.

I never intended to introduce this monster to her.

He cleared his throat, trying to think of an excuse. "There's... I..." He came up short. "It might be better if it's just us, okay? I'll only agree if nobody else plays."

I laughed. "Of course. You're afraid of people," I joked. However, it struck me as odd that he didn't want anyone else to play with us. Aside from murdering people in plain sight and possibly making me his next target.

The corner of his lips tilted upward to one side as he

shrugged. “I’m terrified of humanity, Mya.”

I rolled my eyes playfully. I knew he was joking, right?

Right?

After my classes passed, I let him into my apartment. “Welcome to my humble abode.” I put my bag down. It was really nothing special. Juliet’s side was filled with warm colors, but my side of the room was filled with bold colors—red and electric blue.

Eli’s eyes found themselves a focus on Juliet’s side with her bra sprawled across the floor.

Heat rose to my cheeks. “She doesn’t think other people come around here besides me and Cole.”

He nodded a bit and looked at my side. “You don’t leave yours lying around. Any reason?” Yeah. Because I actually *wore* them.

I snickered. “Because I don’t expect other men besides Cole to see the apartment, either.” Eli was not secretive about his comments. “Let’s get down to why we’re really here.” I clapped my hands before dropping them at my sides. “Shall we establish any rules?”

He shrugged his shoulders.

“The obvious one should probably be sex. No forcing anyone to have sex. I think the rest shall be fair game,” I said. We both sat down, ready for the game to begin. “Who wants to go first?” I put my legs in a crisscross position. I laid my hands in my lap, getting comfortable. I had a pillow under my butt to keep it from getting sore or restless at any point. This could be a long game.

Eli sat back. “I will. I think since I am the guest, I should get the honors of going first. So, I ask you, Mya, truth or dare?” He was staring at me.

I wanted to start safely. “Truth.” I was afraid of dares. I

admitted it.

"All right. I'll give you an easy question, Love. Have you ever shagged someone?" He folded his hands together in a proper manner as if he was trying not to insult me.

"Yes." It had been a simple time then. I thought I was in love with a boy, but I was wrong. We were young and stupid and wanted to try sex. Neither of us had any experience and it was the most awkward time of my life. He had trouble putting the condom on and I was the only one who knew how to do that. Every time after that was better than the first.

He nodded. I waited for a question following, asking what happened or who it was with, but he knew better than to ask me about my business.

"Truth or dare?" I asked.

His eyes shifted towards the floor, not as a way to avoid eye contact but to keep his focus on something other than me. "I think it's fair to start off with the truth."

"Would you rather lose your sex organs forever or gain two hundred pounds?" Hard question.

"Gain two hundred pounds. Never would I give up the sex organs," he answered immediately. "Truth or dare?"

"Dare." My nerves began to ride the edge. It was time I put myself out there and try something that would get my heart racing. To not give away that I was here for a confession. Whether I would regret it or not, I couldn't tell.

"Call a random number and make a scene. It can be any scene you choose." I was thankful he gave me a simple one, something I could ease myself into. How considerate.

I grabbed my phone and called up a random number. The person picked up, causing me to sigh. "Now you have the guts to answer? You've ignored me all day; you have been avoiding me! Don't you think I don't know what you did!

I know your dirty little secret. I guess we'll just have to see what everyone else thinks about it." I hung up.

Eli was laughing, and I had to admit it was a shock. It didn't sound normal to hear such noises coming from him.

I cleared my throat. "Okay, calm down. Truth or dare?"

"Dare."

"I dare you to do my hair, whatever style you decide." I was certain he would pick a ponytail, and even that would be a miserable attempt.

He nodded and scooted closer to me. It took me a minute to realize what he was aiming for. He grabbed the hair tie from my wrist and pulled my hair back gently. He knew how fragile hair could be, which I was thankful for. His cold breath sent shivers down my spine.

No, Mya. He killed people.

Yes, exactly. That's why he sent shivers down my spine, and not for any other reason.

Eli separated my hair into three sections, overlapping each over another. Goosebumps covered every inch of my skin as his fingers brushed through my hair. He wrapped the hair tie around the end of the braid. It felt nice when people touched my hair. I swallowed and cursed myself for thinking he wouldn't be any good. This man never made sense to me.

I touched the braid on top of my hair, feeling how it sat.

Dutch braid.

Not a style many mastered. The fact that Eli had done it intrigued me further.

He pulled back with a slight smile on his face. "Truth or dare?"

"Truth."

"What turns you on?"

I turned red almost immediately. That was meant to be

private, yet it wouldn't be just my fantasy. "Uh..." My heart was pounding. "Well... I imagine being taken by surprise. I come home or something and he's there, waiting. It's dark and when I begin to wind down, he sweeps me off my feet. He warms me up with kisses and his hand keeps me awake until the clothes come off. I fantasize about it happening out of nowhere, but he still goes slow." I averted my eyes, attempting to rub away my rosy cheeks.

After a long pause, I lifted my head towards Eli, seeing his reaction for the first time. He looked deep in thought.

I cleared my throat, grabbing his attention. "Truth or dare?"

"Dare."

"With your eyes closed, I dare you to reach out and touch something. You then have to kiss it on the spot you touched." It seemed so simple. It would keep this game at a somewhat PG-13 version.

Eli stood and closed his eyes. He walked, reaching out when his right hand brushed my forehead. He opened them. He leaned down and barely kissed the skin on my forehead. It only lasted a second. I, however, felt the strangest thing when he did so.

Something about it radiated *protection.*

He sat back in his spot and folded his arms. His eyes conveyed not a single thought in his head. "Truth or dare?"

"Dare." I was going for this again. I would most definitely regret it.

"I will do something you may or may not like but it won't be something off-limits," he assured me, making sure I knew he wouldn't be molesting me or something. "I dare you to follow me blind."

I nodded, then I put a blindfold on and waited.

He grabbed my hand and lifted me off the pillow I sat on. "Where are you taking me?" I asked.

"It's a surprise." He didn't say another word as we walked for a while.

Where were we going? The minutes dragged on, and part of me feared I'd agreed to get kidnapped while blindfolded. Not a smart move for a woman, but I'd fight like hell if I needed to.

I was tempted to rip the blindfold off and demand an answer, as well as the right to feel safe. But I didn't do that. I pushed on for what felt like centuries, begging inside my mind to let him be a good guy after all so I wouldn't be kidnapped, raped, and killed. Maybe for once I'd get my way. If I was going to get my way at all, I'd want it to be in a situation like this, where I was immune to becoming a girl on a missing poster.

My feet passed over carpets, hardwood, and cement, before stopping on something soft. I assumed it was grass right outside the building, but I couldn't be sure of that given the walking distance. "Why are we here?"

Before I could remove the blindfold, my breath was stolen. A pair of lips had taken mine captive as they moved against mine. The kiss wasn't rough, nor was it fragile. It poured just the right amount of addiction.

I opened my mouth a bit, taken back by this action. Why would Eli *want* to kiss me?

To screw with me—mentally.

Eli had received my shock as an invitation. His tongue slipped into my mouth and sent my body to another place—a place where euphoria was heavy in the air. Despite my lack of response, he never faltered. His tongue roamed every inch of my being and his fingers held my chin as if I'd been a lover from a century before.

For just a few seconds, it became easy to forget how dangerous he really was.

He drove me crazy. My fists would always clench, and I'd want to slap him, yet I never did. I stood here, now, letting him explore another side to me that I never thought I would give.

My mind paced back and forth. Should I punch him? Should I accuse him of playing me? I could, or I could relish in the taste of his lips.

He released my lips before I had a chance to return the kiss. I craved more. I was tempted to pull him back, but I never did. I let him go.

His fingers twirled a strand of my hair, brushing against my collarbone. "You can take your blindfold off now, Mya," he whispered against my ear. I had no idea he was so close until his lips touched the top of my earlobe.

I took it off when it was over. Neither of us said a word about it. Instead, I noticed our scenery. The complex was at least a mile away and we were utterly alone here.

Moving back to the game, I asked, "Truth or dare?"

"Truth."

I wanted to ask him why he kissed me, but I had no confidence to do so. Instead, I asked something much bolder. "Do I sexually attract you?" His next answer could make or break my sanity.

He seemed surprised by my question, but he didn't hesitate to give me an answer. "Yes." It wasn't the answer I expected but it *did* break my rationality. Eli would push me away before always pulling me back. We were magnets attempting to create minds of our own.

We had to move on with the game. I only continued

to hopefully distract from it and show him that I wasn't bothered. I didn't want him to think he had an effect on me. His answer was not little in my mind. Surely it wasn't to his, either.

My turn came around again, and I picked truth.

"I want you to tell me about something in your life other than the nightmares that you're afraid to tell anyone about," he said.

Furrowing my brows, someone in the distance flickered back into my view. Owen. "I'm afraid I'm seeing my ex-boyfriend's ghost."

Eli leaned forward. "Ex-boyfriend's ghost?"

"It sounds silly, which is why I haven't told anyone. But last night at the party, I saw him... And now I'm seeing him again." I pointed to him.

He twisted his head. "Is last night the first time you've seen him?"

"Yes." Since the night of the accident.

Chuckling, he faced me again and shrugged his shoulders. "So I have competition it seems." It sounded like a joke, but I couldn't be sure.

Was Eli admitting he had a thing for me?

Was he admitting he could see Owen?

And if Owen's ghost was real, was I tempted to be with him again?

Forgetting about my dead ex, I asked, "Truth or dare?"

"Hm, truth." He looked at me. I wondered if he knew that his answer to being sexually attracted to me had me at a halt. Why did it affect me so much?

"I want you to tell me exactly what happened the night you killed those men." I offered this game for this question. I had to make sure I knew the full truth.

He shifted like he felt uncomfortable. I was no expert, but that meant he may have suspected me. "I noticed those men following you, and I personally know what men like them do to woman who are alone like you."

I closed my eyes, rubbing my forehead. "So shoving me was better?" I didn't entirely believe his story.

"You wanted the truth. You just don't want to hear that I happen to be around at just the right time." He shrugged as if he hadn't done anything wrong. He knew he had.

"You shoved me and made it sound an awful lot like you were trying to have me for yourself. They came to my aid and you were the one who tore them apart like a wild animal. Do you like being the bad guy?"

He pulled his lips into a smirk. "Women love the bad guy."

"I'm not a woman—" I ended my sentence there. "I didn't mean it like that. Please, just forget I said anything." I had intended to say I wasn't that kind of woman, but my brain had an odd reflex moment that just responded back before it processed the thought.

Eli's eyes shot up. "Not a woman? Then what are you? A girl? A little girl who needs to be taught manners, and how to treat others? I got to say, Love, your body is definitely that of a woman." He leaned back against the trunk of a tree.

I looked down at my hands, avoiding his eyes. My face turned tomato red at his comment on my body. This man was sick, and he knew it. How could Eli possibly be this irritating and rude but still manage to make me feel strange? How could he act this way and yet have me fantasizing about his lips at the same time? It made zero sense to me.

"Truth or dare, Mya?" His tone became more mischievous.

I wasn't sure what I wanted. "Truth."

"Have you had any more dreams about killing, and if so, who do *you* want dead?" he asked.

He had no idea.

After a kiss that took me off guard yet had me begging for more, I had to reveal the deepest paradox buried inside. "Yes." I swallowed before our eyes locked. "*You.*"

006 Friday, August 30th

"You heard about the men slaughtered in the alley, correct?" I leaned towards the officer.

He tilted his head. "Not that I'm aware of."

With a shake of my head, I put my phone on the desk. "I have here a recorded confession of their murders. I know the man who did it, and I know where he lives." As long as he had no idea I was here.

The officer gestured for me to go on, so I pressed play.

"I want you to tell me exactly what happened the night you killed those men."

"I noticed those men following you, and I personally know what men like them do to woman who are alone like you."

"So shoving me was better?"

"You wanted the truth. I lied before because you wouldn't have wanted to hear that I always happen to be around at just the right time."

"You shoved me and made it sound an awful lot like you were trying to have me for yourself. They came to my aid and you were the one who tore them apart like a wild animal. Do you like being the bad guy?"

"Women love the bad guy."

I stopped the recording. "Eli Kay. Apartment 201."

"All due respect, ma'am, but we can't use this as evidence."

"Why not? He doesn't say he killed them but when I tell him he did, he explains why he did it."

His eyes filled with concern, and clearly for my mental state by his next words. "There's nobody on that tape but you."

I parked my car in the visitor area again and was nearing my apartment when I noticed something new—no, it was *someone* new. Eli was talking to a girl.

But my mind still raked for answers as to why the police couldn't hear him. Had he known about my recording? Had he edited it himself?

Nonsense.

But what other explanation was there?

Dismissing the thoughts, I focused on Eli's new girlfriend.

The last thing I wanted to do was to be the jealous woman. *We* weren't dating. I'd even returned from trying to incriminate him. He kissed me during a game of Truth or Dare. Nothing went beyond that and he could talk to whoever he wanted to.

However, that wasn't what got to me. It was who he was talking to. The girl I'd met the same day Eli threw me against a wall. She told me she didn't stick around places for long and yet I found her chatting up the same man who shoved his tongue down my throat just yesterday.

I stood from afar, observing their body language all while listening in on their conversation. I noticed she laughed at something he had said and responded with, "Where are you from?"

He was fully focused on her while his eyes lingered to her cleavage. He didn't even attempt to hide his interest in her boobs. Neither of them was bothered by lust. "Romsey, in England. I only came to America in recent years when I was a teenager." She already knew more than I did. What did she have that I didn't?

Confidence.

She kept her ever-so-perfect smile and nodded to his reply. "Do all the British boys have great humor, or is it just you?" Was she flirting with him? Oh my. This had been a side I never saw. She came off as a woman who had no fear, and that included the flirtatious side, too.

I thought you said Eli felt nothing for you? You're just neighbors. He tried to kill you. Why do you care?

"I don't," I said to myself, pressing my lips into a thin line.

She nodded at whatever Eli told her. "Well, I'm Amari. If you ever want someone to show you around a bit, I'd be happy to. I should probably get going." She pointed to the car parked in *my* spot.

I grabbed onto the frame of the door while my breathing grew heavier. "That bitch stole my spot!" Guilt squeezed my chest. I had only called her such a word because I wanted to be the confidence that she so easily could be. I wanted men to look at me the way they looked at her. I wanted them to crave me.

If you don't want her to take it again, then go over and let her know who's parking spot it is. You say you don't care, but you clearly do. If you want Eli to pay for his crimes, then break up the interaction before she gets hurt.

I took a deep breath, taking advice from the voice within my head, and walked right over to them. "I'm sorry, this is actually my spot. It has been for two years." I leaned against the pole. "I do pay to park here." *Also, he's a murderer.*

Eli chuckled as he rubbed the hood of his car in the spot beside what was supposed to be mine. "I should have mentioned that the tenant of this spot is very uptight about parking here."

I growled at him before facing Amari. I saw the glint in her eye. She was definitely upset by my words, but I didn't seem to care how she felt. Eli didn't notice it, being the clueless male he was. She looked at Eli. "Should we meet up later? I'll show you my favorite makeout spot."

The anger began to boil inside me. Eli ignored my red face and replied, "Sure. Thank you, Amari."

She giggled and got in her car, driving off to her next destination. I put my head down, encasing it with my hair. My face was a tomato. I couldn't take it. I couldn't let her just sleep with him, then die for it. I had to make him notice me instead. Target me instead. I had to make her look dull. Difficult was an understatement of how I was going to steal his attention.

During the afternoon, I met up with Juliet to get her advice. I had to make him notice that I was better than Amari.

Juliet's eyes were glued to Amari as she stood with Eli by the pond. "So, we need to take into account what he sees in her." Something in her eyes flashed, something appearing as disbelief. I couldn't quite place where it fit. "Why does

Amari get his attention over you?"

"Because she talks to him. She's confident and nice. But I can be nice. I even invited him to a game. I'm trying. Is it because she's got more cleavage?" I had boobs, too, but Amari's were shiny. That wasn't just a metaphor, either. She put iridescent powder on her cleavage to make them pretty.

Juliet gave me a look. "Damnit, Mya. Why do you always talk about that? Just capture his attention. Talk to him. You cannot let her outshine you. Don't let her get under your skin." She shook her head and let out a sigh. "You managed to capture Owen's attention, didn't you?"

"I'm not even sure how I did that." I scoffed. "But look how that turned out. Now he's dead." Juliet shifted at the mention of his death, so I changed the subject. "They're hanging out. How do I outshine her in that?" I gestured towards them, clearly irritated by their closeness.

She lifted both eyebrows. "I'm supposed to tell you to be yourself. How is that working for you? Listen, you need to do something that you've never done. Break out of your comfort zone."

Amari caught me looking at her. Shit. "Jules, she's coming over." I buried my head into my arms before she could delete all space between us and call me out.

"Hey, Mya, right?" I lifted my head to look at her, nodding a bit. She glanced at Juliet and smiled a bit. "And you are?"

Juliet waved her hand from left to right just once. "Juliet. I'm Mya's best friend."

I took a sip of water to avoid confrontation. What Amari said next had me choking. "It's always the best friend who has the best boobs." Did she just insult me?

Juliet blushed before rubbing her neck. "Thanks..."

Amari nudged me. "And what about you, Mya? See

something you like?"

"What?" I furrowed my brows, puzzled by her question. I saw Eli but I never *liked* him. I loathed him. Him and his dangerous side. Somehow, he got away with it.

And I got recommended a psychiatrist from a sheriff.

Amari let out a laugh. "Relax, Mya. I'm making a joke."

I still didn't understand that joke.

Juliet stood and cleared her throat. "I'll see you later. I'm going to go meet up with Cole." She gave me a nod and left the patio. Such a wonderful friend.

"Ooh, who is Cole?" Amari sat in the spot Juliet warmed up.

"Juliet's boyfriend." I never once glanced at Amari. My eyes roamed anywhere else but her.

She sighed a bit. "Shame. I was hoping she was single."

My eyes snapped up to meet hers. "Juliet? First Eli, now Juliet? Are you trying to sleep with everyone I know?" Now it had been my turn to make a joke.

Amari laughed. "Mya, I'd be more interested in Juliet over Eli any day, but I don't go after taken people."

"Why do you still talk to him?" Shit, well, I sounded like a real bitch.

She chewed on her lip. "Why do you think?"

I sat back in my chair, crossing my arms. "To get back at me, of course," I said with a playful smirk. She had to assume I'd copy her joking personality, right? "I don't understand how you two know each other. Is Eli your ex-boyfriend? He kissed me, but is there something I should know about him to stay away from? Not that I'd date him. He's trouble." Trouble was putting it lightly.

Her smile faltered. Her face didn't display much after that. "You actually don't know why I'm talking to him."

"Please, do enlighten me." I gestured, sweeping my hand over the table.

She shook her head. "I have to go. I'm sorry. If he tries to kiss you again, push him away. Just trust me, Mya. It's for your own good." She got up from the chair and walked away in a hurry.

She didn't need to tell me twice. But I wouldn't tell her. Why didn't I warn her about him? Was I that demented that I wouldn't protect another woman from a killer?

I drummed my fingers on the table as I closed my eyes. Nothing made sense. I thought the adult world was meant to get easier. The same man who wanted me dead had also kissed me. Another woman warned me of him. Yet the police wouldn't take me seriously. I had more questions than answers and I feared I would never receive them.

Someone tapped my shoulder, and I came back to reality. "Yes?" I asked before realizing it was Eli.

He shrugged a little. "You scared away Amari. What did you say to make her run?"

"I told her you're a monster." *Ha,* those jokes again. I straightened my posture. "Is it a problem?" I had no idea what I'd said to make her run away. Something was off and everyone knew more than they were willing to tell me.

"It is when I'm trying to *talk* to Amari. It's something you'd never understand." No friendly tone. No sarcasm. Just pure insults. The confidence was smacked out of me. Why did he have an interest in her? Why murder her for existing? He was a steaming pile of shit for that alone.

"Oh. Right. I apologize for interrupting your flirtation. Nothing like shiny boobs to get a man's dick up." I gestured to the obvious bulge in his pants. Controlling the second head was always harder than the first.

Eli narrowed his eyes at me before turning the other direction and abandoning ship. Maybe Amari had been right. Murder aside, if he could kiss me one day and flirt with her the next, it would be better for me if I pushed him away. The kiss meant nothing, and I'd never let it happen again. I was sure of that.

What was Amari doing to make him desire a woman like her over a woman like me?

Going back to my room, I threw my things down. I wanted to make him pay. How could a woman make a man feel sorry?

I could make him jealous by showing off for other guys and ignoring him, but there was an obstacle in my way. I had no confidence.

What good was I? I was beginning to see why he chose Amari over me. She had everything I could never achieve.

She'd be the one to spill blood.

Looking out the window, I noticed Amari running off somewhere else. Where the hell was she going? Was she so afraid to screw Eli after I exposed her plan? Whatever I'd done, it was working.

There was one plan I could follow through with. It was the one thing I could do to anger Eli, but it would require going outside my comfort zone.

I needed to befriend Amari. Amari had to be closer to me than Juliet if I was going to get to the bottom of this pit of lies.

I could piss off Eli just by making friends with the one person he least expected me to keep on my side. I would pull a reverse uno card. Aside from that, I could also figure out what it was that everyone kept so secret. They couldn't fool me.

Amari warned me about kissing Eli for a reason and I had to know if it played a bigger role than Eli just being a player. It could not be a coincidence that the same man I'd interacted with the most this past week was the target of Amari's games—whatever those were. I had met Amari and Eli on the same day, and now both of them were communicating with each other.

Maybe she also knew he needed to be put behind bars.

They knew something about me that I didn't know. It was my purpose to find out what they hid behind their flawless façades. They were both attractive people driven by lust. I'd be the stake that tore a hole in their hearts, just like I'd done in my darkest nightmares.

007 Saturday, August 31st

A thump hit the floor above mine and I debated yelling at the asshole. It was 3:48 AM, so getting back to sleep wasn't an option.

Cat piss. Rotting. Death.

Three odors nobody wanted drifting around their apartment.

Another thump against the floor above.

Now my anger was rising, and I needed to say something. People around here needed sleep.

Getting up, I went out the front door and walked a bit out until I could peer up the stairs, ready to tell him to shut the eff up. I walked further until I saw a hand dragging across the ground until it disappeared into his apartment. He slammed the front door shut.

No way was I bothering a murderer at a time like this. He was in a certain mood.

Instead, I sat on the comfy bed of my bedroom, laptop in my lap. My whole morning was dedicated to research. I would research him first, then befriend Amari just to get to the bottom of this. I needed more solid information about Eli.

As I glanced at my manicured nails, I noticed the color beginning to peel off. That was the toughest part of using a peel-off base coat.

Amari didn't have manicured nails. She had no nails, in fact. One theory was that she just had a bad habit of letting them grow. Another theory was that she hated long nails. The third theory was a little less family-friendly, and I wasn't wanting to picture such a scene in my own head.

If Amari was going to screw Eli, I was sure that was what they both wanted. It didn't bother me. I didn't have feelings for him. That was absurd.

That's what you like to tell yourself, Mya. We both know Eli gets you all hot and bothered and that kiss was barely the tip of what he has to offer you.

The voice inside my head knew nothing about me. Eli was attractive, and I'd be blind if I didn't admit that. However, I was not so desperate to get inside his pants over a kiss. Was that kiss amazing? Absolutely. But I was not about to let my body win over my mind. I had the ability to think for myself and I was going to use it.

I searched Eli Kay's name in the search bar. His last school was Harvard. I choked on my own words before I could get them out. Did he really come from Harvard? Why was he in Arizona? We were a downgrade, and I did mean a huge downgrade.

I found an article talking about the murder of a student at Harvard. Supposedly, the professor's daughter was killed. I didn't understand much of it, but I was determined to.

From the looks of her wounds, it was very subtle. In fact, she was drained of all blood and only two small holes were found on her body. How was that even possible? I was having nightmares about vampires and a woman from Eli's previous school had been killed by one. I laughed at the mere thought of Eli actually being a bloodsucker.

He sure didn't drink the blood of the men he murdered. He left them to bleed out and stain the city red.

I opened up a picture of this woman. I didn't know if I wanted to go on further.

She looked just like *me.*

A young girl was murdered, and Eli had fled the scene—painting himself a suspect.

Nausea was threatening my stomach. My whole body was heating up. I was trying to process all of this, but how could I begin to fathom what my eyes were showing me?

Right after she was killed, Eli left and came here. Did he realize how it looked on him? To make matters worse, I looked just like her. Maybe this was why he hated me so much. I looked like a girl who got murdered at his last university. Maybe he was the one who killed her. It wouldn't be too far out of his jurisdiction.

Could this be why he was avoiding me and hanging out with Amari? I reminded him of her. Were they dating? Was that why he left? I looked just like the girl. He had to avoid anyone who looked just like her.

Another thump, then something breaking. Like *glass.*

"Shut the hell up already," I muttered to myself.

I read the article further, swallowing my fear. Her name had been Alissa.

In the image they used, she had been turning her shoulder slightly towards the camera. She wore a red tank top, her black hair pulled back into a Dutch braid.

Closing my laptop, I knew just enough to confront Eli.

I knew I had figured him out to the point that he couldn't play games with me any longer. This made sense; this was the story. Showing up at his doorstep wasn't the best idea either way the truth swung. Whether he killed her, or she was his ex. I'd still trigger passionate feelings of some sort.

Getting off my bed, I decided to go to his place regardless. I couldn't stay silent. I had enough to get under his skin and I would use it to my advantage.

Without a weapon?

Apparently.

I knocked hard on his door, but noises came from inside his room. Oh shit. He ripped open the door, annoyance blanketing his face. "I'm busy right now." He was completely naked, and he didn't seem to care that I saw it all. I swallowed and kept my eyes locked on his face.

Blood dripped from a cut along his chest.

"I know about Alissa—why you keep messing with my head." I moved my fingers around my head as I narrowed my eyes.

His face changed and he began glaring daggers at me. I'd hit a nerve. "You know nothing."

"Who the hell is that?" I heard Amari ask from inside the room. It didn't shock me that she was his lover for the night. She had powers I never did. Where did the blood come from? Were they really this kinky?

What did surprise me was the body he dragged in, and the reeking of rotting flesh. She'd been part of his plan. A partner. I was most possibly the victim.

I shook my head, dismissing any feelings I had previously. "I know she was murdered. I know I look just like her and you hate me because I remind you of her. You *also* killed those men. If my theory serves me right, you and Amari are a team and I'm the fool."

His words had all been lies. He had done nothing but tell me lies to keep himself in the safe zone—whatever that was. He was a deceiver. He couldn't wait to get away from me. He used Amari to fulfill his desires. He was an opponent and it was a game I wasn't willing to play any longer.

"But you're right." I turned on my heel and went back downstairs.

I sat back down on my bed, feeling like a total moron. He was just like the rest of the men I'd met. I wanted nothing to do with him. Eli was going to need to find a new victim to play his game now.

I laid back in my bed and stared up at the ceiling. How did some women manage to find good men? Where were they? When and where could I *order* one?

Knowing my luck, I was doomed to be the butt of everyone's joke. I didn't want to die. I wasn't ready.

After hours of lying in bed, still unable to sleep, I decided to walk around instead. I got out of my bed. I was also hungry, so I grabbed a bag of chips from the laundry room. I walked out the back door and sat down to watch the pond. Flooded as of right now.

Monsoon season was my least favorite. Despite the extra rain, humidity, and the storms, we still experienced the heat far worse than most states nearby.

"Late night snacks?" I heard the voice to my left, causing me to jump. I hadn't expected anyone to be awake yet. It scared me.

I turned towards him and sighed. "What, now you want to talk to me? I came to get my snacks in peace. Goodnight." I shooed him away.

"Still mad about Alissa, or is it Amari this time?" I

swallowed and didn't look his way. He had some nerve. "I know it makes you ill-tempered that I won't give you what you really want—another kiss."

I walked right up to him. "You're an asshole and I could never want you. I may have never suspected Amari was against me, but you're the one who kissed *me.* I never kissed back, Eli. Don't you forget that." I'd regretted not kissing back before this, but now I got to use it as leverage. It became a weapon.

He grabbed my wrist and spun me around until my back was facing him. He started to rub my neck and shoulders. "You stress too much. I can feel the knots."

I narrowed my eyes. "You are my stress. I'm calm when I'm not around you. You kissed me because I look like her, and for no other reason. That also makes me your target."

For a moment, he paused, but he soon continued massaging again. "She's gone. No use in bringing up the past."

"Irony at its finest. You're the one who treats me this way simply because of your past. I'm Mya. We might look alike, but we are totally different people."

He chuckled without any trace of humor. "Believe it or not, Love, but you are very alike. You both are very stubborn. She also accused me of being a monster. She was beautiful with a short temper, too. You're remarkably similar." He leaned close to my ear. "She was even an attention whore, just like you."

My blood boiled from his words. "But I'm not her." I blew a strand of hair from my eye. "Maybe Owen really is a ghost. And if that's true, there's no doubt I'll pick *him* over you."

He spun me again and gently placed me against the wall, hands on both sides of my head. "No, I definitely don't want to end your life. Merely just want to see inside that pretty head of yours." He traced his finger down my cheek and chin. I refused to let my knees buckle under his touch. I wouldn't give him the satisfaction. He came closer until our lips were millimeters apart. "But it's much more complicated than that..." He pressed two fingers against my pulse. "Your heart is beating very fast."

I closed my eyes and let the memory enter my mind and I remembered just how it felt when he devoured my lips. At this moment, I wished he would do it again.

He pulled away until I couldn't feel his cold breath fanning me. I opened my eyes and looked at him, seeing that stupid *smirk* on his face. He stood straight, looking right at me. "I won't do anything you don't want me to. When you say the words, I'll give you it all." He began walking away, leaving me to feel foolish. He paused and turned barely ninety degrees. "And if you're really so insistent to pick Owen over me, then I *dare* you to do it. That still won't make me a monster." He disappeared around the corner after those words slipped off his tongue.

I rushed back to my apartment and locked the door. I ran into my closet to find the shirt I wore the night in the alley, to check for blood. I stopped at the sight of something hiding in the corner. I pulled it out, laying it flat on my bed. It was a white gown. The same one I'd seen in my daymares.

Blood splattered it, tainting the purity of the dress. The daymares I got out of nowhere were not just random. They were memories trying to piece themselves back together in my head.

Looking into the mirror, I admired my appearance. My hair was brushed through, my makeup done lightly.

I smoothed my hands over the dress, smiling at my own

reflection. Tonight was meant to be a summer dance before the school year started back up for me to finish off senior year, and I was going to make the most of it.

The gown flowed to my feet, as white as a dove's feathers. The sleeves hung off the shoulders and exposed the tan I'd worked hard to achieve. Whether I met my prince or not, I was going to find someone to get me going.

It had been a long time since I'd had a good time and I wanted to begin the new school year off right.

As I stepped out of my room, I dodged my mother before she could ask questions. I was a grown woman and the last thing I needed was her pestering me.

I got in my car and drove to the place. I parked but I never left my car.

I chewed my lip, debating if I should be here. But I needed it. I craved the escape for just a moment.

People stood, gathering with friends or groups. Everyone was dressed for the occasion and some were even pushing to move to the next step of the night.

A lovely scene to put myself into.

Someone knocked on my window and I rolled it down. I didn't get the chance to ask her what she wanted because she asked first, "Are you Mya?" She even knew my name.

008 Sunday, September 1st

The sun danced on my face as Juliet opened the curtains. Today was a new day and I was ready. I couldn't give Eli the control. I'd pretend he had no power over me. I couldn't be affected by him.

As I left my bed, I put on a black dress to give myself some confidence. I knew I needed it and Eli would be sorry he ever threatened me the first night.

The black dress hung off my shoulders and it was at that moment that I realized my love for sleeves like these. The neckline was a little dipped, barely enough to show my cleavage. The skirt was made of a thinner material that flowed but never passed my knees. I wore some black heels to compliment the entire outfit. My hair had been braided and wrapped around my head as much as allowed. Today, I was expressing my dark side.

I needed some friends who weren't Juliet or Eli. I wanted to actually make friends with people who enjoyed my presence. As my mom said, they didn't end up on your doorstep. Well, they did when you were a kid. But I was an adult now, so I had to actually go out and make them myself.

I left the building, surprised Eli wasn't anywhere in sight. I sat on a bench, eyeing everyone nearby. I needed to study my potential victims first.

People passed by and I noticed a few guys giving me attention. It was what I'd craved all along and now I had the ability to show off what I'd been blessed with.

Someone blocked me from the sun, and it took my eyes a moment to adjust before I could see their face. "Amari, what the hell do you want?"

She took a seat next to me and shrugged. "I've had time to think."

I watched her every move. "You want me dead."

She laughed. "Mya, that isn't why I'm here. I don't want to kill you. I also did not sleep with Eli. It looked that way, but it wasn't. I 'slept' with him for a reason you would never...think of." She put air quotes around the word *slept*. "I didn't enjoy the flirting."

"You sure as hell enjoyed it when you begged him to come back and screw you some more." I crossed my arms. She couldn't fool me.

She sat back and shook her head. "You're disgusting. That's not what I even said by the way."

Maybe I'd misheard things. But she still wanted it. "Mhm, that's coming from the woman who's got no problem exploiting her sexuality."

Amari clenched her jaw. "Shit, Mya. Let me explain and shut your damn mouth for one second." She took a deep breath before looking my way.

I'd pushed a sensitive button.

She gripped the edge of the bench seat. "You're not a

normal human."

"I'd hope not. Normal sucks ass." I snickered.

She slapped her hand over my mouth and scooted closer. Her eyes darted around the area. "No. That is not what I meant." She rested her head against the side of my hair.

"Are you adopted?" she asked in a low voice.

I choked on my next inhale. "Excuse me? How dare you ask such a thing?"

Amari let out a sigh before putting distance between us. "You're a descendant to Kaofi Hunters, Mya. If your mom never told you, maybe she doesn't know. Do you look like your family?"

Thinking back to them, I recalled my mom being blonde. I had hair that was the blackest black of the night, and yet I always assumed it was from my father. Maybe it still was. I didn't want to think about coming from other parents.

"Eff you, Amari. You have no right to tell me I'm adopted. You don't know me. I'm not a descendant or whatever shit you think I am." I stood from the bench in one quick motion.

She grabbed my wrist and pulled me back down. "I'm not just telling you this for some good laughs or whatever. I'm telling you this because I know...you can see Eli."

"What the hell does that mean?" I yelled as I threw my hands up.

Getting up, she began to tap her fingers against her thigh. "Okay, stop yelling before someone hears you." She rubbed her eyes, attempting to gather her thoughts. "Eli is not human. He's immortal. Only the descendants of Kaofi Hunters can see immortal creatures. You can see him because you are one, but you have no idea."

I swallowed my fear. "But you can see him, too."

She dropped her arms at her side. “Exactly.”

Shivers ran down my spine. Amari was a hunter. “I’m so confused. If you hunt people like Eli, why did you sleep with him?”

“I didn’t. I flirted so I could get him alone and kill him. I was trying to kill him the second you came up, but you seem to think we were plotting to kill you instead.” She twirled some of her hair. “That was how I got to him. I got his blood and a strand of his hair. All I have to do is mix the right concoction together before he’s in my control. We hunt people like him, Mya. He’s using you.” She bent down and grabbed my shoulders. “He is the enemy, and he knows that you don’t know what you are. He’s taking advantage of you so he can kill you.”

That was why he hated me yet couldn’t stay away. He despised me for what I was... But he couldn’t pass up the opportunity to wrap me around his finger and snap me in two.

“Only we can see them?” I looked up at her.

She nodded before sitting next to me again. “Yes.”

I laughed a bit. “You don’t have to worry, Amari. I hate him. I knew he was playing me somehow. He killed innocent men in front of me. The last thing I’ll do is fall in love with him.”

“Good. I need your help killing him.” She rested against the bench.

“I’m not a killer.” *Your dreams say otherwise.* “Also, why do you need to control him to kill him?” I leaned back.

“Because I want to force him to do it himself. That’s *my* method.” She shrugged. “Mya, you can pick a side but straddling the fence makes you as guilty as him. You’re with us or against us. I really hope you choose wisely.” She gave me one last stern look before leaving the complex.

What was I going to do? I didn't want to become a killer, but I didn't want to take Eli's side, either.

Everything was beginning to make sense. My nightmares weren't random. They were trying to tell me who I was meant to be all along.

The incident with the recording at the police station had been so obvious now that she mentioned it.

I had to ask my mom about this and get answers.

Leaving the apartments, I drove home. I only lived an hour away and I had the time to spare. It was an urgent matter.

I walked up to the door and knocked before walking inside. "Hello? It's me." I didn't need to pretend I was a stranger here. She was still my family, whether she lied to me or not.

"Mya! Come in!" Mom stood in the kitchen cooking up some food. "Did you hear?"

I stopped and eyed her like she was a suspect. She was. "Hear what?" Did she know that I knew?

Mom smiled. "Juliet told me about the boy in your building. She said you hate him but I said it sounds like love brewing. And remember to always use protection." I groaned as she said that. When she had realized she wasn't going to keep me from having sex, she made it her next goal to make sure I knew how to be careful. She wasn't too happy with me when she caught me with the first boy I'd ever slept with.

After I didn't answer, Mom sat and looked over at me. "Why are you here?"

I halted before taking a step forward. "Am I adopted?"

The room fell silent. Why was nobody saying anything? If I wasn't adopted, wouldn't she had said so by now?

I swallowed before taking a seat. "So, I've lived twenty-one years and you never told me I wasn't your child. Did you think you could hide it forever?"

More silence. Why the hell wasn't she saying a word? She had to know that this news wasn't to be taken lightly. I didn't know where I came from. I had no idea who I really was.

"Mya," she started, "I'm sorry. I didn't want you to think I loved you any less."

My eyes must have been lightening at the fear running through my veins. Mom couldn't stop staring at them. And her stare had never been this intense before.

"That's not what this is about. Most people know their ancestors. They know where they come from and who they are. They are aware of their culture and they embrace it. I can't embrace anything because this family is a lie. You are not..." I choked. "You're not where I come from."

Amari had been right. If I had no idea who my parents were, they could very well be Kaofi Hunters. That's what I could be, too.

Mom put the knife down. "Mya, don't you dare say that. I love you. I raised you. You're my daughter no matter where you came from. Your parents could be Bonnie *and* Clyde and I won't stop loving you like my own." She walked around the counter and grabbed my cheeks. "Look at me."

So I did.

"You are a strong woman. You are so wonderful, and I feel blessed to have raised you. I never wanted you to question your worth. I see so many adopted children feel like they weren't loved but I chose you. I chose you because you are mine." She searched my eyes for any response.

I wasn't sure what to say. I could understand where she came from, but that never stopped the pain inside my heart. "You lied, Mom. I don't know who I am." I wiped a tear as my heart cracked like glass.

Now I had a chance to learn. I needed Amari's help to learn more about my family history and what options I had. Were immortals bad, or were they just like humans?

I had to know who my real parents were. I had to better understand the Mya they created before they tossed me away. Why would they?

"Don't make that face, please," Mom said.

"Easy for you to say." I got out of the chair and walked into the living room. "You're not the one who's adopted."

"You know I still love you. It doesn't change anything except that you don't know your real parents." But she couldn't understand what else had changed. She couldn't know this feeling because she had never experienced it for herself.

I wiggled my finger. "No. You have no right. You are not in my shoes. You don't get to downplay my sadness." She was not going to make me feel bad for being upset. Everything had changed. My entire existence had yet to be uncovered.

"What bothers you the most? I want to know," she asked.

Where did I begin? I had to learn a whole new world. I had parents who were fighters and *warriors.* I could see creatures that normal people couldn't. I had the ability to kill and protect and that was a burden I was given when Amari told me who I really was.

I had the option of avoiding this whole new lifestyle, yet I would be judged. I was given this choice for a reason and I was scared to make the wrong decision. Mom had taught me to love and only judge people once they proved they were no good.

Eli was that guy. He showed me his true desires when he played me like a fiddle, and now I had been shown my own through my dreams. I had to uncover a new identity and nobody else around me understood the kind of pressure I was under, or the toll it could take.

Yesterday I was simply a woman pursuing her fashion dream through college, trying to put a killer away. Today I was a Kaofi Hunter, in which my only option to seek justice was to *kill* said killer myself. But I wanted a choice between the two—and if I made the wrong one—it would cost me my life.

009 Monday, September 2nd

Entering the parking lot, I spotted Eli. As much as I wanted to ignore him, I had to keep up the lie that I didn't know what he was, or that I was meant to take his blood for myself.

I parked beside him, getting out of my car after turning off the ignition. As I noticed his new license in his hand, I lifted my eyebrows in surprise. "Elliot Kay. I knew Eli was short for something, right?"

He didn't seem pleased with me. "It's Eli. I don't like going by Elliot."

A smirk rose on my face. I'd captured his team's flag. "Kay, Elliot." He sent daggers my way.

He quickly circled his car and headed towards the stairs before I could stop him, but something dropped from his bag. I bent down and picked it up. It was a photograph, one of a waterfall. "What is this, may I ask?"

"Go ahead, you already have..." He took it back. "It's just a picture. I'm interested in photography."

Surprise colored my face. That was what those pictures

in his room must have been from. It made sense that they weren't people he knew. He was taking pictures as a hobby. "I think that's really cool. I'm serious. They're really good." We started walking to the stairs. "How long have you been into photography?"

"For at least three years. I like being able to capture a moment that we can never get back. Some think it's easy to take a picture, and sure it is. But the real skill lies in capturing just the right moment to express most of the story."

A tilt of my head, slight drop of my jaw. This man who'd shoved me into a wall actually had a brain. It was amazing what we could hold inside us all at once. We stopped at my apartment and I looked at the door in front of me. "Well, thanks. You didn't have to walk with me."

He shrugged. "Don't overthink it. Why don't we hang out later? I'll even show you more of my photography skills. Maybe I could capture you."

A blush rose to my cheeks. Ugh, why me? "Sounds fun. I'll be there. You can count on it."

"All right, see you then." He walked off to wherever he was intended to get to.

After I ate some lunch, I walked to the mailbox. I heard footsteps until a figure appeared next to me. Their height could be anybody. Everyone was taller than me. "May I help you?" I asked without a glance.

"I was just catching up because we're going to see some more of my skills." It was the English accent that gave everything away.

"Right, sorry. I assumed we'd just meet in your apartment." I shrugged to myself as we went over to his apartment. I took a seat on the bed. "So, Kay. What are these pictures you want to show me?" He brought me his camera and sat, handing it to me.

"These are some of my recent captures." He was close, but my senses were on high alert. I knew better now. Amari taught me that Eli was dangerous, but I would play right into his game the same way she had. He knew her plan, but he had no idea what I knew about Kaofi and hunters.

I went through the pictures. They were random, really, but they were incredibly beautiful. I stopped at a video. I pressed play before Eli noticed, and a girl began laughing. "I said stop it!" The camera panned on her and I gasped.

Eli spoke up next to me, "You shouldn't be watching that."

"Shh..." I watched the girl who looked exactly like me. Alissa. She sat on the grass with a long sleeve shirt and a skirt. It was a terrible fashion choice, but I'd never tell Eli.

"Why must you always insist on filming me?" She looked at someone behind the camera.

I heard a chuckle. "Because someone has to capture the beauty."

Her cheeks tinted as she smiled at him. "But what about my father? He doesn't like you. He'll catch us." Was she a Hunter, too? Now that begged the question if she was actually my sister. Maybe I had a twin.

"I won't let that happen. Let's not focus on that. Enjoy the moment," Eli responded.

She looked down at the grass, hair covering her face. "May I ask why you like photography?"

"There's an old saying that goes: *I don't shoot what it looks like. I shoot what it feels like.* It's exactly what I do. I want to be able to capture your beauty in case you're not always there."

The video ended there, and I looked over at Eli. "I'm

sorry...about everything. What happened to Alissa, it wasn't fair." I didn't know the whole story but something in my gut told me he was telling the truth. He never hurt her. He cared about her. If he loved her, why *would* he murder her?

The cat held his tongue for a few minutes. It wouldn't be long before he compared us again. I reminded him of what he lost. "It was my fault." He balled his hands into fists as he looked up at the ceiling.

"Eli, please, don't. Don't blame yourself." I put my hand on his shoulder to try to calm him. He barely saw it before looking the other way.

I went through the pictures once more, but something caught my eye. "Eli, is this Alissa...?" I studied it until my eyes wanted to distort the image. I hoped it *was* her.

He looked back at it and hesitated. "Yes."

I observed it some more until I saw it. "You're lying." I put the camera down, fear seeping into my bones. "You're lying. That's me. There's something that she doesn't have that I do. That dress. I have the same gown in my closet right now, and I *know* it's mine." I quickly stood, putting so much distance between us.

He finally turned to look at me. "No, you don't understand."

"I understand that you have some image of me in a dress that I own, and I have no idea how you obtained it. I have never met you before this year." But I couldn't be so sure. His brown eyes were from my memories. I knew him long before this and he wasn't about to tell me how.

"If I tell you, everything becomes much more dangerous for you." His eyes went wide while his eyebrows furrowed. His mouth hung open and not on his own accord. I'd never seen him this way before. Why was he afraid for me?

I shook my head. "Eli, I deserve to know why the hell I was even in that picture. You can't keep this from me. I'm already in danger so whatever you're doing, it's not working."

"You can't know, Mya. I can't tell you!" He turned away to avoid looking me in the eyes.

My lips trembled as I pushed my hair from my face. "You're a stalker." Something far worse than just a murderer. He'd see everyone around me as a criminal. They were the ones out to get me if he chose to see them that way. Maybe he'd been the stalker I had to watch out for all along. They carried more danger.

Rape. Abuse. Murder. Everywhere I went, I wouldn't escape him. One wrong move and he'd snap.

Worst news of all? I couldn't turn him in. His obsession with me would lead to my demise if I didn't strike first.

I'd be damned to not strike him first.

I left his place as quickly as I could, making it back to mine and locking the door.

My blood boiled yet my bones rattled. Why the hell did he have a picture of me? I had to find out where he took it, but I was certain I had to kill him.

Between my mom lying to me and Eli keeping secrets, I was afraid of who to trust. My life was in pieces and I couldn't put the puzzle together.

I watched a movie, but I kept my mind focused on what to do with Eli. I told him I wouldn't talk to him again, but I had to still deal with what happened. I needed to jog my memory some more.

I grabbed the dress from my closet, wincing at the sight of the blood. The bottom of the skirt had been torn—missing even. Eli knew what happened that night and eventually I would, too.

I pulled my clothes off and covered my nose after I put the gown on. It didn't seem to work because nothing came to my mind.

What was I doing wrong?

Of course. I was trying to force it and that wasn't how these memories hit me. But patience had never been a virtue of mine. I hardly had any of those.

I thought back to what Amari had asked of me. Would I choose her or Eli? Hunters or Kaofi? The answer seemed clear, didn't it? Humiliation—an understatement of what I felt finding that photo of me in Eli's apartment. I'd let him get under my skin for too long. I had allowed him into my life. But I think the hunter side of me knew who he was before I ever did.

And because of her, that flame ignited within me. It grew and I continued down this path of distrust towards my neighbor. For once, my gut instinct had been right about someone.

Eli was purely the enemy and I'd fallen into his trap.

Laughter passed by outside the building as some girls walked through the complex.

As I stood on the edge of the forest, distinct laughter echoed from within. If they were hurt, why would they be laughing? My gut told me to go inside. I took a step forward, then a few more until I was walking into something I didn't know of, but she told me they were in trouble. I couldn't ignore that. My heart would never allow it.

The laughter grew and it became clear that it came from males. When I approached, they turned to look at me. "Who the bloody hell are you?" The man with black hair asked.

"Mya. I heard laughing."

The second man, one with brown hair, stretched his arm

in front of the other. "Don't. She's a Kaofi Hunter."

"I'm not a hunter. Do hunters dress in gowns? No, they dress in camouflage to hide. I'm not out here to kill animals." I shook my head and looked back at the edge of the trees. "I wanted to check on you. Someone said you guys needed help."

"Help? We don't need help." He laughed and stepped forward.

I crossed my arms. "I can see that now. What are your names?" I turned slightly, ready to head back.

"I'll never tell you my name." He walked over and grabbed my wrist. "You can't fool me."

His nails dug into my skin. "Hey, what the hell? You're hurting me!" I yanked my arm away from him before I stumbled back into a tree.

"Josh, stop," the curly, black-haired man said, coming closer. "She's telling the truth. She has no idea."

"What?" I grabbed my shoes, throwing them at them. "Don't you dare touch me!"

"I'm Eli." He put his hand out. "Josh is an arse sometimes. I apologize on his behalf." He chuckled and glanced at Josh.

I shook my head. "Fuck you both. You're sick." I turned around and headed the way I came. I was not going to get myself killed or worse. Those guys couldn't be trusted and if they didn't need help, I wasn't about to stick around for it.

"Mya, don't go." Eli wasn't ready to say goodbye. That didn't stop me. "Who sent you?" he shouted.

I stopped in my tracks. Who sent me? I spun around to face him, but a word never left my lips. A woman with blonde hair and dark eyes, almost black was who'd sent me. Why did he care?

Eli swallowed, his eyes darting to Josh's. "Lucy is back."

010 Tuesday, September 3rd

Piano music woke me up this morning. It was the most calming way to begin my day before I lost my sanity. I got dressed and ready for school, not giving any thought to my outfit. I threw on jeans and a simple T-shirt.

I walked out to the parking lot, surprised that his spot was empty. He must have left extra early. I didn't know why but I assumed it had something to do with what went down yesterday. If he wanted to take it harder than penis, I'd let him be my guest.

Class went by painstakingly slow. As hard as I tried, I couldn't keep my mind off Eli. The day went on and I never ran into him once.

Telling him I wouldn't speak to him again must have gotten under his skin. I wasn't going to lie and say it didn't satisfy a part of me. Knowing I could hurt him in such a way coaxed the hunter side.

I took a walk near the complex to clear my head. It was the least I could do for myself after everyone turned my world inside out. "All you had to do was tell me why you had a photograph of me. That was all you had to do, Kay." I scanned the area surrounding me.

I wanted to know more. Whether I was talking to him or not, I had to know why he had a picture of me. My ambitions refused to falter.

"Mya." Someone caught up to me, grabbing my shoulder.

That voice wasn't hard to pinpoint. It only came from Amari—deep, yet powerful. "Yes?"

"Have you thought about what I told you?" She stopped me from walking, facing me.

I took a moment to hesitate before nodding. "I have. I'm ready to learn how to be a Kaofi Hunter."

He'd been so worried about telling the truth, but that also had me turning to *his* enemies for help. He sent me into the arms of the hunters. They were the people who made me feel like I belonged somewhere. Amari was willing to tell me the truth that Eli wouldn't.

She smiled. "I'm so glad you've made the right decision. There is so much we have to teach you."

"We?" I gripped the strap of my bag.

She grabbed my free hand. "Yes, come on." She dragged me away from the complex and looked back at me. "We don't use cars. Cars have license plates. They can be tracked and remembered easier, and they're harder to hide. Eventually, your abilities will kick in."

"Abilities?"

She halted. "Abilities. We are gifted with special abilities to take down the immortal creatures. Hunters are trusted to do their job. Vampires and werewolves can run fast. We can run faster." She glanced back with a sly smile.

"What—"

Amari took off into the forest, her feet moving much more quickly than my eyes could keep up with.

A howl echoed around me and I turned my head. Werewolves? As much as I wanted to call for Amari, my pride wouldn't allow me. "Come get me, mutt." I knew that wasn't me speaking anymore. It was the hunter.

Twigs snapped and leaves crunched beneath someone's feet. I spun in the direction of the sound, but I couldn't be sure where it came from. The forest was a maze of echoes that bounced wherever they pleased.

I had no weapons with me but my own limbs. So, I clenched my fists to prepare myself for a fight.

"Kill her..." Whispers rustled the leaves.

I whipped around as my chest tightened from the high-pitched voices of dread.

"We need a bigger army." More whispers.

These weren't human, nor Kaofi. They sounded off. Mimicking something human, but never quite getting it right. Uncanny valley, they called it.

Nightmares were made of it.

The footsteps came closer. "Mya, you good?" Amari came forward.

I brushed invisible dirt from my pants. "I'm good. I just need to know, now that you mention cars and license plates, why does Eli have a car or an apartment if he's invisible? How would a Kaofi attain a human possession?"

"Most vampires pride themselves in their wealth and materialistic possessions. Even if humans can't see it, Hanti and Kaofi can. It's not hard for a Kaofi to sign a lease. Humans are oblivious. As long as someone pays rent and keeps the place nice, nobody questions it. Have you ever met your property management?"

No. I'd never seen them in person before. Everything was handled on devices.

"Don't people notice a car with no driver?" I asked.

Another sly smile. Was this funny to her? "Not if the car was built by Kaofi. They have things, use them in ways regular humans can't fathom with just the naked eye. It's how the supernatural world thrives, Mya. Humans will deny anything just to believe they're going to a better place when they die."

Of course Kaofi had their own factories. Their own jobs.

She said, "Also, we go by two names. Kaofi Hunters, or more precisely, Hanti." Hanti. Interesting.

We both left the clearing and she nudged me. "Try it."

"What?" I looked at her. She couldn't be serious.

"Try it. You'll never learn if you don't try." She pointed at the forest ahead of us.

Ah, running. More precisely, my *ability*.

A part of me feared the worst and yet, I ached to try. Running as fast as Amari looked exhilarating. My abilities needed a push to come out of their shell.

Bending a knee and leaning forward just a bit, I got into position. A long breath passed my lips as I focused on the ground before me. Pushing my foot off, I propelled myself forward. My steps picked up the longer I went, and trees passed me in a blur. I was running faster than any *average* human.

My heart raced as the blood pumped adrenaline throughout my veins. Nothing could stop this feeling.

Except for a tree.

I ran into a tree and cried out, falling back onto the floor. "Damnit!" I yelled.

Amari appeared at my side. "Yeah, I should have warned

you about the trees. You'll have to be more observant on dodging things the faster you go." She helped me off the ground. "Let's go meet the others."

Holding my nose the rest of the way to a cabin, I managed to get it to stop bleeding. Amari pulled me through the front door. "Just sit down and let Ryan inspect it. He can tell you if it's broken."

I took a seat on a chair and used both of my index fingers to rub the sides of my nose. Blood covered every inch of my shirt. Maybe I could use it to scare the Kaofi.

"Who the hell is this?" a man asked.

Amari grabbed some supplies. "Hunter, shut the hell up. She's one of us." She brought them over and pulled my shirt over my head. "We always have extra clothes here for many reasons, as you've discovered."

I laughed a bit. "Hunter. And he's a hunter."

He scowled. "I haven't heard that one before."

"Who's she?" another man asked.

Amari stood and looked at him. "Mya. She's a Hanti, like us. I need you to check if her nose is broken." She stepped back and gestured to me.

He came over and kneeled in front of me. He touched my nose and shook his head to confirm his exam. "It'll be a bit sore but it's fine."

Amari threw me a new shirt, which I put on right away. "She's..." She wasn't sure how to word her sentence.

I wiped the dried blood from my nose. "I'm adopted."

"What use is she then?" Hunter asked.

Amari snapped her eyes to him. "She's a hunter. That's what use she is. She wants to be one. I gave her the choice and she chose us. That's what we do. We can't just turn her away because she wasn't raised as one."

A voice came from the darkness, "She just needs to be trained like the rest of us." A woman stepped forward.

"Thank you, Clara." Amari sighed. "Finally, someone who understands."

She smiled a bit. "Who would I be if I didn't understand your actions?" She walked closer.

Amari smiled in return and I sensed something deeper between the two of them. I could recognize love reflecting from the soul even if I'd never experienced true love myself.

Ryan took a seat on the couch. "Mya, huh?"

I nodded a bit, now paying attention to him. "That's my name."

The inside was small, and nothing was taken care of. There was a desk with plenty of papers and weapons but nothing else stood out. Not a single picture hung on these walls.

"Why are you here?" he asked, sitting back.

"I want to be a hunter," I paused. "I *am* a hunter." I pushed some hair behind my ear. "I met Amari before school started. There was some creep watching me... She came over and bailed me out."

Amari grabbed another chair and sat on it, the back of it was in front of her. "He was also a Kaofi. He noticed you watching him. He knew you were one of us and if I hadn't swooped in, he would have had you killed before you knew anything."

Of course, he had to have been such a creature. "What was he...? Can you tell what kind of creatures you're dealing with?"

She shrugged. "Sometimes. While Hanti share abilities, there are some abilities we don't all have. I see colors. The color glowing from them tells me what they are. Purple was radiating off him, which says he's a fallen angel."

"Colors..." That was an interesting ability to have. I knew it wasn't one I'd gotten. They looked like regular people to me. There were no colors to separate them. They weren't any less visible. However, they did smell different from humans. "We met through Eli officially. Amari 'slept' with him to get control over him," those words left my tongue with poison dripping from them.

"Amari," Clara said.

She looked back at her. "Clara, please. Not now."

"Then when?" She narrowed her eyes. "It's always: *not now, Clara.*" She turned away from her and groaned. "I don't like it when you go and put yourself in danger without informing the rest of us. They're vile creatures and if anything were to happen to you, we'd be devastated."

Amari got off the chair. "Listen to me, it meant nothing. I didn't enjoy any of it. It was just to get his blood and some hair. That was it. It's nothing personal."

"It's personal to me, damnit!" She shook her head and gave herself a moment to calm down. "Whatever." She turned to study me. "So, this Eli, who the hell is he?"

I chewed my lip. "He's...complicated." *No, he's not. He's an asshole.* "That's right. He's an asshole. He knew from the moment I met him that I was a Hanti. He played me as you've played him. He's been stalking me like I'm his latest infatuation but now, I know better. Whatever plans you have to bring him down, I'm in. I want to be the one who does it."

Clara turned her head towards Amari. "You were alone with him when Mya would have easily been a better ploy. He probably has no idea she knows she's a Hanti. She could have brought him down until he begged for mercy and now we have no option because now he probably knows she knows you." She dropped her arms as all anger slipped away from her. "Follow through with your plans. It's not as if my opinion ever mattered." She disappeared into a room and closed the door.

Amari sighed. "Damnit."

I swallowed and thought about Clara's idea. "She's right."

"What?" Amari looked at me. "What are you talking about?"

I fixed the shirt I wore. "I'd be a better fit. He has no idea that I know what I am, right? I could hurt him the most. I could string him along for the ride of his life."

Do you say that because you mean it or because you want an excuse to kiss him?

I was going to go through with this. It would take a lot of training before I could fool him into loving me, but I was willing to be patient. After what he pulled, I wanted him to know what it felt like to be *hurt*. He kissed me and played with my emotions, formulating lies. He'd been stalking me this entire time. Who did that?

Kaofi.

Kaofi who had *no heart*.

I wasn't sure how long it would be before I was going to be ready to pull this off.

Eli kept secrets from me, and these Hanti gave me a home. The answer was clear to who I could count on and call my friends.

This plan would need to be elaborate. He couldn't suspect that I knew anything at all, or it'd all crumble.

"This could work," Amari said as she began to pace while chewing on a fingernail. The stress of Clara being mad at her didn't help. Now we knew why *she* had short nails.

"Only if you're really okay with this plan." Ryan leaned

forward from the couch. “If you’re not, we can find another.”

Hunter scoffed.

I glanced at him for a moment before looking at Ryan and Amari. “No, I’m ready to do this. I’m a Hanti and it’s time I accept my position in society.”

Entertainer

"She becomes far more dangerous the more she knows. We should have taken her out when we had the chance," I said as I circled the haze of shadows.

A shadow stepped forward, his black cloud fading away as a man stood before me. "We tried. She got away the first time."

Excuses.

These pathetic excuses didn't change the fact that she was a threat to all we built. I supposed it should have been mostly on me, but we couldn't dwell on trivial thoughts now. I chose to focus my energy on the best way to tear her apart from the inside out.

Emotionally, she wasn't all that stable.

I'd use it. Twist it. Bathe in it. I'd become everything she'd feared and more.

All I had to do now was search for the weakest spot in her security and yank it from under her.

011 Wednesday, April 18th

"Eli is an asshole and you should forget about him by now," Juliet said with a hint of frustration. She had no idea what I was or what my plan consisted of. All that mattered to her was that I forget Eli ever existed. I sounded like a lunatic who couldn't get over a crush. It was anything *but.*

I looked back at her for a moment. "I'm just saying there's no point. I want *revenge.* It's that simple." I could see her lack of interest as clear as day. "Let's change the subject." I shooed my hand. "So, the masquerade. What about that?"

I stopped to grab some food from the cafe. My stomach was killing me today. Amari suggested to me certain diets to help keep my health in check. I missed eating cake more than once a week.

A smile formed, her nodding along. "Ah, yes, your birthday. You're turning twenty-two. How exciting." To Juliet, the masquerade was a birthday party. She had no idea why it was really planned.

I rolled my eyes playfully and chewed on an orange slice. "No, I'm talking about the ball. It's the dance of the year, and it's my dream dance. The only one I've ever actually cared for." I threw her a small smirk, pointing my finger at her.

Deep down, I wanted one chance to dance with a handsome stranger in case Eli killed me at the end of this.

She laughed. "Yes, you love it. But I think it's so perfect because it falls on your twenty-second birthday, which also falls on a Friday. What's better than that?"

"Nothing. Well, no. If I had a chance to attain a boyfriend, it would be better. But I can't have it all, can I?" I peeled more of my orange before shoving another slice in my mouth.

There was one thing that would make this better. If I survived, I could maybe have it all.

She looked down at her food and back at me. "Yes, a boyfriend. So exciting." Her tone didn't elicit any hint of joy. I'd noticed when I tried to talk about my love life or anything related to it, Juliet wasn't too eager to jump on the bandwagon. I wasn't energized enough to ask her what was up with that—at least not today.

I was ecstatic about this ball, though. I'd spent months training hard. I'd changed my diet and embraced my superhuman abilities to make sure nothing went wrong. Eli would never know what was coming to him. I couldn't let it fail, either, because I was finally going to be the ruin of Eli Kay.

Juliet glanced around the area, but her eyes moved quickly. She was looking for someone.

"What is it?" I asked.

She shook her head. "It's nothing."

"It's not nothing. Don't lie to me. Are you pregnant? Did Cole break up with you?" I grabbed her hand.

She laughed. "No, no. I'm not pregnant and Cole and I are fine. I just..." She took a moment to think. "I don't trust Amari."

I sighed and rubbed the bridge of my nose. "Why?"

"Because she... She's..." She wasn't able to find the words she was looking for. She didn't have to say it. I knew.

"You think Amari has a crush on me." And we were back on the subject that Juliet was never happy about my potential dates. "You can pluck that thought from your head because she doesn't. She likes girls and I don't. Is that why you don't trust her? I've known her longer than you, Juliet. She doesn't like me romantically. She's with another woman." I threw away my orange peel.

Juliet squared her shoulders. "Who?"

"A woman you wouldn't know. You don't need to keep protecting me. You never approve of anyone who isn't you. Stop that, please. Let me be an adult. Let me make my own choices," I said.

She nodded a little. "I'm sorry. I just... It's like having a male friend. It's too easy to fall for someone you're attracted to. You get to know them and next thing you know, you love them, and I don't want her to get caught up in that when you're..." She never finished the sentence.

"Straight, Jules. I'm straight. Amari is bisexual. They're not bad words. They just...are." I cleared my throat. "Why would you be so interested in friends falling for each other?"

She shrugged her shoulders and looked out the window.

I laughed. "Are you in love with me?"

She didn't smile, nor did she blush. Instead, her eyes glossed over. "Because I know what it's like to fall for someone. I know what it's like to be rejected by someone you love the most."

My smile faded out like a movie scene. "You never told me."

"It wasn't important then. Before we met, I was friends with this boy. He was...so special. He made me feel like I mattered. We did everything together. One day, I kissed him. I was tired of not knowing. I couldn't live like that anymore. When I pulled away, he apologized. He told me he was sorry because he didn't see me that way." A tear slid down her cheek. "After that, our friendship was never the same. We fizzled out."

I reached over and wrapped my fingers around hers. "I'm so sorry. He missed out on a wonderful woman."

Neither of us said another word. Juliet just wiped away her tears before looking at the clock. She rushed out of the cafe before I could stop her.

"What was that about?" Amari asked from beside me.

It wasn't my business to tell Amari Juliet's private thoughts. "How's the plan coming?"

She grabbed a book from her bag and laid it on the counter. "Well, actually. I finished. It took me so long, but I finally found the potion I was looking for."

"What? Potion?" I looked at the page she'd opened. It had a spell for inflicting pain on a vampire.

Being undead made them more tolerant of pain and injuries. This would penetrate that barrier.

She nodded and grabbed something, showing me a bottle of *yellow liquid.* "Vampires. This is the color I see when a vampire is around, and this is what I can use against them. His blood, his hair... I have two means of DNA, enough to get him to talk. He will tell us what we need to know."

"What do we need to know?" I had no idea she'd been so focused on this for so long. She was obsessed with bringing

Eli to the ground. It almost instilled fear in my bones.

She groaned as her head fell back. "Mya, you're killing me here. We need to know where the vampires live. We can get rid of them for good if he tells us what we need to know. We can find out where they breed, sleep, eat, hunt... We can destroy them."

We could kill every vampire that ever *existed.*

Don't let her go through with this, Mya. You know you don't want Eli dead. You never did. The hunter side of you is trying to poison your mind. What was the worst thing he did? Kill gang members? Lead you to think he was interested in you when he wasn't? Play with your feelings? That doesn't deserve the death penalty.

"What about the ball? I thought we were going to hurt him through me." I furrowed my brows.

"We don't have to. The masquerade can be another ploy to get through to the Kaofi world. They'll be there and they can't see our faces. They can't tell who's a Hanti and who's Kaofi. We blend in. We have the ability to know who's who, and we can bring all of them down. This is it, Mya." A grin spread across her face as she gripped the bottle. It was the same excitement I got when I skipped my period.

We had come up with the masquerade ball to lure out the Kaofi. It also created a great excuse for me to lure in Eli and twist him around my finger like a puppet on strings.

"Amari, I love you, but I'm going with my plan. I've been focused on it for a while, and I want to bring him down myself. You knew what he was doing when he kissed me and 'slept' with you. I didn't. He used me for his own pleasure until someone came along to give him what he wanted." I clenched my jaw. "He's mine."

"Mya." She put her potion away. "Are you still hungover

about that? You didn't even love the guy."

I closed the book in my hands. "No. You don't get to say that. He knows things about me that neither of us can answer. I'm sticking to my original idea and you can't take that away from me. If you want me to be your *marionette*, let me prove myself."

She grabbed the book from me and returned it to her bag. "Marionette? You're one of us. We gave you a choice."

"You're right. I made a choice. Let me follow through with it my way." I walked past her and left the building.

She only wanted to be around me because I was easy to manipulate. The choice was between kill or be killed. She never let me be just human.

When Eli left early the day after I stopped talking to him, he stayed absent for a week. He returned after that and we never spoke. We haven't said a word since that day. I missed talking to him. I missed the banter.

You miss the way he made you feel.

Where the hell had this voice come from? She was always invading my privacy.

As I took a seat on a bench, I observed the humans walking by. Their lives were so simple. They had to focus on establishing their careers and following dreams. I didn't understand why I was here if I was shoved into a new identity regardless of what I wanted.

I never got the choice to be a hunter or not. I was born as I was.

When the smell of death floated in my direction, I followed my eyes to see Eli by the fountain. He wasn't talking to anyone because they couldn't see him. He had nobody but himself. Why was he still *here*?

I observed the way his nose crinkled when he was deep in

thought. His eyes displayed the sorrow plaguing him. A part of me wanted to run over and hold him until he smiled again. Guilt washed over me as I focused on his stalking. He was a danger. Nothing more.

Deep down, I wanted to kiss away whatever it was that kept his mind locked up. He seemed so cold and empty. If only I could fill the need for something missing...

Eli thought I had no idea who I was and yet he never killed me. I had to wonder why he didn't just snuff me out right there. Was his obsession so strong? Why obsess over the predator?

If I was the hunter, why was he letting me live to find out who I always was inside? He was digging his own grave and he was giving me the chance to bury him.

I wasn't supposed to be romantically interested in him in any way, and I knew he wasn't interested in me. Yet, I let myself dig deeper into the pain.

It had been a long time since I had a boyfriend or anyone to care about in such a way. I wanted him to rest his head in my lap as we watched a movie. I wanted to run my fingers through his hair and lift his spirits when he had a bad day. I craved something real.

He'd never once pretended to be someone he wasn't, at least not entirely. He had shown me his ways.

We came from two different worlds that could never come together. We would always be at each other's throats.

Eli was making the same choice as me. He couldn't choose to be human. It was kill or be killed, and he chose to kill the same way I had. Now, I wasn't so sure I wanted to be the predator, and I think he wasn't so sure he wanted to be the prey.

012 Friday, April 20th

Every glance I made at him, he never returned. Curiosity piqued my interest when it came to Eli, but after all these months, mine never piqued his. Why wasn't he looking my way? Maybe he found someone else to hold his interest instead.

As hard as I tried to ignore him, I couldn't. I'd told them I would spend my time training and luring Eli in to mess with his heart, but I wasn't so sure I wanted to do that anymore. Something about him drew me in, and who was I to say no?

Anyone else would have thought I'd lost my mind. Here I was, watching Eli from afar as if he were something mesmerizing. In my mind, he was. The way he walked told me he didn't fear anything that anyone could actually see. His secrets were larger and whatever they were, he was determined to keep them buried.

He leaned against a wall of the building and ran a hand through his hair. I figured he was a vampire the moment

Amari told me she was going to use the potion on vampires and it'd work on him. Also the moment she told me vampires appeared yellow to her, the same way Eli did.

I almost followed the scent that wafted my way because it wasn't the smell of cat piss this time. It couldn't have been coming from Eli. I scanned the area to locate the source, but I didn't know who it was. If only I had the ability to see colors could I then see who the Kaofi was here.

Whoever they were, they smelled of rain and mud, and it was a nostalgic scent. I wanted to hold them tight and never let go. What kind of creature smelled so amazing?

I took a few steps, pretending to be walking mindlessly around the area. I was attempting to see which direction it came from, and as soon as I got closer, I followed the trail just a bit.

Did any other immortals know who I was? Surely Eli knew, and Amari did, too. But they knew because I could see Eli.

As I glanced over at a figure, his eyes met mine and his whole posture shifted. He immediately turned away from me and began walking, and then I knew. He was the one who smelled like heaven.

He took off running, and I didn't have time to look back and see if Eli was looking my way. Instead, I ran off to keep up with him.

I just wanted to ask questions. I couldn't forever be left in the dark.

Pushing faster, I reached out to grab him, but he escaped my grasp. I jumped forward and tackled him to the ground. It wasn't my best plan, but it did the job.

I turned him over and pinned him to the ground. A gasp escaped my lips. "Owen." I probably did appear as a monster to him, treating him the way I was. In my defense, I didn't want him running off or using any power against me. I still had no idea *what* he was. "What are you?" I asked.

He scowled as if I'd done something wrong. *Had I?* "Why do you think I'd tell you?"

"I'm not here to hurt you. I just want to know what you are." I cleared my throat and let go of him. I stood and lent my hand to help him up, but he stood up on his own.

He narrowed his eyes. "Can't you figure it out?"

I lifted my chin. "I've discovered that vampires smell like cat piss. That's all I know." Essentially, I had no idea what creatures really existed because in my world, they were referred to as Kaofi. It was never specified which Kaofi they were. "But...I have an idea," I whispered.

Owen crossed his arms. "It's none of your business."

"All I ask is what are you. I just want to know what kind of creatures exist. Why are you giving me the cold shoulder? We used to make out in the pouring rain." Rain. Mud. That's why those scents seemed so familiar. That was why I appreciated them so much.

"You're a hunter, can't you figure that out? Can't your new friends help?"

I swallowed. "I don't know how to ask them that question."

He dropped his arms at his side for a moment. "Mya, I've been trying to contact you all year."

"I don't know what that means."

Ghost gone missing.

He squeezed his hands into fists. "I've been trying to get your attention. But you're far too focused on being a Hunter now. Far too focused on *him*."

"Eli? Owen, I'm training to kill Eli. He's got a picture of

me and I'm afraid he's been stalking me for a while. If I don't train, I lose. And I cannot afford to lose."

Owen let out a laugh, but it wasn't the same laughter I'd heard when we were together. "I see the way you look at him, Mya. It's hard to miss."

"Why do you care?"

He clenched his jaw. "Anything else?"

"I have many questions but I'm sure you aren't ready to hear them." Like why did he smell of rain and mud, and what kind of ghosts existed? Did that mean that after we died, we *all* became ghosts?

Owen threw his arm out towards me, pointing at my hands. "Try me. You seem like you're nonthreatening."

"Yet you ran away."

He scoffed and leaned against a tree. "Well?"

"Why couldn't I see you earlier?"

"Because I wasn't ready, mentally speaking."

"Why?"

"Because the way our relationship ended left me a mess."

"You were hit by a car, Owen. You make it sound as if one of us cheated."

He stepped forward and grabbed my chin, lifting my head. "But I was dead for a long time. You had to grieve me, Mya. You would get drunk at parties and make out with strangers because the pain was too much, and I know you still haven't accepted my death."

"It was a summer fling."

Owen brushed his knuckles across my cheek. "I don't think it was."

My breath hitched as I screamed inside my head for him to kiss me. It had been so long. I missed everything about Owen. He'd certainly been the most romantic man I'd met, and I was certain I'd been falling in love.

I think I already had, too.

Then the car hit him.

Swallowing the lump and fighting the butterflies, I said, "I'll go now so you don't feel threatened any longer." I turned on my heel.

He made me pause when he said, "What about us?"

"What about us?" I glanced back.

"Nevermind. You should get back. If you want to kill Eli, you need more training."

I gasped at the insult but he only chuckled in response. Despite our disagreement, it couldn't mask the question: *what if.* What we could have been. What we still could be. A hint of sorrow lingered behind both of our façades.

The complex came back into my view and Eli wasn't anywhere to be found. My heart almost dropped from my chest to my stomach. It had been far too long since we spoke, and I missed talking to him. How could I lie to myself and say I didn't?

I headed to my apartment and plopped onto my bed. I didn't want to be bothered anymore today and thankfully nobody did. Amari was probably with Clara while Hunter and Ryan were training.

Training.

I needed to be doing that. I'd been training with them on being a hunter for the last seven or eight months. After Amari introduced me to the group, I was put through strenuous tests to see if I could take this seriously. Well, I could, and I did.

They had trained me in combat fighting as well as using my superhuman abilities. I'd learned even a bit about the history of Hanti and how we came into existence.

Long ago, a human met up with a Kaofi. That Kaofi had taken loved ones, and the human was rightfully pissed off. That was what started the hatred for Kaofi, but when the human knew they were no match for a creature, they went into research about how to defeat them.

After many empty books and useless information, she finally found some kind of spell that would end Kaofi lives. However, written in small print was a price to pay and she ignored it. When the spell was performed, the Kaofi didn't drop dead. Few did, and she didn't understand, but days later, the truth came out.

She could feel when a Kaofi was around. She could feel the death, or the life, or whatever they were. She knew how to tell them apart from the humans and it wasn't long after her superhuman abilities kicked in.

From that day forth, the spell had created a line of hunters who were now gifted abilities to help them take down Kaofi, and it was forbidden for any Kaofi or Hanti to fall in love. The price we paid was giving up our dreams to fight a war we never asked to join.

I couldn't be sure if any Kaofi or Hanti had ever broken these laws, but it wouldn't have mattered. Eli and I would never speak and when we finally did, I was supposed to make him pay. I wasn't sure if I wanted to, though.

I told them I was ready to bring Eli down and be a Hanti, but I wasn't wholly sold on the idea. I still had dreams to be a fashion designer and those weren't going to change. Besides, why was I obligated to kill someone?

It didn't seem fair to put such a burden on my shoulders. I had no idea what I was for twenty-one years. I didn't know who my real parents were. I barely knew who *I* was.

Yet here I was now joining a group of hunters to take

down Kaofi. As far as I knew, most of them weren't even horrible people. They were just trying to survive like the rest of us. Could we really fault them for that?

Sure, one killed humans. Many of them probably did, and I wasn't going to say they were all innocent. But they weren't all villains, either. So, who was the villain here? Was it me?

As I laid back, I stared at the ceiling. My phone pinged and I checked it to see a text from Juliet. She wasn't coming back tonight because she was staying with Cole. It was typical. Ever since he entered the picture, she'd spent most time with him. That was one of the reasons I didn't really like him. However, it wasn't my choice who she dated so I had to let her make her own mistakes.

I closed my eyes for just a moment and Eli entered my mind. He took that picture of me, no doubt. How could I lose so many memories? How could I lose the biggest memory of when I *first* met Eli? It couldn't have been the day before the first day of school, could it?

Maybe so. Maybe he took that picture without my knowledge and he was stalking me. Maybe I had no recollection of that night because something awful happened and he did something vile before erasing my memory. Maybe...my own mind erased the memory to protect me.

If Eli had done something awful, I was thankful we weren't on speaking terms anymore. I would eventually find out and a part of me hoped he wasn't a bad guy so we could be friends, but the other part hoped he was just so I could kill him with the hunters and not feel guilty for doing it. I wanted it to be so easy to pick a side, but I knew deep down that wouldn't be the case.

Like humans, Kaofi must have had both the good and the bad and it wasn't always black and white. There were those who were trying to do good, and those trying to do bad.

If only Eli knew that I knew what I was... However, he didn't, and that was what put him in more danger. He was my target, and he had no idea what we had in store for him the day of the masquerade ball. It was only a week away now, and I hoped he prepared himself or his blood would be on my dress next.

013 Saturday, April 21st

"Ready, set, go!" Ryan yelled as Amari and Hunter raced through the trees. Part of our training was going against other Hanti.

Clara nudged me, pointing to Hunter. "Amari is good but she's never once beat Hunter in a race. He's not just named Hunter for no reason. He's one of the best."

I nodded as Hunter returned to the group before Amari. She groaned in frustration as Hunter downed a bottle of water. "You always assume you'll win but I've been training since I was able to walk."

It never occurred to me that some of them have been Hanti since birth. They were raised in this lifestyle, so this was all they knew. They never had any chance to build dreams and go for them only for it to be ripped away in a flash. No—that was me.

"How do you train as a toddler?" I asked.

Hunter looked at me, giving me a weary look. He still didn't trust me. What had I done to prove I wasn't in this wholly? I wasn't, but he didn't know that. "When you have two parents who are also Hanti, they don't give you a lot of time to be a kid. You're homeschooled to learn about different Kaofi, and what their weaknesses and strengths are. I've been running, fighting, and using all my abilities since I could walk because my parents wanted me to carry on the legacy."

"Sounds strict."

"It has to be if Kaofi are threatening lives."

"Have any Kaofi you've ever come across been threatening?"

He cleared his throat. "Yes. Plenty have been threatening. If you're implying that we kill innocent people, I can assure you that isn't true. These are monsters. They're not loving."

"But why are Kaofi specifically bad? Because the ones you run into happen to be? What about being immortal makes someone a bad person? Being cursed to live forever isn't their fault. They can't help being born in that species."

Hunter stepped towards me. "Are you here to convert us or are you here to train?"

"You've been raised with one view of the world and no chance to tackle any other perspectives. Excuse me if I think your view is skewed because you've never challenged it yourself." I closed the gap, not allowing him to intimidate me.

Hunter narrowed his eyes, but Ryan pulled him back. "It's not worth it. You know she's been raised in a world where she's learned many views. Just accept that she disagrees with you and move on."

Hunter grumbled and walked away from the group.

Amari patted my back. "Hunter knows nothing but this life. You're telling him everything he stands for is wrong, and you can understand why that might piss him off."

I let out a sigh. "I know. I'm sorry for bringing it up." Hunter and I were from different worlds and I knew we'd probably never agree.

Ryan looked at me and approached me with slow strides. "You and Hunter might always collide on your ideas of hunting, but this is our group. I get the sentiment, but you can't nudge your way in and try to change our minds. It's not your place."

So many people had always told me it was never my place. It wasn't my place to be at home with Mom who wasn't my real family. It wasn't my place to know why I was in a photo Eli had. It wasn't my place to be just a human. It just wasn't my place to exist as I chose to.

I left the hunters and headed back to the small cabin. I ignored Hunter's glare as I made my way to the room in the back. I pulled my hair back into a ponytail and punched the bag hanging from the wooden beam. I had to release my anger and I also needed to train to be better than the Mya of today.

Punching the bag again, I kept going at it with all of my strength.

One swing. "It's not your place, Mya." *Another swing.* "You have to be a hunter, Mya." *Third swing.* "You have to trust me, Mya!" *Multiple swings.*

After many punches, I took a deep breath and rested my head against the bag. "Maybe I don't effing trust anyone. Maybe I don't want this life. Maybe I just want to be a fashion designer and find someone to love and grow old with. I just want to be normal and fit in somewhere," I whispered.

Nobody had ever asked me what I wanted. They all just

told me what to do as if I wasn't capable of making my own choices. I was about to turn twenty-two and I was very capable of making those decisions myself.

I heard a knock on the door, and I glanced back at Clara. "What?"

"Can I come in?"

I gestured for her to come in, but I didn't say a word.

She cleared her throat as she leaned against the wall. "Everyone here is a bit on edge."

I snickered.

"I know it doesn't seem like much," she said," but we do care about you. We like you. Hunter does, too, in his own way. I know that Amari just sprung this life on you without really giving you a thought, but she means well."

"They all mean well, don't they? Telling a grown ass woman what to do means well. Maybe I should just focus on making my gown for the ball." It had been coming along nicely.

She shrugged. "Sometimes. I know we can't make your choices for you, but we just want to help you. You are what you are, Mya, and nobody can change that. You're a Hanti and it's in your blood. You have the ability to see these Kaofi. You can smell their true scents. When they see you, they will know what you are, and Kaofi feel threatened by us at all times. They will take advantage of you and try to kill you whether or not you choose this life. You don't have a choice to be a part of it or not, and you have to at least know how to defend yourself and kill these Kaofi when they do threaten you. Do you understand?"

I turned to face her. "You're just trying to prep me for the worst-case scenarios." I rubbed my eyes. "But what if I don't choose to be a full hunter? What if I don't want to spend every waking hour searching for these creatures?"

"Nobody can really force you. We might judge you, but we can't do much about it, can we?" A small smile creeped up.

"I spent my entire life with one dream in mind. I want to be a fashion designer and I can't just pretend I don't want that. Then Amari told me I was a hunter when I was beginning my senior year of college. I'm so close to finishing school, and I don't want to make it this far just to drop it all. I don't want all this debt to be for no good reason. I want to be a fashion designer, not a hunter." Well, that wasn't entirely true. I wanted both. I had been designing and making my own gown for the ball—the ball in which I was going to *hunt* at.

Clara swallowed, lifting her chin. "Why are you here if you don't want this?"

I dropped my hands to my sides. "I think...a part of me wants to be a hunter. I want to learn about myself and my parents. I want to learn about these Kaofi, but I don't want to do it at the expense of my dream."

She nodded and approached me after pushing herself off the wall. "Well, what if you can have both? I'm not saying it would be easy but why should you have to give up both?"

"Because society teaches us that women can only have one dream. We never get told we can attempt it all."

Clara laughed. "Then ignore them. It's your life you're living. You deserve to get the most out of it."

"But I don't want to just kill Kaofi with no reasoning. What if that Kaofi has a family and they've never hurt anyone? I'm not going to kill them because that's just what we do. I don't want to kill innocent people who never chose to be what they are. They're killing me because they think

I'm a threat, but I don't want to make that same mistake."

Shrugging again, she said, "I can't tell you what to do."

"No, but if I'm going to be a hunter, then I want to make it clear I only kill Kaofi who are evil." I was like a detective who killed the bad guys.

"I can work with that."

"But can Hunter?"

"He has to try."

I looked at the bag and punched it one last time before leaving the room. My knuckles were looking pretty beat up, but it didn't bother me much. Clara got the attention of everyone in the room, and that was when I noticed that everyone was back at the cabin.

Clara gestured for me to break the news, but I shook my head. I wasn't going to talk to these assholes about something they may judge me for. "Mya says she wants to be here, but she only agrees to kill those who deserve it."

Hunter's eye twitched. He didn't want to hear that. To him, I was the girl who had infiltrated his group and forced him to accept me. He had a right to be upset, but I wasn't going to change my mind, either.

Ryan and Amari looked at Hunter, waiting for his answer. Ryan and Amari could probably deal with my decision, but Hunter was the one who needed to give his opinion. It was him or me in this group, and I didn't doubt they would choose him without a second thought. He was the best Hanti there was.

He narrowed his eyes at me. "Why do you think you can change the rules?"

"Because the rules were changed for me when I grew up without any clue I was a hunter." He could judge me all he wanted because I expected that. But he couldn't make me feel guilty for not wanting to murder people without mercy.

"That was on your parents. That was not our fault."

There was a dull ache that formed at the mention of my parents. I longed to know them. I just had to confirm if they were still alive, and I hoped they were. If they weren't, I didn't know how I would take it.

"But you can understand why they did what they did. My parents were like you, Hunter, but they gave me this life. Surely you must respect their decision from one Hanti to another."

Amari stood in front of him. They communicated through their eyes, and after a few minutes, he relaxed. Whatever she told him, he seemed to calm his temper and I was thankful I didn't have to worry about being kicked out of the group.

She moved out of his way and he crossed his arms to make sure I knew I still couldn't be fully trusted. "Do what you must, but I will kill *all* Kaofi because that's what I must do for our planet."

I didn't agree with him, but we'd have to take baby steps. I was only glad I could stay and do what I needed. Maybe this would work out and maybe I wouldn't have to kill Eli at this rate. However, Hunter might do that for me if I didn't. Eli was my responsibility now and I had taken on that task when I promised the group I would break him.

He'd spent his time ignoring me when he used to taunt me, and that was fair. However, that didn't make him a villain and maybe I never *truly* believed he was. I wasn't quite sure who the real villain was here. It could have been me.

I'd still need to show them that I was still on their side and I somehow had to prove that at the masquerade ball.

014 Sunday, April 22nd

I took a seat on the stool as Mom held out a spoon. "Does this taste right?" she asked. I gave her a thumbs up as I tasted it, and she went back to stirring the sauce. She'd always been a wonderful cook.

"Do you know anything about my birth parents?" I asked her.

She looked at me and shook her head a bit. "I don't."

"Someone must know who they are." I swallowed. "I want to know where I come from." I knew it was hard for my mom to hear me talk about my birth parents when she loved me so much, but I still wanted to learn about them and more about myself as a Hanti. Did I have other siblings?

Mom shrugged and sprinkled in some spices. "I don't think it'll be too hard. Even sealed records can be opened."

I chewed on my lip and straightened my back as I folded my arms on the counter in front of me. "Why did you pick me? I mean, did you pick me out of the other babies or were you just handed a baby?"

She stopped stirring the sauce. "I wasn't just handed a baby. I was introduced to you. They called me and said you were in need of a home and I wanted to meet you, so I came to see if you would be my new daughter. I wanted a child so bad." She laughed. "And God knows I wasn't about to get pregnant and deal with that, so I went through adoption. It was a long process, but I walked in that room and they brought you in, and I just...I knew right away that you were the baby I wanted to hold forever. I had this connection with you, like you were my own."

Chills ran up my arms as I cleared my throat. "So, you chose me?"

"In a way, *you* chose me. I could see it in your eyes that you wanted me to be your mom." She closed the distance between us. "I don't regret adopting you. I know you'd probably choose to change things if you could, but I never would." She grabbed my hands and squeezed them. "You are my daughter and you always will be."

For so long, I'd assumed that maybe I looked like my father. Before I discovered I was adopted, I'd been told that our father left after I was born. However, I knew that wasn't true now. My mom never loved anyone, and I came along through the adoption system.

"What if there were things about me you didn't know? What if they were scary things? Would you still love me?" I asked.

She frowned. "I could never stop loving you. Why would you ask that?"

I wanted to tell her everything. I wanted to tell her what I was and what I saw on a daily basis. I wanted to tell her about Amari and the hunters I trained with, but I was scared she would call me crazy. She'd make me feel like I didn't belong.

"Nothing."

She let go of my hands and went back to stirring her sauce. "I will never not love you. Being a mother is about loving your child unconditionally. You could kill and I would still love you. Would I support you? No, but I couldn't just stop loving you." She glanced at me.

Mom was close to the truth, but there was so much more to it. If I told her the truth, I could be putting her in danger. She could forever be a target and I couldn't live with myself if I did that to her. This was my life, and I had to keep it that way.

"What if you find out my parents were killers?" I asked. "Will you be afraid of me ending up like that?"

This caught her attention the most. Maybe she suspected I knew who they were. Not quite, but I knew just enough.

"I raised you. They didn't. I don't believe killing is genetic. You've always been kind to people, and I doubt you'll change that if you find out they happen to be killers." She grabbed the pasta and drained it into a strainer. She returned it to the pot, then mixed it with the sauce.

Unfortunately for me, it was genetic. I was a Hanti just like them. I was supposed to kill Eli without a second thought, but I couldn't. I didn't want to kill him. I just wanted answers, and if those answers were terrifying, I would reconsider murder. However, I couldn't confirm whether or not those answers were horrible.

Mom set out a plate for me. "Don't worry. You never have to question my love for you."

I nodded before devouring my pasta. Some days I wondered if my mom ever got lonely. I had my own life now and she didn't have many friends. "Do you feel alone without me here?" I asked.

She sat beside me and looked at her pasta. "I see Martha all the time."

"That weird lady down the road?"

"She isn't weird. She's eccentric. There's a difference, and I want to make sure she has a friend." That smile of hers appeared right where it always belonged. Genuine.

I squinted my eyes as I ventured deep into thought. Who made sure I had a friend? Was it Amari? Was it Juliet? Juliet was hardly around anymore, so I couldn't really count on her like that. We were beginning to drift apart after all these years, and I'd be the one left behind.

After my visit with Mom, I tried to look up who my parents might have been, but I got nothing. I wasn't tech savvy, and not enough to unseal records that my parents didn't want me getting into.

Maybe I could ask Amari to do it for me.

Someone knocked and my heart leaped in my chest. Could Eli be at my door? No. Could he?

I jumped from the bed and answered it, but my heart sank at the sight. "What are you doing here?" I asked.

Hunter walked in without being invited. He faced me. "I thought we should talk."

"Without the others around? I don't think it's a good idea to let you lose your temper. You aren't fond of me." I gestured, closing the door.

He growled. Where the hell did that come from? "I can control myself."

I stood in front of the door in case I needed a quick escape. "Why do you want to talk? Are you threatening me to leave the group?"

"Stop asking so many damn questions and let me explain."

I shut my mouth.

He rubbed the bridge of his nose and closed his eyes. "I know I've been tough on you but it's only because that's how I was raised. You have so much potential to be one of the best Hanti and I have to be hard on you, so you prove to me that you want this."

I laughed. "That is a load of shit. That is such a cliche excuse. You hate me and it's because I wasn't raised a Hanti."

Hunter rolled his eyes, and that was the first time I'd ever seen him result to annoyance over anger. "No, but it's not exactly your fault. I can't hate you for something out of your control. I know it sounds cliche but it's true. Being able to smell the creatures is an especially useful tool, and the fact that you weren't raised a Hanti will make plenty think you're less skilled than you really are."

Swallowing, I lowered my head. I think Hunter just said I was doing well with my training, but I wasn't about to call him out and have him take it back. "Why is it useful? Don't all hunters have abilities to tell them apart from humans?"

"Hanti, Mya. We prefer to be called Hanti more often than hunters. Most times when we're called hunters, it's derogatory coming from the Kaofi. But by also calling ourselves Hanti, we can shut that down. Kaofi don't know of the term Hanti much, and if they did, they'd never use it."

Yet we used Kaofi. Ironic.

He scanned the living room and saw the bra in Juliet's room. I wasn't even surprised that every male I knew now knew what Juliet's undergarments looked like. He returned his gaze to me. "Yes, and no." He shrugged. "There are Hanti who don't get extra abilities. They have to work extra hard.

Amari's gift is useful because she doesn't even have to search for them. They just glow and she knows which ones are Kaofi. However, that becomes a problem when she looks at them. She sees them glowing and they know she can see them. It gives her away. You, however, can smell them. You know they're around without having to look at them. They don't know you're a Hanti and they don't know you're able to smell them because it's not an obvious ability."

He had a point, but it wasn't the whole truth. "I still can't tell where the scent is coming from. I can't just spot them in a crowd like Amari. How does that make me useful?"

A sly smile met his eyes. "Because together, you and Amari can scope out every Kaofi and we can take them down."

I wasn't about to tell them about Owen. He'd been nice and he wasn't a bad person just because he was a ghost now. He was still my ex.

"So, what? I sniff them and Amari points them out? But then they'll know she's able to see them which defeats the whole purpose of having me around." I shrugged.

He sighed. "You're really not making this easy for me." He rubbed his face until he gathered himself. "You can tell us if someone is around with a simple signal. If they are, Amari can tell us exactly who. Then, we can go in without them ever spotting us. Amari can hide if she needs to. You will make it easy for us because you can walk in a crowd, smell a Kaofi, and leave that crowd without them ever knowing you were there in the first place. You'll be safe and we can swoop in to end them without them seeing it coming."

It made sense. I could, but I didn't want to do this to innocent Kaofi. "Did you not hear what Clara said? I don't want to kill every Kaofi."

He cleared his throat. "Yes, I heard. That's where Ryan

comes in." He walked to my window and pointed to the ground. "Ryan doesn't see colors like Amari, but he senses impure thoughts. He can emotionally get inside of their head if he just pictures himself in their shoes. He can see all of their motives, desires, memories, and everything else you can think of. He can tell us if they are wicked."

This must have been why hunters, or Hanti, would hunt in groups. They could use their abilities to work together.

"But will he be able to tell us if they feel remorse? I don't want to kill one if they're overcome with shame and guilt. That's not fair to them."

"Why would that matter? If they've killed innocent people, their guilt shouldn't play a part. They've hurt others." He shook his head. "I'm not going to let them live because they feel remorseful. They are a threat if they've made the big choice to take a life and hurt others. That doesn't just go away because they feel sorry for themselves."

This argument wasn't going anywhere, and I knew that. He wasn't about to budge, and I wasn't either.

"We can talk about it later," I said. "However, thank you for seeing me as part of the group. I really *do* want to be a Hanti. It makes me feel more connected to my real parents." It was stupid to say that, especially because I loved my mom. But a part of me still wanted to know my biological parents because they gave me the Hanti gene and I couldn't just deny that part of me.

Hunter smiled a bit, and it was an authentic smile this first time around. "Mine, too."

It was that response that made me realize I wasn't the only one who couldn't talk to my real parents. I'd never even taken the time to get to know Hunter. I'd always assumed things but now I knew that he, too, lost his parents and this helped him feel connected. We both shared that need and I couldn't blame him for doing what he did just to remember them. It was a risky business and being a Hanti meant life or death. For me, I could lose my life to this decision, and somehow, I was okay with that.

015 Friday, April 27th

I wasn't so focused on being a Hanti tonight, despite that we'd all agreed this was exactly what the masquerade was.

A hunt.

Instead, I wanted to enjoy my birthday, and I was going to, whether anyone else liked it or not. I checked my own reflection one last time. "I look beautiful." Glancing at her, I jokingly said, "you look decent, too."

Amari smoothed out her gray gown. "Clara will love it, no doubt. I've been trying so hard to make it up to her."

"You'll win her back over. Just show her that you're sorry and you care about her. She'll come around, Amari. I know she will." As for me, I was ready to feel like a sexy woman. I wanted to enjoy myself and let my worries slip away because nobody would know I was the enemy.

My makeup, including my dress, were all made up of red shades. As for my mask, it was made of diamonds, my birthstone. I wore a strapless dress that stopped at mid-thigh to bring it all together. I wanted attention, and I wasn't going to deny it.

A few pairs of eyes watched our every move as we entered the ball room. Most stayed glued to her but that was because of the way she walked. She *owned* this dance.

We walked over to a table of drinks. The snacks were few and far between. Not many Kaofi actually ate food. I tapped her shoulder as I licked the frosting off a cupcake. "Is anyone looking over here? I don't want to seem desperate." I was.

She chuckled. "If he comes, I'll let you know. He's got a yellow glow." She scanned the area. "Maybe he didn't come."

I nodded. Deep down, I wished he would. I needed him to. Not just because it was part of my plan to figure out the reason for that picture, but because I missed him. I wanted to see his meaningful eyes on my birthday. I wanted tonight to go right.

"Hey, Clara," she said, smiling up at the woman with blonde hair standing next to us. She'd been stunned by the gown Clara wore. It was gorgeous. Forest green looked amazing on her. "That is quite the eye candy."

Clara gave her a wink. "Me or the dress?"

Amari grabbed her hand, pulling her closer and whispering, "Both."

I nodded to them, peeling back the wrapper of the cupcake. "Go on. Go dance. You deserve to. I can stay here for a few minutes. I won't break down just yet." I sat down in a chair, savoring every bite of the sweet treat. I was filling the void inside me—the emptiness that had taken over inside my heart.

Amari gave me a pitiful smile and took Clara's hand as the two of them walked into the crowd. I had my food to keep me company, so I knew I'd be okay.

As I looked at the table, my eyes landed on a bottle of wine. I needed to get drunk if I was going to enjoy this at all. I got up and grabbed some wine, pouring it.

A hand landed on my arm. "I know what you're thinking, and trust me, you don't want to do this. You'll regret it." *He came.*

It wasn't the English accent that told me who it was. I recognized his voice either way.

"They do say: *no rain, no flowers.* You bloom when you deal with things naturally, even the anxiety of coming out of your shell," he said in a whisper.

Spinning to face him, I nearly stumbled in my heels. Handsome was an understatement. My body and my brain agreed on one thing tonight—he looked divine. His curly hair was a lovely mess. Stubble formed, attempting to become a beard. He wore a black tux and a black mask that made his brown *eyes* pop for the occasion.

He took pleasure in my distraction, a curve forming in the corner of his mouth.

I cleared my throat to dismiss all thoughts. "It's not your choice."

"If you want to dance with me, I suggest staying sober. I don't need you puking on me." He put his hand out, asking for me to take it and dance with him, and I *took* it. "The birthday girl deserves a dance at the ball of her dreams." He took us to the dance floor.

"How did you know all that...?" Something was still off, but my plan was now being put into action.

"I just do," he whispered into my ear and put his left hand on my waist. His right hand rested in my left one. "Now put your right hand on my shoulder."

I did as he said, mumbling, "I already knew that much."

The next song started, and I looked at him. Dancing had my nerves on edge.

Damn, I should've drunk that wine.

For the moment, I had to wonder if Eli had planned all of this. Had he wanted me to ignore him for so long so he could take me by surprise? This could be an idea of his to get me wrapped around his finger. Something about his expression screamed mystery. He knew so much more than he was letting on, but that part didn't come as a surprise.

And tonight, he didn't smell like cat piss. He was *vanilla.*

"Did you know I love the scent of vanilla?" I asked.

He pulled our chests together, letting his lips fall near my ear. "I know more than you think."

I didn't know how that made me feel. How much did he really know? There were things I didn't want him to find out.

"Are you a stalker?"

His hand pressed against the small of my back, keeping our chests connected. "What I am, is much different. Who's to say I didn't secretly talk to Juliet about this? Romance and stalking are separate things. They should be kept that way."

Lies. Juliet couldn't see him and that was a fact.

I scoffed. "Says the man who keeps a picture of me in his room, a memory of which I have no recollection of. Is that not stalking?"

"You were aware of where you were before that picture. Now, your memory of that event is a whole other issue, but that doesn't make me a stalker. I wish I could tell you more, Love," he whispered. He didn't want anyone else in this room to hear our conservation. I didn't know why, considering he was keeping his secrets to himself anyway.

He moved to the beat. Surprisingly, I was able to follow

along without looking like a one-legged cat. We both danced to the rhythm and our steps fell into utter harmony.

Eli spun me in his arms until my back rested against his chest. "I forgot to tell you that you look absolutely gorgeous." He breathed against my neck. Shivers ran down my spine. He spun me away from him, but brought me back as the song ended, dipping me. "Do I make you cringe?"

I swallowed, seeing his bottomless eyes staring through my soul. "A little," I joked. To combat the urge to kiss him, I'd chosen comedy.

His hand slid down my abdomen and thigh as he opened the slit down my dress. "What's this for?" His fingers brushed over the dagger strapped to my thigh.

It would be easy to kiss him here. It would be a breeze to just take this to the empty hallway and unleash all the built-up tension. But that wasn't part of the plan. Not yet, anyway. "Would you believe me if I told you I came here to kill?"

"Kill?" The corner of his lips twitched before he settled on amusement—and something along the lines of *pride*. "And why the bloody hell would Mya need a dagger to kill anyone?" He knew. All this time he had known that I knew what I was. I'd been training with the Hanti. I couldn't fool him.

"You remember my nightmares, Eli. You know exactly what I want. You know exactly what I *am*," I whispered.

The doors burst open, catching everyone's attention. I noticed Eli clench his jaw before he pulled me up and pushed me behind him. "What do you want?"

"We aren't here to play games, Elliot. We want her." Their words were vague and could mean anything. What I couldn't miss was the arm the man lifted to point in my direction.

They were desperate for *me.*

I swallowed, looking at Eli and taking a step back. What made my hair stand up was the fact that the man standing amongst these people was the same one who'd been watching me the day I met Amari.

My adrenaline told me to run but I wasn't sure if I was ready for that just yet. Amari wasn't running. Neither her nor Clara were leaving this room.

The leader stepped forward, locking eyes with Eli. "Elliot, I would suggest you don't toy with us. Hand her over."

Eli turned his head and whispered, "Run."

I didn't have time to ask questions. I took off running while Eli and the Hanti fought them off. Knowing they were working together for me wasn't something I asked for but it sure as hell helped. I was thankful I wore a dress that didn't drag behind me or snag. I'd prepared myself for the worst as a real Hanti would. Bursting through a door, the clicks of my boots echoed through the halls as I raced out of the room.

"She's a fucking menace to society, Eli. Trusting her is a grave mistake," Josh said.

Eli shot him a firm look.

As I walked over to them both, I traced an X over my heart. "I should be the one who's worried. I'm out here, alone, with two men who could rape and kill me, and yet something inside me tells me that you won't do that."

Eli gave Josh a nod. "She's right."

I looked everywhere, searching for a safe place to hide. These men were angels or Kaofi of some sort and if they knew that I knew what I was, they'd kill me sooner.

I came upon a dark closet and got inside, hiding away from the enemies. I turned the lock on the door and backed away, keeping the light off. I covered my mouth to quiet my breathing as much as possible.

Hands reached from above me and grabbed my shoulders, causing me to squeal. They pulled me up into the blackest of the ceiling. Musty air surrounded us, making it harder to breathe. Their arms covered my mouth and wrapped around my body to keep me quiet and restrained. I was dragged through the darkness until a blow to the head ended my struggling.

Eli left to check on something, leaving me with Josh. Josh kept giving me the death glare. I didn't understand why he was so against me. I was the woman. I was in more danger than he was.

I looked back to see Eli emerging from the trees. His eyes went wide as he shouted, "Josh, no!"

I was thrown to the ground and a large wolf hovered above me and saliva dripped from his teeth. The size of this monster was larger than any wolf I'd ever seen, and I knew I was about to get my throat ripped out. Before he could, I let out a scream that echoed into the sky, bouncing between trees.

Eli rushed over and tackled the wolf to the ground. "What the bloody hell?" he yelled at it.

I scrambled to my feet and grabbed the skirt of my dress. "You're effing nuts. I can't..." I couldn't gather my words. My breathing was unsteady as I stumbled towards the trees.

A man came from the trees and ran at Eli with a blade. "You are poisonous vermin!" He plunged the knife into Eli's back, and I screamed once again. Eli threw him off, and the man landed on the floor.

The wolf stood in front of Eli, growling and baring his teeth. The man pulled something else from his belt, something that appeared to be a dagger. He barely turned towards Eli before Eli came and tripped him, knocking him to the ground. I took a step back, but just as I had, Eli took the man's knife and used it against him, plunging it right into his neck. His blood would forever stain my memories.

I opened up my eyes to darkness once again. I tried to squint and take notice of my surroundings, but they were too disoriented by the lighting. My vision had to readjust itself when the door opened to let in some light, and in stepped the man who kidnapped me.

As he turned on the lights, he glanced my way, noticing the fear in my eyes. "I don't bite." He sent a small smirk my way. "At least, not like dear Elliot."

I knew what that meant. Eli smelled like death and he was Kaofi. It could never have been more obvious that Eli was a vampire.

Surrounding me were tools of many types, and they weren't the kind you could just use to build something. They weren't doctors' tools, either. They were torture devices. I didn't want to know who had been in this room or what happened in it before me.

He walked around the room where the tools all hung on the walls. The guy faced me and approached with ease as if I was not at all a threat. He bent to my level, squatting right in front of me. "Do you know anything about Elliot?"

"Not much." I would play this little game as long as I could. Eli knew what I was, but I suspected it had to do with reading my mind. These guys couldn't do such a thing. I could play dumb quite well.

"Elliot is not human. You must know that."

"I don't understand." It would be so easy to take him down right now.

As if he read my thoughts, he grabbed something from the wall. He smiled at me, but nefarious intentions covered it.

He closed the distance and grabbed my hair, pulling it back. He used his foot to hold down mine, and I didn't have enough time to register his comment before the mallet swung into my ankle.

Bones cracked and my cries pierced the air. The spot was left throbbing, forming bruises that would take weeks to heal.

He put the mallet back on the wall and began walking back and forth in front of me. "Most Kaofi come in groups to help protect each other. However, Eli was never in one. The rogue vampires have to find a source of food—*blood*—but vampires with mates are much different. Their body requires a different kind of blood. They need one specific kind, which is only attained through their mate."

The pain surged through my foot and I wanted to scream, but I couldn't give him any more satisfaction.

"But Alissa couldn't hide her blood forever..."

The story sounded solid, but I couldn't decide just yet if this guy was telling the truth. Vampires couldn't have mates.

I looked up at the man, gritting my teeth to keep myself from screaming due to the pain. I mumbled to myself, "I'm nobody's mate."

"We'll see."

It was at that moment I realized he heard me, making me think about the abilities these creatures had. Could Eli also hear me? Could he read my mind? The idea of my thoughts not being my own private thoughts was something I couldn't handle.

"Were you ever good, or did something change you?" I asked.

He leaned down into my bubble. "None of us really change over time. We only become more fully of what we really are."

Looking towards a wall of torture devices, he made his way over and grabbed yet another tool. Aside from the raging pain in my ankle, I could still move my arms. I wasn't retrained...yet. This still wasn't looking good for me. I needed to escape.

He came close with the tool in his left hand. "My solution to revenge is to take the one who Eli cares most about. You." He pushed some curls back and I tried to stay still, not showing him any fear.

I swallowed and blinked a second faster than normal. I knew this was going to be my end. Eli wasn't going to come to save me, and I didn't expect him to. I had to save myself.

He smelled my hair and smirked. "Hunter, are you?" The insulting tone was hard to miss, and now that Hunter had opened my eyes to it, I couldn't unhear the way disgust dripped from their lips when they referred to us as hunters.

We were Hanti.

I pushed him away. I couldn't hide that I was well aware of my origins anymore because he knew. I was going to find a way out. I had to fight him off. I couldn't allow some malicious man to abuse me, and especially because Eli was his enemy and I just happened to be the girl who was dancing with him tonight.

Eli was my enemy as much as he was his.

He laughed. "You think you can hurt me? I do admire your persistence." He rushed over to me and stopped just inches before our lips touched. "What do I smell like, Mya?"

It wasn't enough that my cover was blown, but he also knew what my *unique* ability was. Somehow, he knew things about me even Eli hadn't figured out. Maybe this guy was the real stalker when I had tried to pin it all on Eli instead.

Unfortunately for him, I wouldn't tell him what he wanted to hear, that he smelled like smoke, the burning ash after a fire had died down to nothing.

I glared daggers at the man before me. If I hadn't had my ankle smashed, I might have had a fighting chance. I was hoping he'd make one wrong move and I could escape for my own safety. I just needed to survive a little longer.

"Having fun without me?" A woman walked in. She looked just like the woman from my memory.

I was cautious of her right off the bat. "Can I help you?"

Blood covered her front. "You have to help me. I tried but I couldn't do it myself. Someone over in the forest needs help and I'm scared they won't make it until the police arrive."

How could I trust this woman? I'd seen those rouses used before. I didn't want someone to die but I wasn't obligated to venture off alone into a dark forest. I was obligated to call the police.

"Please. He said he had a little brother. He wanted to make it to his graduation, and I don't want to let him down." Tears flowed down her cheeks as they puffed out. Her eyes were stained red.

I took a deep breath and got out of my car. "All right. Where is he?"

He wanted the satisfaction of me screaming and begging. He wanted me to fight back. What if I didn't fight; what if I chose to be silent? One might think I was giving up, but I was just refusing to play the devil's game.

I sat back, looking as calm as I could in such a situation as this. "Do your worst."

He chuckled as he came closer and grabbed my face. The woman watched from behind, relishing in her sadism.

He slowly traced his fingers down my neck, shoulder, and

arm before grabbing my fingers. He used the mallet, again, to smash into my forearm.

I promised not to scream but that was easier said than done. I screamed from the pain, cursing like a sailor. My training had been for nothing.

His smile widened. "I knew you couldn't resist." He grabbed my leg, and I whimpered as he moved the bad ankle. He held my leg straight out and took a swing at my toes.

I cried out once again. The pain wasn't like anything I'd ever felt.

Not a period, not a rupturing cyst, not even getting an IUD implant hurt this much.

He put the mallet back up and looked at me. The fear in my eyes spoke for me. He took his sweet time picking his next weapon. The suspense might even have been worse than the torture itself. I held onto the arms of the chair and watched him carefully.

He grabbed what looked like a double-sided fork with two prongs on each end. He grabbed a collar with it. "Humans have always been so cruel to each other."

I even knew what the double-sided fork did.

The angel came over and put the leather collar around my neck and fixed the fork as it rested against my chest, and chin. If I even let my head fall, it would stab right through my jaw. It could also go into my chest.

I kept my head back in an extremely uncomfortable position to keep me from killing myself. The prongs had already broken the skin as stinging hit and blood dripped without means to an end.

He trailed his disgusting fingers on my thigh. He got dangerously close to that area between my legs, and I squirmed in discontent. "Stop!" I jolted from the touch, but it caused the forks to dig into my skin on *both* ends. I let out another cry of pain.

The door swung open, crashing into the wall. Eli stood there with his eyes glowing a deep red, angrier than I'd ever seen before. I could frustrate the guy but not to this extent. Only the angel could elicit such emotion.

He grabbed the angel and pulled him up to his face. As the woman attacked Eli, I removed the double-sided fork from my neck.

I slipped out of the chair and began limping along, mostly dragging my left leg with me. Eli threw him against the wall as tools shook and clattered to the ground.

The other Hanti entered the room and helped him fight off the two angels. I clenched my jaw to focus on anything but the pain as I dragged myself out.

Hunter abandoned the fight and approached me. I was quick to react, stepping away. "Don't touch me." He hated me and I couldn't trust him. He could be working for the angels. Anything was possible.

One arm was completely unusable. My blood dripped onto the concrete and dress, bold enough to stain it ruthlessly. I made my way from the room and into the halls, and it was only when I neared the front door that I smelled the burning smoke, not coming from angels this time. I looked back and saw bright orange flames eating the place alive.

I quickened my pace, forgetting about the constant pain throughout my body. Everything ached.

An arm snaked around my waist to help guide me out of the building quicker than I could manage on my own. I made a slow exit in the torn-up dress, seeing the light of day. Blood poured from my wounds. I looked dead without having actually died.

The tall structure burned into the sky, sending smoke in the direction of the wind. The flames ripped away at the material, bringing the wood to nothing but ash.

This had now become a *war.*

Hunter stood beside me, watching the destruction play out. "They'll make it out, Mya. They have to make it out." He never said that to reassure me. He said it to make sure he believed it himself.

016 Sunday, April 29th

The bright lights kept an eye on me while the hospital bed kept me secure in its cold touch.

The doctors had put casts where my bones shattered—arm, ankle, and toes. Stitches were placed under my chin and on my chest as well. I was thankful for the painkillers in my system. For once, tranquility took hold. Well, as much as it could knowing what I knew.

"I was so worried, Mya. You scared me." My mom sat at my right side.

I wanted to know more about my biological family. I decided if I was going to be healing for many weeks, now was a better time than ever.

I smiled a bit. "I know. I'm okay now."

"How did this happen?" she asked.

"I ran into the wrong guys when I was at the store the other night." That was the story I was sticking to. I told everyone that a bunch of guys beat me up and ran off before they got caught. No witnesses and nobody could ever prove my story wrong.

I hadn't heard much from everyone else, but Amari had visited the other day. We'd lost Ryan to the fire and it was devastating to hear such news. According to her, everyone else made it out alive.

Eli was somewhere, processing everything that happened the same way I was. If I could just ask for one more dance, I would do it without a second thought.

In the end, he cared about my safety despite what I was to him. Of course, he went about it the wrong way. He still had a heart even if it wasn't beating.

Mom asked, "You okay? You look worried."

"I'm okay. I just wondered about someone else who was there after they guys ran away." Eli had many things I still needed to ask about and I wanted to ask without my mom pestering me about boys this and boys that. The last thing I needed right now was being told how to use protection. I didn't want to have any adult talks at this moment.

I didn't consider Eli and I friends anymore, but I know I felt *something*, no matter the amount of feeling.

Now I knew it wasn't hatred or fear.

Someone knocked on the door and Hunter poked his head in. I was surprised to see him of all people, and my mom immediately assumed he was a boyfriend. "May I come in?"

Mom nodded, leaving so Hunter and I could talk. I wasn't in much of a mood at the moment because I couldn't leave the room if he said something stupid. *Lucky me.*

"What are you thinking about?" he asked as he sat down where my mom once sat.

I pulled the blanket over me some more. "About what my parents were like. I always wonder who they are and why they didn't keep me."

"You haven't stopped wondering about them, huh?" He ran a hand through his hair.

With a shake of my head, I said, "Nope. I want to know who they are. I always ask myself if they're still alive, and it seems silly but that's something that consistently runs through my head."

"Do you know how to find them?" He turned the TV on, keeping the volume was low. It made for good background noise.

"Not really. I doubt Google is going to tell me. I have to unseal the adoption records to know and I'm not quite sure how to even do that." I laughed a little. I grabbed the water from the table and gulped down a few sips.

He slapped his thighs as he fixed his posture. "How are you going to do that when you're broken?"

"I'm okay. Just a few cuts and broken bones. I can heal. I just need the rest to do so, and because of the resting, it's a perfect opportunity to find out who my parents are. Amari is good with this stuff. She can crack open some files and tell us. I just...never asked because she was helping me exercise and get healthier." My eyes rested on the blankets. At the mention of rest, I remembered I had a month left of my senior year. I'd be damned if I let it all wash down the drain now. "How am I going to finish the school year? Crutches aren't an option because one of my arms is also broken. Walking definitely isn't an option. I need to be there for the lessons." I sat up some more.

Hunter shrugged. "Don't worry. I'm sure you'll get everything you need to finish."

"Don't sound so enthusiastic that my dream is on hold." I laughed. "I'm sure Amari could help me."

He leaned forward. "And I'm sure she could if you asked."

I questioned if part of him was plagued with guilt, but none of this was ever his fault. He wasn't responsible for me just because he chose to keep me in the group.

I wanted to ask him why he was visiting me but I had a feeling I knew the answer. Hunter lost Ryan who was like a brother to him. If he didn't want to be alone, I wouldn't turn him away.

I enjoyed the comfort of talking with people who had been there for me during different parts of my life. I couldn't talk about being a Hanti, or Kaofi, but it meant I could be a human for a few days. It eventually led me to a peaceful sleep.

Something woke me up in the middle of the night. Amari was shifting around in her seat. "It was too easy, Mya." She chuckled.

Hunter was passed out in the chair while Mom had been sent home. I looked around the dark room. The only thing that lit up was the screen of the laptop that Amari had open.

I slowly sat up and reached over to the little table on my left and sipped the cup of water. My throat was parched.

"What was easy?" I asked.

She shrugged. "Finding your parents. I searched your name and that brought up some sealed adoption records. It was only a matter of time before those records could be unsealed. Your parents are Emily and David Morgan. Now you ask if they're still alive." She looked at me, but her eyes gave it away.

They weren't.

I wondered how I would get through this. I had to face reality. I had been kidnapped and tortured. I had seen some serious shit. I was living in a world that barely made sense, and that was with the evidence at my hand.

I knew stuff I shouldn't, stuff I didn't want to know

anymore. I was brought into this mess because of my own genetics. I was put through serious pain all because I knew *one* guy.

Maybe it meant something, but I couldn't be too sure. Even though we never spoke through those months, Eli still might have felt something. He couldn't dance like that if he truly didn't care about me emotionally. I'd been the enemy and yet, he *saved* me.

Sure, anyone could remind me that he'd been a stalker and that's how they began. They saved you and attempted to make you fall for them in return when at the root of things, they were dangerous. Obsession would eventually become too much.

However, what Eli couldn't lie to me about were the emotions that couldn't be entirely locked away. His eyes had been the answer to every question I had. He hadn't been lying when he told me he wasn't a stalker. Not a single tell had been obvious.

He could have been that good of a liar, or he could have truly believed he wasn't a stalker when he was. But the eyes would never be able to hide the truth, no matter how hard people tried. Kaofi couldn't lie to me, either.

I set the cup of water back down on the little table and sat back against the pillow. I looked up at the ceiling and wondered if my parents had given me up for a reason or if they were killed before it happened. I would like to think they didn't do it to me on purpose.

"How did they die?" I asked in a quiet voice.

Amari reached over and grabbed my hand, giving it a light squeeze. "They were killed by Kaofi, as you would suspect. The police report doesn't tell you that. I just know because the report says the murder was fueled by rage. Key details about the profile told me that it had to be Kaofi. They gave you away to protect you."

"Protect me... Everyone seems to do a lot to protect me." I sighed as I shook my head. "I'm sick of being a target. Between my parents being Hanti and Eli being a vampire... It's getting ridiculous."

I wondered if Eli would come back or leave forever after what happened. I didn't know if the whole event built up the need for him to leave just so I'd be safe again. We both knew I was in danger regardless.

I felt a ping in my heart at the thought of never seeing him again. But I didn't want to think about it any longer. I wanted to be independent, but even that wasn't much of an option. How did one be independent when they couldn't use half their limbs?

"Who the hell were those guys? The woman and man who kidnapped me, they knew Eli somehow and despised him this much," I said while gesturing to my injuries. I looked down at her hand still in my other one. She removed it as if it were on fire, mine the stove burner.

Amari's head tilted to one side as she went into thought. "I'm not sure. Kaofi tend to stick together. They don't have feuds with each other this way. It's us against them on any given day. Boy, have the tables turned." She let out a sigh.

I didn't respond. There was nothing that I could say to answer my questions. All I knew was that allies had turned against each other.

She nodded while shooting me a look of concern. "Mya, we need to talk about it. You can't pretend it didn't happen or that you're okay. They tortured you. I want you to properly deal with this. Might be harsh at times, but I advocate for some kind of therapy. Mental health is crucial.

Healthy mind makes for a healthy life."

"I'm fine," I simply said.

She shook her head. "No, you're not. I care about you. You can't expect to just forget about it and go back to your regular life."

"I—" I choked on my words. I didn't know how to force them out of me.

"Just promise you'll see someone or feel your feelings. Maybe a diary, or a therapist, or even just me. You choose what works, but you need to let it out." She grabbed my good hand again, her eyes fixed on me and my soul buried inside.

"I guess I'll try to..." Maybe I was making a promise I couldn't keep. I didn't want to lie to Amari, but what other choice did I have?

"Good. You didn't deserve what happened to you. It will not be something you can forget and we both know that, but you have to find a way to deal with it." She let go and watched me as I attempted sleep.

I tried to get back to sleep but my thoughts wouldn't shut up. I was at a total loss on how I was supposed to deal with this in a healthy way. Nothing about my life had been healthy. It was just *all* about survival.

017 Monday, April 30th

Amari pushed me into the classroom in a wheelchair and placed me at a desk on the end. "I'll see you after." She bid her goodbye for now and left for some errands.

I scanned the classroom for any signs of danger, but none were to be found. I hadn't seen Eli at the apartment complex either lately. I knew he wouldn't be around, but part of me still hoped. He refused to come out of his hole after what happened. Most people didn't. The only person I knew who did was me. I didn't have time to waste sitting in my room and moping about my life. I only had a month left of school anyway. Life went on with or without me.

Pitying myself didn't do me any good, so with life I went.

The day dragged on without Eli in it. I even debated going to his place to check for him there, but I decided against that idea. I couldn't barge in just yet.

People did ask some questions while others respected my privacy. Confidence wasn't my strong suit, so I barely answered them. I'd rather not be noticed for something like *this.*

We went to the bathroom, and as in we, I meant Amari and I. I didn't let her help me get my pants down because that was pushing it. I had to start depending on myself at some point.

I closed my eyes for a second and the images raced through my mind.

The sound of my bones snapping. The pain that overtook my body. The stress of having to hold my head up to stay alive. Most importantly, the putrid feeling of hopelessness that I would never make it out alive.

When my eyes shot open, hot tears rolled down the hills of my cheeks. Sobs soon followed.

Attempting to make my way back into civilization was much harder than I anticipated.

Amari stood outside the stall, not letting a word slip her tongue. Someone else made their way in, but she had kindly ushered them out.

This went on for at least twenty minutes. I was out of tears—dehydrated by the time my emotions had finished pouring out of me like a waterfall.

After getting my pants back over my hips, Amari came in and helped me into my wheelchair before she leaned down, wrapping her arms around me and promising she would always be here.

I didn't know what I would do without her. I didn't want to say it, but I most likely would have ended my own life or wallowed in depression for ages. Her support was everything and more. I wasn't the strong woman who could hold herself up. Something this devastating couldn't be felt alone.

We got back to my apartment and I sat there with a blank look on my face. Cheeks were swollen and raw as a faint sting left its mark. "Will you promise to listen to my suffering?"

She sat beside me on my bed. "Of course. I told you, I'm here. I will listen to whatever you need me to listen to." A pat to the hand before her fingers laced through mine.

I didn't know how to start. I didn't know where else to go.

I began with how I felt about Eli the night we met, when he murdered those men and said they were the bad guys. I'd accused him of stalking me, being a threat, but then the dance happened. Something changed that night and I became obtusely aware of how little I hated him—how much I began to believe him about what I once thought were lies. I went on about how it made me angry, how sad it made me that he didn't visit me after saving my life.

Telling Juliet the truth about Hanti and Kaofi wasn't an option. But with Amari, I could be honest about everything. I vented my frustrations about everything that had really gone through my mind in the last few days, including how painful it was to shut out my best friend.

"Every time I close my eyes, I see *their* faces. I feel the pain all over again. Painkillers can't mask what I feel in my mind." I grabbed my pillow from the bed and hugged it.

Bones healed, but trauma... Trauma scarred. There were things I'd experienced. Going back to the Mya from a week ago wasn't an option. The pain was seared into my skin as if I'd been branded by an iron rod—and I may as well have been.

I squeezed my eyes shut to block out everything I feared that waited for me tonight. The darkness waited to scoop me up from the shadows and keep me prisoner.

What an honor.

Amari scooted closer, pulling me into her arms. "Trauma

is never easy on anyone."

Why couldn't I just be the exception?

Sure, it was selfish, but I still wished.

My screams echoed in my head as he smashed my bones into smithereens. What I couldn't answer was if knowing Eli or ignoring him was what put me in danger. It was too difficult to decide, and I didn't want to believe that either of those options were valid.

Ignoring him for so long had worn down on me, and when he danced with me during the masquerade, I felt like I'd *belonged* somewhere.

Until now, I couldn't place why I trusted his words when he promised he wasn't a stalker. I had joined the group of Hanti to find a place to fit in, and I had but not completely. I was the one still adopted, the one still raised human. At the end of the day, I wouldn't be *just like them.*

But that was what made Eli so fascinating.

He, too, would never fit in with Kaofi. They despised him in ways I couldn't fathom, and he'd come to me for company. He was like me in many ways that others couldn't be for me, and in that same sense, I fit perfectly into his world and he had let me right in without too much push-back.

Together we defied what both sides expected of us.

I wanted to cherish that feeling even if I never saw him again.

"What's on your mind?"

I exhaled before shaking my head. "I miss him. It's a constant war inside my head and I can't make it stop. I only hope he doesn't leave for good, but yet I understand if he does."

She glanced at our hands. "Are you talking about Eli?"

Eli had changed from the man who used to toy with

me. Now he avoided me altogether. I liked it better when I was the one avoiding *him.* But our memories would never change. We now connected on different levels and I could never deny that.

Juliet knocked on the door. "Sorry to barge in. I was just checking in on Mya." *Look what the cat dragged in.*

Amari stood as she slapped her palms against her legs. "I'll let you two talk. I should get back to the cabin anyway."

When she was gone, Juliet sat beside me. "You can tell me anything."

Could I?

"We were talking about Eli."

Juliet swallowed. "Go on."

Releasing a sigh, I said, "I know it doesn't make sense. He refused to tell me how he knew me. It's silly, but I still want to be around him whether I admit it or not. I can't be mad anymore. I just want to hug him and never let go. I want him to ask me which color of shirt he should wear with his suits. I want to hear about his bad day and make him feel *better.* That's not realistic, though. It's just a stupid fantasy that I can't achieve."

There was a certain edge to her voice that I couldn't pinpoint. "Will I ever meet Eli?"

She couldn't see him, and she could never gain that ability. According to Amari, she would forever be blind to this side of the curtain.

I met her gaze. "At this rate, I don't know. He's disappeared again." Sigh...

"He seems to do that a lot." She shrugged a little.

I narrowed my eyes. "What does that mean?"

She shooed the idea. "Nothing."

"Tell me." A shiver slid down my spine as I prepared for

anything.

Juliet swallowed. "It's just that... I've never seen him and yet he's the most important boy in your life. It seems odd to me that you talk about him so much. I want the confirmation that you're doing okay. You went through traumatic events and you've been acting odd surrounding it. You exercise and diet. You have horrible nightmares. There's blood on your gown in the closet." Her eyes roamed my walls, then the ceiling. "I *worry* about you." She met my stare.

How did she know about the bloody dress?

"It's complicated, Jules." That was an understatement. I wasn't about to drag her into this world if she didn't need to be part of it.

"Then explain it to me. I'm willing to listen." She smiled.

Her smile couldn't fool me. "I didn't make up an imaginary love interest. I'm not crazy. There's just so much going on. I've been struggling with memories I can't place and then I found out I was adopted. It's a lot to deal with. Holding on to the odd relationship Eli and I shared for just a moment—that keeps me sane."

Juliet coughed before clearing her throat. "You're adopted? Mya, I didn't know."

"How could you have? I didn't know for twenty-one years. It's just a lot to handle amongst other things. Amari found my parents" —I paused for effect— "they're dead by the way. I've been doing a lot of self-discovery lately." It was enough of an explanation to keep Juliet somewhat in the loop.

She gave a little nod. "I'm sorry. I am."

"I know you don't believe he's real, *Juliet.* But is it so wrong for me to hope for romance? It makes me feel normal. Why can't you just hope for the best for me? Every time I talk about a boy in my life, you're making him out as a bad guy or something. Why?" I grabbed a small blanket from my bed and wrapped it around my shoulders. Well, almost.

A laugh left her. "Mya, I'm not making Eli out as a bad guy. But I've never seen him. I've asked others about Eli and they've never heard of him. Think about it. Has Amari talked about Eli?"

"Yes!" my voice squeaked. "She talks about him. You're just not around when she does." It was done purposefully, and I hadn't minded until now. Now I was the one looking a fool to my own best friend.

Thanks for that, Amari. Would it have killed you just to mention his name once?

"When you first spotted him with Amari, what did she say to you?" she asked.

I shrugged. "She told me not to trust him."

"No. She came over to us and asked you if you liked what you saw."

"She did. And she was referring to her being with Eli. I clearly didn't like that."

Juliet groaned. "No, Mya. Amari was making a joke. She's bisexual and she was making a joke about you staring at her. It was clear as day. You can ask her what she meant." She gestured to my phone.

I flipped my phone face down. "Okay, so she was asking me if I liked staring at her, but she was joking. What does that prove?"

"It proves that Amari thought you were weird." *Ouch.* "If Eli was real, she would have come over and asked about that. She came over because you were staring at her in a creep-kind-of-way. That's what it was about."

"No." I shook my head. "No, Juliet. After you left to hang

out with Cole, Amari talked about Eli. She mentioned Eli's name, and not as if I was crazy. He exists." She just couldn't *see* him.

Both of us turned away, not daring to say another word.

I let the silence speak volumes. There was nothing more to contribute about Juliet's disbelief in Eli.

As hard as I tried to sleep, memories rushed through my mind. I laid in the darkness, and sounds began to worm their way into my ears until my brain believed the worst. Was I being watched? By who?

I gasped as a *shadow* moved in the corner. I reached over and turned my lamp on but nothing reared its monstrous form. Nobody was in here but me.

I was hallucinating.

This trauma had me living in a house of cards, and if I didn't set the fire, I'd be the one to burn.

018 Wednesday, May 2nd

A small but distinct knock on the door.

"Come in," I said. My heart sped up almost instantly at the person entering. "Eli," I breathed. "Why are you here?"

He walked into the room and closed the door behind him. "I think you want to speak to me."

"I do." I nodded my head a bit. Awkward filled the air like smoke. I'd changed my mind; I wasn't ready to talk.

His focus was determined and set solely on me. "Can I sit?"

"No," I joked. It helped break at least some of the tension.

He smiled a bit and made himself comfortable next to me. "I'll try my best to answer any questions, but I have one question first." His smile dropped. "Knowing what you know, do you hate me?"

"No," I said without hesitation. A reflex. I knew I didn't hate him. I couldn't possibly do such a thing. "But I do have questions. They all will revolve around what you are and what happened at the ball or moreso, what happened afterward."

I was a target, and I had no idea as to why those angels wanted me dead. If I was being forced to protect myself, I deserved to know why and hopefully Eli would finally agree.

Nodding, he said, "I'm ready." I was thankful he was because I wasn't quite there. I couldn't be sure how long he knew that I knew about my origins.

"First question. Were you always a vampire? Were you born a vampire?" I turned my body towards him the best I could.

"I was. My parents were both vampires. I'm a purebred as you could call it. We lived in a quite different society than what we have today."

"Tell me about that society."

"I come from Romsey. Back in the era when I was born, there was no freedom. When a vampire couple wanted children, they had to seek approval from the king. The king would decide if they were worthy enough. My parents had to go through this process. There are extensive background checks and tests to determine the fate of this couple and their future with children. The king was the only one who held the medicine that would fertilize a couple who was otherwise dead inside and out. As he put it, he couldn't just give it to anyone because it would risk our destiny as vampires. Some vampires believed we should never mix with any species different from our own."

I tilted my head. There was so much I didn't *actually* know about him.

"He wanted us to be purebred and to thrive as a society. That meant keeping it controlled. He eventually decided my parents were good enough to have a child, so I came along.

Society changed over time. They no longer have a king who decides. The secrets of that formula got leaked and now any of us can procreate with whoever.

"That's when Alissa came. We started dating, much to her father's disapproval. I thought everything was fine, because why wouldn't it be? A vampire dating a fallen angel. But it became clear the moment she turned on me. I had no choice but to kill her. Then I met you." He peeled his eyes from my carpeted floor before they settled on me.

My breath caught in my throat. Had the angel been telling the truth? Was I considered his mate? Absurd. I was nobody's mate, and certainly not the enemy's.

Eli ran a hand down his face. "I had never smelt blood like that. I had never wanted blood more than I wanted yours. It scared me. I hadn't learned how to control such a need. I desired your blood and it brought about...destruction."

I straightened my posture and put my pillow in my lap to support my arm. "Did you want to kill me right away because you had to kill her?"

"No," he started, "I never once harmed her, Mya. When Alissa and I dated, Lucas and Lucy, the fallen angels, found out. It shouldn't have been a big deal but it was to them, and something about me had them turn her against me. In turn, I defended myself and killed her. I had to flee. I could never explain myself, and her father would always blame me no matter which story he was told, or what proof he was showed." He released a sigh.

"I'm sorry." I inhaled, holding just for a few seconds before exhaling. "She was just a romance but they took it all." I shook my head as I repositioned my arm. "We're enemies, though. I'm supposed to kill you. If the Hanti knew I was here with you, just talking, they would kill me themselves."

The gears in his brain could be heard a mile away. "In the human world, do they get a second chance?"

"Sometimes."

"Sometimes we get those second chances, too."

I swallowed. "So that means..." *I* was his second chance. "What did you do to make Lucas hate you so much?" My question came out barely above a whisper.

"Even if it seems like we're on two sides of the same coin, it doesn't mean we don't hate each other. Before I met Alissa, I chose to drink from a girl who was too easy to catch. Well, it attracted attention I didn't know existed. The girl was dating someone."

"Lucas. You killed his girlfriend."

"Yes. I killed his girlfriend and his sister got angry. They consider themselves siblings. They both were pretty pissed. I didn't realize that the girl I killed had a connection to him because she was a hunter, and we aren't supposed to interbreed. I defended myself anyway."

I chewed on my lip. "Eli..."

"She ran off and told her brother when she caught me. He vowed to get revenge. That's why he took you. I hurt his partner, so he wanted to hurt mine. You're not exactly my partner, but you get the idea."

I fiddled my fingers. "Did you ever apologize?" Eli didn't strike me as the type to apologize, at least not after the way we met.

He cocked a brow. "Vampires don't apologize."

Of course. "So, if you played with my feelings and wanted to take it back..." I couldn't finish the sentence.

"Then I would apologize." He leaned in but his lips never touched mine. He trailed his breath over my skin until it hovered over my ear. "I am so sorry for making you feel like that."

For a few minutes, we sat in silence and I just soaked in his proximity. I wanted to kiss him, but it would ruin what we shared. The silence, the intimacy was all that we had right now, and I wanted to hold onto that for as long as I could.

"I have to know, Eli," I whispered. "Do you crave my blood?"

He pulled back just a bit, looking into my eyes. "I've been drinking other blood for now. I'm trying to survive, but eventually, I will starve. When I do, I will lose *myself.* I will lose my sanity."

I fell silent for a while.

I couldn't believe what I was subjecting him to. He wouldn't be able to last forever. But it was my blood first and I wasn't obligated to give it to him on the same line either. Would Alissa have offered her blood if she was given the choice?

The picture of me in the woods popped into my head. "That picture of me, why did you have it." It was formed as a command and not a question for good reason.

"It's a long story." He wrapped his hands around mine, attempting to bring life back to my pale skin.

"I have time."

"Before we met in the alley, we met in the woods. It wasn't a pleasant encounter—"

"And the first meeting in the alley was?"

He sighed and continued, "You looked so much like Alissa that day. I swear you were, but you weren't. You said you were Mya. I asked you what you were doing up there. You said someone told you we needed help. Lucy told you that. I took pictures of you after we got to know each other a bit.

"I left for a moment to go grab a new battery for my

camera but when I returned, Josh attacked you. I hated him for doing that. A hunter came out and attacked us to save you. I killed him to defend myself, and then you ran off. When I asked about you, they said you had no memory of that night. I decided to forget about it all." Something was being left out, but I didn't think he was going to reveal what that was.

I remembered half of those memories. They'd been coming back to me in bits and pieces, but I knew for certain they were mine.

Eli got up from my bed, facing the door across from me. "It's going to be hard to process this." He glanced back at me. "And sometimes you should stop looking for happiness in the same place you lost it."

I didn't understand what he was implying. After everything we knew about each other, this was where he wanted to call quits?

"I hope you understand." He headed for the front door.

He wanted to leave me again.

It all hit me at once, but I now knew the feelings coursing through my veins were mine to feel. I wanted him. I refused to let Eli just abandon me and cut me out of his life forever.

I couldn't stay away from him. I couldn't stop thinking about him. He always pulled me in no matter how hard I fought to push him away.

Pushing myself off my bed and onto my black boot, I limped over. It was not easy in the slightest, but I was too determined to stop. He turned back and looked me up and down. "What are you doing?"

I stopped just inches away. "Eli, I know you're scared you'll repeat what happened with Alissa, but what if you don't have to? We both feel *something* for each other. I want this. You want this. Let's stop pretending we're happy about it. I know how we can make this work."

"What are you talking about?" Suspicions raised and he inched his way to the door until his back was pressed against it with nowhere else to run.

"I want to change the way people think, including myself. Hanti and Kaofi can't always hate one another. We cannot become what we want by remaining what we are." I grabbed my dagger from the table. "I want to be with you." I cut a small slit into my neck, allowing the blood to seep out of the wound.

He widened his eyes. "Mya, what are you *doing*?" the question came out rougher—frenzied.

I closed the distance left between us. "I'm offering you the chance to be with me. Take it."

He shook his head, but I could be *just as* stubborn. I grabbed the back of his neck. "I give you permission." If I didn't establish consent here and now, I would never reiterate to him that I had to give my blood in order for him to take it.

He wrapped his arm around my waist, checking my eyes one last time. Slowly, Eli began to lick. Within seconds more, he placed his lips against my neck, sucking.

This was who Eli was. Our ancestors had been enemies for centuries, but that couldn't overpower the craving inside me. Nothing could destroy what was growing between us, and maybe that meant both of us were poisoned to the core.

019 Thursday, May 10th

I stared down at the gauze wrapped around my palm. "Am I accident prone?" I'd stabbed it with my pencil when I played around with it.

Eli chuckled at that. "I think you just attract danger."

I choked on a laugh. "You can say that again." I gestured to my arm and leg. "Don't pretend I can't handle this. I think I handled that angel pretty well. Oddly enough, I feel like I belong here."

"That is odd. You're a hunter." Something in his tone made me clench my jaw. *Hunter.* It was a filthy way of demeaning me to a killer of his kind.

"I'm meant to be the hero or the villain, depending on which story you want to look at." I scooted closer to him, reaching for his hand. "But I am sure of what I want. I hope you want it, too."

He gave me a look, brows knitted downward like I was the one unsure of what I wanted. "Mya, I don't know if it's safe for you. I don't want you to end up hurt."

"Did you just assume I'm weak?" One glance at my broken frame. "Don't answer that."

Eyes glued to my casts, he pulled his hand from under mine, walked over to the wall, and leaned back.

Following his movement, I said, "I know what I'm getting into. Let me make my own decisions. The entire time we didn't communicate, Amari and the others were training me to be a Hanti. I like to think I know what I'm doing."

"What are you talking about?" He eyed me warily. I guess that destroyed any worries I had about my thoughts being private. He couldn't pry into my head.

Taking a deep breath to prepare myself for what I was asking, I stood. "Eli, you're Kaofi. I'm not. It's a terrible fate to be stuck in a world where you watch the one you care about die. I'd be leaving you with that kind of pain."

He cut his hands through the air like knives, crossing them back and forth to tell me he wasn't having it. "No, no. Absolutely not. I will never allow you to do this."

Once I realized what I'd implied and how he took it, I laughed and threw my head back, hand over my stomach. I'd scared the poor guy nearly to death. "I'm not telling you to turn me into a vampire. Trust me, I don't want that." I had to grow into being a Hanti, and I wasn't about to take on *another* identity. "We have to talk about this, though. I'm going to die someday."

Approaching me, he grabbed hold of my face as he peered into my dark eyes. "No." Lots of *nos* lately. "I don't want you to go without me. I won't let you. I'm making a promise right here, right now. When you die, I'm going to die right with you. I won't live an eternity without you in it."

It was too easy to get lost in his beautiful brown eyes.

So I did. "Eli."

Eyes full of promises. Every brown stroke painted with such precision and purpose. Perfection was the only word that described him in this exact moment.

"What?" he asked with caution.

"Kiss me."

His lips crashed onto mine, passion pouring from every crevice.

I returned the kiss and grabbed hold of his neck.

Deepening the kiss, I pulled him further against me as if I needed him to become me the same way I'd been him. When he tried to pull away, I used my teeth to pull him right back.

This time, he accepted every last bit.

I longed for this moment. I wouldn't allow him to leave me wanting more.

Our desires melded together as our breaths mingled. The taste of his lips was an addiction I could not kick, and one I never wanted to.

We carried this moment to the bed with me on the bottom.

Lips moving in harmony, I struggled to get his button shirt off him with only one good hand. He helped me finish the job. His hands played with the hem of my dress, testing the waters as he pushed it up my thigh.

I laughed as my stupid sling got in the way. "Sorry." I took it off my head.

He lifted me up, unzipping the dress and pulling it down my legs. He looked at the black boot that encased my leg.

I leaned my head back into the pillow as I laughed yet again. "I'm so sorry. Not really setting the mood, am I?" I sat up and looked at him. "Here, let me help."

I got the boot off and chewed on my lip. "Just be careful." I grabbed my underwear, struggling to lift myself while being gentle enough with it.

Eli helped me get them off. "I suppose the bra is next," he said as his eyes darted to my black lace bra.

I nodded a little. "Help me get it off." He wasn't hesitant about that. Reaching behind me, he unclipped and pulled the straps down before tossing it off to the side.

"What are you still doing with your clothes on?" I shot him a glare and unbuckled his pants. It was still impossible to do with one hand. Eli shook his head and guided my fingers, and when the clothes all laid on the floor, I laid back.

We'd been from two different worlds, but tonight we were the same soul.

Eli kissed me, but short and sweet was all it was. "May I?" His fingers pushed my hair from my neck, tracing along my skin. I gave him a simple nod. He then took a liking to my pulse.

Within seconds, he bit into me, only taking a little blood in the process. The pain resembled a bee sting for me, but it brought him pleasure.

When he pulled away, he leaned down once again, and my hand shot up to cover my mouth. "Eli Kay, don't you dare kiss me with my blood in your mouth. That is disgusting."

He groaned. "Mya."

"I'm serious. Wash your mouth or don't kiss me." I gave him a stern look.

Eli agreed. He grabbed the thigh of my good leg. "I'll avoid kissing you." He planted a kiss on my throat.

We spent our time bonding in ways other people could never, sharing pieces of ourselves with each other that we could never take back—and I would never wish to.

He fell to my right side, careful not to hurt what was already broken.

I was the one in some kind of trance, lost in a world of fantasies. He was no stranger to what he was doing, and he managed even better than past boyfriends while I had multiple casts on.

He peeled my hair from the sweat on my forehead. "Did it make up for getting you nearly killed?"

I frowned. "Don't joke like that. I don't want you to blame yourself. I never blamed you." I rolled onto my side, placing a kiss on his cheek.

He grabbed my chin and kissed my lips, whispering against them, "I want to give you everything you deserve."

"You are..." I kissed him more before pulling away. I turned my head up at the ceiling. "How do you cope with it? I find myself stuck on the events and moreso on the pain. I can't think of anything else half the time. How do you deal with it?"

He reached forward again, moving hair from my face. "It's not easy. When you've lived as long as I have, you experience so much trauma. Somehow, you learn to live with it. I've had to go out to the edge of the forest and escape reality. I...enter this other place inside my head, reliving the happy memories before I let go of my pain.

"I had a rough past. I made some choices at my old school that ended in murder. It pissed off many Kaofi. They went after you to hurt *me*. The world is a cruel place, Love, and we weren't given the choice if we wanted to be in it or not." His gaze found mine and together we confirmed what we already suspected. We'd choose each other over arbitrary rules.

I was afraid to speak because he had mentioned Alissa, and I remembered her as his *first* love. I could never match up to his first love, even if he had to kill her in the end.

"Is something wrong?" he asked me, concerned.

I laid my head on the pillows, half of my face finding its way into the fluff. "No."

I had to accept it and move on.

I let out a sigh as I gave into his pleading eyes. "I know I'm probably being selfish *and* rude, but I just can't help but feel like I have to match up to your first love."

Eli didn't shoot me a look of judgment like I'd expected of him. Instead, his brows knotted together as he pursed his lips a bit. "Yes, she was my first love, and I can't forget about her, but I want to spend forever with *you.* I may have loved her, but I can't live in the past. Vampires learn that trait early on. She betrayed me and that's all I remember of her."

No smile. No agreement. Insecurities would be the death of me.

I said, "It's hard to be reminded of how much you loved another girl just like me. She's dead, but she is still competition. Oh shit, I said that wrong." I widened my eyes and buried my face.

He grabbed hold of my chin and turned my face towards him. "I refuse to be *that* guy, Mya—the guy who dismisses how women feel or what their concerns might be. For that, I see how the alley situation could have looked. I slammed you against a wall and made myself look like the danger when my goal was to just protect you from another gang of vampires. I'm sorry for ever making you feel that way."

All the anxiety that'd been rattling my shoulders dissipated. I knew if I had to confide in him about anything, he'd take me seriously. Even if what he heard wasn't painting men in a good light.

"Thank you," I breathed. "Most people wouldn't

intervene in rape, and it's the downfall of society. Women get blamed for every little thing they think or do. *'What was she wearing?'* As if that matters. Men should have self-control regardless. They attempt to gain dignity by shaming us, without realizing they're further digging their grave. Not all men, but enough to force us to take too many precautions just to stay alive and safe in a world built for men and by men."

Not all men, but it was all women taking fear into account in every scenario just to keep themselves safe.

We couldn't as much help a child alone in fear of being trafficked. We couldn't politely say no to a date without fear of being stalked and killed. Most things we did, we planned accordingly with the intentions to stay safe. It had been a terrifying world, and self-defense was recommended to us only because there were men waiting in the darkness for us to make one *wrong* move. Like I had done just by walking near an alley when the sun had still been setting.

His thumb brushed over my cheek. "I'm an arsehole and I'm aware, but I'd never invalidate what she experiences. I gain nothing from it except her hatred, among other women alike. My mother taught me that the more we respect, the more we achieve. We reap what we sew." Pause. "I won't sew a world of silence for women."

The tears threatened at the surface, but I fought to keep them back. I wouldn't cry over something I shouldn't have cried over in the first place. It was the basic decency that should have existed among everyone. It was so little to ask, yet they would never give.

Whispering, I scooted closer, "And I won't end up like her, either. I won't turn against you."

He planted a warm kiss. "I never doubted you would."

I began to hum a tune. "We should probably get out of bed."

He pulled back enough to look at me, mouth agape. "Why is that? Do you not want to be here with me?" he joked.

"I have to pee." A soft smile.

"I don't want you to pee on my bed." He chuckled as he got me to the bathroom and left me in there, waiting by the door.

When I washed my hands, he came back in. "We should probably get dressed. You'll have to help me." I looked at him through the mirror, saying what we both knew. "We have to keep this relationship a secret. A Hanti and a Kaofi is probably the worst thing to happen in the supernatural world." After he nodded, I asked, "what exactly are we?"

He helped me back to his bed, giving me my clothes. "Do I have to answer that?"

"Eli, just answer it." I laughed. He rubbed his neck, his eyes darting everywhere but me. Why couldn't he answer a simple question? "Are you ashamed of me?" I asked.

He sat beside me, helping me get my shirt over my head. "No. I am not ashamed of you. It's complicated. You're right about keeping this a secret, though, because I'm not willing to risk your life for any reason."

"I know I'm in danger no matter what. Don't give me that shit. What are we?" I asked again with a more authoritative tone. I wasn't interested in a fling, and I'd make it clear. If it was, Eli would have so much more coming to him.

He scratched his neck and glanced at me. "I don't particularly like to think or talk about this stuff. What does the question mean?"

"It means: *what are we?* It's a simple question. Are we dating? Or am I going to be degraded to just being your one-night stand?" My patience was starting to run thin.

He exhaled, something vampires didn't *need* to do. "Okay. Okay. I would like to be together."

"Was that so hard?" I lifted my eyebrow.

He nodded his head like a child who had just gotten out of getting punished. He confirmed what I wanted and so serenity settled in my bones.

And despite what Juliet said, I had a real boyfriend.

"I've had a fling before with Owen, and if I'm being honest, it ended poorly. I tried to keep it as just a summer fling but it ended up being more." I met his eyes. "And he's been here and there."

Eli shifted. "Here and there?"

"Yes. And I do believe he still has feelings for me." Did he always have feelings?

He pulled my underwear over my hips and stopped to stare at me. "Do you have feelings for him?"

That was not the question I wanted him to ask me. I didn't know the answer. Owen was my ex and we didn't choose to end our relationship. He was killed and those feelings never properly healed. I didn't hate him, and he didn't hate me.

"Mya, do you have feelings for Owen?"

I tugged on my bottom lips, scraping my teeth over it. "I might. I don't know. I'm confused."

"It's simple. Do you want to kiss him?"

Shivers ran up my spine.

I did. I wanted to kiss Owen. I wanted to feel his arms around me one more time. I wanted to feel his skin on mine. I wanted everything that Eli and I were doing.

Now that Owen was back, I couldn't just pretend I'd stopped loving him. I was in love with two men at once.

But if Owen found out, I'd be asked to choose.

I didn't want to *have to* choose.

020 Friday, May 11th

"I'm heading out here in a few minutes," I told the Hanti.

Hunter grunted. "Did you at least sharpen your blade? Oh, wait, you haven't killed anyone yet."

"Ha, ha, very funny." With a roll of my eyes, I checked to make sure my dagger was in my sheath. It was, right where I left it. "I'm getting there. After I heal, I swear it."

"Couldn't even kill Eli," he said with a *tsk-tsk*.

He turned back to the sharpening machine, sliding his blade on it at an angle.

It had once been a question on my mind, but they answered it among others. Why did our daggers kill vampires, wolves, and others alike, but not all Kaofi?

Iron.

Our daggers and weapons alike were made of heavy traces of iron which most Kaofi were allergic to. It wouldn't kill them on the spot, sure. They'd suffer in pure agony as their body turned against them by attacking the blade.

The way Hanti had mastered our weapons was by coating them in a way that iron would be left behind even if we pulled it out of their body. They wouldn't stand a chance. Because of that, it was important for us to keep our weapons maintained. They could last a few battles if needed, but Hunter made it clear it was a good habit to get into by keeping it sharp and prepared for every battle we went into.

It was crucial for our kind if we wanted to stay alive.

"Come one," Amari said as she walked out the door. I followed her out and she took me home.

When we arrived at the apartment, Eli waited for me outside. Amari shot me a look, but I tried to play it off as if he wanted to talk.

Eli came to my rescue by pointing to my car. "You can have your stupid spot back. Leave the notes out of this."

Amari flashed him a fake smile. "Such a gentleman."

"Hunters have no room to talk about gentle," he retorted.

"Okay, okay." I cleared my throat to break them up. "No notes. My parking spot it mine. Thanks, Amari. Goodbye."

She nodded one last time before giving a glare to Eli.

He turned and began walking up his stairs and I started towards my front door.

Amari headed back to the cabin.

As I looked back, Eli peered over the railing. "You coming?"

A smile filled my face as he hurried down the stairs and helped me to his apartment. "Good acting, by the way." I pointed.

"I am the best." He showed his pearly whites.

I teased, "Don't push it."

I moved my body to the beat of the music, but Eli wasn't taking any of it seriously. His laughter clogged up the air.

Narrowing my eyes at him, I sat on the bed. "Something funny?"

He shook his head and coughed. "No, nothing. Your dancing is spectacular."

I stood up and swayed my hips. The laughing began again. "Eli! What the hell?" I dropped my arms at my side.

His laugh faded out after a minute or two. "I'm sorry, Mya. You just look like a wild monkey."

"Screw you, too!" I threw my arms up. "I was trying to dance like a stripper, and I can't even do that." I bent my knees and leaned them against the edge of the bed.

He scooted closer, pulling me between his legs. "Is it selfish to not want to ever share you? It's okay that you can never be a stripper."

My heart swelled. "I don't want to even think about you being with another woman when you're with me." I leaned down, resting my forehead against his. "And I'd never expect you to have to share me with another man. I only want you." I was trying to forget about Owen, and so was he. I could do that right? If I ignored him enough, my feelings would disappear the way he could.

He traced the bite on my neck. "What if people ask?"

A shrug. "Then let them. I'll explain myself." I planted a quick kiss on his lips. "I have to get back to my apartment. I also really need a shower and the only person who can help me is Juliet."

He snickered. "Juliet?" He definitely didn't like her. "I've seen you naked. In case you forgot, we've shagged."

"Juliet is home and I don't need the neighbors listening in and thinking I'm masturbating. Don't make me explain something that obvious." I patted his shoulder and straightened my legs. "Besides, I only need her for backup. I'm going to attempt to do it on my own so I can learn to be independent again." I made my way over to his front door.

Eli leaned back onto his hands, still glued to the bed. "If you ever do need me, I'm always around. I'd love to *wash* you."

I shook my head and rolled my eyes. "Not today." I left his place and went downstairs to mine. Every now and then, pain would surge through my foot. I had to ignore it and keep walking.

After I arrived, I scoped Juliet out. "Hey, can you help me cook?"

She looked at me, nodding. "Of course. How are you feeling?"

I shrugged. "I feel fine, aside from my limbs cursing me." I grabbed some things I would need, but I couldn't carry it all.

She helped me grab the rest of my ingredients and set it by the stove. I was able to mix a few of the ingredients after chopping some vegetables, but Juliet helped with the majority.

I ran my fingers through my hair, gesturing for Juliet to help me tie it back, which she thankfully did. "So, it's official. Eli and I are dating. We kissed and all."

"And all?" An eyebrow raised.

Turning tomato red, I then cleared my throat. "Yes, sex. That is what I meant by all. And Juliet, it was damn good sex."

"Mya, you're having sex with Eli now after everything he put you through." Skepticism laced her tone. I couldn't blame her there.

"I do get that. There are just some things about him that you could never understand." I nodded a bit.

She let out a frustrated sigh. "I love you, but are you stupid?" *Harsh.* "You talk about how he ignores you for so long and plays with your feelings, then you sleep with him. What makes him special? You are going against everything you are."

I swallowed the lump in my throat. "It's been a very rough year. A lot has changed. I'm not the same Mya you knew. I've been through hell and back and I've had to discover things about me that I never suspected before. Why are you mad at me?"

"You mean, why am I mad at you for giving it to a guy who ignored you for nearly nine months? Let me think," she said with sarcasm dripping from her lips.

I threw the vegetables in a pan while placing a lid on top. "I know, Jules. Eli had come back, and he explained so much. He didn't do it with ill intent. Let's just move on, shall we?"

She grumbled. "Fine."

I smiled a bit. "Good. I can't do much because I'm kind of broken," I joked.

After my vegetables were steamed and my chicken was baked, I ate the plate in comfortable silence. Juliet was the one to take it to the kitchen for me when I finished. It was thoughtful. "What do you want to watch?" I looked over at Juliet.

She sat down, her head lowered. "I can't let this go, Mya."

"Let what go?" I asked.

She hit the chair's pillow. "You made a stupid decision! You slept with a man who doesn't exist, and you think he loves you. This is not Romeo and Juliet. Romeo and Juliet was not even a good love story. It was complete crap."

I laughed a bit. "Of course, because you are Juliet. If it was you instead of me, then it would be Romeo and Juliet."

Crossing her arms, she said, "This is not funny. He is not that special. You could have found love somewhere else."

"Nobody has ever made me feel the way he has. This is different. You have Cole. I have Eli. I want him. I did what I would do. Can't you be happy? I found it, and you're not happy about it."

She rubbed her eyes, pinching the bridge of her nose. "This is not the way you find love. You slept with him to ignore the flaws. You keep making up all these lies about him, and I'm convinced he's all in your head which only makes it that much worse. You want to ignore the red flags of an imaginary man. That is not normal."

"I can't pretend that this isn't real because you say so. He apologized to me for everything he did. The worst thing he did was lead me on when we were merely enemies in the beginning." Not entirely true, but I couldn't tell her the other part. "I don't blame him because he let me in, and he isn't a bad guy like everyone makes him out to be." I sat up some more and shot her a look.

She groaned, trying to brush me off. "I'm still mad at you. You don't seem to understand the repercussions of this situation. Can you at least try to see it from my side?"

"I am seeing it from your side. I see that every time I try to be happy, you want to rip it away. You never want me to have a boyfriend. You make them out as bad people. You hated Owen, even, and he didn't have a single red flag. I can't continue to do this if you're always going to make me feel like shit. You have a boyfriend who loves you." At that moment, I remembered Eli mentioning Juliet flirting with a man from the party we went to at the start of the year. "But when I try to get the same for myself, you try to convince me that he's a villain." A tear slipped down my face, and a few more followed right after.

"Don't do that, Mya. Do not try and blame me for this." She turned away from me, holding her arms and rubbing them up and down.

Dizziness swayed inside my head. I laid down.

My best friend wasn't even denying my accusations. "I didn't do this to hurt you or myself. I did this to be with him. Nothing else about me has changed. I am still Mya. I am still the same woman who wants to finish college and become a fashion designer." I closed my eyes to keep myself from feeling any dizzier than I was.

"I know you don't have ill intentions, Mya. I'm your best friend. I only want what's best for you. But sometimes, you can be an idiot. I have to tell you when you're being an idiot. You're *being* an idiot."

"You're calling me an idiot because I called you out on your bullshit. Admit it, Juliet. Admit that you..." I didn't finish. I didn't want to even imagine a world without her.

She choked on a sob. "Mya, please don't say that."

"What?" I asked.

"I want you to admit I was right, and then break it off with him, for *your* safety."

I sat up in a hurry, feeling that dizziness overcome once more. "Are you serious? You're asking me to break my own heart because I can't make you understand something you say you can never understand. This is a losing battle for me, isn't it? Do you want me to be alone? I deserve to be happy just like you!"

"That is not what I meant. You do deserve happiness, but this is not it." She shot up off the chair and came over to me.

She had the upper hand. I was still crippled.

"No. You don't know a damn thing about me. I know what I feel. I know more about how I feel than you do, so don't you effing tell me how I feel! You keep saying you want me to find someone, but you can't accept it when I actually do. Do you want to be the only friend in a relationship to feel superior? He makes me feel worthy. What is so wrong with that?" I *yelled* at her. That was my weapon of choice. It was all the power I had.

She grabbed my shoulders. "Please, don't do this. I am not trying to say anything bad about you. I am not saying you're worthless. You are freaking beautiful. You are worthy. You deserve everything and I want that for you. But this isn't everything. Take a moment to really think about what it's like to lose your best friend. We can talk then." She stood from the couch and walked to the other side of the apartment.

I hadn't really understood it until now. She felt like she lost me because I was catching up with her. "You didn't lose me. I'm still here. I'm just a little better than the Mya I was at the beginning of the year and that pisses you off. You don't want me to be at your level. You want to be above me because you want to be *better* than me."

"You would stoop that low. You would actually accuse me of wanting to be better than you." She turned towards me, tears falling. "You're supposed to be my best friend, but you've been losing yourself."

The tears started flowing without permission. "Oh, Jules... I wish I could say that was true, but I found myself. This is me. I've changed. You just weren't prepared to change with me."

Juliet started mumbling. She knew she couldn't deny the

truth. She never tried. She always pinned the blame on me, as if I were the bad guy for even suggesting that this was the person she was.

Defensive.

Deflecting.

But never denying it.

I knew better, now. I finally discovered the Mya I had been all along, and Juliet had never been prepared to see it. She wanted to be friends with the Mya who would hide away instead of sticking out. She wanted to be the prettier of the two of us. I transformed into a better version of myself, but Juliet had never wanted to make that shift with me, and now she never would.

She went mad when she lost control of her doll.

When night fell and darkness coated the earth, I turned in for the night.

I no longer had the option of asking my best friend for help, so when I couldn't get back to sleep an hour past midnight, I decided to get up and take a shower.

After making my way to my bathroom only a few feet away from my bed, I got my clothes off and jumped in the shower. Once the shampoo was lathered on my scalp, the lights went off and I poked my head out to see if Juliet was messing with me. Would she stoop that low? No. She was the subtle hater, but she wouldn't go this far.

Eli was just upstairs but I didn't want to yell for his help just to find out we forgot to pay the bill. And I was the only one who noticed since the rest of the complex was asleep.

I washed the shampoo from my hair first before getting out and attempting a piss-poor version of a towel around my chest. I flipped the switch but it wouldn't come back on, and I went to test my bedroom light as well. Again—nothing.

I went over to the living room and tested a few more lights before figuring out our entire apartment was out. Had we forgotten the bill?

I wasn't about to wake up Juliet and ask her now.

Knowing Eli was awake, I grabbed my phone and texted him to ask if his power was out. When he replied with, 'No', he shot another text asking if I needed him to come check it out. I didn't want to have to rely on him all the time, so I told him it was fine. We probably forgot the bill.

Croaking started from the closet.

That was the moment I knew we paid the bill and someone else was in here.

I texted Eli again, only the text never got sent. My phone *died.*

I reached for my dagger and held it out in front of me, mustering up every ounce of courage to go and investigate. I knew Owen was dead, so ghosts didn't particularly scare me. I still hadn't met or heard of demons so who really knew if they existed? But I had heard stories of shadow creatures growing up, and I had always believed in them. Right now, my closet was their playground.

Pulling the door open, I shoved my dagger forward and swiped through the air.

The croaking began again, a little quieter at the back of the closet. I wasn't all that eager to go towards it but what was my other option?

Slowly, it grew louder as I drew closer. I brought my blade down into the corner, hitting nothing but carpet. I stood and exhaled as I thought maybe I had begun to hallucinate everything. It'd been only two weeks since the attack.

Two weeks and I had become crippled.

Vulnerable.

A *perfect* target.

Then a whisper in my ear, “Boo.”

Manipulation

The plan had been coming together nicely. If this hadn't scared her from the group, maybe something else would.

Plan B.

For now, Plan A would have to do.

Take what she loves most.

When Owen almost spilled those secrets of his that never belonged to him, we made sure he would never see the light of day. Eye for any eye. Or, I supposed, an eye for a lie.

Nobody was going to take the control away from us—from me.

Squeezing my fingers into a fist, I watched the shadow before me crumble to his feet, begging for the mercy I'd never give.

His screeching tore through the walls. Paint crackled. Lights flickered.

Everything went dark.

"You have no power over me, *puppet.*" My voice bounced around the room, venom laced along my tongue. "And eventually she will realize that, too."

021 Sunday, May 13th

The Arizona heat was not to be reckoned with. Especially when you were being dragged into the forest and forced onto your knees butt-ass naked.

Lucas stopped in front of me, grabbing my chin. "Nowhere to go, no way to fight back. This is what we call justice." His palm met my cheek. It stung like a bitch, but so did I. However I got out of this situation that was.

Lucy stood back and crossed her arms. "Justice for all the Kaofi wronged, and justice for what Eli did to Alissa."

I could hardly be blamed for that event unfolding. Alas...

Lifting my chin higher to expose my neck, I encouraged Lucas with, "Go on then. Kill me. I can't even fight back." It was my subtle way of calling them cowards for grabbing me at my worst.

Without hesitation, Lucas grabbed me by the jaw, but before he could snap my neck, I threw my mouth against his wrist and bit as hard as I could, tearing a chunk off. He yelled out and sent a blow to my head. I fell to the ground and spit out the dirt that got caught in my mouth.

He went for my hair but I rolled out of the way, swallowing the pain in my shoulder. I shoved my good foot right into his knee, watching it bend backward. Such a pleasant sight.

Lucy grabbed my arm and dragged me across the floor, throwing me into a tree. I swore I heard my spine crack but I could still move everything below the waist, so I'd only been imagining it. I could also unfortunately feel every ounce of pain coursing through my nerves.

Her hand flew into my hair as she ripped my head back, forcing me to face her. "Fight back all you want. You have absolutely no strength here." She slammed my head into the tree and a groan left my lips.

She'd stop at nothing, and I knew that. Eli had hesitated in killing me, knowing full well I was a Hanti. Lucy and Lucas never hesitated once.

The only way I'd escape this was through my own doing.

The question was: *how did I save myself?*

The wind whipped through my hair despite knowing no wind had made it up to this forest at this hour of the night.

A small smile etched its way into my lips as I recalled the person who used cues like that to get my attention. Someone who'd been haunting me since the day he died.

Owen Castillo.

Lucy snickered as he formed before her out of thin air. "Your ghost boyfriend is gonna fight? Ghosts can't do shit."

Owen laughed like it had actually been funny. "What most people don't know about me is that my father was a hunter. You tend to pick up on things." He pulled a dagger from behind his back and plunged it right into her thigh.

She screamed out and shot him the darkest of all looks as

he rushed over to me and picked me up. Badass.

I had no idea his father was a Hanti, either.

"The dagger won't do much to her, it just slows her down and gives us time," he said in a low tone as he vanished.

In that second we vanished, I became a feather. A slight breeze hit me, but it was the kind of breeze you'd feel subtly that would keep the weather unmoving.

I discovered I liked it there, wherever we went.

But then we showed back up at my apartment and Owen plugged my phone in. "It'll take them a second to get here, so I'll go inform Eli."

Like that, he went to Eli's apartment and informed him of the event and Eli came to watch over me the rest of the night. I just couldn't seem to escape my damsel nature.

The cool air of the fan brushed against my skin, comforting me and my sorrows. It was no secret that I'd been down since Juliet and I got into a fight. She'd been my best friend for so many years. It was hard to just let go.

"I always seem to find you here," Amari said as she sat.

I sighed. "Yes, it seems so."

She nudged me. "What's wrong? You look like shit." I felt like shit, too. Everyone kept kicking me while I was down.

My heart ached. Everything inside me was tightening with every breath I took. I was afraid I would never make it without Juliet. "We had a fight."

"Who?" Amari didn't know Eli and I were together. She would kill me when she did know.

"Juliet and I. She thinks I've made Eli up in my head and she's saying I changed too much." Juliet was never around. Amari and my family were at the hospital. Where had Juliet gone? She'd been screwing Cole because he was more important. But she'd been screwing others, too. It never made sense as to why Juliet called us friends when she spent more time with them than she did me.

Amari scanned the area. "Why does it matter if she knows Eli is real or not? She'll never see him."

"Amari..." I coughed before I went into a coughing fit over saliva in the wrong pipe.

She eyed me. "What?"

Lowering my head and closing my eyes, I said, "Eli and I are together."

"Mya, tell me you're kidding. That... That is disgusting. You're supposed to kill him. He's a vile creature. He drinks blood." She got off the bench. "How could you be so stupid?"

More tears. "Amari, everyone has their weird kinks." I grabbed my hair with one hand and pulled it behind my shoulders.

Her gaze landed on my bite. A shake of her head. "This isn't a kink, Mya. This is against *nature*. He lives forever and drinks blood to survive. That doesn't scream danger to you?"

"No!" I wiped my cheeks with the back of my hand. "Eli doesn't hurt me. He's never called me a name or silenced my issues. He had never even laid a hand on me."

She laughed but it wasn't humorous in *any* way. "He tried to kill me when you thought we were sleeping together."

The despair vanished and rage replaced it. Amari couldn't get to me anymore. "So. Fucking. What. We weren't dating. I have no right to judge his private affairs. You're a Hunter, Amari, and I know for a damn fact that you initiated it. You did it to murder him. You're the one I should blame if anything." I stood up on my boot.

Amari stepped back. "What?"

"Murder is a *two*-person act—is it not?"

"Well, yes." She folded her arms.

"You both fought each other and it's not my place to control what he did before we got together. Do not destroy our friendship, please." It came as a demand.

"He's the enemy, Mya."

I narrowed my eyes. "He's *your* enemy. He was never mine, at least not in that sense. You promised sex for revenge, Amari. I did it because I genuinely wanted to be with him."

A sharp sting exploded on my cheek as her hand collided with it, my face turning to my left. But I looked back at her, eyes locked together.

"Mya..." She gulped.

"What the hell?" I sat on the bench, rubbing my cheek. "I was not born with a hatred for Kaofi. I was not raised like you. Why can't you understand that? What if Clara were a vampire?"

She shook her head. "No. That doesn't count because she's not."

"But what if she was?" I whispered.

Amari's shoulders slumped. "I would have to resist."

"You know you couldn't. You can't help who you love. If she was a vampire, you would do everything you could to be with her. That is how I feel for Eli." Goosebumps covered every inch of my skin.

Amari sat beside me, but it took her five seconds longer than normal. "How the hell do I tell Hunter and Clara?"

"Don't. That's my job." I pushed a strand of hair behind my ear. "Juliet hates me, so I'm prepared for any reaction now."

She grabbed my hand. "Let her. She's a bitch."

"Amari!" I gasped.

She shrugged it off. "Am I supposed to lie? Juliet has no reason to hate Eli."

"She hates him because he threatens what she has. She has a perfect life, and I don't. She wants to see me in misery, so she never has to be jealous of what I have. She even tried to say you were toxic to me." I squeezed her hand and smiled a bit.

"That bitch." Amari sat back and spread her knees, laughing. "I'm not surprised. She was jealous of our friendship because..." Amari was weary to say it.

My smile grew and I laid my head against her shoulder. "You're a better friend than Juliet. Juliet was never there when I needed her the most. We grew apart. *She* was the toxic one. She never wanted me to grow as a person because she refused to grow herself."

"Have you cut her out of your life?" Amari asked.

I frowned. "How do I do that? She's my roommate. Both of our names are on the lease."

Amari tapped her foot against the pavement. "Well, you can move in with us. Oh, wait, you can't run that far." She pressed her lips together. "Also, we couldn't hide your car."

Sitting back up, I squinted. "Lucy and Lucas attacked me this morning. They're still going to be after me."

"There's only one option, dare I suggest such a thing." Amari scoffed. "You'll have to move in with Eli. He can keep an eye on you until you heal. Plus, you can cut off that toxic bitch."

"When I'm no longer broken, I'm going to bring them down." I got off the bench and scanned the trees. "They're probably watching us right now."

Another shrug. "Let them. They're pieces of shits!" she said the last word louder than the rest. It gained us some glances, but it didn't bother me.

"Amari, what—what is it?" I fixed the skirt of my dress. "What kills a fallen angel?"

She smirked. "I see your game." She leaned forward. "It's simple, but only Hunter knows the answer. He doesn't want the word to get out so easily."

"Then when you get a chance, bring him to me. I need to get ahead of those assholes. I'm going to bring those fuckers to the ground." I gestured to my leg.

Amari laughed again. "Good. They deserve it."

My eyes lingered on my leg.

Bones shatter. Screams echo. Pain explodes.

"Mya?" Amari broke me from my trauma.

I choked on my air. "Y-yeah?"

She stood up and caught my attention. "Mya, you don't look okay." I lost my balance and Amari caught me, holding me against her. "Mya." She wrapped her arms tightly around me. "I've got you."

But she couldn't catch the joy falling right from my body. It splattered onto the ground, and I was nothing but desolation.

Amari didn't let go of me, but people began to stare. "Fuck off!" she shouted at them.

His fingers trail up my thigh. I squirm. It cuts me. His touch poisons me.

A cry erupted from me, blending with the screams in my throat. These memories couldn't be erased. They did not resemble a tape you could record over. They were not a blank disc you could burn into. No, they were none of those. These memories resembled the scar on my heart that could never repair itself to its original state.

Amari sat us both down on the bench, but her security never faltered.

My heart pounded against my ribcage. Everything inside me ready to burst. My mind was a playground for sorrow, and I couldn't bully it away.

Amari stroked my hair and whispered, "I'm here." She repeated this phrase until my body was no longer shaking.

"Hey, Amari, Mya, what's going on?" someone asked.

"Can you take Mya somewhere less public? I have to do something." Amari looked up at Hunter.

He gave me a look. "Is she okay?"

Amari stood, nodding. "She just needs someone by her side. This is important. Thank you." Before he could protest, Amari left in a hurry.

Hunter swallowed. "Well, uh, where should we go?"

I shrugged, unable to say a word. There was nothing I could say that would make this less awkward for either of us.

Hunter helped me onto my feet, and we left the complex and ventured off to a park in the middle of seven other apartment buildings in the complex. Nobody was here. I didn't want to even look at another person right now.

"What is it?" he asked.

The words barely escaped in a whisper, "It just hits me."

"What does?"

I shook my head and turned to him. "The...torture." I choked on another sob.

"Oh..." His lips curved downward. "I'm sorry. I know we started off on the wrong foot, but nobody deserves that."

"Ryan died because of me. If I had just figured it out sooner..."

He patted my hand. "No, it was never your fault. Ryan

died because he did what he loved. He kicked some Kaofi ass. He didn't die in vain."

I faced the sky. "I'm fine one minute, then I'm not. One minute, everything is normal. The next minute, I remember the pain and I break down. I can't even control it. I thought I had already grieved."

Hunter let out a sigh. "Mya, this job isn't easy. Being alive is never going to be easy. There is no clock you can set on your grief. It comes in waves sometimes. Everyone grieves differently and it'll take time to heal. It's barely been two weeks since you were tormented. You can't expect your brain to just bounce back so quickly. What you experienced was hell."

Sobs came once again, but tears did not. I'd been dehydrated from crying. "I want it to go away! I want to go back to my life."

"You can't just will your mind to forget, Mya." He twisted his body to face me. "That is not how this works. We try so hard to forget everything that happens, but we cannot control *everything*. The brain doesn't forget trauma so easily. Some people can bury their pain, but we all function differently."

"I can't even tell the truth!" I shouted. "I can't tell my mom what really happened! I can't explain the severity of the trauma that was inflicted on me that night because nobody else knows what I do!" I sobbed until my head dropped.

He lifted his arm to rub my back in an attempt to comfort me. "What do you think it is that will help you get better? What is it that will help you deal with this in a healthy way?"

I couldn't answer the question. As hard as I tried, I couldn't think. Nothing made me smile. Eventually, the bones would heal. That didn't mean my bones would go back to being what they were once before. There would always be a piece that would be off.

"Mya?"

The worst part was that I was trying to love a vampire in the midst of it. Eli was immortal, and I couldn't keep it hidden forever. I was the Hanti who was supposed to take his life and yet I didn't have the guts to do so. I didn't want to think of such a despicable act.

I wanted to be everything Eli would need and knew without a doubt he was that for me. He was not going away anytime soon, but the abuse I suffered was the result of knowing him. I had to deal with this somehow. I had to get rid of the threat, too.

What conflicted me the most was who I was vs. who he was. We were from such different worlds. I had to pick a side. I could not continue to kill the very people that Eli associated with, but I could never be just a regular human, either.

Quietly, I said, "I'm not sure I can heal."

022 Monday, May 14th

A gentle hum passed my lips. "It strikes me as strange that autumn is so beautiful, yet everything is dying." I stared out the window at the sky. The stars were still out, shining down on us.

A low chuckle rippled through his throat as Eli glanced my way. "It's spring."

With breathing steady, I scooted myself closer to him. I wrapped my arm around his waist, pressing my cheek into his side. "Because you are autumn. You are dead, but you are still so mesmerizing. This is my cheesy way of saying...I love you."

"You do?" He wrapped his arm around my body.

"I do. It took me a while to realize it, but... I know I can't deny it. I would do anything for you. I gave up everything for you. That is called love."

"Yes, it is, Love." He kissed my head.

I didn't understand if that was his way of telling me he loved me too or not. He was a man but *also* a vampire. I let go of him and twirled myself around the room, but my steps were choppy and slow. *"I can't help...falling in love with you..."* I sang. This song had been stuck in my head for a while. Definitely my wedding song.

Eli watched me with curiosity etched on his face. "Is something on your mind?"

I looked over at him as I began chewing my lip. "I wish I could say no but... So much is going on. I have to take down Lucas and Lucy when I get better, but I have to choose to be a Hunter or be with you. It's too much."

He grabbed my hands, pulling me closer. "I wish I could take it all away for you."

I sat beside him. "What about... If we have kids someday, how does that work? We both have abilities that would probably pass on. Our children would basically be smelling like death all the time." But I'd remembered what Owen said. His father was a hunter. So did Hanti become ghosts when they died?

Eli rubbed his thumb on mine. "They don't have to. We know more than we like to admit but when you smelt cat piss on me, I knew that you had the ability to sniff out Kaofi. When we danced at the masquerade, I masked my original scent. I knew you wouldn't want to dance with someone who smelt the way I did. What do other creatures smell like?"

I laid my head against his shoulder. "Lucas smells like a fire burning out. You smell like a cat peeing all over everything. I haven't met enough of the other creatures to pick up their scents." I smiled a bit at him. "Except Owen. He smells like rain and mud."

He chuckled. "*I* sound so wonderful." He rested his head against mine. "I can't answer any of your questions. I wish I could, but I don't know how to make your decisions for you."

"I didn't expect you to. My problems are mine to solve." I closed my eyes. "Thank you for just listening to me."

"Always, Mya," he whispered as he placed a gentle kiss on my nose.

I rolled my eyes and stood up, pacing the room a bit. "That's different."

"No, it's not." Juliet shook her head.

I stopped and looked at her. "This is a big deal to me. You don't want me to change. I don't get to choose how to deal with my trauma. I just deal with it however I can. You're the one calling me crazy and telling me that when I kissed Eli, that wasn't real."

"So, you're going to move out because we got into a fight? Is that how this is going to work? You're very mature, Mya," she said with sarcasm. She got out of her bed and started getting ready for class.

"Juliet, I'm not moving out. I'm telling you right now that I'm *done*. With all of this. We're not going to be friends. I don't want to talk to you. I don't want to text you. I never want to see you. Amari treats me the way I want to be treated. She's my friend. She's become a sister to me." I released a sigh. "I'll be packing up my stuff and getting out of your hair. This is where the road ends. I hope you can find yourself and be happy, too."

Before she could say another word or stop me, I grabbed my bag and went to my car. A hole filled the place where Juliet once stayed.

When I glanced to my left, I chewed my lip. Eli was

leaving, too. I was going to ask him if he loved me. That was all I could really do, if I wanted to quiet the loud voice in my head. Nobody could read his mind. *Wait.* Could I read his mind? Was it an ability that Amari never told me about? I could try.

I barely peeked at him. He smirked at me, already noticing my stare. "Is there a special reason you're giving me the googly eyes? Does it have something to do with our little confession this morning?" He lifted an eyebrow.

My cheeks heated as I smiled. "Maybe." He did mention *our* confession, so was that his way of saying he returned the feelings? Was that a thing? It couldn't be believable in my world, but then again, vampires were real. What was believable anymore? Everything. Anything and everything could be the truth.

I looked at his head, trying to pry into his brain. Was there some sort of trick to this? He made it sound so easy.

"Are you trying to read my mind?" he questioned.

I nodded, not really saying anything else.

He chuckled and patted my hand that laid flat on the hood of my car. "You can't. Only shadows can. Hunters don't get to have every ability that we have. Sorry, Love."

I scowled quietly, realizing my dilemma. I knew I now had to ask him myself. *Damn.*

"Oh, I meant to ask, do you prefer spoons or forks for your pasta? Or both?" Eli grabbed something. "I found this cool utensil that is double-sided. Spoon on one end and fork on the other."

I gripped the hood of my car. Beads of sweat dripped from my skin as memories flooded back. My lungs refused to take in any air, leaving me struggling to breathe.

Eli hurried over, and the attention was far from wanted.

He rubbed my back. “Hey, look at me. Look at me and just breathe.”

I couldn’t catch my own breath. My lungs were failing me when I needed them most. I could only relive the pain I went through during that night in that room. The pain was overtaking every inch of my body, sinking its *claws* and drawing blood.

Eli pulled me from my car and rushed me inside his apartment. I might have needed more than just him. He gave me some water. “You’re safe now.”

Everyone knew what had happened. It was no secret as to what I dealt with in that place. They just heard the knock-off version of me being beaten in a parking lot.

Eli sat on a chair next to the bed. “What can I do to help?”

I rubbed my palms along my thighs. “Everyone else recommends therapy but you and I both know the issue with that. I will need to take the time to get help. This stuff doesn’t go away.” Eli was there to make sure everything was under control.

I didn’t know how to come back from this. I needed help. I couldn’t get over this without it. But I guess nobody truly got over it, did they?

“I’m okay. I just... The memories are so overbearing. When I saw something similar to a double-sided fork, it brought back too many painful thoughts. I know it was humiliating, and I don’t want those memories to resurface.”

Eli moved next to me, encasing me in his arms. He stroked my hair while shaking his head. “Don’t ever feel embarrassed. You don’t get to control when it comes to you. You’re still a human and trauma is trauma. It doesn’t go away with the snap of a finger.”

“I need to get into therapy, don’t I?”

"It would be good. You don't have to mention everything. I just want you to find peace somehow. I care about your health, and that includes your mental health. You should find joy in some form again." He placed a small kiss against my temple.

I released a deep breath I'd been holding. "Okay. I will go to therapy. I will do it for myself, so I can get better." They infested my nightmares. Awake or asleep.

He continued to stroke my hair to comfort me. "I'm sorry. I am so sorry I didn't protect you sooner."

"Stop right there, Eli. Don't you blame yourself. I would never ask you to rely on me like that, or vice versa. You are not responsible for it. I'm just glad you stopped him when you did. Let's focus on the good. If you want therapy to do me any good, start by not redirecting blame to yourself." I sat up and lost myself in his eyes almost immediately. He had a habit of doing that to me.

He smiled a bit, pushing a strand away from my face. "Okay."

"Can we talk about something else?"

"Like what?"

"Love. Us." I gestured between us.

He studied my face for any answers to his questions.

I cleared my throat. "This refers to this morning. I admitted I love you. You called me Love right after, and then earlier in the parking lot you referred to it as *our* confessions. Is that your subtle way of returning the love? I want to know if you love me or not.

"I mean, if you don't, it's okay. I don't want to rush or pressure you. Please, don't say it if you don't mean it. Do you understand what I'm saying? Sometimes you are direct, but I don't think that way. I still have a part of me that assumes little clues are hidden in the words."

He chuckled and pushed my hair back using his thumb. "It's okay, Mya. You don't have to worry or wonder what my words mean, or attempt to read my mind," he joked.

I wondered if this meant he did love me back. Did he?

"I do, Mya. I love you in return," he confirmed.

A smile formed as I laid my hand over his, giving it a light squeeze. This was the one good thing that had come out of today. "You have no idea how much this means. Now, if only I could fix this trauma issue, then would my life be perfect."

"Don't you worry. I will help you through this."

I started to feel a bit better, but not quite. I still had to take care of the memories that haunted me, with or without an ability to heal myself.

Therapy would be my lame attempt to bring back a piece of me that was running away. Maybe it would work, or maybe it wouldn't. I couldn't say for sure.

The one thing that was resolute was the end of my abusers. Lucas and Lucy would not escape my wrath. Hunter had given me the secret ingredient to taking their lives from them for good. This world would do better with fewer angels in it, anyway.

023 Monday, June 11th

Eli was waiting outside the building, leaning against the railing. He saw me approaching and he pushed himself off the metal. “Ready for our first date?”

“I’m not even dressed for a date.” I looked down at my denim shorts and T-shirt.

“Don’t worry about it. You don’t want nice clothes for this date.” He chuckled and grabbed my hand, pulling me in the direction of the forest.

I looked back at the building behind us, remembering everything I told the therapist. I had kept careful to not mention the supernatural, but I would have a long way to go before I was able to function normally.

We trod through the forest.

The smell of pine was something I had always loved. We would always buy a fake tree during Christmas and it made me miss real pine.

“Where are we going for this first date?” I asked.

Twigs snapped beneath my boots, echoing in the space

around us and getting trapped between all the tree trunks.

"I never told you one little thing. I hunt for my own food. I find a thrill in hunting," he said as he shot a look back at me.

"Hunting?"

"Yes. For animals. We do drink blood and snacking on animal blood is not a crime. It's better than humans." He shrugged.

Nodding a bit, I focused on every root we avoided. "You have a point. It's not like I was ever a vegetarian anyway. So, hunting animals for our first real date? Show me how it works."

"I will. You have super hearing due to your superhuman abilities, and this will be of use. This is the springtime, so we should be in the ripe animal season." He chuckled and came to a stop.

He listened. I followed suit.

He drank blood and I was meant to kill people like him, so the way to come together was to hunt little creatures. I could still hunt, keeping my abilities alive, and he could be himself without killing humans.

He put a finger to his lips. "Do you hear that? Now, what you do is stay as quiet as a mouse. You have the upper hand because your speed can outrun the animal. Your main goal is to quietly follow the sound and spot the animal, and once you have a sight on it, you are ready to pounce."

He demonstrated this method by sneaking off in the direction of a sound, which I also followed. He gained sight of an animal and kept his eye on it until he went full speed and attacked the prey. He snapped its neck and gave it to me. "Now I want you to try."

I nodded and looked around the woods. I listened for

some sounds, chewing and squeaking. I followed one that stood out to me. It led to a little squirrel. I ran and attacked, but the squirrel got away. I groaned in frustration. "Shit."

Eli shook his head, smiling as if this was funny to him. "This is normal. It's okay, it was just your first try. You just have to learn these skills. We can always go again. Now come on." He waved me over to him.

We tried a few more times until I finally caught some kind of bird. It was an accomplishment in my eyes since birds had a better escape route than squirrels. The sky. "I did it! I caught one! I am finally learning something useful." I squealed. If I could catch and kill a bird, I could catch and kill a fallen angel or two.

He tapped his stubbled chin. "Shall we evolve in our hunting? I want to try something new. I want to hunt you."

I lifted my eyebrows. "Hunt me? What does that mean?"

"I want to hunt you. If I catch you, I get to drink your blood." He smirked.

I looked at the forest floor. "You mean like some kind of vampire-hunter roleplay?"

"Exactly." He came closer to me, his shoes coming into my view.

"I'm down for it. Will we have sex?" I met his gaze.

He poked my nose gently. "If you want to. But I think hunting you would be beneficial. It really gives us some more variety of what we can do and expands on your skills of being able to hide and mask yourself." Vampires had the ability to sniff out different humans. By now, Eli had my scent down to a T with how much time we spent together.

"I like it. Sounds great to me." I smiled.

I started off in one direction. I stopped and tried to rub dirt and leaves on my skin. Eli never told me what my scent was, but if he was vanilla, maybe I was chocolate.

My speed picked up as more trees flew by. I dodged every single one, remembering what Amari had taught me. I knew my east from my west. The Hanti taught me so I could always find my way through the forest. It was a required skill to properly hunt or outrun a Kaofi. I could look at the sun and always tell what direction I was going.

If it was a new moon, then I'd be screwed.

I climbed into a tree and stayed there for a while. I listened for his footsteps, wondering how well I could keep myself hidden.

"Boo," someone whispered behind me.

I screamed and slipped from the branch, but his arms caught me. He chuckled and rubbed some dirt off my arm, rubbing it between his fingers. "Really? Dirt? You have to do better than that." Except this time Eli wasn't the one catching me.

"Owen," I breathed.

"Hello, Mya." He flashed me that smile that had me swooning the day we met.

"You shouldn't be here. What we had is in the past and I'm happy with Eli."

His smile faded as he pulled his arms away from me. "I understand."

My heart cracked when he said those words. I wanted to grip his collar and yank him into my arms. But I couldn't do that anymore. "I'm sorry."

Owen glanced to his right and gripped the branches. "This was supposed to be our *second chance*. But I suppose those aren't real, are they?" He looked at me one more time before he vanished into thin air.

Eli hopped up into the tree, climbing branches before

facing me. "That was too easy."

I looked at him and smiled a bit. "Maybe I wanted to be found, Eli. Now come on, why would I pass up the chance to be touched by you? I'm with a vampire now, and my desires have changed. The thought of you sucking from my neck actually turns me on."

"Well, then it's probably bad if I tell you I won't do it." He bopped my nose again. "I like a good chase. This is not even a chase."

"That is so mean! You can't lead a girl on like that."

"I'm not. I am simply motivating you. Just keep practicing. It will be much more fun that way." He kissed my nose.

I sighed. "Why don't we do something else for the moment? You like photography. Let's go sightseeing. That would be fun. I get to watch the man in action. You can teach me your tips and tricks."

He climbed down a branch. "Sure, why not? You can be my model."

"I'm not dressed to be a model." I laughed.

He grabbed me and jumped down from the tree, landing on the ground. He set me down on my two feet and stood back, looking at me. "No, you're perfect for this. Let's go."

"Excuse me. I am not ready. I'm in bland clothes with a naked face." I crossed my arms.

"A naked face? You can remove your clothes and give me a naked body, too. I won't complain." His lips did that curving upward thing again.

I rolled my eyes playfully. "No. You will just have to use your brain like a camera, England."

"England?" He lifted his eyebrow.

I nodded, a small smile plastered to my lips. "When

we first met, I called you that. You're pretty irritating sometimes."

Irritating. He was so frustrating, and Amari had been too. But now she was my best friend. She replaced Juliet when Juliet decided I was never enough.

A part of me still missed Juliet, but eventually, I would feel better that she wasn't in my life to hold me back.

No, you're not here to think about her. Focus on this.

"And you are, too." He grabbed my hand and pulled me along. We went back to his apartment so he could grab his camera.

"So where are we going to have this photoshoot?" I asked him.

He looked over at me as he packed his equipment. "Well, I would say nature. Preferably a forest, or creek. You with that backdrop? Perfection."

My cheeks burned bright red. "I like creeks."

We made it back to the woods and put me up against a tree. "Stand right there. And move your chin up a bit." He got his camera ready and put it to his eye. He snapped a shot, then a few more. "Okay, I want to see you move this way." He waved his hand to the left. I moved to the left. He snapped a few more pictures.

It felt strange being a model. I was always too short to actually be one, but Eli didn't think so. He could make me his model and teach more about photography while I designed my own clothes. We would be the perfect duo.

"Technically speaking, we never got a chance to take final photos for your college graduation," Eli said. "We will need to do that one of these days."

With a smile, I nodded. "Let me just make the perfect dress."

We continued this for a good thirty minutes to an hour.

Eli looked up at the sky as the sun was starting to rise. "We should probably go back to the apartment. Everyone will be waking up and I don't want to be out here when people are hunting."

We headed back to his place.

"What are we going to do now? I'm not tired." I opened up the curtains just enough for some light.

He looked at the pictures on his camera. "I can't really think of anything. What else do women like to do on a date?" He looked up at me.

My laugh bounced off all four walls. "Well, for starters, you don't usually ask us. But we are limited on our options, considering Hanti and Kaofi are now out and about." I sat next to him and put my head on his shoulder. I looked at the pictures. "You're really good at this."

"Thank you." He smiled and kissed my forehead ever so sweetly. "I meant to ask, what is Hanti? You say it quite a bit."

Chewing my lip, I said, "Kaofi Hunters. We call ourselves Hanti. Calling us hunters is too shallow. Like that's all we are. So, we call ourselves Hanti."

"Noted. Hanti." He cleared his throat. "Maybe we should do something for you. I want you to be able to fight off the enemies and defend yourself in case I'm not around."

I lifted my head, furrowing my brows. In case he wasn't around? I knew he meant it in the sense of not being around me all the time, but a small part of me feared he meant death. "That's a good idea. I apologize for not having already known how to defend myself. I'm a poor excuse for a Hanti."

"Don't go putting yourself down. Just accept my offer to help you train to protect yourself."

"Of course. Right. I'm sorry. It would be good for me." I continued scrolling through pictures. "These are so beautiful. You make me look elegant." I admired the angle and lighting.

He glanced at me. "You always look elegant. I remember a specific night when you stole my breath, metaphorically speaking of course. Your birthday, at the masquerade."

"I remember. I didn't plan to stand out. But I did, and you danced with me like I was the most beautiful woman ever. I love that. It was the best night of my life."

His eyebrows shot up. "It was? You were kidnapped and nearly killed." He set the camera on his nightstand.

Shrugging, I said, "I was, yes, but it was the night I knew everything about you. It was the night that a romantic dream of mine came true. I got to dance with you at a masquerade ball on my twenty-second birthday. Yes, I got kidnapped and tortured, but I also really enjoyed being with you. It's the only good memory I hold onto about that night. That's what my therapist helps me focus on."

"I don't understand how, considering you're traumatized. You still have nightmares. They overpower you." He smiled a little but nothing about it was genuine innocence. It was filled with mourning.

"I won't let them. If they overpowered me, I wouldn't be smiling. I would be stuffed with pills or in a bathtub with my wrists slashed. But I want to fight this. I want to get better and move on. I want a future, and I want it to be with the people I really love."

Eli rested his forehead against the side of my hair. "You're stronger than I ever was when my mother was attacked." Sigh. "I want to help you find peace in your life." His lips pressed against my hair. "We should probably get started on your training. I want you to be able to murder the arseholes who put you through this woe. I want to hear them beg you for mercy."

024 Wednesday, June 13th

"I promise not to take up too much space in your apartment. I'm going to look for some apartments." I faced Eli. "Fair?"

He shrugged a bit. "I'm not asking you to move out."

"I know you're not. But it doesn't seem fair that I'm coming in here and taking away your space and free time just because it turns out my ex best friend is actually a bitch. I'm a grown woman. It's not going to kill me." I sat back, putting my feet up on the desk.

Eli laughed at that. "If you say so, Mya." He stood and grabbed my ankles, putting my feet down on the floor. "Maybe I don't want you to leave." He leaned forward. "Maybe I want you to stay." He began tracing his fingers up my thigh.

Heavy were my eyelids as my breathing shortened. "I mean...maybe."

He gripped my hips. "I'd miss our parking lot banter."

I grabbed the collar of his shirt. "Would you?" I pulled his lips onto mine and tangled my fingers in his curls.

Just as things were ready to escalate, Eli's phone rang. He grumbled and pulled himself off of me and answered it. "This is a terrible time, Josh." A pause. "Are you bloody serious? Fine, I'm headed over." He hung up and looked at me. "I'm sorry, but things have gotten out of hand at his place. I have to step in."

"Maybe I can come." But my suggestion hit a nerve.

"That's not a good idea. We should keep this under wraps for a little longer." He pulled his jacket on and grabbed his keys. "I'll be back when I can." He hurried out the door and down the stairs. I peeked out the window long enough to watch him jump in his car and burn rubber.

On one hand, I enjoyed the thrill of having to hide our secret. But on the other hand, I hated being nothing more than unknown.

"He leaves just like that, huh?" Owen asked from behind.

I jumped and whipped around. "You cannot be here. Not in his apartment. That's breaking and entering."

"It would be. If I were still alive..." He scanned the place. "But when you actually don't have a body, things change. I'm merely just a soul wandering." He took a few strides towards the dresser. "I woke up and you'd moved on without me."

"What was I supposed to do? You want me to be hung up on you forever? Owen, that isn't possible. It's not fair to me that I have to give up a chance of being happy because of what happened to you. I didn't kill you. I wasn't the one driving that car." I pointed out the window just as it began raining. How convenient.

He looked at me. "No, you weren't. But we were dancing in the rain in the dark like you wanted."

I dropped my arm at my side. "You blame me for your death."

"No, I'm sorry. That's not what I meant."

"But it's what you said." I leaned against the wall. "You don't get it. After you died, I pretended to be okay because I didn't have the guts to kill myself. But I wasn't okay. I went to parties. I drank until I was numb. I made out with strangers and who the hell knows if I happened to sleep with any of them. But that was how I tried to handle it. There was so much happening inside me that I was afraid to sort out. We met at the beginning of the summer and I was absolutely happy. But you died. And I was still expected to start my senior year as if you hadn't."

Owen closed the gap between us. "I was trying to reach you. I just couldn't quite get through. Not until...you *became* a hunter."

"And by then, I was already into Eli. I just couldn't admit it. I love him. I do." I knew that not being able to talk to him sucked the life from me.

"Then let me ask you this." He swallowed. "Did you love me?"

I averted my gaze and that told him everything he needed to know. "I never stopped," I whispered.

He placed his fingers under my chin. "Then why did you choose him the moment you saw me?"

"It's more complicated than that." I stepped away from him. "It's not so black and white."

And it never had been. Owen died and I had to grieve for him. I had done it the wrong way, but I still grieved. Then he came back, and I couldn't pretend like we could go back to normal. Like we could pick up where we left off. So much had changed between the time he died and when I tackled him.

I had changed in new ways. Eli had kissed me. Owen came back at the worst possible time and now he was demanding that I figure out my feelings. I didn't like that. Eli had never asked me to sort out my feelings in a matter of minutes. He trusted that I would eventually.

Yet here I stood, in love with two men. But I could only have one, and I chose Eli.

"Just tell me to leave, Mya, and I will. I will leave you alone and never bother you again." How could he say that? He made it sound like it was so easy.

"Owen, you know I can't do that."

"But we both know you chose him and I can't be the one who steps in the middle of it."

"Then why are you here?"

His gaze lowered. "I came to say goodbye. To tell you that I enjoyed those two months with you, but it's time for me to move on. I suggest you do the same." Turning around, he headed for the door as if he needed to use it and he couldn't just vanish with the wind.

In a split second, I reached out and grabbed his arm, pulling him back. I neared his lips, stumbling. He wrapped his arm around me and kept me from falling just as he leaned in.

I'd forgotten the taste of him, and how he made me feel inside.

The first time Eli kissed me, he elicited feelings of hunger. The first time Owen ever kissed me, he elicited feelings of bliss. And this time I hoped it wouldn't be any different.

He was the first to pull away, but he was barely a centimeter farther. "This is wrong on so many levels."

I debated going in for the kiss, but I took the moment to

put space between us as I wiped my lips. "What have I done?" Total shame washed over me as I stumbled back onto the bed. "I'm a horrible person."

"I wouldn't say that."

"You're not the one who cheated on someone just now."

"But I am. I almost kissed you, too, knowing full well you're dating Eli."

With a few shakes of my head, I hunched over. "I am the worst." I ran my fingers through my hair. "Why couldn't you just vanish like you always do?" Desperation dripped from my tongue.

"Mya—"

"No." I stood. "This is on me. I almost kissed you. And I shouldn't have. And there's only one way to make this right. I have to tell Eli."

He nodded a little. "Understood."

"And it's best that I do it alone. It's my sin to bear."

"Fair enough."

"You should leave. Now."

Before I could tell him again, he disappeared.

I wasn't sure how I was going to tell him, but I had to. I was a grown adult. If I truly loved Eli, I had to tell him so he could make a decision to either stay or leave.

Or in my case, let me stay or kick me to the curb.

A door opened and closed and a figure came into my view. "Hey. Sorry I'm late," Eli whispered as he started to undress. "Things got ugly tonight."

I sat up and turned on the lamp, seeing the blood staining his clothes. "What happened?"

He snickered. "Well, you know. Lucy and Lucas showed up. Those two are always trying to cause trouble." Eli took a seat, exposing his bloody back. I reached out to help but his wounds had healed just seconds later. "As if I need any more trouble." He glanced back at me.

Trouble. Like what I had done earlier.

Tugging his pants off and leaving nothing but his boxer briefs, Eli grasped my hips and pulled me on top of him. "Now, where were we earlier?" He moved my hair to one side and planted soft kisses along my neck.

It would be so easy to just enjoy this and let it lead to sex. It would be the highlight of my night. But I couldn't back down just because I was scared. If I waited longer, the repercussions would be much worse.

"Eli," I sputtered. "We have to talk."

He chuckled. "I don't think that would be much of a turn on." His fingers trailed up my waist, pulling my shirt over my head.

Shivers ran up my spine as I attempted to catch the truth before it ran away. I couldn't let it go. No matter how wonderful Eli's hands were. "Please," I whispered.

He leaned me back onto the bed and climbed on top. "Please what?" He gently tugged at the skin of my neck with his teeth, slipping his hand into my shorts. "Please satisfy you?"

I almost nodded, but I caught myself. I just needed to say it before he had me under his spell. "I almost kissed Owen." He froze. "I pulled him to me and we were so close. Another inch and I would have."

He didn't say a word.

"Eli?"

Taking his hand out, he got up from the bed and clenched

his jaw. "When?"

"Today..." I sat up, pulling the sheets up to cover my chest. "I am so sorry. If you need me to pack up now, I understand. There isn't any excuse. But you deserved to know."

He threw a plain shirt on. "I'll be in the living room."

Knowing what that meant, I jumped off of the bed and grabbed his arm. I dropped it as soon as I squeezed the tension in his muscles. "No. I'll sleep on the couch. And if that's too awkward, then I'll sleep at Amari's. This is your apartment and I'm the one who hurt you. I don't deserve to sleep in your bed just because." I began pulling clothes on.

I'd have to stay at her house. Or wherever it was that she lived.

Eli looked at me. "Why did you almost kiss him?"

I finished buttoning my jeans. "I...I still have feelings for Owen and I was scared of him leaving forever." I found some socks and pulled them on.

For a minute, he seemed to be thinking. But then he said, "Stay at Amari's for a few nights. I need time to process this."

That was the last thing I wanted to hear, but I couldn't just say no. I made the move. I was the one completely in the wrong. So I packed up a bag of my things and put on my shoes last. "I'll see you in a few days, I hope."

I grabbed my keys and left the apartment. I wanted to cry about it, but I had no right to. And on top of that, I had no energy.

Hurting him had *hurt* me.

My car was now parked on the other side of Eli's since I had moved apartments. Every apartment came with two covered spots, so I took the empty number he didn't use.

I hopped in and started it up, but I couldn't go to Amari and have her ask me questions. I couldn't go to Juliet, either.

There was only one place I could go where I would always be welcomed even if I had killed someone.

Pulling out, I left the complex and headed somewhere else. I glanced at the clock that read 2:05 AM. I arrived at my destination about 3:09 AM, and the moment my mom answered the door, she scowled at me for waking her up so early.

So lovely to be home.

025 Friday, June 15th

I sipped my wine, then the doorbell rang.

Mom rushed to answer it but she came back to me. "That's odd. Nobody was at the door."

"Maybe kids are playing pranks." I shrugged, drinking some more.

"Or maybe she can't see me at all," Eli whispered.

I screamed and spilled my wine.

"What?" Mom yelled. "What's wrong?"

"Nothing. I thought I saw a spider is all." I cleaned up my mess and glanced at Eli. "A spider that came out of nowhere, *unannounced.*" A glare.

"Oh, I announced it. But you didn't check your phone." He pointed.

Mom gave me a weird look. "Let me make lunch."

Clearing my throat, I nodded. "You do that. I'll be outside for a moment. Fresh air sounds good right about now." I stepped outside where she couldn't see me. "What the hell,

Eli?"

He walked in front of me before facing me. "I think scaring you is the least bad thing that's happened in the past few days."

My heart sank and I fell into the chair. "Right."

"Mya, listen to me. I'm upset about it. But I want to give us another chance. You almost kissed him, yes, but you *didn't*." No, because *Owen* pulled away first. "You also told me right away and you didn't try to play the victim. That shows me that you're willing to own up to your mistakes and learn from them. And I can't stop loving you, so there's no reason to give up on us."

I began chewing the skin from my lip. "Really? I mean, I'm glad to hear that. It won't happen again. I won't even see him again. I'll make sure he knows that there's nothing between us and he needs to move on. We both need to move on."

Eli bent down to my level, pulling my lip from my teeth. "Let's go train some more. Fair?"

I smiled a little and nodded. "Fair."

I informed my mom that I was going out for a bit. Eli and I headed to the forest. I strapped my sheath to my thigh before placing my dagger inside it.

As soon as we found a spot, Eli had run off in some direction. I narrowed my eyes, mumbling, "This is how we're going to train, huh?" And I sprinted into the trees after him.

I used my senses to follow the scent of vanilla, and when the time came, I pushed my legs to carry me faster than Eli could run. I tackled him to the ground and pulled my blade out, pressing it up against his throat. "Not bad, eh?"

"Not bad."

Sitting up, I put my dagger back. I'd expected a smirk, kiss, or any kind of remark. I was left with the Eli who'd said he didn't want to give up, yet he couldn't let go how he felt. I'd screwed up big time. I slid off of him and stood, brushing away dirt. "The chase is good. But I need a real fight."

Eli got on his feet and furrowed his brows. "No, Mya, I'm not going to resort to that."

"It's good for both of us."

"Hitting you is not good for any of us."

"It's not real, Eli. I'm asking you to give me your best fight so I can learn to take you down. Besides, I think after what I did, it should be easier to want to fight me."

He shook his head. "I'm not entertaining the thought. You emotionally hurt me. Physical violence isn't the answer."

"It is for me."

Without giving him a second thought, I whipped out my dagger and aimed for his chest, almost plunging it into him. He blocked it, but the slices in his skin made him hiss. "Mya!" He ducked when I swung around, then he tackled me to the forest floor. He knocked my weapon out of my hand and it flew to the floor a few feet away. Eli brushed his knuckles across my throat before grabbing my chin. "I am not going to fight you just because you hurt me."

My eyes fluttered shut just as my breath hitched. His lips began at my neck and traveled down my collarbone.

But I took my chance.

I threw him off of me and rolled to my dagger, grabbing it before he could catch me. I ended up with one knee on the ground and the other against my chest. "This isn't the time for sex. It's time for fighting."

Eli ran towards me and I pushed myself off the ground just as he flew under me. I landed on the forest floor behind him and turned around just as he pushed me against a tree.

He buried his face in my neck. “Don’t you think that’s my goal?” With a chuckle, he unbuttoned a few buttons, but he couldn’t finish before I pushed him away. I’d worn a black pair of shorts that only had like ten buttons on it.

“You’re testing me by seducing me? Very classy.”

“What does that mean?”

“It means you think I’ll be easily seduced by every man who comes my way. I was seduced by Owen, wasn’t I? I was seduced by you. I’m stronger than that. I almost kissed Owen but I’m not going to kiss just any guy that gropes me.”

“That’s not what I said.”

“But you were thinking it,” I whispered. “You think I have no control.”

He stepped back. “I wasn’t insinuating that you’re easy to seduce.”

I leaned back against the trunk of a tree. “Forget it. You made your point. I screwed up and I’m easy to seduce.”

“Mya, that wasn’t what I said.”

“Yes it was. It’s on me. I nearly kissed Owen. I’m the one in the wrong.”

Eli scowled. “Bloody hell, just let me speak.” He circled the tree. “I was not trying to say you’re easy. I was trying to say that it’s good for you if you’re not always easily seduced by *me*.”

I furrowed my brows.

“We both know I’m hard to resist. If you can resist me, you’ll learn how to be the best fighter. That was my intention with what I said. Don’t twist my words, *please*.”

I gasped. “You said please.”

He gave me a little smile. “I did.” His smile dropped from his expression. “Mya, I think maybe it’s time I tell you my darkest secret. Something nobody else knows.”

"I thought I knew all of your darkest secrets. You killed Alissa."

"This is different," he said in quieter tone.

I nodded for him to go on.

"When I was younger, I wasn't the man you know today. My mother hammered it into my head that I respect women. That I treat them with the utmost respect possible. I was taught to be a gentleman, which probably sounds unusual for you. Vampires aren't normally so kind."

"Hanti teach us that. But I'm sure you're kinder than we give you credit for."

He leaned back against the tree. "Mum took me out one night to pick out a suit. Another girl had no date and I promised to take her. We tried on so many, and they were all so sharp. But the classic black was my favorite. That's what we chose."

"You *do* look amazing in classic black," I noted.

"We headed back home, but this group of men stopped us. Mother told me it would be okay. We just needed to sort out everything with my father. But when I tried to call him, they broke our phone. And all my mum could say was, *'take me; let him go.'*"

Swallowing, I realized how dark this story would be.

"And so they did take her up on her offer. But not without teaching us a lesson first." His hands began to shake. "Two of the men held me back and forced me to watch them rape and *kill* my mother. From that moment on, I stopped being the nice guy. What was the point of trying if the only person I cared so much about was gone?"

"Damn, Eli. I'm so sorry. I can't even..." I couldn't imagine the horror—the trauma that came from that kind of thing.

Everything in the alley began to piece itself together. A

gang of vampires followed me, and he had no choice but to stop them for the sake of his mother. Suddenly, that event seemed so miniscule to this one.

He'd been all too familiar with men like that.

"I'm a dick. I know that. But I still do my best to give respect where it's deserved," he said.

Something echoed in the distance, and both Eli and I could pick up on it. Breathing. A heartbeat here and there. The echo of a metal blade sliding from its sheath.

Based on the blend of wet dog, cat piss, and burning ash, I knew right away Kaofi were here. Had they followed us? Regardless of the answer, we knew we had to get out before we met our end. Who knew how many there were, and based on our heightened senses, there were tons upon tons. It was suicide to stick around and find out.

Eli gave me a look and I nodded a bit, taking slow steps in the opposite direction. I attempted to calm down my heart, but I didn't think it was working. If I could hear them nearby, they could certainly hear me.

I'd walked too close to a tree without even thinking and I scratched my hand against a branch. I widened my eyes when beads of blood seeped through. "Oh no..." My heart pounded louder as I looked at Eli. I could hear the vampires already catching a whiff, making their way through the forest. "Run!" I yelled, sprinting through the trees.

Unfortunately, I wasn't fast enough. Especially since I didn't have *wings.*

The fallen angels landed first—right in front of me. I tried to backtrack but that's where the vampires were, which made it easier for the wolves to follow. Shadows followed the sounds, and then a few extra immortals I couldn't quite recognize yet appeared.

I gripped the handle of my dagger, backing into Eli. "They're everywhere," I whispered. "And I know I'm not supposed to admit I'm afraid but I'm really afraid." An owl swooping just within our distance before disappearing once again.

I swallowed my fear, realizing they were mostly targeting me. It was like zombies going for the humans. They knew their own kind weren't the villains. No, I was the Hanti. So when they all charged, I put everything I learned to good use. I was aware of all surroundings, never turning my back for too long.

When I threw one to the ground, two more came. As hard as I tried to fight so many at once, I couldn't. There had to be thousands of them against just me.

Eli helped me fight against his own kind, but his attention was redirected towards me when a group of them pushed me into the tree, squeezing my throat. I lost my grip on my dagger, dropping it and clawing at his arm, trying to loosen his grip. My lungs burned and the world started to slip away.

Seconds later, air rushed into my lungs as I fell to the ground, coughing and trying to gather what strength I had left. I felt for my dagger, but I couldn't find it. Something caught my eye, a glint of light reflecting. I saw my dagger in the hands of another vampire, but he wasn't focused on me. No—he was paying attention to Eli.

"No!" I yelled as he threw him into a tree.

I jumped to my feet and hurried over, but before I could get there, someone else knocked into me and I flew back. I groaned and rolled onto my hands, refocusing.

I looked up at Eli.

The vampire came towards me, but Eli tried to stop him. The vampire swung his arm back as a reflex, plunging my dagger into Eli's neck.

And I *screamed.*

My heart was about to jump from my chest as I kept screaming while he grabbed his neck and fell to his knees.

Nothing else mattered. I stumbled to my feet, running towards him. Anyone who got in my way was thrown to the ground. I got there just as he fell, catching him in my arms. "No, no, no. No, you're okay. You'll be fine. You have something for this, right?" I swallowed.

He choked, eyes rolling back into his head.

"Right?" I yelled, starting to cry.

His blood stained my hands and my shirt. I didn't even care.

"You're going to be fine," I choked out.

He tried to groan, tried to shout from the pain of his body attacking the little bits of iron digging through his neck.

I hadn't even paid attention when the immortals began backing away.

A hand landed on my shoulder, and I screamed, "Don't fucking touch me!" I hadn't even registered that they were Hunter's.

I just held Eli, savoring every bit of him. "Don't leave me. Don't you dare effing leave me." I grabbed his face, pressing my forehead against his. "I can't survive without you." As if convincing him, I kissed him. It was a soft yet sweet kiss, one that begged him to stay for me.

But he *never* kissed back.

"Eli," I whispered as I pulled away. He wasn't moving anymore. "No, Eli."

Everything broke inside me.

I *shattered* like my bones at that very moment.

The Hanti pulled me back, and I started screaming and

crying.

He couldn't leave me. He couldn't just leave me like that.

They dragged me away from his body, and I fought every ounce of them. I couldn't let him rot here, but they were more worried about getting me out of the legion before they devoured my soul.

"Anyone want to explain to me why Mya was dating Eli? Isn't this what we all wanted? To kill him?" Hunter asked.

Amari slapped his arm. "You fell apart after Ryan died. He was like a brother to you. Mya was in love with Eli. We can't control who we love, and she just watched him die. Try to understand, dickwad."

"Mya?" Clara sat beside me as I curled into a tighter ball on the couch. I never made any effort to look at them.

It couldn't be real. Eli couldn't be dead. This had to be just a horrifying *nightmare*. Anything but real. I couldn't survive without him. How could I grieve yet another dead boyfriend?

Another sob rippled through my chest and I broke down.

Who was going to train with me? Cuddle with me? Who could I tell my darkest secrets to? Nobody. The man I loved had been ripped from my heart, and it destroyed me more to know that I'd cheated on him by loving someone else. Eli left this world knowing I didn't wholly *belong* to him.

026 Monday, June 18th

I spent hours trapped inside my head.

Hours upon hours.

My entire world had been ripped away from me. I thought maybe if I wished hard enough, it could be reversed. But no. After the undead were killed, they never returned. My dagger made sure of that.

I laid back, staring at the ceiling. I put my earbuds in, shutting out the world. Closing my eyes, I placed myself in a different reality, one where Eli never died.

Instead, we barely made it out of the crowd of immortals, but we were alive and together. He tended to my wounds, and I tended to his, but one thing led to another, and we had sex. Afterward, we stayed in his bed, and he told me a few more games he used to play as a child. Listening to him made me happy. I would sit up and lean over him, telling him that I needed pajamas, but I wanted to wear his clothes instead. He agreed to that, and then he made a comment that I looked better in his clothes than he did. I blushed at that comment. It warmed my insides.

Something sharp poked my back, in multiple places, dragging down and tearing open my skin. Stinging seared.

Opening my eyes, I was back in my old bedroom, curtains drawn with the moon barely shining through. I had been lying on my side now, arm stretched above my head, and when I sat up, I scanned the room.

The stinging on my back intensified, and I got out of the bed, going to the bathroom across the hall. I turned my back towards the mirror and lifted my shirt, widening my eyes. Bloody claw marks ran all the way down.

I took off my shirt, going back to my room to grab a new one and do my best to clean up what I could. I couldn't tell my mom, but I didn't want to call anyone else either.

Pulling a shirt from my closet, I turned around, running into a shadow. I swallowed, trying not to show fear. "You really shouldn't scare people like that. It's rude, you know." I tried to step away but another shadow blocked my path. Now I was starting to worry. I'd been training so hard to kill all Kaofi that I hadn't focused much on how to kill something made of *smoke.*

Because shadows couldn't be killed.

I slowly tried to slip out from another angle, but more shadows appeared. "Listen, I don't know what you've heard but you can't just barge in here. This isn't even my house." I came home after his death, fleeing the world that brought me to my knees.

One shadow grabbed my shirt, ripping it from my arms and tearing it to shreds. "We heard about your little affair with the vampire."

"He was killed by his own kind. What do you expect me to do? I'll take my revenge."

"And now it's our turn." He nodded to some others and they grabbed me. I tried to scream, but they shoved cloth in my mouth, throwing me against my bed. Before I could get up, every inch of my skin started to burn as they dragged their claws down my body. They flipped me over and did the same thing down the front, and as hard as I tried, I couldn't gather the strength to get them off of me. There were too many, and I knew nothing about them except the smell of cigarettes.

A hall light turned on, and one of the shadows slowly brought his long finger against my lips, whispering in my ear to stay quiet. I stared at the light, wide eyes, begging for my mom to come in here.

The light turned off, and I started to cry. The shadow pressed his hand against my head, shoving nightmares into my mind. I tried to get away, but I couldn't get out of his grasp, and every single nightmare I'd ever had while I slept or lived filled my head.

The shadows disappeared, leaving me behind with my own mind as it attacked itself.

Eli's death. The moment the Kaofi attacked me at the ball, planning to rape and kill me. When Owen died. Not knowing my own father. All the nightmares I had of dying or being chased, unable to get away. Everything blended together, and I couldn't get them to go away no matter how hard I tried. They just flashed inside my head like horror movies, and I couldn't look elsewhere.

I started to scream and cry. They didn't stop. They replayed over and over. I begged for death to take me. I wanted my heart to stop, but instead it pounded and raced right in my ears.

My mom ran in, but she stopped dead in her tracks at the

sight. She eventually rushed over, yelling, but I couldn't hear what she said. I just continued to scream and cry. She called anyone and everyone she could think of, and at one point, I had to be sedated. It didn't make a difference, because I kept screaming and crying even when I was asleep.

It lasted so long that I lost my voice at one point, and I couldn't cry real tears at another. So I was left there, trapped inside my own head.

027 Wednesday, June 20th

At one point, Juliet was called, then Amari.

And every single Hanti I knew.

Amari made something that shut down my mind, but it didn't solve the problem. It only temporarily kept my thoughts at bay. "I need time to figure out another solution," she told everyone.

"What the hell is wrong with her?" Mom asked her, on the verge of crying.

Amari studied my eyes, but I couldn't really focus on the details. "The shadows got to her. That's what they do. They instill terror into their victims. It's like... I can't explain it well, but they extract every single fear she has, then they shove it into her head like it's a gumball machine. She can't access anything in her head without the shadows' permission, and all she has access to now is every nightmare she's ever had or lived through."

"What the hell does that mean?" My mom put her hands on her hips. "What did they do to my baby?"

Amari looked at her. "Imagine if you couldn't access the happy memories in your head. All you could see were the nightmares. That's what they did. For days, she's seen nothing but terror, and they trapped her in that state of mind. She's the projector, and the shadows inserted only horror movies in her head."

It was exactly like that. I was trapped in my own movie theater, strapped to the seats. My own horror movie played on screen while the Hanti and my mother walked into the theater room, trying to get my attention. But my mind was too focused on the screen to be able to respond.

"How do we stop it?" she asked.

Amari snickered. "Like I said, you can't without a shadow's permission. It's their work, and I can only control it so much. That's why I need to find another solution. Something more permanent."

My mom sat beside me, kissing my head. "We're going to get you out of there. I promise." I just stared at the carpet, my mind completely blank. On one side, my nightmares were held back by a dam that kept cracking at the seams, daring to flood my head again. On the other, my happiest memories were locked away and the key was long gone. It was barren inside my head, *for now.*

The dam tore open and the nightmares flooded my head. No tears this time. No screams. My voice was gone.

My mom tried her hardest to get through to me, but nothing worked. She did the only thing she knew how to do. She just held me while my nightmares raided my mind.

"This isn't helping," my mom told them. "We just need a

solution. Anything." She stroked my hair. "I want my baby back."

Hunter clenched his jaw. "I'll be back."

He disappeared for some time, but I didn't know how long. However, when he returned, everyone was glad to see him and whatever plan he came up with.

Using something small and shiny that I couldn't quite make out, he extracted the nightmares, unlocking the gate to my other memories.

The theater lit up and I became aware of everything. I had *control* again.

Everyone around me seemed relieved. Maybe I was, a little, but it didn't bring Eli back. And all the nightmares I'd been trapped with were my own. My life had been one mess after another.

I thanked Hunter while Amari brought me some food. Mom brought me blankets, but I refused all of it. "I know where I need to be," I said in a whisper.

Mom was unsure about letting me leave on my own, but Amari assured her that I'd be okay this time.

Nobody could be sure. But I could. And the last place I needed to be was at my childhood home where the shadows attacked me, or the cabin where I was reminded of all of the loss.

I returned to the one place I connected to.

Eli's apartment.

The moment I stepped foot inside, shame and grief came flooding back. I fell against the door, trying hard to regain my composure.

Dead and gone.

With some strength, I pushed myself onto my feet and took a walk to his bedroom. "Screw you," I said to the air.

"For leaving me here alone. I could have handled a breakup, Eli, after what I did. But to watch you die? That is so *cold.*"

I hadn't been inside his apartment since the night I cheated. It was as if he hadn't erased a single memory of me living here. I packed a few things, but he kept all of the stuff I left behind where it was. Maybe he didn't hate me. Maybe he really did want to move on.

Sitting in his bed, I hugged his pillow. It still smelled just like him. The wonderful scent he would put on just for me.

"I miss you so much," I choked.

Of course I did. It had only been barely a few days since he died. I'd be a fool not to feel anything.

But I felt *everything.*

From remorse to anger.

Without another thought, I decided to move back into his apartment. Staying at my mom's was dangerous, but staying at the cabin was too much for me.

The safest place was here. Physically and emotionally.

I got up from the bed and looked in his closet, searching his clothes. I ripped everything off my body and pulled a shirt of his over my head. It eased a bit of the ache.

And to ease some more, I pulled some briefs up over my hips. I smelled just like him now. It killed me inside that he wasn't here anymore but knowing that this was all for me now made it better. I didn't have to worry about having no home or being unsafe. I didn't have to worry about someone else ending up with *his* things.

Alissa had died. Ironically, though, now it was Eli who lost his life. I was the one left to pick up the pieces.

Part of me wanted him to come back as a ghost but that wasn't plausible. Vampires didn't return. They weren't living souls. And maybe Lucas and Lucy knew that.

After Owen died, I didn't want to bother healing. Now that Eli was gone, too, I didn't want to focus on myself at all. There was one thing on my mind now.

Revenge.

028 Thursday, June 28th

"How are you feeling today?" Amari asked.

"Good. Because I'm going to find that vampire and rip his effing throat out, after I rip his penis off and feed it to him." I faced her. "I'm going to take such great pleasure in watching him suffer." I opened the door, letting her walk out first. "I want him begging for mercy." I scanned Eli's room, promising him that I would avenge his death. I closed the door and we made our way back to the cabin.

Amari followed and nodded. "I'm sure you will. You're strong. Better. They fear you already."

"I know." I smirked.

She laughed. "You know that smirk reminds me of Eli."

I shrugged a bit. "He rubbed off on me. We spent a lot of time together. I refuse to let his memory die."

We began training. I trained against Amari, Clara, Hunter,

and Josh. He'd come after finding out about Eli's death. He put aside his differences and we dropped ours so we could kill the vampire together. I trained endlessly.

Going against Amari, I channeled all of my rage. She got the upper hand multiple times, but I let my anger boil in my blood until I used it to throw her to the floor, dagger at her throat.

She got up and nodded. "You've made such a huge improvement this past week."

"Well, it turns out when you have nobody to love, you have a lot of time on your hands. I've been training nonstop." It was the one thing that distracted me from doing something stupid. "And I don't intend to ever quit."

When our training session ended, I returned to Eli's apartment. I promised I would find an apartment and give him his space, but now that he was gone, I had no reason for that. I couldn't leave now. Not ever.

I drove back to the apartment late at night. Sitting on the bed, laptop in hand, I began my deep dive. I needed to track them down. The vampires, shadows, and all of the Kaofi who had been there the night Eli died.

I put my music on to fill the silence. "Where the hell did you go?" I searched the dark web. "I know you're out there, hiding," I whispered. Wherever he was, he was terrified. He knew he'd taken the life of my love, and that had given me the strength of a hundred men. It had built me up to be the killing machine Kaofi feared.

With a groan, I closed my laptop. I couldn't even find him, but I knew he was still alive. Or as alive as a vampire could be...

I got off the bed and went to the bathroom, taking my phone with me. I looked at myself in the mirror.

"Here you were upset with me because you thought I suggested becoming immortal. I'm the mortal. The one with an expiration date. The one supposed to die someday." I snickered. "And yet that's what you did to me. You left me, forcing me to live without you." I ran my fingers over the scars on my neck. I glanced at my dagger, pulling it out and observing it.

My eyes flickered to the girl in the mirror, not giving it a second thought before I pulled my sleeve up, dragging the blade down my wrist. It wasn't deep, not enough to cause me to bleed to death. I put my dagger down, leaning my hand against the counter. I swallowed, closing my eyes.

All those times I craved watching him bleed, craved hurting him and taking his life—now my dagger was the culprit for his demise. I was left picking up the pieces, and in some way, bleeding for him, for myself, was a way to keep his memory here.

029 Sunday, July 8th

I refused to even think about him at all. I kept myself distracted through training, and anything else I could, and then I had a breakthrough. I'd located the vampire, finally. I could finally enact my revenge.

After arriving at my mom's house, I went straight for the kitchen to grab some food. "I found him."

"Who?" Mom asked.

Glancing at her, I said, "The man who killed my love. I found him."

"Why is that...? Do you plan to kill him? That's dangerous. You'll get arrested for that."

"I doubt that. If the cops could never find him, they won't find him even when he's dead." I grabbed a bottle of water and took it back to my room. I looked at my phone, debating if I should tell Amari or Josh. I decided to wait, for now.

But that night, I got dressed. I couldn't wait any longer.

After ripping seams and sewing the sleeves higher to my corset, it felt like a good change. A change that would signify the modifications I'd make to my life for now on.

Straightening my posture and strapping my dagger to my thigh, I glanced in the mirror. My blood was boiling. Heart pounding. Everything inside of me was itching to watch him bleed and beg for mercy.

I left the house, traveling in the dark. When I approached his hideout, a few odors blended together. I was ready, and far more ready than ever.

Approaching, I made sure to stay as quiet as possible. As soon as I got to the front door, I kicked it open, pulling out my dagger. "Where is he?" Nobody wanted to answer.

They came charging, and I sliced into their necks, cutting off heads and making my way through the halls. I stopped to stare at the monster who killed him. He looked at me, and right then, another Kaofi came up from behind, but I stabbed my blade into its chest, dragging it down and cutting him in half. The vile creature dropped to the floor. "I've been dying for this moment." I licked the blood from my dagger. "Tastes very rotten, like all of the useless bodies here." I blocked him as he tried to leave, pointing to the chair using my dagger. "No, you are going to sit your ass down."

He slowly sat back down, not saying a word.

I walked over to him, unbuckling his pants. "You don't even get the satisfaction of knowing the pain you've caused me." He opened his mouth to say something, but I grabbed his tongue, cutting it off and watching his eyes budge from his head. "Did I effing tell you to speak?" I threw his tongue on the ground. "Unlucky for you, my favorite movie franchise happens to be gore porn. So don't you dare test me," I spit in his face.

This vampire didn't make another move. I relished in the face of fear. Pure terror. He'd ripped my heart out and it was time for me to take away what he loved just as much.

"I think it works out perfectly. Don't you?" I reached into his pants, pulling his penis and balls out. "Without your disgusting tongue in the way, it'll be easy to feed you." I gripped his junk tightly, cutting it off. He tried to scream, but nothing came out. I cut off the tip, shoving it in his mouth and covering it. "Swallow." He tried to fight back, but he wasn't much use with a gaping hole in his crotch. "Swallow, or this blade is going right where it doesn't belong." His eyes went wide, but he swallowed. I sat back a bit. "That's what I like to see. Cooperation." He was already trying to puke it back up. I grabbed some cloth and gagged him. I stood up, watching him squirm.

After a few minutes, I took my dagger and plunged it into his chest, over, and over, and over.

Overkill. Rage. Anger. Hatred.

Whatever you wanted to call it, that's what it was.

When I got tired of that, I ripped his head off, reveling in the suffering. Then I stepped back, admiring my work.

"Holy fuck," Josh whispered from behind me.

I took a deep breath. "He deserved it. He really deserved it." I fell to my knees, shivering. My work still wasn't done. Somehow we had to destroy the shadows. I pressed the back of my hand against my mouth to keep from throwing up.

Fingers faintly brushed my shoulder and someone whispered, "I'm proud of you." But when I looked back, *he* wasn't really there. I pushed away the aching pains in my abdomen, looking at my dagger. Then I stood from the floor. "I'm done here." I left the building in a hurry and ran back home. I found myself in the bathroom, puking up everything. Mom came in, and when I finished, I just stared into the bowl.

She sat beside me and pushed some hair back behind my ear, wiping blood from my cheek. "What did you do...? We told you this was dangerous. You can't just kill people. You can't take justice into your own hands like that."

I leaned away from the toilet and into her shoulder. She wrapped her arms around me, but I couldn't cry anymore. I'd already used my tears.

The vampire was dead, but nothing had really changed. I was just as alone, and he was still nothing more than a memory. It had been only two weeks since his death, but it never got easier to live with.

After I left my mom's, I went home to Eli's and cleaned myself up. I smelled badly like cat piss. I looked through my closet for anything that was clean. I found the gown I wore to the ball the night I danced with Eli. It was mostly intact, aside from a rip in the chest when Lucas put the double-sided fork on me. Eli had come to save me. He always did that, though. He always knew how to make things right.

I dropped the dress and rubbed my head, stumbling over to my bed. I fell onto it as my head started to spin. I rolled over on my side, closing my eyes. But no matter how hard I tried, my head kept spinning and I couldn't fall asleep.

Josh kept calling.

Then Amari.

Then Hunter.

Then Clara.

Everyone tried but I couldn't muster up the energy to answer. Josh told them what I did. They wanted to ask why I had been so careless.

I wasn't in any state to answer those kinds of questions. I was just here to exist. Here to suffer, and to take the lives of Kaofi.

So much for my fashion career.

How I wished for Eli to appear out of nowhere and kiss me with every fiber of his being. To rip my clothes off and show me that he was never letting me go.

He used to love me enough to stay.

Juliet still lived in the apartment right below me, but she had no idea. When my mom called her for help, Juliet told her what happened and hung up. That's what my mom told me, anyway.

I wanted someone to come and hold me. To kiss my head and promise everything would turn out okay. But I couldn't reverse the clock and I couldn't demand lies.

It sounded so stupid of me to be angry with Eli for dying just like that. But it was how I felt. He didn't fight it. He didn't say anything to help his case. He just let my dagger cut through his neck. He allowed his body to give in to demise. Wherever he was, he was happier there than I was here.

All night long, I stared at the wall, begging it to manifest into the man himself. When it wouldn't, I ended up chewing the skin off of my cheeks, and I wasn't gentle about it.

The same way Eli wasn't gentle about letting me witness his death.

Nothing about him screamed *gentle*—even if that's what his mother taught him to be.

Nothing about any of this screamed forgiveness.

No.

Everything inside my head yelled at me to continue to fight for a good cause. It yelled at me to continue to get revenge on the shadows who had tried to take the only joy I had left.

All I asked out of it was to feel happiness once more.

030 Friday, August 17th

"What were you thinking? You weren't!" Amari yelled.

They weren't going to let me live this down.

Clara grabbed her shoulder. "Take it easy on her. When you watch someone die, your better judgment is clouded."

She mumbled, falling down into Clara's lap.

"Maybe I didn't think. But what does it matter now? I can't take it back. And what's so wrong with it?" I looked at them. "He's dead. I murdered that entire house."

Hunter studied my face. "Yeah, Josh filled us in on the details."

"Isn't this what you wanted?" I asked. "For the longest time, you wanted me to accept my Hunter side. To not love a Kaofi. Eli is dead and I'm a killing machine. And I want more." I swiped my tongue over my lips. "I want to continue to slaughter them."

Amari narrowed her eyes. "You think we wanted this? We

wanted to hunt *together*. We didn't want you to go rogue. To murder an entire house by yourself. To shove a vampire's dick down his throat. That is not the Mya we trained."

Laughing, I threw my head back. Were they pulling this card? I dropped my head again. "You don't get to back out just because you don't like what I've turned into." I clenched my jaw. "When I feel like this, I'm immortal. And it makes me feel closer to Eli." I leaned back. "And I'm never going to stop if it's the closest I'll get to him."

Hunter pushed himself off the chair. "No. Don't you use that excuse." He pointed at me. "I lost someone who was like a brother to me. To save you! Because you can't save yourself."

"Is that what this is really about? I'm not allowed to grieve Eli because Ryan died trying to save me?" I stood. "I didn't ask anyone to effing save me!" I got in his face. "I never once asked anyone to save me. I was trying to save myself. Eli died trying to save me and I regret *every* effing second of it. You stupid asshole." I turned around and went to the kitchen for water. I slammed the glass on the counter when someone followed me in. "What?"

Clara appeared beside me. "Hunter is just terrible at expressing himself."

"He made it pretty clear what he thinks of me. I'm just the damsel in distress. Further proves my point as to why I never asked anyone to back me up when I found the location of Eli's killer. I don't need anyone else coming to save my ass. Ever." I faced her. "I didn't get to grow up with the luxury of knowing how to defend myself. I didn't know about Kaofi. My parents didn't want me, and now they never will. My entire life is stained with bloodshed. My parents. Owen. Eli. Ryan. Some Hanti I can barely remember the night I met Eli and Josh." I chugged the water. "I won't let anyone else die because of me."

"Is that what you really think?" She crossed her arms. "Mya, you are not the reason everyone dies. You can't refuse help just because a few people died."

I squeezed the glass until it broke. "If I had been enough for my parents, maybe they would have kept me. Maybe I could have been trained. I could have saved them. Ryan wouldn't have died trying to save me. I would have seen that car before Owen was hit. I could defend Eli before he was murdered. Yes, I am the exact reason everyone dies. Because I'm not the hero. I'm not the villain. I'm the damned damsel."

Clara sighed and left me to think. Instead of getting wrapped up inside my head, I took my anger out through training. I went to the other room and began punching the bag, also kneeing it here and there.

It felt good just to hit something.

Hunter despised me for letting Ryan die. Now that I was strong enough to kill on my own, he was angry about that, too. I couldn't win in his eyes.

But this wasn't about him. I wasn't here to impress him. I was here to impress myself.

After a good hour of practice, I went to drink more water. I walked outside and scanned the area. Everyone disappeared on me.

"Headed home so soon?" Hunter asked.

I whipped around. "None of your damn business."

He stepped forward. "I'm not the enemy, Mya."

"Sure act like it."

"I'm trying to teach you that revenge is dangerous. We serve a purpose greater than revenge. And living at Eli's apartment is not going to help you move on."

I choked on a laugh. "Excuse me? Now you're telling me where I can and can't live? You're not my father."

"I'm not trying to be." He shook his head. "I'm trying to be the brother Ryan was to me, for you."

I fixed my ponytail. "You're doing a shitty job at that. I don't need anyone else." I stumbled over the twigs.

Hunter was right there to catch me, pulling me into his chest. It wasn't expected. It was an odd feeling, but it gave me a bit of comfort. "I know that even though his killer is dead, you don't feel any better. You still miss him just as much."

All the warmth seeped out of my body, leaving me feeling numb. "How could you know that?" I mumbled against his shirt.

"Because killing my parents' murderers never took away the pain. I continued to fight in their legacy. That was all I could do," he whispered, resting his chin against my hair.

A sob came out before turning into many more. It was humiliating to be so vulnerable in front of Hunter, but I wasn't going to push away at a time like this.

"I know it hurts. It always will. We promise to be here when you can't stand on your own two feet."

My cries got louder. I hated admitting he was right. Living at Eli's apartment made it much harder to live without him. I needed him back so bad. I needed to feel his arms around me. Why did everyone have to die when they knew me?

"Oh, this is a bad time," Amari said, backing away.

I pulled away from Hunter and wiped my eyes. It didn't hide any of the emotions. "We're done now." I glanced at Hunter for a split second but he wasn't looking at me. Pushing loose hair behind my ear, I squared my shoulders. "How much space do you have for one more Hanti?"

Amari smiled. "We always have more space."

Nodding, I looked over at the sunset. "Let me just spend one more night at the apartment. Then I'll move in."

Scanning his bedroom, I took a deep breath. Could I really leave?

I went to the bathroom and took a cold shower. I sat at the bottom, hugging my knees. "I miss you so much," I whispered. "How am I expected to survive without you?"

A form of Eli manifested from the air beside me. "Don't. Don't leave me."

I wiped away the tears before they came. "No. You're not real. You're just a figment of my imagination. I need to accept that, and I can't do that here."

"What if I am real? Why can't I be a ghost like Owen?"

"Because..." I squeezed my eyes closed, stifling a cry. "Owen had a soul."

It was wrong of me to wish that Owen was here for me now. But I wanted just anyone to hold me. Someone to kiss away the pain.

As if proving me right, Eli turned into mist while the water washed away any last memory of him. The shower became lonely again, and I hated myself for sending him away.

How could I?

Screaming, I grabbed the ceramic soap dish, throwing it at the glass door. It shattered to the floor and I pushed myself upright against the wall. I hadn't *intended* to break anything.

Turning off the water, I stepped out, getting some shards in my feet. I sat by the toilet and pulled them out before I grabbed a broom and cleaned up my mess.

Once the mess was said and done, I dried myself, looking in the mirror. "You really mess everything up, don't you?" I snickered at my reflection. "No wonder your parents didn't want you. You were a curse from the moment of conception."

It was harsh to say that to myself, but it hadn't been any less true. How could I be anything but a curse?

Tomorrow I'd have to move out because Eli was dead and eventually his lease was going to need to be renewed. And he wouldn't be here to do it. I'd be kicked out either way.

At least by choosing to leave, I had some control over my grief.

I removed the towel from my body, dropping it to the floor. The scars ran up and down my front and backsides, reminding me of the aftermath of his death.

However, the pain of having my skin clawed didn't match the emotional pain of watching Eli die for days on end. Even to this day, I still got stuck in nightmares watching his life flee his body all over again. But it had only been two months. It was expected.

And Hunter promised to be there every time I broke down.

It wasn't very fair that everyone else got to be happy. Juliet got to happily live with Cole while both men I loved were killed. I had two chances, and both of them had been torn from my grasp. How did it happen?

And why me?

I turned off the light, leaving the bathroom. I sifted through his closet, grabbing a shirt and some briefs. I changed into them before laying back in his bed. My entire head ached, and eventually I fell asleep.

I woke up in the middle of the night from yet another

nightmare. My heart was pounding as sweat coated my skin. I rubbed my eyes, trying to get rid of the heaviness so I wouldn't have to go back to sleep. I grabbed my phone, ready to text Amari if she was awake so we could train a bit, but something moved out of the corner of my eye. My head snapped up and I pulled my dagger from under the pillow.

Squinting through the darkness, the moonlight gave me a glimpse of the outline of a figure in the corner. I slid off the bed, tightening my grip. I refused to let a Kaofi take this from me, too. Not the only place I felt safe.

Before I had time to register, the dark figure solidified and shot out of the corner like a bullet, throwing me on the bed. He grabbed my dagger, ripping it from my fingers and pressing the blade against my throat. His scent filled my nose, but it wasn't like any other immortal. It was...sweet. And woodsy. Cedarwood, mixed with...vanilla. His face became clear and my heartbeat started to race as I breathed, "Eli."

Something about him was different. He wasn't the same Eli who had died in my arms.

I badly wanted him to kiss me, to make up for all the time we missed. But he didn't. His eyes were darker than usual. What had happened to him?

He pressed the blade deeper, drawing blood. Something flashed in his eyes, like he had forgotten that I could bleed. He pulled my dagger away, staring at it before licking the blood.

"Are you okay?" I swallowed, tempted to throw him off. He didn't respond, instead running his tongue across my neck to clean up the cut.

In seconds, he vaporized into a cloud of black smoke, then vanished. I sat up, swallowing. I immediately called Amari, and she picked up on the first ring.

031 Saturday, August 18th

"You aren't going to believe what I just saw. And maybe I'm crazy! It's plausible, given everything that's happened. But hear me out." I tried to catch my breath, then steady my heartbeat. "I had a nightmare and I woke up but I saw something move, and then out of this dark corner came some kind of...thing. He smells different, yet familiar and before I can realize what's happening, Eli is about to slice into my neck. But he's different, Amari. He's like...not wholly himself. He doesn't know how to react, like he forgot that I'm supposed to be his mate. And then he just turned into black smoke and vanished! Just like that." I snapped my fingers.

Amari exhaled. "That's rare, but not unheard of."

"What? What is?"

"To be a mix between two different species. You can't forget that shadows are made of black smoke, right? And you said he turned into one..."

"I watched him die. How could they bring him back...?"

"Shadows have their tricks," she said. "And one of those tricks is using it for their personal gain. Do you want to know what makes shadows the worst of them all?"

I swallowed. No, not Eli. He wasn't like them, was he?

"They're truly immortal, Mya. Shadows can't be killed." That much I knew. "They can only be controlled. They're walking nightmares. Horrendous creatures. They crave fear. And sure, it sounds great that he's back, but you said he was different, and...that means the shadows got ahold of him. He's going to hate you. The shadows have been building an army, and Eli was just one of the pawns."

All the energy drained from me. She had to be lying. I couldn't lose him just like that. No. Could I? He was now filled with darkness. He was confused, unaware that he had died and been dead for the past two months.

"They brainwashed him?" I asked.

With a sigh, she nodded. "To an extent, yes. That's their goal. They saw him as an opportunity, as one of them, and so they did what they had to. He only knows what he's been familiar with for a century." Meaning he hadn't known me for at least a hundred years, and so he didn't remember everything we shared. That explained why he was confused when he made me bleed, and why he didn't know what made him want to lick it. What he knew was his hatred for Hanti...

And now one of those Hanti had been living in his apartment. There was no telling what he would do to me now.

But that wasn't going to stop me from living in his place. He'd just have to sit in the corner. I couldn't lose the only thing I had left connecting us.

Footsteps echoed outside the bathroom door. I finished buttoning my top, the same one I wore the day he died. The same white corset that was still stained with his blood. Maybe I was crazy for wearing it, but I was afraid to wash it off. Besides, it was Kaofi blood and it scared the other Kaofi. I needed that fear from them. "Come in."

I jumped, seeing him through the mirror. It wasn't him. He wasn't the same Eli anymore. I had to remind myself of that. My Eli was long gone.

Drying my face, I looked at him and cleared my throat. "I don't know why you're so persistent on having this room, or this apartment. You're a shadow. Go live with the shadows instead." I wanted to tell him that nobody wanted him here, but I couldn't bring myself to say that. He may not have been my Eli, but he still looked like him. It eased the pain just a little.

"You don't belong here. *I* do."

My heart stung when he told me I didn't belong here. He definitely wasn't the same man I loved. "You wouldn't understand. You've been gone for months. A lot has changed since then." I was afraid to tell this version of him that he loved me once, and that was why I lived here. If I told him that, he would respond with something just as soul-crushing about how he could never love me. I was barely surviving as it was. "Forget it." I shook my head and went back to the bed, laying down and curling up.

His presence could be felt from behind me. So much wickedness radiated off of him now.

"If you're going to kill me, you need to try harder than a few nightmares and threats. I don't scare as easily as you think I do. A wise man once told me that he loved me, and I'm not going to let him down." That was my promise to him. I knew he'd be angry if he knew I gave up so easily and wallowed in my pain. That was why I tried so hard to use my pain to motivate me to train and become a better Hanti instead. I wanted him to be proud of me, even if living without him was torture.

I swallowed, turning on my side. What was I supposed to do, let this evil version keep his apartment while I got thrown back into the house an hour away? I couldn't. If I didn't wake up to the smell of vanilla every morning, I'd lose my sanity. I'd have no reason to stay alive. I wasn't going to give up this space that easily.

"Come and get me, Eli," I said.

He yanked my shoulder, pinning me to the bed and shoving his hand into my chest and squeezing my heart.

Getting noise out was harder than it looked. My entire heart exploded with pain and I struggled to fight back. Maybe it wasn't my place to.

Maybe I could give into the anguish...

The cloud of smoke vanished above me and my heart began beating again.

"Mya! What the hell was that?" Hunter hurried over.

I grabbed my chest and closed my eyes. "Eli..."

"He was going to kill you, and you were going to let him."

"Hunter, no. Stop. He can't kill me. He's been trying for a while. He can't."

He scoffed. "And you're trying to test him."

Sitting up in the bed, I rubbed my chest. "I'm trying to remind him that he's not the one in control."

"But he is. He's the one who's the shadow. He's the one who can't die. Don't go playing with fire after dousing yourself in gasoline." He pulled me from the bed. "Let's go out for a bit. It's better if you get out of this dark room."

I sighed. "I want him to kiss me just one last time..." I leaned my head against Hunter's shoulder. "But he won't. And maybe this is my punishment."

He found some clothes for me. "For what?"

"For getting Eli killed in the first place. For falling in love with Kaofi."

"How can I argue with the second part?" Hunter gave me the clothes and sent me into the bathroom.

I changed and fixed my messy hair. "You can't. Now Eli is back, and he's this version of pure poison. But you don't have to worry. He doesn't remember me." I walked out.

"You told us."

"Oh. That's right. Well, we can leave now."

Hunter and I went out to get some late dinner. It was awkward knowing what he saw back there. Eli tried to kill me. I was going to let him. I had even asked him to.

Hunter ordered us some food. "So, this Eli. What has happened so far?"

Sipping my beer, I shrugged. "Aside from him trying to kill me? He talks, too, sometimes. He hates me, like Amari said. He doesn't know me. He wants me gone so he can have his apartment back. But I don't think his vampire side hates me. I think he wants me. My blood. And it conflicts him."

"That's more than I needed to know." Hunter took a big gulp.

Goosebumps rose on my skin. "I know he's not the same Eli who died, Hunter. But I can't just brush him off that easily. I can't make myself stay away."

He nodded a little. "I can help. We can help. That's why you told us, right?"

"I'm not so sure." I leaned against his arm. "I'm still in love with him. And I haven't accepted his death. How can I be expected to accept it if he's not really dead?"

"Because that Eli is the version the shadows created. He's not the one who died. He's the one who was *born*."

Our food arrived and we both munched on some fries.

He had a point, and yet I couldn't allow it in me to let him go. I couldn't do it. So maybe instead, I would try to call a truce. Somehow, I would make Eli a better version of himself. I couldn't let him suffer inside this form. I'd be a horrible person if I didn't kill the zombie or save him from himself.

"How do you stop loving someone?" I asked.

Hunter met my eyes. "What kind of question is that?"

"Just answer it, please."

"You don't. Love is everlasting. You can only learn to let go and move on."

"And how do I do that?"

He gave me a look. "Do I look like a man who's been in love?"

My cheeks burned red. "I mean, maybe. Do you like anyone?"

"There's no time for romance when you're a Hanti."

"Yet two of our friends are in a relationship with each other. So that clearly is a fat ass lie." I pointed a fry at him.

He chuckled. "Okay, so I'm not right a hundred percent of the time. Is that a crime?"

"It is if you're a Kaofi Hunter named Hunter. You're given the title of expert. Of perfection. Of knowledge." I took a bite of my burger. Food never tasted better before tonight.

We both devoured our food like we hadn't eaten in days.

Hunter paid the bill.

"What is your day job?" I asked him.

He shrugged. "Don't need one. My parents were loaded. I inherited everything from them."

"Damn. Wish mine did the same." We both laughed and left the diner. "How is Josh doing? I haven't heard from him. And I know it has to be difficult for him, too."

"He's been taking it rough. Then you dropped the shadow bomb on us and he's been a mess since. Doesn't exactly excite a man to hear that his best friend is one of the cruelest creatures to exist. Shadows normally don't target Kaofi, but they've officially started a war between Kaofi, Hanti, and shadows alike. They're essentially the highest of the food chain in the Kaofi world."

"Which makes some sense. They can't be killed."

"Exactly." He nudged me. "You're learning your way around this side of things. Is it so bad now?"

"Well, before I became a Hanti, I was just an aspiring fashion designer. Now I'm the girl whose boyfriend was killed. It's not exactly the life I would have chosen had I known Eli was going to die in my arms." I held back the tears.

Nodding, he dropped the subject. The rest of the walk was built on silence, and it was fine for the night. Just having his support was enough.

Blind and oblivious. That described my love for Eli perfectly. I'd been too blindsided by his death, and now I was oblivious to his dark side to care that he was out for blood.

It was tragic yet beautiful, the way Hunter and I had become so much closer over our grief for the people we loved. Once he had despised me, and everything I stood for. Now he was the shoulder I could cry on.

And just maybe—I could do the same thing to Eli.

032 Monday, August 20th

I didn't tell anyone else about what I saw. Not yet at least.

So I trained, then I went home and retreated to his room, closing the curtains to block out the sun. I faced the other side of the room, anxious. Maybe I was crazy to try and lure him back, but I still wanted to see him, even if it *wasn't* him.

I waited, but he never actually showed up. I sighed and went to the kitchen to eat some food, but that food made me sick. Then, I found myself in the bathroom, throwing it back up. I knew I wasn't pregnant because I had already double-checked to make sure I wouldn't become a single mom after he died. No, I was just sick. Every now and then I couldn't stomach any food. It had been part of the grieving process.

Rubbing my eyes, the day came rushing back. We had worn matching outfits somehow. He'd worn his white button-up and black pants. I'd worn a white corset top with off the shoulder sleeves and black, high-waisted shorts. It never occurred to me that I would have been the last time I got to do that with him.

As I sat down beside the toilet, I fixed my gaze on the wall. Everything inside me started to ache again. That day, every single thing about my future changed. There would never be a wedding. We'd never hold each other again. I'd never hold or love anyone again. I didn't know how anyone could live for an eternity this way. I was mortal, and I could barely survive living with this pain. There was no way I could do it forever. I was at least thankful I wasn't *immortal.*

I closed my eyes and took a deep, shaky breath. I wouldn't cry. I was tired of crying. I turned back around and puked some more, only this time I had nothing in my stomach, so I was essentially just choking. When that ended, I got off the floor and washed out my mouth before drinking some water to ease my throat. I left the bathroom and went to his closet.

Maybe it was weird to everyone else, but sleeping in his clothes and in his bed was the only way I felt safe at night. It wasn't enough to keep away the nightmares, but it gave me an inkling of comfort, so I changed and laid down in his bed, hugging a pillow.

On the bright side, now I knew for sure I'd never had kids. There was no way in hell I was going to fall in love with someone other than Eli. It was better to just be alone.

And maybe he was back in some way, but he was still gone in general and that had people questioning why I went on. I took my revenge, yes. But even if he wasn't my Eli, I had a duty to stop the shadows. For whatever reason my parents gave me up, I'd do it for them. I'd do it to also ensure my own mother's safety.

After a few minutes, I fell asleep. My dreams were no better than the night before. Not by a longshot. A snake latched itself onto my waist with his fangs, then it tore open my skin and burrowed inside of me.

I shot up from the bed, feeling my abdomen. I was relieved it was only a nightmare. Unfortunately, the lasting effects of a snake slithering around in my gut made me sick, and I was puking over the side of the bed. Except I still had no food in me—which left me dry heaving. It was far too painful. I rested my head on the edge, closing my eyes. Unfortunately, I was still too tired and I was already diving back into another nightmare.

I hadn't expected this nightmare, but I should have. For two months, I'd been having dreams of anything and everything hurting me. But no, after I fell back asleep this time, I had a nightmare of something that was very real. I had to relive his death all over again, reminding me that he wasn't here anymore.

The feeling of pure dread when that vampire turned and plunged my own dagger into Eli's neck. The moment he fell to his knees. Then I was holding him, begging him to stay with me. But he never did, and in seconds, he was utterly gone. I woke up crying, but it never got easier. It would be so easy to just go to Amari and drink our minds into oblivion. That was how I coped with losing Owen.

But I sat up, dangling my feet over the bed and trying to stop the tears. My heartbeat was too loud, ready to jump out of my chest and leave me for good. *Was that such a terrible idea?* I didn't even want my heart anymore. It caused me nothing but pain.

I got up and went to the bathroom to clean my face. He used to wrap his arms around me—cold—but it was a comforting kind of cold. Now, I stood here by myself and the icy air it left behind froze over my heart instead.

Eli quickly appeared and looked through the mirror. "You are a fool to want me here."

"Who says I want you here?" I didn't even look at him directly. No, I didn't want to give him the satisfaction. I pulled my dagger from my thigh and dragged it along my wrist, just enough to draw blood that would make him squirm.

"For starters no sane *hunter* chooses to reside in the apartment of a Kaofi, much less one who is half vampire and half shadow." He grabbed my other wrist and spun me until I faced him. He lifted the one seeping just a small amount of blood, tempted to lick it.

"How cute, you thought I was sane." I pulled my wrist away. "What tipped you off? The fact that I'm living in your place? Sleeping in your bed? Wearing your clothes? Oh come on now. How long have you really been spying on me? You expect me to be afraid of you? None of your tactics work. I'm not a puny little human. I'm a Hanti, and we both know I've been training nonstop to kill people like you." People like him, but not him exactly. I don't think I could ever try. He looked *too much* like Eli. "I've been training to *control* you."

"You could never control me."

I glanced at my wrist, watching the blood drip. "I already have. I know your weaknesses. I know your darkest fears. I don't just live in your shoes. I know everything about you." I fixed my hair, facing the mirror. "Why is a Hanti the only person who knows that when you were a boy, you watched a group of vampires rape and murder your mother? You embraced the dark side and disconnected yourself from reality for a long time. Josh doesn't know that. He has no idea that you watched someone you love die in front of you just like I did."

He stepped back. "Y-you... H-how? Who told you this? How could you know that?"

"Because I am you." I relaxed my shoulders. "In a way... I'm a lot more observant. Intuitive..." I wasn't going to tell him that we were in love just yet—or maybe ever. "I'm not going anywhere. If you want me out of this apartment, you have to kill me." I looked back at him. "Now if you don't mind, I came in here to shower. I doubt you want to watch your enemy take a shower." I shook my head, removing my shorts and hanging them back up.

"Why would I leave? This is my bathroom." He growled.

Lowering my head, I stared at the floor. "The love of my life was murdered, and I have nowhere else to go, so I stay here to comfort myself. You understand what that's like..." I rubbed my face, sighing. I removed my shirt and hung it back up. I'd probably never wash his blood off. I got in the shower, which had three stone walls and one glass door. I took off my underwear and threw it out, turning on the cold water. I preferred it over hot water now. "That's why I can't just leave."

"Someone murdered someone you love? Did I know him?" He walked to the shower door.

My heart pounded just thinking about it. "You knew him." I took a deep breath, hugging myself. I couldn't erase the memory no matter how hard I tried. I still saw his eyes. Heard my screams. Felt his blood all over me. It amazed me that I survived this long without him.

I shook my head. "They killed him right in front of me. That isn't even what hurts. He was collateral damage. A casualty. They only killed him because he was trying to save me. I was the target and he got in the way. Yet I'm the one standing here. He died in my arms like Alissa died in yours, and it was also at my own hand." I grabbed the shampoo. "So as much as you want to take credit for my nightmares, you can't. The one person who understood me perfectly is dead and that's why I can't sleep. And that's why I stay here."

Eli stayed silent the rest of my shower. When it was over, I stepped out and pulled on some of his clothes. He watched, but it didn't bother me. He knew I wasn't giving up.

"Any reason why you won't kill me given how much you hate me?" I asked. Risky, sure. But a valid question.

"Something doesn't add up, as to the real reason—that of which you won't mention—to why a Kaofi Hunter is living in the apartment of a Kaofi. I want to know why. Do you want me to kill you?" He cocked an eyebrow.

With a shrug, I said, "You're just wishy-washy. Pick a side. Kill me or don't." I slipped into bed and grabbed his phone.

"That's not yours," he said.

"I know," I whispered. "Everything here is yours. It's your room, remember?" I put in my earbuds and closed my eyes, listening to the music. The moment we first danced at the ball. He was having too much fun with it, and so was I. The first time he kissed me. It had been the best kiss ever, and so good that I needed more. I blamed myself for cheating on him by almost kissing Owen. I drove him away. I ruined our entire relationship.

Eventually, I fell asleep to the music.

I'd manage to keep this evil Eli away from Josh. At least until I could tell Josh would be okay.

But when I woke up at one in the morning, I decided to tell him.

I texted him, afraid to change my mind. To prove my point, I told him we'd been sharing his room, or it was

mostly a situation where I hogged his room and he sat in the corner. But some nights I woke up unable to breathe or move. *Sleep paralysis.* He got into my head, my nightmares. He controlled everything while I slept, and then I'd wake up with him trying to kill me. But he never went through with it.

He'd want to meet him, but I knew it was far too risky. So that was when I told him he didn't remember me at all to keep the questions at bay. He wanted me dead now.

It was impossible to sleep after that, so I slipped out of the bed and trained for a few hours, and when the sun began to rise over the horizon, I took a cold bath to relax.

I closed my eyes, pushing away the dark memories. I pictured him wrapping his arms around me, whispering in my ear. Time did not fly by without him. Since his death, the time went by so slowly and it killed me. So, when I said it felt like a lifetime since I had felt something, I meant it. I wanted to feel something other than anger, or pain. I imagined him right there with me, chuckling like he used to. Placing a few kisses on my neck and shoulder. His fingers traced right down my torso, one hand on my thigh and the other headed right down there. I arched just a bit, slipping down under the water, and a hand shot out to hold me under.

Struggling, I gripped the edge of the tub and pulled myself up from the water. I looked back behind me, seeing nobody there. No, it was just me here... Just me, almost drowning at the thought of him. I shook my head and rested my chin on the edge of the tub, sighing. "You stupid bastard... Leaving me to fend for myself."

That cloud of black smoke hovered behind the tub, and I thought maybe for a second he felt guilty or he remembered me. Both guesses were wrong.

Deep down, he knew he was the man I loved. But neither of us were bold enough to admit it.

I laid my cheek against the tub, closing my eyes. "It doesn't matter anymore. You're not him. The man I loved died that day, and I have to accept that eventually." I didn't want to accept it. If I did, it made it feel that much more real. By accepting his death, I accepted that I would never love again. But I did. I still loved him, even if he was long gone. "Lucky for you, I'm mortal. I won't be around forever, you know? I'll grow old and wither away, and you'll eventually get your apartment back to yourself." Then, with tears escaping the prison I locked them in, I whispered, "I only need it for a little longer."

Pawn

A *little* longer indeed.

Satisfaction was an understatement. I relished in her agony. The torment saturating her stare. Her hardened expressions. Her crumbling soul.

Plan A was a success.

Few shadows made it to my cave, and I scolded the few who did about what they'd seen. Rarely did they leave this room unscathed.

"He's been doing exactly what he trained him to do," a shadow said lowly.

"Is he going to kill her?"

"He's trying. Something keeps stopping him, though. However, we've seen her cut herself a few times."

I turned to face the shadow, stepping down a few stairs. "What the hell is getting in the way? You figure out what it is and fix it. I don't just want to play with her sanity. I want her to take her own life if nobody else will."

I'd be her downfall—what made her *shatter.*

"We leave no heart beating."

033 Tuesday, August 21st

After spilling wine on my shirt, I had to throw it in the wash immediately. I grabbed a new shirt and turned around, bumping into Eli. "Damn, didn't know you were here."

His lips didn't curve in the corner. His eyes didn't lighten up at all. Why was he so stoic?

Right, he was a shadow.

"I don't need to announce my whereabouts to you in my own apartment. In fact, there's the door." He pointed to it.

I threw a new shirt on. "We've been over this a million times. I know your brain doesn't work anymore but I told you I'm not going anywhere."

Eli scowled at me. "Don't talk to me that way. In seconds I could have all of your nightmares shoved front and center again."

Furrowing my brows, I stepped back. "How do you know about that?" The counter hit my back as I gripped the edge, reminding myself that he wasn't him. I needed to prepare for anything.

"Because shadows know everything."

"Did you send them to attack me?"

"What?"

"You sent them, didn't you?"

Laughing, he shook his head. "I wish I had. Maybe then you'd be gone."

"They attacked me in my own home. I had nowhere else to go. So I came here. I feel safe here. Even with you trying to kill me." Shivers ran up my spine, and I badly wanted to kiss him. But I couldn't. I never could. He wasn't *my* Eli anymore.

"Safe—of course. Because I'm somehow better than the other shadows." He grabbed a knife from the rack, eyeing it. "I'm not. I'm the monster that hides under your bed. The demon who crawls under your skin. I'm not here to be your friend." He stepped forward, trapping me against the counter. "I will rip your heart out." The tip of the knife poked under my chin, bringing back memories from the ball.

"You already have," I whispered. My knuckles turned white while my heart began to race. My own screams filled the space in my head.

Pulling the knife away, he stabbed it into the cutting board behind me. "Good. I'm glad the message is received." Eli backed away and turned on his heel. "You should fear me, *Little Hunter*. And I will make sure that you do." He vanished in a cloud of black smoke.

I dropped to my knees as tears began to flow down my cheeks. I couldn't make them stop, yet I couldn't seem to get any sound out either.

The old Eli would have comforted me and taken away the pain. Now, he was the direct cause of it.

And it just reminded me over and over again that he was gone *forever.*

"Mya?" someone asked in a quiet voice behind me.

Turning back, I hugged myself. "Don't. Please don't look at me."

"I'm not here to make things worse. But someone needs to help. You don't deserve to suffer alone," Owen said, getting closer.

I wanted to yell at him. I wanted to pound his head in. Anything to make him feel what I felt when I hurt Eli, then watched him die. But I didn't have any energy for that. He was right. I didn't want to suffer alone, and now that Eli wanted to watch me rot in the ground, I had to turn to the only other person who understood me.

I nodded a bit, leaning into his arms.

When my tears dried up, Owen pulled my hair from my face and rested his head on mine. "What happened? I'm here to listen."

"Do I not deserve to be happy?"

"Who said that?"

"Everyone I've ever killed."

He pulled away, looking at me. "You can't be serious. You think you've killed everyone in your life? People die, Mya."

"Of course they do. But why is it that other people get to live life and nobody they love dies, but everyone I love does? It's not fair. I must be the reason." I peered up at him.

Shaking his head, he tightened his arms around me. "No. You are not the reason. I was hit by that car because if I never died, you never would have wanted Eli."

I laughed. "Is this your way of saying I belong with him? Not that it matters now."

He shrugged. "I mean, I was jealous at first. But I can't

dwell on the past anymore. I died and you had to move on. Eli was there. I would have done the same if I were him."

Nodding, I sighed. "It's ironic because you are him now. He died, and you're having to comfort me. And that's why I'm so miserable. I'm trying to accept this, but I don't understand it, Owen. I don't understand how I'm expected to get back up after this."

"I don't have the answer to that either."

As I closed my eyes, I relaxed in his arms. I wasn't completely alone. "Just let me stay here forever."

Minutes passed, and they felt like hours. Hours I couldn't get back. I opened my eyes and sat forward. Owen loosened his arms. "What's wrong?"

With a shrug, I pushed my hair behind my ears. "Where do I begin." Pinching the bridge of my nose, I added, "my life's a mess and I'm struggling trying to figure out how to put it back together."

"I can help. I mean, I didn't come back as a ghost just to look pretty," he joked.

I laughed again. "You are very pretty." I glanced at him. "I'm sorry. I'm sorry that I never picked up on your cues."

"Don't be sorry. You wouldn't have understood them easily."

He only said that to be nice, but I knew better. Somehow, his green eyes seemed to shine so bright at a time like this. How?

This time, I was fully aware of my surroundings and my next move. Even after a second thought, I leaned in and kissed him. And he kissed back.

Owen's arm slipped around my waist while I leaned back on his shoulder. As opposed to previous kisses, this one was different. It bloomed with a longing sensation that I didn't get anywhere else. It reminded me of why I had loved Owen in the first place.

He pulled away first, again, and kissed my forehead. "As much as I want this, I don't want to be the rebound boyfriend. I know that you loved Eli more."

"That isn't true."

"*But it is.* And you know it. You chose him."

"And he's dead. So what do you want me to say?"

He brushed his knuckle over my cheek. "Exactly my point. He's dead and you want someone else to love you in that sense. I don't want this to be something we both end up regretting."

I sat up and twisted myself around until I faced him. "Regret? You think I regret loving you? I could never. I regret a lot in my life. I do regret letting Eli stay. I regret going to that ball. I regret so much, Owen. But I don't regret falling for you. Was it complicated? Yes. Loving you, and loving Eli. It wasn't ideal. But I had loved you first. You always respected me. You always showed me that I mattered and I was worth something.

"What was supposed to be a fling turned into this beautiful romance, and I was devastated when you were killed. I pretended to be okay because Juliet never felt comfortable being my shoulder. And I didn't have anyone else to support me. So I drank away my problems. I made out with strangers. But all I really wanted was you. And then I had you..."

He didn't move when I grabbed his hands. I knew he wanted to say something but whatever it was, he couldn't seem to form the sentence.

"And I gave it all away. And maybe it sounds dark and twisted but I deserved to watch Eli die. For cheating on him.

And for...choosing the wrong guy." I exhaled. "You died and you came back the same man. He didn't. He wants me dead, and that's making my grief much worse.

"And maybe that's why everyone around me dies. I make all the wrong choices. I was so worried about my parents even though they chose to get rid of me." *Dead.* "I clung to Juliet for the familiarity even though she was trying to keep me from growing." *Broken.* "And now I'm homeless because I can't seem to grow up. I choose what makes me happy for a fleeting moment over what is healthy for me in the long run. Instant gratification is a dangerous poison. It doesn't kill right away. It lingers. Slowly takes over. Then, it drinks up all of my sanity and leaves me with nothing but a hollow shell of myself."

Owen rubbed his thumb over the top of my hand. "It's not your fault. He made you happy. I was the one who died. You moved on."

I shook my head violently. "But I didn't move on. I never did. Never. I only chose Eli because he made me feel those butterflies. Clearly that was the wrong way to go. I chose my heart over my head, and now I'm the one paying the price. But it's not just me. It's all of us. You. Me. Eli. Even the Hanti. They're all putting up with my shit because I made the wrong choice." I lowered my gaze.

"Mya, look at me." He cupped my cheeks. "You can't blame yourself for this. You might have felt mostly physical attraction at first, but it grew into something else. You loved him. Nothing will take that away. Cherish that feeling. Don't regret it."

It was easier to say than to believe. I wasn't oblivious to all of those romances where the girl chose the brooding guy over the nice guy. I'd fallen into the same trap, hadn't I? What a fool I was.

Maybe it was for my own good that Eli died. I just wish he hadn't been the victim of my recklessness.

I needed to work up the courage to say no. I desired the confidence to choose myself over others. If I could give up my friendship with Juliet after a decade, it was possible to remind myself and others that I was important, too. And there wasn't any shame in being single for a while.

If only I could believe that...

Taking a shaky breath, I closed my eyes. "It doesn't matter anymore. Eli is gone. It's been two months and I need to accept that. It's time to begin living my life for me, and not for anyone else."

"And how do you suppose you'll do that?"

I'd chosen Eli when I was still in love and grieving Owen. I wasn't ready to make the same mistake twice and choose Owen when I was still grieving Eli. Maybe I could give it some time. Then I could finally be happy...

"I'm going to focus on training. Focus on my fashion designs—the original path I wanted to follow. I'm going to focus on my life and what I want. No more will I let others take away what I enjoy. Which means I'm going to learn how to control the shadows, then kill Lucy and Lucas." I placed my hands over his. "I want my revenge, Owen, and I'm never going to be the damsel again."

I loved fashion dearly, but I was afraid to admit aloud that I hadn't been as into it lately after everything that's gone down. Something had shifted inside me and the things I thought I once wanted weren't quite the vision for me anymore. I had other things that took its place, and fashion had become more of a back-burner kind of dream.

A small smile formed on Owen's lips. "Sounds a bit dark

but I can get behind it. And I will be by your side every step of the way."

I planted a soft kiss on the inside of his wrist. "Good. I wouldn't want anything else."

He seemed to blush the second my lips made contact with his soul, *if* ghosts could blush. The memory appeared to be still embedded in his system.

And with time, I could see what had made Owen so special to me. He had once been the peanut butter to my jelly. Now he had become just the bread while Eli turned into my peanut butter.

But someone needed to be both this time, and Owen was the only man willing to step up to the challenge.

034 Wednesday, August 22nd

His lips dragged across my shoulder as he hooked his thumb in the strap of my bra, pulling it off. I grabbed his face and crashed my lips against his, climbing into his lap.

Pushing him back against the sheets, I removed his shirt.

I sat up and rubbed the blush in my cheeks. "Owen," I breathed.

Owen materialized and came to my side. "I'm here. What happened?"

Was I about to blab that I'd had an intimate dream of just us? Not a chance. "Nothing. Just a nightmare." I looked around for my phone. "I'm going to get ready for the day."

Owen nodded and left me to get dressed. I picked myself up out of bed and put music on to keep my thoughts under control.

"A liar, eh?" Eli asked. "Didn't you used to date? You confessed your undying love for that incel, and yet here you are afraid to tell him you have wet dreams about him."

Facing the English dickhead, I snickered. "Afraid is a strong word. It's better to say considerate. I'm being considerate of both of our feelings."

"Considerate." He rolled his eyes. I'd never thought I'd see the day a shadow rolled his eyes. "Bloody lie. Just shag him already."

I narrowed my eyes. "That's none of your damn business."

He stepped forward, and I pulled my dagger from my thigh, ready to stab him. "You think that will hurt me?"

"It's not for you." I stretched my arm and dragged the blade against my skin. Beads seeped out and dripped down my arm. "I'd like to see you try to kill me, Elliot Kay."

His eyes swirled into black smoke. "You're playing with fire."

"It was no accident soaking myself in gasoline." I brought my arm to my lips as I licked up the blood. "You can't kill me."

"You want to bet on that?" He vanished. "Because I'm willing to bet I can," he whispered in my ear from behind. Before I had a chance to face him, he ripped the dagger from my hand and pressed the tip against my side. "Dare me."

Knowing he could never do it before, I spit out, "I dare you to fucking kill me." I choked on my own words as he slipped the blade into my abdomen. I'd never expected him to prove me wrong, yet my own blood now stained my weapon.

"Is that proof enough for you now?" He leaned in, letting go of the dagger.

I tried covering the wound as blood poured through my fingers. I stumbled back onto the bed. "You..." I coughed up some blood.

He squatted in front of me and peered up at me. "Spit it out," he said with a smirk.

Grabbing the dagger, I pulled it out.

He stabbed me. He had actually shoved my own weapon into my body.

Laying back on the bed, I coughed up some more blood. The world faded from my view and I was certain I had died this time.

Peeling my eyes open wasn't easy. I fought to keep them open, but the world around me was dark. I sat up and yelled out from a horrid pain in my side. Certain I was in some void, I lifted my shirt to see stitches along my wound. Who…?

I scooted back on the bed and reached over, turning on the lamp. No, I wasn't dead. I was just in his apartment.

"Was it enough?" he whispered.

Owen hunched over in the chair beside the bed.

"What are you talking about?" I asked.

"Was it enough proof that he's out for your blood? You almost died, Mya. That's reckless behavior. Forgive me for calling out your shit, but you need to get a handle on reality. He is not your Eli. He isn't afraid to kill you. Don't wiggle the bone in his reach. Learn when enough is enough. Please, for your sake."

His words incited anger. Unfortunately, he was right. I needed to stop trying to antagonize the shadow. He made it clear tonight that I was just an obstacle and nothing more.

"I'm sorry," I said in a quiet tone. "I'm sorry for making terrible decisions."

Owen smiled a bit. "You're just lucky I saved you."

Ah, yes. *Saved* me. I was the damsel, and once again it had been my own fault.

"Thank you. I'm reckless, and I need to get out of that

habit." It became clear that neither Eli nor I were planning to leave. Somehow we'd have to put up with each other and I needed to quit tempting him.

Swallowing, I debated telling Owen about the bad routine I'd fallen into. I never imagined it could be me who'd harm herself, but I was afraid to stop. I was terrified to ask for help. I had been enough of a burden as it was.

"What do you plan to do now? I mean, you mentioned training and focusing on being a better hunter. But I want to ensure that I see you make that come true." He folded his hands together. "I want the best for you, Mi Cielo."

Chills ran up my spine as those words slipped from his tongue. "I—" I wasn't sure how to answer him. "I'm not really sure. Surround myself with people. Never listen to my own thoughts for too long. Bite my tongue when I want to curse someone."

Owen chuckled. "Interesting suggestions, but it's a start."

I scooted closer to him. "There was also a day when I asked you to teach me Spanish. Why not try again?" My heart fluttered as his green eyes lingered on my gaze a little too long. Was that a yes?

My heart screamed at me to grab him by the collar and kiss him. I wanted to do that with every fiber of my being, too, but I had told myself that I wouldn't.

Owen dropped his stare and smiled to himself. Why was he afraid to show me his smile? "Mya, you have the worst skills when it comes to learning a language."

"No, no. Don't say that. I can try!" I leaned over the edge, trying to think of something simple. "Mi..." I furrowed my brows as if it would help. "Damnit, I can't remember the Spanish word for name." I released a sigh. "You're right, okay? I am the worst person to teach Spanish to." I fell back into the pillows.

He laughed. "How about this? I'll say a phrase and you try to guess what I'm saying? If you guess correctly, I'll consider teaching you again."

"That sounds fair."

"Te amo."

I smiled. "I know that one! It means I love you. Okay now you're making me look like a dumbass. Everyone knows that."

Owen leaned back in the chair. "Fine. I'll make it a little harder." He folded his arms across his chest. "Te quiero besar."

My smile faded. "You love me a lot? Owen, is that your way of saying you love me? Because I told you the—"

"It means I want to kiss you."

My cheeks reddened. "Oh. So I was close? I mean love and kiss are not the same but they sound similar." I wasn't sure I was supposed to respond to that the way he wanted me to. "Why don't we go train?"

"Are you in any state to train?" He pointed to my wound. Of course not. But I needed to get out of this small room. A room I'd already had intimate moments in multiple times before.

Getting up from the bed, I hurried to the kitchen and searched the cupboards for snacks. I grabbed a bottle of tequila and faced Owen. He stood there by the counter, lifting an eyebrow. "I'm an adult. I'm legally allowed to drink and you can't stop me."

I set the snacks down and began eating, taking a swig every now and again.

Owen didn't make any moves to stop me, which was the right move. It wasn't his place.

"This is what I did." I put down the bottle, feeling the buzz kicking into my system. "I'm sure I told you. But I drank after you died. A lot." And now I was heading back into that rut with Eli, because I couldn't rebound with Owen or train with the Hanti.

"Do you want me to take the alcohol or let you have it? I mean, I'm not sure what you're asking of me here. I don't want you to hate me forever." He shoved his hands into his pockets.

Staring at my tequila, I grabbed the bottle and downed the rest. "My tolerance was always very low." I dropped the bottle as it shattered along with my heart.

I stumbled into the glass and Owen caught me, carrying me over to the couch. He picked the glass from my feet. "If it makes you feel any better, from this side of the fence you seem to be handling his death better than mine."

I was aware of my surroundings, but I had this urge to do whatever came to my mind. "Feeding a man his penis is better?"

His face burned from embarrassment. "In other words, maybe? I'm not condoning it, but the guy wasn't innocent either."

"So it's better to hurt a killer than to destroy my own mind."

Owen lowered his eyes to my wound. "Certainly better than tempting a killer to make his move."

I'd believed it to be a ruse. Oh how wrong I'd been.

Before anyone said another word, I grabbed his shirt and pulled him against me. I kissed him slowly at first until it grew into something more. Owen pulled away from me in seconds. I stayed frozen, unsure of his next play.

As if testing the waters, he kissed me again. My own

heartbeat pounded in my ears, knowing he didn't have his own. It became so loud—all I could hear.

Heartbeat. Hearts pumped blood. Blood...

Everything that had happened over the past few months had been complete despair and I deserved to forget about all of it.

Owen's fingers dug into my waist. It drove me crazy. My mind was all over the place tonight, and part of me wanted this but the other part said no. But a third part wedged its way in, taking full control. Maybe it was the Hanti in me. I couldn't be a hundred percent sure about it.

I pushed his shirt up his torso, begging for more. His kiss had my mind running in circles—dizzy. "You are so damn slow." I pushed him onto the cushions and climbed onto his lap. I took off my shirt and tugged at his. "Come on, Owen. Are you trying to seduce me or screw me?" Deep down, a dark urge surfaced. I desired to rip his head off. It would have been too easy. "The two are not the same and you know it."

His grip on my waist didn't waver, but the look in his eyes did. "Mi Cielo, you're not sober. I am not going to have sex with you in that state."

"What, you're afraid of a little alcohol? You're dead. Grow a pair." I scowled as I stood from his lap, not even worried about the little cuts on my feet.

He fixed his shirt and followed me to the bathroom. "I might not have a heartbeat but I didn't lose my heart along with it. I don't believe in having sex with a woman if she isn't sober, and definitely not if I am the *only* sober one in the situation."

"I'm not drunk." I whipped around and faced him. "I'm mentally capable of consenting."

"And I'm not comfortable with the situation given what

it's stemming from."

Narrowing my eyes, I walked forward, forcing him out of the bathroom. "Then leave if it's so wrong. I don't need to deal with this shit right now." Was I horny? Maybe. Was I pissed? Hella. "Get out before I rip your head off and feed it to the wolves!" I yelled at him. I wanted to blame the anger on the alcohol, but I wasn't so sure that's where it came from.

Grief snuck in like a black cat in the night.

035 Friday, August 31st

Some nights dark thoughts raided my mind. Some nights I wanted to do things much worse than skip a meal or add a cut to the collection on my arm. Some nights I debated giving up on this life.

I'd be lying if I said those thoughts were fleeting. They were anything but. And if I let them linger just long enough, I'd be lying on the bathroom floor right now. Instead, I was at the cabin punching the bag. Anything to get my mind off it. The anger I wanted to take out on myself was used to train.

"Mya?" Hunter entered the room.

"I'm not in the mood to talk, Hunter." I kneed the bag and then turned and kicked it from a different angle.

"Then why am I here?"

"Because you walked in." I punched again a little too hard and the bag came back full swing, hitting me in the gut. I groaned and stumbled back.

He snickered. "No." He grabbed my shoulders and spun me to face him. "I'm talking about the empty bottle of vodka I found this morning."

"I'm legally allowed to drink."

"A whole bottle? Of vodka? We talked about this, Mya. You're still grieving. You had agreed to move out of his apartment and now you're staying behind because he's there. It's not really him."

"What if Ryan was still here?"

Hunter stepped back, straightening his posture. "What?"

I removed my wraps. "What if Ryan came back? Maybe he was darker, maybe immortal, but what if he came back and you saw him? Could you just drop it and say you were done with him? Cut him out?"

He swallowed. "I'd have to. That's our job."

"Bullshit. Amari tried pulling that same shit about her and Clara. But she knows that if Clara was a Kaofi, she'd do anything to be with her. If Ryan was here, somehow, you'd change your views just to hang out again. So why am I the one expected to move on? It's not my Eli, but it is still *Eli*—and I'll be damned if I give up on him like that." I drank my water.

With a sigh, he rubbed his face and said, "You are such a pain in the ass."

"You are such a pain in the ass, too, you know. And you could probably be less of a pain if you stopped seeing everything in black and white. I fell in love with a Kaofi. Get over it." I exited the room and entered the kitchen to make myself some food.

Hunter followed, but he never said a word as my gaze lingered on the counter.

Thoughts ran through my head. "It hurts. Every single

day, it continues to hurt just the same. I try to push it away. I try to move on, but I can't," I said.

He didn't respond.

"I keep replaying it in my head. What I could have done right. What I did wrong. How I could have saved him," my voice grew quieter. "I screw up everything. I should have been able to save Eli."

His presence grew closer. "I think that about Ryan. Every day. It doesn't get easier, Mya." He grabbed my shoulder, turning me to face him. "Ryan was a brother to me. And I've tried to deny that he's gone but I wake up and he's never there."

"But Eli *is*," I whispered.

Eli was there when I woke up. Physically, he was still around. And even if Hunter hadn't said it, he implied that I still had Eli around. I needed to focus my grief on trying to befriend this new Eli. However that was possible...

"Did I ever tell you I cheated on Eli?" I forced myself to meet Hunter's eyes. If he was surprised, he didn't show it. Not to me, anyway. "Before he died, I cheated on Eli. We were on that date in the forest, to train, because it was the only way we could be around each other after what I did. If I hadn't done it, maybe he'd still be himself. I'm a shitty person, and I know that. If I run from him now, I can never truly apologize. Helping him find some part of who he once was is my way of redeeming myself, even if I can only redeem myself just a little. He never truly understood how sorry I was. I can't let him scare me away now. That's how apologetic I am." I screwed the lid from a water bottle and drank it.

His voice lowered. "Who was he? The other guy?"

With my eyes now glued to the floor, I whispered, "Owen.

He's been haunting me. We dated before I met Eli. And what's worse is I've kissed him since Eli died. I don't seem to learn."

He snorted this time. It was odd to hear him snort. Hunter wasn't very friendly around me, on a normal day anyway. "We all figured that much. But if Eli doesn't actually remember you, does it matter anymore that you're seeing Owen after he died? He can't be hurt."

"It isn't about him being hurt. It's the intent. The implications." I shrugged a bit, licking my lips before my eyes settled back on Hunter. "And we aren't seeing each other. I just kissed him. Drunken mistake."

A flash of judgment passed. There it was. The Hunter I knew.

"Drunk? You admit you use alcohol to cope with your grief. It's not healthy and you should probably quit before it grows out of hand. You know, like becoming an alcoholic. We don't need a Kaofi Hunter violently acting out on something altering her perception. It wouldn't only be bad for you but the entire community. Humans and Hanti alike."

I forced a laugh. "And what's the worst that could happen? I scream that I can see vampires? Are people really going to believe me? I'll end up in an asylum, maybe. I doubt it would hurt anyone else."

Hunter's eyes trailed over the sandwich behind me. "Are you going to eat that?"

As a smirk rose to my lips, I grabbed it and licked the bread. "Did you still want it?"

He didn't seem all that fazed. "Germs never really bothered me. Besides, am I supposed to be afraid of a little tongue? I've French-kissed before."

Growling, I took a bite. "Don't be gross," I said with a full mouth.

He muttered, "Chew with your mouth closed."

"Mya! There you are!" Amari came running in, cheeks tinted peek and sweat forming a thin sheet across her skin. "You are not going to want to miss this."

I glanced at Hunter who only shrugged in return. I set my sandwich on the plate, following Amari out of the cabin. She grabbed my wrist as if I hadn't been quick enough. When Clara came into view, we stopped beside her.

"We've found something." Clara pointed to a tree, or the trunk of it. From a distance it might appear normal. It might have appeared normal to anyone not paying any attention to the trees at all. People like me.

The trunk was anything but.

Carved into the bark was a symbol. Not one I recognized but one that stood out. "That looks like something you'd see from some kind of witch," I said.

Hunter stood next to me, taking a bite of my sandwich. "Not a witch. A shadow."

I narrowed my eyes. "The shadows? They're out here? I know that they're trying to build their army, but what do they want to do out here?"

Amari touched the mark. "Shadows want to instill fear, remember? Marking this area as territory they own is their way of saying they're always watching. Nobody is safe."

She didn't say it, but I heard between the words. I put us all in danger by living in Eli's apartment and interacting with one of their pawns.

"Maybe I can help," I whispered.

Hunter choked. "Well, yeah that's the whole point of you being part of the group."

I elbowed him in the rib. "I meant with digging up more information. Figuring out the goal, maybe even figuring out their weaknesses. Aside from us having to control them. I live with a shadow. I can try and get inside their plans."

Clara shook her head. "That's dangerous. If Eli even suspects what you're doing, he will kill you without second thought. He doesn't know who you are anymore. He has no use for keeping you alive."

"I'm surprised you've lasted this long," Amari said.

I wanted to admit that I lasted because I was stronger now. But that wasn't entirely true. Eli proved to me he could wipe my name from existence if he wanted. He was skilled. He was a vampire and a shadow, and he had two-hundred years under his belt. I had what, *barely a year?*—if that.

"The shadows are making their territory. They're sending us a message. A warning if you will. If we are going to save anyone at all, it's our job to find a way to control them. Somehow. They're not just targeting Hanti or humans. They're targeting Kaofi, too. Eli is proof of that. He didn't get any say." I pulled my phone out and took a picture of the mark.

"Maybe." Clara shrugged. "But they're not taking perfectly healthy Kaofi. They're taking those wounded, with fatal injuries. People like Eli."

I spat. "Would he even have chosen this? Would he have chosen a shadow over death? A creature that has no idea who I am, except that I'm a threat? I know he was pissed with me, but I doubt he wanted this to be the outcome. The shadows stole that choice from him. The other Kaofi stole his life."

Without another word, we all headed back to the cabin. I packed up my things and went home for the night. I needed a cold shower, anything to get this feel of sweat from my body.

When I approached the front door of the apartment, I stopped in my tracks. The same mark was now carved into the metal. "Screw if I let you scare me off that easy. Bastard," I said with a scowl. I unlocked the door and went inside, locking it behind me. As if that would help. The monster was *inside* these walls.

The temperature was at least sixty here, but it didn't bother me as much as he wanted it to.

After my shower, I put on some of his clothes to reclaim my territory. He didn't get the upper hand. Sure, I told Owen I wouldn't tempt him anymore. However, that didn't mean I wouldn't stand my ground and not show him I was here to stay. Where else would I go?

I sensed he was watching from the shadows. The chill air nipped at my skin. Owen wasn't around. I knew that much.

"I'm only going to say this once so listen good." I glanced up at the ceiling as if he were there. "I'm not going anywhere. I have nowhere *to* go, Eli. This is home to me now. I won't try to piss you off if that's what you want. We can call a truce. That means no more stabbing me with my dagger. I won't tell you to kill me."

He didn't respond. Would he agree? I was probably wasting my time, but what did it matter? At least I *tried.*

"Yes, you're probably thinking to yourself: *why is this Hanti trying to make a truce?* Well, this Hanti knows things about you nobody else does. So if you're going to try anything again, I'll have to expose those secrets."

Ah, yes, blackmailing him into a truce. That's a good idea, Mya.

I snickered.

"But if you let me, I think we could be really good friends."

Yeah, sure. "Or at least tolerate each other. We both aren't going anywhere. We may as well stop trying to go at each other's throats and expecting a different outcome. We may as well live life the way we were supposed to, now that you have a second chance." I meant to say *together*, but that wasn't going to happen now. Not ever.

It was best for me to focus on training anyway. For the shadows, and for whatever else was coming. I had to be the best of the best.

"Let me know if that's something you'd be up for." I laid back in the bed, watching what I swear were a pair of eyes flashing in the moonlight from the corner of the room. "Goodnight, Eli." That was if he let me *survive* the night.

036 Sunday, September 2nd

Owen stood outside of the shower but he didn't dare look in the curtain. "There's something I need to tell you, Mya."

"Tell me." I ran my fingers through my hair to get the last of the conditioner out. "Nobody is stopping you. You've been free to communicate your thoughts to me for the longest time."

His next words had almost stopped my heart. "My death wasn't an accident."

Exhaling, I reached out and grabbed the towel and dried myself before wrapping it around my body and stepping out to face Owen. He leaned against the wall with his hands in his pockets and one ankle crossed over the other.

"What the hell does that mean?"

"Exactly what you think. My death wasn't an accident."

My eyes fell to the floor. "And how do you know?"

His eyes must have burned through my soul. "I have known you were a hunter for the longest time. I didn't bring you out to that spot for a date. I was going to tell you the truth about everything. But...they stopped me before I could."

My eyes snapped up to his. *"Who?"*

Owen shook his head. "I'll let you get dressed." He vanished before I could stop him. Screw him for leaving me like that.

I grabbed my clothes and hurried to get dressed but even when I left the bathroom, he didn't return. "Damn you, Owen," I muttered. Then and there, my stomach grumbled. "All right, I'm going." I went to the kitchen and pulled out the ingredients needed to make a sandwich. Simple. Yet filling.

A chilled breath hit the back of my neck. "What secrets do you know?" his English accent came out in a whisper.

Glancing at the knife I'd been using to cut my tomato, I set it down. "Are you sure you want me to tell you?"

He snickered, grabbing my wrist and spinning me to face him. My back pressed into the edge of the counter. "Are you bluffing then? Because that's expected of you."

I slipped my wrist from his fingers. "Your mother taught you to be a gentleman." He stiffened. "She wouldn't be very proud to see you threatening a woman weaker than you with no place to go." Admitting I was weaker had me biting my tongue to keep the curses at bay.

He took a few steps back but didn't budge after that.

"You were born a vampire. So it was part of the family. Your father was in charge, had more power than you'd admit at times. But I always suspected you were rich to an extent none of us could fathom. But you were a gentleman, nonetheless. And when you agreed to take a girl without a date out, you picked out a classic black suit with your mother.

"Things took a wrong turn, unfortunately. Before you could get the phone to be of use, they broke it, and then your mother begged them to take her and let you go. They did. But they made you watch the horrors they inflicted on her before they ended her life. I told you a few weeks ago I know about what happened to your mom, and I do. I also know why that made you who you are today. You stopped caring after that point."

I dropped my gaze to the floor. "I understand. I don't know what that's like, but I can see why your first instinct is to kill a Hanti living in your apartment. But I'm not the threat, Eli. They are. The shadows. Lucas and Lucy. They're the ones I'm after and I know you're after them, too. I take no pride in having to house myself here, in a Kaofi's apartment. If I had options, I wouldn't be here."

He stayed silent for a few minutes.

"Then there's Alissa," I whispered. "Your ex-girlfriend, someone who looked just like me."

This time, he replied, "She was like me and yet she turned on me. I had no choice but to kill her to defend myself. I had to live off animal blood for a while to stay off the radar and gain my morality back."

He'd never told me that, but I didn't tell him. Instead, I agreed.

Something shattered in one of the rooms and Eli and I shot each other a look of concern. We knew nobody else had access to this apartment.

Without thinking, Eli walked toward the hall when something shattered again.

My dagger was immediately in my hand from that point forward as I walked up behind Eli. He shot me a look, furrowing his brows and shooing me away. He lost his mind if he thought I'd give up that easy and let him fight alone. He didn't remember me, but I certainly remembered him. I'd be damned if I allowed him to be brainwashed a second time.

I grabbed him by the shoulder and pulled him back as I walked in front of him. He owned the apartment but I was the one actively living here. It was my duty to check it out.

As I approached the door, I pressed my back against the wall next to the frame, grip tightening on the hilt of my blade. I turned my head and peeked into the room. I quickly pulled my head back before they saw me. I tilted my head up and breathed in the scent, scrunching my face.

Cigarettes.

Shadows—in other words.

Eli lifted both eyebrows up when I looked at him, in which case I mouthed "shadows".

In seconds, Eli had rushed over and clamped his hand over my mouth as he pressed me against the wall. His eyes didn't dare stray from mine, and whoever was in the room was not willing to leave anytime soon.

As much as I hated to admit it, I missed being this close. I missed every little thing about him, but most of all, I missed the Eli who'd once bickered with me without a second thought. Now he sent nothing but threats my way.

From this close up, I could see the irises of his eyes. Dark gray, almost black. It felt off. Wrong. And yet Eli seemed to pull it off well.

No.

His irises hadn't just lost their color and turned gray. It was *smoke.* Gray smoke was swirling in front of his irises and that had been all that was left of this man.

"Boo," someone whispered from behind Eli.

Eli whipped around so fast while I used my dagger to swipe at them. It cut through the figure made of black smoke but did no real damage. They were untouchable in this form.

The shadow pushed Eli out of the way and came for me, grabbing me by the neck and squeezing. How he managed to get a grip on me when I couldn't do the same in return was beyond me. I clawed at my throat but the air wouldn't pass no matter how hard I tried.

My dagger clattered to the floor. My vision began to blur and before I could get a chance to breathe, the world went dark.

When I came to, Owen sat at the foot of my bed, eyes focused on me. "You almost fucking died."

My throat was sore and it hurt just to swallow. "Eli didn't do it."

"No, but he might as well have. That asshole could have gotten you killed."

A snicker echoed in the corner of the room and when I turned my head, Eli was sitting on the floor, back to the corner with his knees up and arms dangling over his knees. "I'm right here."

Owen shot him a disapproving look before scooting closer to me. "Why are you still here?"

Sitting up, I situated myself against the headboard. "Where do I go? Juliet and I are over. Going back to my mom's isn't an option when she lives an hour away. Have you seen rent prices? Owen, I have no other option."

"Yes you do. Amari. Hunter. Clara. Any of them would be willing to take you in." He leaned in. "That's safer than here."

With my own snicker, I threw my arms up. "What about *this* is safe? What about being a Hanti makes my life safe in any situation? I was never safe from the start, and you know damn well none of them would want to be burdened by me. It's a miracle I wasn't killed before I found out who I am."

Eli decided to put in his two cents then and there. "You should listen to your boyfriend."

"He's not..." I rubbed away the stress in my temples. "Eff this." I reached for the water on the nightstand and took a long gulp before giving Eli my full attention. "I'm not going anywhere. Build a bridge and get the hell over it."

Owen wasted no time grabbing my hand. "My death was a homicide. You asked me who did it. I'll tell you right now that shadows did it. For the longest time, I knew about you being a hunter. But it occurred to me you didn't know. I was going to tell you everything that night in the woods, by the highway. But the car hit me before I had a chance. Shadows have been planning a massive war for a while and you're at the heart of it."

"Why me?"

"The question is why not you? A hunter who wasn't raised that way. If the shadows can get a hold of you and use you as their warning towards hunters, they can establish their leadership over all the other creatures. They want ultimate power. At some point along the way, after you discovered the truth, they made it their goal to target you. Now it's just because they refuse to go back on their word and look like the losers." Owen squeezed my hand.

I glanced at our fingers. "How would you have known, Owen, about this world and who I was before I did? Humans can't see Kaofi."

His breath came out slowly. "I wasn't human."

I whispered, "What does that mean? Were you a Hunter? You mentioned once your father was."

"Once Kaofi, always Kaofi, unless killed by the hand of a Kaofi Hunter. Eli was killed by your blade. Only shadows could revive him. I was killed at a shadow's hand, and I came back as a ghost. But before I became a ghost, Mya, I was a werewolf. You—you were my *mate*."

My breath caught in my throat as I met his eyes. Longing, yet filled with such sorrow.

Mate. That had been a word I heard in passing at times. It was when the universe or some higher power paired two together. They'd paired us, and a part of me felt sick about it. Had my feelings for Owen been a sham? Had we been forced together by some cruel fate? Was any of it ever real?

I could ask the same about being Eli's mate, too. Why me? And how had I ended up as both of theirs?

Regardless, it didn't change that I'd had feelings for Owen. As irritating as he could be, I also felt safe in his arms, or as safe as a girl could when her boyfriend had been murdered because of her.

Which meant it had happened before. A Hanti fell in love with a Kaofi. Owen was the product of an abomination. Maybe that's why he'd been mated to me. Maybe fate knew he'd die, and Alissa would die, and I was then mated to Eli, too. But why this mess? Why—if Eli was going to die at all? Why—if Owen would return as a ghost to love me all over again? Why give me two options to rip them both away?

Owen stood seconds later. "I have things to take care of. In the meantime, I trust you can stay alive."

I looked up at Owen as my face softened a bit. "Thank you for saving me. Not that I needed it, but thanks."

Eli choked on something. Owen, on the other hand, shook his head. "I didn't save you. Eli did." He vanished before I could even open my mouth. Damn him.

Eli shoved his hands into his pockets as he approached the bed, knees touching the mattress. "For the record, you did need help. You passed out."

Silence was exchanged for a few minutes before Eli dropped himself onto his bed, right beside my feet. The question finally seemed to form on my tongue. "Why did you save me? This was your opportunity to get rid of me like you wanted."

Instead of answering my question, he said, "Shadows are not what you think they are."

I laughed at that. "What, evil? Let me guess, you're all a bunch of misunderstood villains?"

He gave me a serious look without even entertaining my joke. "No. Shadows are cruel. Ruthless. There lays no emotion behind eyes. What that shadow wanted from me, I can't say. I can say he would have torn you apart had I not stepped in. No mercy. You should be bloody grateful I haven't taken your life by now. By their standards, I should have."

I pulled my legs from under the blanket as I crawled closer, sitting back on my calves. "So why didn't you?"

His breath came out slow and ragged. "Because I believe you might be able to help me."

037 Monday, September 3rd

A shin to the bag.

"Because I believe you might be able to help me."

Another punch.

"How can I help you?"

Two punches.

"I want to take down the shadows, too."

Kick.

"Mya?" Hunter leaned against the frame, ankles and arms crossed.

I rolled my neck and swallowed some of my water. "You need something?"

He shrugged a little as he came closer. "You know what Amari can do. Do you know what I can do? What ability I may have?" He looked at the bandages wrapped around my hands. My knuckles had begun to bleed, and for good reason. Eli made it so damn hard not to kiss him. I was doing everything in my power to see him as nothing more than a nuisance now.

After removing the bandages and cleaning my knuckles, I gestured for him to go on. "Tell me."

He chuckled and grabbed my wrist. "I'd rather show you."

Hunter led us into the city but we never ventured farther than the shadows. We kept ourselves hidden from plain sight as not to draw any attention.

Pointing to a creature that smelled of wet dog, he said, "Werewolf." He pointed to another. "Fallen angel."

I looked at Hunter. "How do you recognize them?"

"I see them for who they truly are. Fallen angels can't hide their wings. Werewolves appear with their wolf form. Vampires show up with fangs and dark eyes. Shadows? I only see them in shadow form." He put his hands in his pockets.

Shadows. After what Owen told me, I knew I needed to warn the others.

"Hunter, I need to talk to you. All of you." Without another word, we headed back to the cabin. It had been the safest place to discuss anything and all things immortal.

Clara leaned forward while Amari made her some food. Hunter was leaning back against the couch. "Go on."

I balled my fists together and leaned my chin onto them. "Have I mentioned Owen?"

Clara shrugged. "A little."

Hunter nodded. "Enough to know you had cheated on Eli with Owen."

I wanted to shout that it was just a kiss, and one that never happened, but he was right. Even an almost kiss was considered cheating. Feelings, and knowingly being around him with said feelings was cheating. I couldn't erase that. "Owen was my boyfriend over a year ago. Before I met Eli. We'd dated for a short time and it was never meant to become serious, and yet it did. Owen was hit by a car that night and killed. I spent months trying to recover. By recover, I mean I drank all my sorrows."

Amari frowned. "That sounds like torture."

Nodding, I looked at my hands. "Owen became a ghost."

Clara nodded as well, like she expected that answer. Did she? "And?"

"And he told me he wasn't hit by accident." I exhaled. "He knew things we don't know. The shadows are planning a war on all Kaofi Hunters and they intended to use me as the warning."

Amari's eyes darkened. "What the hell does that mean?"

I stood. "It means they wanted to kill me in front of the world for show, to remind you that they're not afraid. And even if I can fight back this time, they're not going to give up. They are determined to follow through. He meant to tell me the truth before they murdered him."

Amari cursed under her breath. "We can't even kill them. How are we supposed to take control of all these shadows? We're screwed. We're actually screwed."

Hunter put his hand out. "Hold on now. We aren't screwed. We may have to go on a search for more Hanti. That's our only option."

Clara stood. "Hunter is right. If the shadows want to wage a war on us, we need to be prepared. The four of us alone can't take them down."

"Five," I muttered.

Hunter furrowed his brows. "There's only four of us."

I shook my head and turned my head to look at him. "Eli wants to take them down, too. If I'm lucky, maybe I can get Owen in on it. He was a werewolf before they murdered him." I didn't tell them about what his parents were and what it made Owen. It didn't feel like my place. "He has better reason than anyone to go against the shadows. Maybe Josh might want to help. Eli was his best friend."

Clara nodded. "That's great. And in the meantime, we need to be on the lookout for more Hanti. The more, the merrier. We have to go down fighting if we must go down at all."

"And," Amari started, "we should also be figuring out how to gain control of the shadows. If we can control them, we can win this war. We know they don't die."

No, they didn't. Eli was no longer a victim if he couldn't be killed. But they could still control him if they wanted. They knew how to control their own kind. If Eli would tell me, I might be able to help. However, that was assuming they told him how to control shadows or that he'd tell me his weakness at all. He asked for my help, but that didn't mean he trusted me.

Amari saw the look on my face and took from that what she would. "You have to get close with Eli. Get him to talk."

I snickered at that. "Eli wants me dead. You really think he's going to spill all their secrets to me? That would be obvious." I folded my hands together and brought them to my lips. "But I might have a better idea." As horrendous as it was... "I'll make him fall in love with me all over again."

Everyone went silent at that, like it would be an impossible task. Was it?

"Shadows can't love," Amari said.

I met her gaze. "Then I'll change the rules. I'll make them love. Nothing about my life has been quite run-of-the-mill. Owen believes they're after me because I didn't know I was a Hanti and I was the perfect warning for shadows to show to Hanti. However, I fear that maybe there's more than the shadows are letting on. What if I'm more than just the Hanti who was raised human?"

Clara smiled a little. "Mya, we love you, but your gift is no more extraordinary than ours. It's normal to want to believe you could be the chosen one but the reality is you probably aren't."

Hunter choked on the water he'd been drinking. "Wow, that was harsh. Normally you're the nice one."

Amari sat beside her, resting her chin on Clara's shoulder. "Let's be real. There was never any nice way to say that."

I stood from the couch. "I appreciate what you're saying but I refuse to believe that Eli is gone forever. I'll make him love me. Anything is possible in this world." I left before they could get another word in. It seemed cruel to play with his feelings that way when I truly loved him. But the man I loved died months ago, and this was not the same one who took his place. I'd be able to believe they were separate people when I treated them as such.

When I arrived at the apartment, I noticed the pot was boiling over. "What the hell?" I rushed to take it off the stove.

"You enjoy running away?" Eli asked.

When I whipped around to face him, he sat at the counter with his feet up while he twirled a knife in his hands. That bastard.

"I didn't run. I went to train. If I'm going to help you, I have to train. You know, build muscles? Skills?"

His gray eyes met mine with animosity. "Tell me then, Little Hunter, what is it that makes you run."

I rolled my eyes, ignoring the little flutters in my abdomen. "I'll do you one better and tell you what makes me stay." I circled the counter and ripped the knife from his hand, stabbing it into the countertop. Except it didn't get stuck like I had aimed for. Instead, the tip of the knife chipped off. They were *stone* counters after all. "And it's Hanti, not hunter. Hunter is rude." Deflection. *Nice.*

Eli snickered. "Good bloody job at that." He lowered his legs and grabbed my wrist, yanking me between him and the counter. He slowly stood and grabbed my chin. "Well then? What makes you stay?"

A damn shiver ran down my spine. "Fear." *You.*

His hand dropped from my face and he gave me my space as he walked away from the counter. "How did the training go then?"

I warned myself not to spill our plan but part of me trusted Eli wasn't going to blab to the shadows. "We're going to find other Hanti to team up with us against the shadows."

He glanced up from cutting tomatoes. Wait a damn minute... "Yeah? Does that mean you're finally leaving my apartment?"

I hadn't quite asked that question but I assumed it meant something along those lines. "We might be on the road a little but I won't be leaving here much if that's still your goal. They're the ones searching. My plan is to stay here most of the time and train." *And make you fall in love with me, Little Shadow.*

Eli finished with the slicing and assembled a sandwich. He handed the plate to me. "Eat up, then. If you're going to train, we have work to do."

Did the mothereffer just make me a sandwich?

"We?" I furrowed my brows.

"Yes, we. Your friends are off looking for other hunters and I doubt you can train by yourself. That only gets you so far. I'd be the perfect candidate, shadow and all." He gestured to himself.

As I took a bite of my sandwich, I tried not to gag. He

forgot the mayonnaise and it tasted hella dry. "So if we are going to train together, then I guess that begs the question. Are you really still a vampire? I mean how does that shit all work? Owen died as a werewolf and became a ghost. Why didn't you become a ghost?" We'd been over this once, but I needed just a little more clarification.

"Vampires are already dead. It wouldn't make sense to become another dead thing. The shadows are the ones who made me invincible. For their little game of revenge, that is."

Right. If a Hunter's blade killed a Kaofi, they died. If another Kaofi killed a Kaofi, they became a ghost. Owen made that clear. And it was easy for them to kill werewolves, among a few other Kaofi. Vampires—not so much...

Kaofi were called that for a reason. Without interference—death—they could live forever. They didn't age like the rest of us. But they all had weaknesses. They could all be killed, aside from shadows. Some were easier than others like a werewolf vs. a vampire.

But immortal didn't mean indestructible.

I tilted my head. "Wait, are you trying to say that the shadows intentionally targeted you because you're linked to me?"

He narrowed his gaze. "How exactly am I linked to you?"

Reality came crashing down on me. Clara tried to remind me that I wasn't the one at the center of this war, because why would a measly little Hanti be so dangerous? However, maybe it *wasn't* me. Maybe it was the idea that I gave Hanti and Kaofi alike. Through Eli and I, we had brought years of feuds and beliefs to the ground. They targeted me because I had made one of their own fall in love with me. And I was going to do it again.

I took a blow to my chest the more I thought about how

Eli became a target because of my own doing. They killed him intentionally to turn him against me. It was the only way for them to hurt me and save the fate of our worlds colliding.

"Eli, I'm going to say this as carefully as possible so you don't take it the wrong way." By the wrong way, I meant he didn't kill me on the spot.

He hissed. "How the bloody hell am I linked to you?"

After ripping the skin off my lip with my teeth, I rubbed my thumb against the hilt of my dagger.

Just in case.

"I may or may not have played a role in your death. You became a shadow because of me," I breathed.

His eyes darkened. "What the fuck does that mean?"

"It means the shadows intentionally killed you, sending that vampire and the others to surround us. It was never an accident, and now I know that no matter what we do, they are two steps ahead of us."

He rushed around the island and ripped my dagger from its sheath, pressing the blade to my throat. "I could kill you."

But he wouldn't. Eli tried, and now he knew that I was the key to also ending this. Just as his eyes bored into mine, I debated grabbing the dagger from his grasp. I decided against it. There was no need to light the fuse.

I cleared my throat. "We really should begin that training now."

038 Wednesday, September 5th

Hills rolled by first, then mountains. Was it a good idea to allow my enemy to drive me into the far forest? No. But here I let him anyway.

"We could have run there," I said.

"Could have, sure." Eli shrugged as I looked at him. "But where's the fun? No sightseeing? Besides, I'd miss the look on your face, wondering if I'm going to murder you out here alone in the mountains."

I scowled. "Well, are you?"

"Little Hunter, we made a fair truce."

I lifted a finger. "To be *fair*, we never did agree to that truce. I called a truce and you didn't show up until the next morning. And you never actually agreed to it. You asked me questions."

We approached a car, but Eli's patience had been tested. He failed. In seconds, we were swerving around the car while I hung on for dear life. "What the hell? You're Kaofi, and I'm not! Does my life mean nothing to you?" I rubbed my head. "Don't answer that!"

Eli chuckled. He actually *chuckled.* Granted, it lasted no more than a second, but it counted as something.

As he took his foot off the gas a little, he glanced at me. "All right then. I agree to your truce."

I almost stopped breathing. *Almost.*

"Really? You're calling a truce now? You know that means you can't kill me for any reason, right? Are you prepared to live by that promise?"

"I know what a truce is. I wouldn't have agreed if I didn't plan to stand by it." He cleared his throat. "You just sit back and keep quiet the rest of the trip." He turned up the music to tune me out even if I didn't agree.

The rest of the trip passed by in his vastly different music tastes—mostly R&B. When the road began to wind around cliffs, I knew we were getting close. And as the trees parted, a massive mansion came into view. Gates and all.

"Shit, Eli."

He pulled up as the gates slowly opened to their master. "Welcome to my humble abode."

I choked. "Humble, sure. Why do you live in a measly apartment if this is what awaits you in the mountains?"

As we pulled up toward the front doors, Eli parked.

The mansion had to be at least three big homes combined into one. The home hadn't been kept up with all summer and now the vegetation was withering, preparing for winter when fall had yet to arrive.

The driveway came from the gate to the front door, circling around a fountain just a few feet before the front steps. The fountain hadn't been watered in what appeared to be years.

"That's why I'm planning to move back when this mess is over," Eli said as he got out of the car and closed his door. I hurried out behind him, nearly tripping over a few missing bricks in the driveway.

We approached the contrasting red door against a house of white. Well, it must have been white once before weather wore down the color. It was nothing a good pressure wash couldn't fix.

When we stepped inside, nothing prepared me. The outside appeared unkempt and untouched for years. The inside had been anything but. Inside the floors were made up of a dark-stained wood throughout while the windows stood from ceiling to floor to let in all the natural light in the world. Chandeliers hung from every light fixture and a grand staircase waited front and center, curving up and around to two hallways where anyone could plummet from had rails not been installed.

Everything in here had been a dark-stained wood, except it all pulled together well. Someone had been here recently. Maybe the outside was left that way to scare off potential criminals. One could only guess.

Cozier than any small home I'd ever been in.

Eli waved me back through the foyer and into the kitchen. He gestured to the fridge. "All the sandwiches your heart desires."

"No effing way." The fridge was double the size of our fridge at home, and our fridge at home had been big to begin with.

"As much as I'd like to gawk at all the beauty, I must show you where we'll train." He grabbed my wrist, which we both sent each other weird looks for. He dropped it before leading me down the stairs into the basement. Of course he had a basement. Which mansion didn't?

When we approached, I almost stopped dead in my tracks.

"Eli. This..."

"This what?" He lifted an eyebrow and shoved his hands into his pockets.

"This is a home theater. I've always wanted one!" I ran over and gasped at the chairs. They had to be the comfiest chairs in the world, and I'd bet my life on it.

"Mya, please. Let's not get ahead of ourselves. Training." He waved me to follow him, and I did. We exited out through the back doors which led to a balcony.

The balcony had been the size of a small house, and that wasn't even the best part. The balcony was overlooking a cliffside off the side of the mountain. As terrifying as it seemed, it was far more breathtaking than any trip I'd ever take.

"We train here?"

Eli shrugged. "Would you prefer the home theater?"

"Never! If we ruin those pristine chairs, I'd never be able to live with myself." I pulled my dagger out, eyes the sharpened blade. "Let's get to it then."

Eli pulled out his own dagger. "Don't hold back. I can't be killed."

"Yeah, thankfully," I mumbled. "You too."

He approached me, sticking the dagger under my chin. "I have to hold back a little. Otherwise our little truce is a lie."

I swallowed as his dark chocolate eyes unraveled my every waking desire. Why did this man have to be the most stunning creature to exist? Why couldn't he have been another average Joe?

"Then let's get started," I said. I attempted to swipe my dagger while grabbing his but he was far too quick—and calculated.

He pressed his dagger against my throat as the rail dug into my lower back. I scooted my boot back and a rock rolled off of the balcony, skipping along the cliff as it made its way down the mountain.

Eli snickered. "You really are untrained."

That boiled my blood. Coming from anyone else, it wouldn't have been a huge deal. Coming from him, however, it was a huge blow. If he'd known I had ripped a man's penis off for him, he would have been singing a different tune.

But I was determined to prove him wrong.

I moved my foot back behind his ankle and swiped, sending him back onto his ass. I pulled my dagger from my sheath and pointed it at his throat while hovering over him. "Not as untrained as you'd like to think."

Knowing his next move, I twisted myself out of his grasp as he sliced his dagger through the air. Eli jumped to his feet and in seconds the two of us were at it again.

Our daggers barely missed each other as we dodged the attempts. I dropped down, sweeping my leg to catch his foot, but he jumped just before I could make contact.

I rolled across the wood deck as he lunged for me, barely missing by just a few inches. I stood to my feet and stepped back. "Is that you not going easy? Come on, Little Shadow."

His eyes blackened as he stepped forward. In seconds, he was swirling black smoke and when he charged at me, I didn't move quick enough. Eli had me pinned to the railing and no matter what I tried, I couldn't get a grip. My dagger was useless against shadows. I knew nothing about their weaknesses.

"All right, you made your damn point," I spat.

He shifted back into his vampire form, appearing as human as he could. "You didn't manage to even pin me down more than once. It should come second nature, Mya.

Until you master that, you will never be able to learn how to subdue a shadow."

I snickered. "I tortured a vampire before I killed him. I'm not a rookie."

His eyebrows shot up, but not out of bewilderment. It was more condescending than that. "Oh, but you can't manage to get a grip on me. Interesting."

I shot him a glare. "It's different. With him, I had my emotions controlling me."

"And with me?"

"With you, I..." I cleared my throat, shoving my dagger into my sheath. "My emotions control me in a different way."

This caught his attention. "Are you saying you want to shag me?"

"Don't flatter yourself." I did, but he didn't need to know that. "With you, I want to strangle you. But I can't because you're not the real enemy here, and deep down I know that. The real enemy is them, those shadows out there. When I killed that vampire, I was fueled by pure anger. He had taken something from me that I had loved. He crushed my world, so I trained hard for months to be able to get revenge."

Eli popped his collar. "Revenge? Did it help?"

I shook my head, eyebrows knotted. "Helped by getting me to work my ass off training. But it didn't erase the pain. It didn't bring back what I loved. It didn't fix my situation. It only made me feel emptier inside, and as much as I hated that vampire, I realized he wasn't the real issue. The real issue is the shadows. They're watching my every move. They're targeting my friends and trying to scare us. And it sucks because I can't do a damn thing about it. Shadows are new. I know not a damn thing about them. I know absolutely *zero* weaknesses."

Eli shoved his hands into his pockets. He seemed to do that quite a bit now, and it told me that he trusted me. Well, maybe a *little.*

"I doubt you're going to tell me any weaknesses."

"I have to know I can trust you first," he said as he looked out from the balcony. "I know we have this truce, but it's a huge step giving out information like that. And even if you have it now, you're not ready to use it. That leaves a lot of time for the shadows to figure out I told you and then use me while they kill you. It's best if I keep that information to myself for now. Until you're ready for this war."

That seemed like a fair option.

Eventually we retreated back inside and found our rooms for the next several days, unpacking all we brought with us. When I finished with my bag, I went to his room and leaned against the doorway.

Eli was staring at something in his hand, but he shook his head and threw it down before he spotted me. "What do you want?"

"I want to know if it's true. You said you want to move back here when this war is over." I crossed my arms.

He rolled his eyes. "Of course. Why wouldn't I mean it? Are you scared because you have nowhere else to go? I can't help you there. You're an adult. I've already done more than enough not killing you for staying in my apartment."

I wanted to beg him to stay, but I couldn't do that anymore.

He wasn't mine to love.

"Why did you move into the apartment?"

He walked over to me. "Because, Mya,—" I hated when he said my name. It felt so disconnected. I wasn't more than an inconvenience to him. "—I wanted to be closer to the city. I see that was my mistake. There's a reason my father left me this mansion. He knew what was best for me. I have no reason to return to the city."

Right. Vampires were supposed to live in solitude because screw socialization, right?

I swallowed. "I'm sorry. I'm sorry that the shadows did this. I can honestly say you didn't deserve any of this."

His eyes roamed my face to find where the lie began, but he never found it. "Go to bed, Little Hanti." He shut the door on me.

I stepped back, frowning at the piece of wood. Fine.

I headed back to my room and glanced at the hall. Little Hunter had just been an insult. For once, he called me Hanti. It'd become a step in the right direction. But why did it also irritate me so much? Because he meant it to tease me, the way I did him by calling him Little Shadow. Well, I called him that because he called me it first.

Deep down, I knew I enjoyed it. It felt more intimate than when he called me Mya. And I knew he'd never call me Love again, so I gave up on trying with that. But why did his death erase just the past year from his life?

Why just me?

That was the answer. Because he had loved me once, and the shadows were doing everything in their power to take away all crutches I had. They wanted to make a spectacle of me. They certainly killed him just to target me.

Would they have done the same to Owen if it had been him over Eli? Possibly. They didn't care who they had to hurt to make me scream.

Eli just happened to be in the wrong place at the wrong time.

039 Thursday, September 6th

My dagger managed to pierce his abdomen, but it didn't make a difference. Eli was *truly* immortal now. Unstoppable.

He grabbed my hand and pulled it out. "Again. You need to master this."

So we went again. He took swings at me but I blocked his blows with my own arms, and just when he had aimed for a lower hit, I spun around with my dagger pointed outward before plunging it into his neck.

The vampire swung his arm back as a reflex, plunging my dagger into Eli's neck.

And I screamed.

My heart was about to jump from my chest as I kept screaming while he grabbed his neck and fell to his knees.

Nothing else mattered. I stumbled to my feet, running towards him. Anyone who got in my way was thrown to the ground. I got there just as he fell, catching him in my arms. "No, no, no. No, you're okay. You'll be fine. You have something for this, right?" I swallowed.

He choked, eyes rolling back into his head.

"Right?" I yelled, starting to cry.

His blood stained my hands and my shirt. I didn't even care.

"You're going to be fine," I choked out.

He tried to groan, tried to shout from the pain of his body attacking the little bits of iron digging through his neck.

I hadn't even paid attention when the immortals began backing away.

A hand landed on my shoulder, and I screamed, "Don't fucking touch me!" I hadn't even registered that they were Hunter's.

I just held Eli, savoring every bit of him. "Don't leave me. Don't you dare effing leave me." I grabbed his face, pressing my forehead against his. "I can't survive without you." As if convincing him, I kissed him. It was a soft yet sweet kiss, one that begged him to stay for me.

But he never *kissed back.*

"Eli," I whispered as I pulled away. He wasn't moving anymore. "No, Eli."

Everything broke inside me.

I shattered *like my bones at that very moment.*

"Mya?" he whispered.

I stumbled away from him. "I'm sorry. I'm so sorry."

"Sorry for what?

"I'm sorry I got you killed." I grabbed my dagger and put it into the sheath around my thigh. "I'm sorry you were turned into a shadow, and I'm sorry your life was obliterated and your memories of the past year were erased."

He tilted his head. "My memories weren't erased. I remember this past year."

"You do?" How long had he known? My heart began pounding rapidly in my chest. "Like what?"

"Like over a year ago, Josh and I were drugged and kidnapped. We managed to escape, however. And we went to a masquerade ball for hunters to target us, although things went south fast. Instead war broke out," he said with so much confidence.

I kept waiting for him to finally say, "And you. I remember you."

But he didn't.

"I remember everything. I'm just not quite sure where you fit in."

My heart shattered again. He remembered everything and everyone *but* me. They truly had ripped away everything that gave me joy. They had taken his, too.

I swallowed. "I don't fit in quite like you think. But that's not truly important. I can make one thing clear, however."

He waited for me to go on.

I put my hands up as if confirming what I said next. "I swear to you that I'm not the bad guy. I'm not the enemy. I never was and I never will be. I won't hurt anyone you care about, either." As much as I tried to come off as the scary one, we both knew I wasn't.

Eli stepped forward, taking enough steps until he was merely inches from my face. "They do say that the most dangerous monsters are those who don't know they have teeth."

In other words, he didn't trust me. He expected me to snap, or to hurt someone eventually. And he was right. I'd let my dagger get into the hands of a vampire who then used my own blade to murder the man I loved. Intentionally or not, it didn't change the outcome. Eli had still been the victim the entire time. I only had myself to blame.

"Let's have a picnic." His words took me out of reality. There was no way he'd just announced that. None.

"A picnic?" I asked. "You're not the picnic type and to have one, you need food, too, which you don't have at the moment." I gestured to the mountain behind us.

"You think I don't keep the fridge here stocked? Vampires need to eat, too." He fixed his button-up and I followed him into the mansion, up the stairs, and into the kitchen. I grabbed what I needed for food, and he looked in the fridge for blood. When he pulled some out, he set it on the counter, eyeing it. "It'll be our little secret."

I wasn't sure what he meant by that but I was afraid to find out. I didn't ask. I focused on making myself chocolate strawberries, a PB&J, as well as some salty chips to top it off.

When I glanced at him, he unbuttoned his cuffs and rolled his sleeves to his elbows. What was it that made men that much hotter when they did that? It was almost the equivalent of a woman undoing the top buttons of her shirt and leaning back onto her hands in the sun as if she wasn't attempting to look more attractive than she was.

After he poured some ice, alcohol, and other ingredients in with his blood, he mixed it around before leading me to a different balcony. This one had been higher, yet smaller. It was much cozier. I'd say intimate, even, but we would never go there.

We sat down at the table and I munched on my food while Eli sipped his drink.

I chewed a little too wildly, and I'd bitten my tongue in the process. I pulled it out to see if it was bleeding, but Eli immediately had already scrambled from the chair and moved himself away. "What the bloody hell, Little Hanti?"

Bloody sounded right.

"What, you think I did this on purpose? Really?"

"I think you're trying to get under my skin."

"By biting my tongue? Really? Eli, I'm a female. I don't have to intentionally hurt myself to bleed. I do it naturally once a month." I took another bite.

But I had intentionally hurt myself in the past and we both were acutely aware of that. It had been something I found myself tempted to do again, yet I fought the urge for the both of us.

His face contorted at that statement. "Period blood is not the same. It smells different, and not a *good* different."

Ah, so that was the million-dollar question. For vampires, it wasn't all black and white. It wasn't *all blood was good blood.* It was more like *some blood was good and other blood smelled awful because of where it* came *from.*

"Eli, I didn't intentionally bite my own tongue. My point stands. I was genuinely enjoying this view with my lunch." I snorted as if it was the most amusing thing to hear his accusations. I quickly sucked the blood before he said something else labeled unremarkable.

Eli sipped his blood and carefully walked to the rail. As he admired the beauty, I admired him. Once mine, and never forgotten.

He turned his body and leaned back against it, crossing one ankle over the other. "What is there to know at this point? You accidentally injure yourself and then I'm left here wondering why I want to taste your blood so desperately. It doesn't make sense. I've been around other hunters in peril. I've smelt their blood, but nothing has ever been quite like yours."

I had an answer, but I couldn't reveal that to him. He

wouldn't take that news so well. "Beats me."

"Beats you?"

I shrugged. "Beats me."

Eli shook his head, looking out upon the horizon. "Tell me what it is that makes you special."

"All I know is my parents gave me to a human. I was raised that way. There's nothing more I can add to that statement." Although I was certain there was more to it. The shadows picked on me for more than just that reason alone, but I wouldn't discuss that with Eli now. Even my friends didn't believe there was anything else about me. I was normal. As normal as a girl could get—seeing creatures that didn't exist in the human eye.

"You're not the chosen one?" he joked.

"Even if I was, I wouldn't tell you that." I shot him a cunning smile as I took the last bite of my sandwich.

Eli nodded a little before his gaze rested on the mansion behind me. "And what abo—"

"Stop talking. Just let this moment be."

And like that, he shut up. He didn't make any snide comments or irritate me further. He instead kept his mouth shut as I pondered how my life ended up here. A year ago, I had barely found out I was a Hanti. Now here I was, endlessly training for a war that I was at the heart of, and possibly the cause of.

Lucky me.

A year ago, I was certain I wanted to be a fashion designer. Today, I wasn't certain of what exactly I wanted. My dreams were ripped away, and I was given this ultimate title of being Hanti to save humanity from what—I didn't know. Kaofi weren't all bad. Neither were all Hanti. And maybe there was a reason I hadn't grown up with skewed views because

I could see Kaofi for who they really were. They were like us. People with different DNA, and they wanted to love as much as the rest of us.

But even if that dream had been torn away from me, I still wanted to pursue it in some form. Even if I wasn't supposed to anymore.

My parents were dead. Both of my boyfriends were killed. Death followed me even when I hadn't been entirely aware of my ancestry. No matter where I ran, I couldn't escape the inevitable.

Just when I thought I had a family, I lost it. That was all my life consisted of. I believed things happened for a reason and that reason was that I was meant to get used to being alone sooner rather than later. I was born a Hanti, and we didn't get the opportunity to watch people find their happy ever afters. I'd still be alone in the end. And maybe my reason for being here was to discover my abilities. But it wouldn't last forever.

It never did.

Eventually they all would slowly stop talking to me or the group would just fall apart and I'd be left wondering what happened. Every friend I'd ever made had eventually left. Even Juliet gave up. They *always* left. I was just used to it by now that I expected it.

So I didn't get my hopes up.

I didn't get attached.

I distanced myself to prepare for what was already paved from the start.

I'd certainly never make the same mistake of falling for Eli again. But making him fall for me? That could happen. And I needed to make it happen if I wanted to get any real information to stop this war, to control the shadows. It was for a *good* cause.

The wind picked up and as it did, the temperature dropped.

Higher elevation meant we were closer to winter, to put it simply.

And oh how I despised winter.

The cold did bother me. The cold was something I despised just as much as the heat, and with monsoon coming to an end, all my dreams were slipping away.

I'd had all these plans with Eli over the summer but his death squashed those into dust. Fall was coming, but up here, fall didn't exist. We skipped the transitioning season and went for the freezing temperatures and the icicles.

And maybe if I had been an active kid during winter, I might have enjoyed it. But snow sports were not my thing. Snow sports were not the same as summer sports.

Snow sports were a cruel mix between being too cold and being too hot at once. You could never find the right temperature or the middle ground. At least from what little I did do, I never could. And if you went snowboarding or skiing, you had to be careful putting on too many layers because if you got too hot, you could sweat and that led to other bad winter things. Hypothermia, or frostbite.

Summer...

Now that—that came with sports that made sense. Swimming, for example. Surfing. Wakeboarding. All these activities keep you cool enough under the summer heat.

However, with the high temperatures came the risk of heat exhaustion.

And I'd been unfortunate enough to experience that.

As a child, I'd come up with the idea of getting as hot as possible right before swimming. That meant no rolling windows down or turning on the AC. And I took it like a mantra.

Until a few years back, I went swimming with Juliet, and while she had taken her time blowing up her paddleboard, I waited in the hot sun. It hit me, and I was lightheaded and unable to speak properly. I was on the verge of passing out, and I had no idea what it was at first. At first I thought it was just a dizzy spell, and so I sat. But that only made it worse.

Juliet helped me to the water and when I stepped in, I cooled off and immediately I could stand on my own and speak coherently. I knew I'd experienced heat exhaustion and I never dared do that again.

With Eli, it was different. He made my body heat up the way the sun did, and he made it impossible to think of the right things to say. But in all honesty, I liked the way he made my body feel. I'd never be able to tell him that because my goal was to accept the death of the man and move on.

It was just easier said than done.

040 Friday, September 7th

Lying back on dead grass, I stared up at the sky. "Is the temperature always this unpredictable?"

Eli held a little bit of mischief in his eyes. "It fluctuates a little bit. But it doesn't get too unpredictable until winter fully hits."

Right then and there, the sprinklers came on. I screamed and jumped up, giving Eli the glare. "What the hell? You could have warned me!"

"Could have. Didn't want to." He shrugged.

The lack of empathy irked me, and there had been only one way to combat that. I had to show him I wasn't taking it personally. Instead, I walked into the sprinklers and faced Eli while pretending it didn't bother me. It was still Arizona, and the weather here was warm enough for this kind of activity. It was never too early or too late for water fun.

He began pulling his shoes off, then his socks. "It's the perfect time to get a little wet." He ran into the sprinklers.

It was odd, seeing Eli of all people enjoying himself. Sure,

I had seen him like this once. But he had become a whole new person. He tried to kill me and scare me away when he came back from the dead. To see this darker, sadder version of him enjoy some sprinklers was heartwarming to say the least.

He ran around, expecting me to chase him.

I did.

I chased him through the sprinklers and eventually I tackled him to the ground, straddling him and pinning his arms. "I win."

Mischief gleamed in his eye. "I don't think so."

My vision blurred a bit and his voice grew quieter—more muffled as my eyelids grew heavy. "I'm not sure if this is supposed to happen or what you're doing, but we had a truce," I forced out.

His brows knitted together as he tilted his head.

The world around me went dark, and in place of it was a new world. No, it wasn't just any world. It was my own head, except it had been under attack.

Shadows emerged from every corner and I reached for my dagger but it wasn't there. Why wasn't it there?

Now powerless, I backed away.

They stalked closer, darkness closing in as they engulfed all the light left in my path. I crouched down into a fetal position and covered my head as their cold fingers reached for me, pulling at my hair strands, and tugging my clothes. They aimed to devour me and leave me with nothing left. Not even a heartbeat.

041 Friday, September 7th

Something bright blinded the shadows. They screeched and cowered, backing away from me.

I looked up as they vanished, and Eli was standing there with something in hand. "I need you to trust me." He crouched beside me. "I'm going to do something, and I need you to trust it's going to keep you safe."

After what I'd just experienced, I had no other options.

I nodded.

Eli reached forward, grabbing my head. Walls began to go up around us, and it was uncomfortable at first but when they were built he stepped back. "You're going to wake up now."

And I did. When I opened my eyes, I was on the couch in the mansion, Eli leaning over me. His expression had been that of genuine concern.

I sat up quickly, gripping the edge of couch cushions as I scanned the room. "What did you do? What the hell was that?"

Eli grabbed my legs and moved them as he sat. "I never explained quite the extent of how powerful shadows really are. We can access minds. Our main source of fear is getting into people's heads and screwing with their mental state. I knew the shadows were after you but I forgot to keep them from accessing your mind."

I'd felt violated. I'd felt so violated the way they had stolen my own body from me the way they did. They attacked, and for what? To see me beg for mercy. To see me scream. To see me become nothing but a battered vessel of a woman.

"Correct," Eli said. "And what I had to do was...create my own blockade around your mind. They can't access your head from here and it's only a matter of time before they figure out I'm the reason. They're going to find out that I'm not on their side and they *will* use me against you when they do."

That sounded way worse than what had gone down inside my head. As if we needed more reasons to run. As if we needed more reasons to fight. Aside from training for this war and figuring out what controls them, now I was going to constantly worry for Eli's safety.

"It is worse. They're not kind creatures. They never show mercy." He rubbed his eyes with his thumb and forefinger. "*We* are not kind creatures."

Shivers ran up my spine as I started to question what was going on. He was talking to me. Except I hadn't said any of it out loud.

He sat back. "The block protects you from them, but it also gives me access to your thoughts. I hear everything going on in that pretty little head of yours."

Everything? I wasn't sure how I felt about that. What other choice did I have, though?

Right. Control the shadows, then win this war. That would be the only way he could safely remove himself from my head.

"Then that begs the question. How far does this thing go? If I'm in a closed room, can you hear my thoughts?"

"Yes. Because if you're in a closed room, I still have to have that block up. The second it comes down, they attack." He gave me a look like I was the dumbest person he'd ever met.

I stood from the couch and went straight to the kitchen, ignoring his insults.

After cooking myself something basic like pasta and barbecue chicken, I sat with my plate. I decided to scream inside my head as I snuck a glance at Eli, who then winced. A triumphant smile appeared on my face as I thought of all the new possibilities this could entail.

I just hoped he didn't hear the thoughts I didn't want him to know.

"I'll eventually hear them. They always slip." He came into the kitchen and sat in the chair beside me. "Well, eat." He gestured to the plate.

As much as I wanted to defy him, I couldn't help it with the growling in my stomach. I ate the pasta first per usual, and then I grabbed the drumsticks and ate the meat off the bone. It tasted amazing, too.

When I finished with my food, I licked all my fingers. "That was absolutely a delicious lunch. Or dinner. Whatever time it is, it was perfect. I cook a mean, basic white girl meal if I do say so myself."

Eli leaned closer, and I thought he was going to kiss me but he licked the extra barbecue sauce off of my cheek. "You're messy."

I swallowed, trying to keep all my feelings at bay so he

wouldn't sense them and use them against me. But deep down, I was melting on the spot. Wasn't I supposed to be making him fall for me? Shit, he heard that.

He smirked. "Indeed. But I think that'll be a little difficult." He stood from the chair and grabbed my plate. "And for the record, I like messy."

My entire body fired up. Every inch of me was a burning flame. Why did he have to go and say things like that to bring me to my knees? No doubt if I stood up, I'd collapse.

Eli turned to face me. "Tell me about Owen. How did your boyfriend die?"

"You heard."

"I want it from your perspective." He shrugged like losing my boyfriend hadn't been a big deal. It had been. I'd spiraled, and I turned to drinking to cope.

I averted my gaze toward the floor. "Well, let me remind you that Owen and I had only been dating for barely a month. It was meant to be a summer fling. But somewhere along the way, it dug deeper. We were going up to the forest to have a date, but it was raining and Owen pulled over to try and find some road markers. I was already tired, so I got out and decided to dance in the rain to combat it."

Eli leaned against the counter. "And?"

"At first, he questioned what I was doing. Thought I was crazy, and even got a little argumentative. Then he joined me and we let our troubles wash away. Together, we rejuvenated so we could get back on the road later on with a clear head. But we'd parked right at a curve and the car was driving too fast. In seconds, the headlights came flying around the corner and I didn't have time to stop Owen."

Thump—the sound of his body hitting the car before falling to the ground. The car disappeared.

That didn't stop the rain. Everything went to shit from that moment on. My screams could be heard for miles, and even if the rain washed away my tears, my face still prickled. Owen had died on the spot, and his blood still stained the pavement to this day.

Now that I knew the shadows did it, I had more incentive to win this war. Not just for my sake, or Eli's, but Owen's, too.

"Is that why he's haunting you?"

I nodded a little. "Like he has to avenge his own death. I'll do it for him, though. We're not going to let the shadows win. Owen never deserved such a fate just for being my boyfriend."

Eli shook his head. "Nobody deserves that fate. Except for a select few."

A select few indeed. Like shadows who targeted innocent people. Shadows who targeted their own allies. Shadows who targeted anyone just to gain something in return even if it harmed those they targeted.

A thought occurred to me. If Eli didn't remember the past year of his life with me in it, that meant he could never explain the picture he took of me in the forest—or more importantly what happened *after.*

"What picture?" Eli asked.

I pulled a blanket over my legs to warm myself up, picking at the fabric. "You took a picture of me. Said I had modeled but then Josh went berserk and a Hanti attacked. I sensed something else happened after that. Unfortunately, I no longer remember it."

"When was this?"

I shrugged. "I'm not really sure. I asked about it last year. Around the same time. Still haven't gotten closer."

Eli tapped his chin but no thoughts came to him. I'd lost the memory and now he had, too. All I could remember were bits and pieces and none of them were any good. Not a single memory following this was any good. They'd all consisted of blood and screaming and horrors I didn't want to relive. However, I needed to somehow remember them if I was going to gain more answers and possibly win this war.

"Maybe I can help. Get some of my own memories back," he said.

I gave him a slight nod and pulled my knees to my chest. "Then it's settled. We need to somehow figure out what happened during the summer that Owen was murdered, the same one where I ran into you. I have a feeling that we play even bigger roles in this forsaken game of the shadows than we ever guessed. I no longer want to be just another puppet for the shadows to toy with."

042 Saturday, September 8th

As the sun had set behind the horizon, the moon leaked in through the windows. The power had been out all day and Eli was struggling with getting a hold of someone to deal with it.

Rich vampire problems I suppose. Or would it be rich vampire *and* shadow problems?

"Can you be quiet for two bloody seconds?" he growled.

After a few minutes of silence, he hung up the phone. "I've been on hold for two bloody hours! Does anyone in this state work at a power company?"

When I opened my mouth to say something, thunder boomed and lightning struck not long after. Rain began pelting the roof and everything outside the mansion. "Well, what use would they be now in this weather? We're all the way out in the middle of the mountains and we have no power. In fact, we're supposed to leave here tomorrow. So what good would it be now? Just light some damn candles and deal with it. We had power outages all the time when I was growing up. They're not bad." I sipped some of my water as I grabbed a towel from the laundry.

Eli gave me a look. "Where do you suppose you're going?"

"To take a bath. I still need to take a bath after today's training. I smell like a sweaty oaf." I scrunched my nose in disgust. "I'm taking candles with me."

I took a few candles to the bathroom and lit them, placing them on the shelf by the tub. I started up the bath and stripped down, slipping into the warm tub.

Closing my eyes, I relaxed and slid under the water until the world couldn't hear me scream.

Down in the abyss of my soul, the nightmares haunted me. The moment Owen had been struck by the car, and the moment Eli had been killed by my own dagger. Both had been my fault. Both should have blamed me and kept their distance, yet they were trusting me to win a war they had been dragged into the middle of—again, because of me.

I didn't forget the agonizing pain of claws slicing into my back as I screamed for someone to help me. I didn't forget the horrifying experience of being trapped inside my own head with nothing but the nightmares that had plagued my waking and sleeping hours.

I wasn't safe. I never would be until the shadows were under our control.

I came back up and pushed my hair back, glancing over at Eli. I squealed as I covered my chest. "What the hell are you doing in here?"

He wasn't actually looking at me though. "I knew they did horrid things, but never to that extent. For that, I'm sorry."

"Sorry?"

He nodded a little, his face only half lit by the flames. "I've been around monsters for months, being trained and programmed to think and act exactly like shadows. When I found you in my apartment, my first instinct was to kill you. I only knew you were a hunter, and I had to do anything to protect myself. But I'm starting to see that maybe you're not so...bad. You're less of what they say and more of what I see." He scoffed. "Not to say you're not unbearable most of the time. You just don't deserve to die for it."

"Thanks?" I slipped further down until the water covered my body.

"But you never deserved that. Your biggest crime is being insufferable. Not enough to warrant such...suffering." He sat just outside the tub and leaned his upper body against it. "And as much as this hurts to admit, it's only fair I'm a little honest with you given that I can see all your honest thoughts about me." He lifted his head more.

I leaned closer to the side of the tub, gripping it with both hands and resting my chin. "Which is?"

His eyes darkened—or maybe I'd been hallucinating. It was hard to tell in this lighting. "If the shadows ever fuck with you like that again, I will find it within my power to burn their entire world to the ground."

As tough as I was and as independent as my mom had taught me to be, something inside me warmed at the idea. Even as much as he hated my guts, he hated theirs *more*.

"Now I must ask," I whispered. "What was the world like back then? What did you notice the most?"

"Women." He wasted no time giving me that answer.

I furrowed my brows. "Women? Really?"

"Really. Women have changed fashion many times over the years. And men, too, of course, but women have changed the most." He shifted his gaze toward mine. By now, I was too close to the tub and he was not sitting up high enough to be able to see below my neck.

Ah, yes. From big gowns, corsets, and crinoline to just basic crop tops and shorts. Or in my case, I still wore corsets from time to time.

Eli cleared his throat. "There was a day in which men used to fantasize about seeing women's ankles. That was not me, no. I had seen enough by the time I was born. Women liked to throw themselves at me. Part of the vampire charm."

"How old are you?" My eyes narrowed at the thought.

He shrugged a little. "I was born in 1852."

"Ew. You're an old man." Why had this just occurred to me?

He chuckled. "Depends on your version of old. Vampires age at a different rate than humans. Some species age quickly and mature within a day or few weeks, only to die weeks later. However, vampires live forever, unless killed by your blade. But because our lifespan is so long and stretches until eternity, we mature a lot slower."

"Physically and mentally, how old are you?"

He leaned closer. "Twenty-two." He reached his hand into my hair, tangling his fingers. "I thought you knew everything about me."

My breath nearly caught in my throat, my eyes growing wider. My plan was shattering like a mirror. "I knew dark things. I never learned your age." Dark things, like the way his mother died. It was not something I'd ever wish on my worst enemy. And Eli played that role perfectly and yet all I felt for him was empathy and despair.

In this moment, however, I felt fire in a few different areas of my body.

In a perfect world, Eli would lean in and take control of the situation. He'd kiss me with the same amount of rage he had for the shadows. I'd return the kiss without hesitation, relishing in the taste of the past.

But this wasn't a perfect world.

Eli didn't remove his hand, nor did he make any moves to scoot further even after knowing I was daydreaming about kissing him. "Tell me your darkest trauma. Since you know mine," he said in a quiet voice.

Almost as soon as he said it, he let go of me and twisted his body until he was facing the door. He leaned his head back onto the edge of the tub, right beside my hands, staring at the ceiling.

I nodded a little. "It's hard to pick. There's so many." It was meant to be a joke, but he never laughed.

Once I had settled on just one, I shifted my body before releasing a sigh. "When I was younger, life wasn't any easier than it is now. People always say they miss being a child and they miss when things were more innocent for them. But unfortunately for me, that's not true. Not every child has a fond childhood to look back on.

"I love my mom and I am so happy she chose me. But on the same coin, I also wish I'd had a dad like all the other children. I wish I could have been the daddy's girl other girls were. How does the saying go? You miss what you never had?"

"I don't think that's a saying at all."

"But I still felt like—like part of me was missing." I sighed. "It's silly to everyone else, of course. But to me, it was never silly. I never questioned too much about being adopted because I thought maybe I looked like my dad, and when I asked about him, mom never really answered. I assumed it was another case of a dad running away." I tapped my fingers along the edge.

Eli glanced at me. "It's not silly."

Not silly. At least he thought so.

It wasn't something I liked admitting to anyone, and certainly never to my own mother. I didn't want to make her feel bad that I didn't have a dad. Not that I ever really blamed her. But it just never felt right.

"And that's what happened. I spent so much time looking through my mom's yearbooks and photos and social media. I tried to hunt him down so I could speak to him. I found one guy from her past, and even managed his number. He had other kids and a wife. He was excited to have these kids, too, and it made me question why he didn't want me.

"I did what any daughter would do and I texted his number. But he had no idea who I was even when I said I might be his daughter. He didn't even reply back to my text. He simply disappeared and that was that. At that age, I barely understood and I certainly didn't immediately assume I was adopted. I was too afraid to ask my mom about it, either. The only thought going through a mind like mine was that my own dad didn't want me. It messed me up for years."

He leaned his head forward. "How old were you?"

I remembered it like it had been yesterday. "Sixteen. Actually, fifteen but I was a month from turning sixteen. I contacted him before my birthday, asking him if he knew what was coming up."

"And so," he started, "you grew up for years, thinking your own father forgot about you."

I nodded just a bit. "It didn't help. As a child, you blame yourself because that's all you can do. You think they left because of you. It wasn't my idea of an ideal childhood and it's still painful. Even if I know I was really adopted, the truth is my real father is dead. I still will never know what that kind of love is like, or how that kind of relationship can make a girl feel."

I never blamed my mom even when I found out I was adopted. When she told me, it made sense. The man didn't know me. No father left me except my real one, along with my real mother. And I couldn't have blamed her for it because she couldn't make up lies to make me feel better. There had never been a man to get her pregnant and leave in the first place.

But as a child, I still always craved that father-daughter bond. And sure, maybe it was easy for people to tell me that it wasn't a big deal and I could get over it, but it wasn't so easy. And it was even harder to explain that to people who already had a father or who'd been happy without one. I was neither of those.

It became my normal, but I didn't have to like it.

"That's it. My biggest trauma is never having a father. Maybe I didn't scream and cry when it happened. Maybe I didn't drink myself into oblivion. However, it's something I will never be able to have and I'll always wish for. I'll always wonder 'what if' because that's what I was given. And knowing I'm adopted makes it far worse. I know why my parents gave me up but it didn't hurt less and it still has a part of me questioning my worth and if there's possibly more to the story and that they didn't just give me up for that one reason alone."

And sometimes you'd never find the answers. You'd never find peace in a situation like that.

The biggest trauma was not always the one you'd expect it to be, not always the most painful or the one that had you screaming for someone to come back from the dead.

It was the one that you blamed yourself for and the one that lingered the longest.

It was the one you'd *never* be able to fix.

043 Saturday, September 8th

"You should know I despise being asked questions about history," Eli said as he walked into the living room with his glass of blood.

The power was still out, and I had to wrap my hair in a towel to dry it a bit quicker. It was too cold to leave it out to air dry all night long, and Eli also mentioned something about keeping my wet hair off his furniture.

"And why is that?"

"History bores me. People think I should know but I don't care all that much." He shrugged as he sat.

I shivered. "I'll keep that in mind for the future then. In the meantime, we need to pass the time. Power's still out."

He snickered. "Obviously. I'm not blind."

"You are in the dark," I joked. "Or maybe you aren't. I forget you can see in the dark. Shadow and vampire." I gestured to him as I grabbed the bowl of chips. "Now what should we do? Before you say I should sleep because it's almost midnight, I'm not even tired. I'm just trying to pass the time. I can sleep in the car on the ride home."

"Do you promise?" He laughed.

I shot him a glare, which I knew he could see. I just couldn't quite see him all that *well,* aside from the few candles we'd lit.

I got up from the couch and walked to the window, peering out into the darkness. "You sure they don't know we're here? They attacked my mind."

"I'm sure. You'd know if they knew. We can attack minds from far away—the outside. We don't necessarily need a location to attack mentally speaking."

But what if they were holding back? What if they had been hiding amongst the darkness and they planned to terrorize us a little bit before they stole our entire sanity? Shadows were evil and far more calculated than I'd ever expected from them.

"Then get back from the bloody window," he said.

I threw him another glare, but the shattering of glass echoed as an arm shot through the window and grabbed me, trying to yank me through. They'd succeeded, too.

Pieces of glass scraped along and sliced into my skin as the shadows dragged me through the dark. I tried to pull back and find my way out of this situation. My dagger wouldn't help. And without any light, what could I do?

Rely on Eli, sure. But that was too much to ask for and embarrassing.

My towel had been ripped from my hair and left by the window. I tried to grab hold of the fountain and free myself, but it wasn't long before Eli was already there, yanking me from the shadow's grasp. If they didn't know about his disobedience, they certainly knew now.

"Eli! Watch out!" I yelled as more shadows emerged from the trees. I'd smelled so much smoke, and I knew they'd been nearby. But Eli hadn't wanted to heed my warning.

He turned and dodged the few running at him. "Run, Mya!"

I didn't have to be told twice.

I booked it into the trees, through the shadows. I dodged branches the best I could but a few snagged my clothes. I glanced back every now and then only to have my wet hair cling to my face and obstruct my vision.

I reminded myself over and over that they couldn't kill Eli. They could torture him, or do horrifying things, but they'd never be able to kill him. Was that any better though?

No. I couldn't leave him alone. He'd promised he'd defy his nature for me and I'd be a fool if I didn't do the same.

I grabbed onto a branch to stop myself on a whim before I turned and faced the shadows. "Come and get me, mothereffers!" I pulled out my dagger, knowing it wouldn't do me much good. I still had to try. I wasn't going to go down without a fight.

Behind every puppet was a puppeteer. If shadows were the puppets, who was the *puppeteer*?

"Mya!" Eli yelled as he ran towards me. "What did I tell you?" He grabbed my wrist and pulled me behind him as we ran through the forest. "You never listen, do you?"

I swallowed. "And what, leave you? You wouldn't do that to me so why would I do it to you?" I glanced back but faced forward as Eli dragged us through, pushing our speed to its limits.

"I know how they think. I'm the one who can't die. You can! This isn't up for argument!" He stopped and wrapped his arm around my waist before grabbing onto a branch and hoisting us up. He climbed higher into the tree with me not far behind, and when we got high enough, we stopped and held our breaths. Well, I held *mine.*

I wasn't sure how they searched for what they wanted, but I didn't dare make noise or move a muscle. It wasn't worth my life.

Something slithered up my ankle and I almost squirmed, but Eli's hand covered my mouth. I wasn't sure if that was a snake or something else. Snake? Snakes didn't slither up pine trees. What the hell was it? I'd feel better if it had been a snake! At least then I'd know what it was.

It couldn't have been a shadow, because it would know I was here whether I made noise or not. It was something else. Something that lived amongst this forest daily.

Before I screamed or wiggled my body, I gripped the branches and filled my head with something else. Anything that was enough of a distraction. Or someone, in my case—like Eli.

I pictured the memories of us, memories when Eli and I had been physically close. His hands all over my body, his lips all over my skin. It certainly worked to remind me that I was safe now. Or as safe as I could be, in a tree, hiding from shadows.

In my head, instead of allowing myself to interrupt Eli when he got home late and wanted sex, I gave in. In this version, I let him do what he wanted to me. Deep down, I wished he'd do it all over again, but that wasn't plausible. Not in my reality. My reality had always been crushing and this was only a small example of that.

His hand disappeared from my mouth and I held onto the branches.

It didn't stop the memories from taking hold the way they always did—harsh and without permission. Reminding me of my worth, I was left screaming and crying inside my head as I watched Eli drop to the ground all over again.

He stopped moving *in my arms* and the Hanti ripped me from him before I had a chance to give him a proper burial. That was the last memory I had of him before he showed up to kill me.

"We were friends, weren't we?" he whispered in my ear.

"Something like that."

Nausea swirled in my stomach as the forest grew eerily silent. Where were the shadows, and why weren't they coming? Running? Attacking? They weren't making a single sound. What did that mean?

"I need you to trust me," Eli said.

I looked at him. "Eli, I already trust you."

"Good." He immediately shifted into shadow form, slipping through the darkness with me in his grasp. It all happened too quickly for me to understand where we were going or what was happening.

All that touched me was thick chill and crowned panic.

As we came out, trees stood in front, but behind us was the side of the mountain.

Eli looked back, not a hair out of place. "I need you to hang on." Before I asked questions, he wrapped his arms around my form and threw us off the cliff.

Wind rushed at us.

I wrapped my arms around Eli as we fell into a void.

Then the bite and trembling I'd felt just moments earlier brushed by. Then nothing.

We never hit the ground, but rather landed softly.

When we stopped, we were in some place I didn't recognize. Where the hell did we end up?

"This is further from the mansion, but you'll have to keep an open mind," he said as he returned to vampire form.

Unsure of what he meant, I wanted to protest, but he didn't give me the chance. We were squeezing between rocks and hard places. Literally, too.

When we were far enough, Eli turned to face me. "They shouldn't be able to find us here."

"Why? Where did we go?" I swallowed.

Eli glanced back, and that's when I heard it. The rushing of water. We were near a river. It glowed a faint blue, illuminating the rock surrounding us. When I turned my head up towards the sky, I realized I couldn't see the sky. It was dark, and even then I should have been able to spot the stars and the moon.

"We're at the base of the mountains." Eli pointed to the walls. "Those are the mountains. This is the river. We're far below the forest. The shadows won't find us here because this is the opposite direction we ran." He pointed to the river next. "And shadows can't touch water."

Shadows couldn't touch water.

A weakness. Eli had revealed to me one of their weaknesses.

Why couldn't they touch water?

Like the blink of an eye, something faint came into view. I couldn't quite grasp it, but it appeared like a tether—from me to Eli. No, that didn't quite look right. It traveled from him to me.

Why? How?

Because he had revealed a weakness. He had made himself vulnerable in my presence. He had willingly lent me his most intimate emotions.

He stepped away from the river. "It's like...quicksand. We sink to the bottom and we get stuck there. And as Kaofi, we don't die. But we also can't swim. All we can do is sink and spend eternity at the bottom of the water. It's a cruel fate."

A cruel fate indeed. And yet one idea to get rid of the shadows. However, to do that, we'd first need to control them and lure them into the water. I'd be able to bring this back to the Hanti. We were taking a step in the right direction.

"We're safe down here," he said.

"I'm safe. You're not." I pulled him further from the water. "Which is ridiculous, but I feel responsible for you. You shouldn't have to put me first. You're the one they killed first."

He leaned back against the rock wall. "My first worry is making sure you're safe. Your safety is much more important, Little Hanti, and you can't fight me on this."

My safety was more important. Had Eli really just said my safety was more important? No, I'd misheard that.

"No, you didn't. You're the one in danger of dying." He turned to face me but his body never lifted from the rock. "And we should really talk about those thoughts you're having of me."

"What thoughts?" My cheeks burned as I already knew what he meant.

He took a few slow steps towards me. "You know which ones."

After swallowing my humiliation, I straightened my back. "You're attractive, Eli. I'll admit that much. But I still hate you all the same."

He laughed. "Excuses."

"Do you hate me?" I crossed my arms.

Eli closed the gap between us and leaned in, whispering, "More than you'll ever know."

It didn't surprise me in the least bit. He'd hated me from

day one. Both day ones, or was it three now? I couldn't quite remember the first time we met but I wondered if there was some hatred lingered there as well. Maybe it was our fate to always meet in less than wanted circumstances.

"Are we sleeping down here?" I asked to break up the tension.

He pulled back. "I don't think we'll be sleeping much. It's already the middle of the night."

It was more like the middle of the morning, given midnight had passed. But I wouldn't say that out loud. I didn't need to anyway. He heard.

The two of us sat down but we kept our distance from the water. However, I couldn't take my eyes off it. The river had been the most beautiful thing I'd ever seen. Why did it glow like that? If it had been just a little warmer, I'd go swimming in it.

"What if the water isn't deep enough? What if you can touch? Can't you go in the shallow part and be fine?" I asked him.

Eli shook his head. "Water absorbs shadow. Even if we take human form, or in my case vampire form, it senses the shadow form and without even trying, we revert back to it and it takes control. It sucks us in, to the deepest part until we get stuck at the bottom. Shadows are no match against water."

"And cement pools? Kiddie pools? The sprinklers?"

"The sprinklers aren't bodies of water. Kiddie and swimming pools don't do anything because there's nowhere for us to go. But you don't find shadows lurking in rich people's swimming pools. You find them in the forests. Mountains. And those are where the dangerous waters are. We must steer clear, Little Hanti, or I will meet a fate much worse than death."

Strings

"*We lost track of them.*"

Not the words I wanted to hear. They lost track of Mya and Eli, and who was to blame this time?

The shadows.

Worthless. Good for nothing but wrecking plans and failing the simplest of tasks. All I'd asked of them was to kill Mya, but even that deemed too difficult.

The girl had been trained for barely a year and these vermin had been trained their entire lives.

How had they become that incompetent?

"Find them," I seethed. "The next time I see your face, she better be dust or I will have you banished to the depths of the ocean. Clear?" I faced the shadow as he gulped down his fear. *Good.* I loved the taste of it.

"Crystal, master."

044 Sunday, September 9th

I'd slept most of the car ride back home as I promised Eli. He appreciated that, and he made it clear, too.

We'd gone back up the mountains when the sun began to rise. Although it took hours before we saw any light illuminating down the side of the cliffs.

I'd even discovered how Eli traveled so quickly. He essentially glitched through dark spots. It explained the anxiety in my bones and the frost coating my skin.

As we got in the front door, Owen was waiting as if he'd been a worried parent. "Where did you guys go? I couldn't find you anywhere."

"I think that was the point," I said. Not that it did anything. The shadows *still* found us.

Eli snickered. "Relax, lover boy. I got her back in one piece."

Owen shot him a glare before stepping towards me. I'd noticed the feelings right away—or lack of feelings. When I'd left this apartment, I still felt things for Owen. Those things had been a result of rekindling what we lost before he was hit and killed, but now as I stood here, I felt nothing of that sort.

Eli snorted. "That's rich."

Owen tilted his head towards Eli. "What?"

"Nothing," I blurted. "He was talking about something else."

I shot Eli a glare before turning back to Owen. He had something he wanted to say, I just wasn't sure what it was.

"I can't do it with the vampire watching. *Or* the shadow." He grabbed my wrist and pulled me out of the apartment. Loved talking to dead people out in public.

In fact, I loved talking to *any* Kaofi out in public.

I gestured back at the apartment. "What is this about? Eli didn't hurt me or kill me. We had to go somewhere a lot more private to train so the shadows wouldn't attack." What I didn't tell him was that they did attack us regardless. "You couldn't come. I'm sorry but that was just his rule. Since the shadows clearly have an eye on you as much as they do the rest of us. The less people that went, the better."

He rubbed his face. "I was trying to research the shadows. How to control them. I don't need that bloke listening in."

Because Eli was a shadow. Right. What I also kept to myself was that Eli *was* listening in. He didn't have a choice. And Owen couldn't know that.

"You should know that we found a weakness. Well, Eli *told* me. One of the shadows' weaknesses is water. Not cement pools or little solid pools. I'm talking lakes and rivers and...the ocean." The ocean was a guarantee they'd never return. It was so vast and deep. So deep that even the sun couldn't reach how far down it went.

His eyes narrowed. "You trust him? You trust him to

actually tell you their weakness?"

"Of course I trust him." It was difficult to explain to Owen. In his mind, I had no reason to trust Eli. Eli had almost killed me if Owen hadn't stepped in. I didn't entirely blame Owen for being this upset with me. He had a right to believe Eli was lying.

But something buried inside told me that Eli had told the truth. Owen didn't experience what we did. He didn't see how close we had gotten, and Eli could try to deny it but the past four days were different to us. We'd become...*frenemies*—in a way.

"This is what I was afraid of Mya. You're trusting him too much because he used to screw you." He ran his hands through his hair.

Absolutely uncalled for. Was he calling me a slut? Saying I only trusted men who'd screw me? What in the hell?

I swallowed, pushing that thought away. "No, that isn't true. Sure I had possibly cared for him once but this time it's different. We hate each other but we also know that we are not each other's enemy in this war. That's the only reason."

He shrugged. "Maybe. But not with you."

"What the hell? What has gotten into you? Are you mad that he helped me train? Are you jealous of him or something? He's been a trained fighter since birth. He's spent his whole life hiding and running from Hanti like me. You should know, you were just like him! He has the skills needed to teach me how to be better at this and why can he teach me better than you? Because he's a shadow now, Owen. He is the one who knows their secrets. He is the perfect ally."

"But also the perfect enemy, Mya. You said it yourself. He knows their secrets. Why do you think you're special?"

The tears threatened right at the rims of my eyes. "Because

I was special to you once, *and* to him. Why should it change now?" I believed I could put things back to the way they were. I desperately needed that.

Owen didn't say much. I wish he would because the silence only felt much more overbearing and crushing.

"What the hell did you want to tell me? Did you find out how to control them?" I needed to change the subject before I said or did something I'd absolutely regret.

He ran a hand down his face and shook his head. "No luck."

"Let me give you some." I pointed to the apartment. "The shadows are not the ones we need to fear."

"Mya—"

"No. They're not the ones behind all of this. A whole species doesn't decide on their own that I'm suddenly the enemy for what, being the easiest target of a Hanti? There's more to it. I believe someone else is controlling the shadows. A puppeteer if you will. We need to find them and steal that control."

I knew Eli would suggest that we relinquish the control altogether and shadows might actually be tolerable to coexist with. But that wasn't a risk I could take after what they did to him, or me.

And then it occurred to me that Eli could have possibly met or heard about this puppeteer. And he would have kept that secret to himself for as long as he wanted.

Owen tilted his head. "You believe someone else is behind this? Like a shadow king?"

"If that's what you'd like to call them, then yes. Someone is guiding them. Every army, every group, every legion needs a leader or a mastermind behind the plans. Someone is at the head of this war and we need to find them. Before they kill me." I ran the side of my forefinger over my upper lip to wipe away the sweat. "I'm still trying to figure out how I fit in there." Because I was simply a Hanti and one raised by humans. Why was I that important to target? It still never added up.

We eventually retreated back into the apartment and Eli didn't say a word even after every thought he heard. What could he have said? I didn't want Owen to know everything that happened at the mansion and neither did Eli. Thankfully.

Cramping stabbed my uterus, and immediately I grabbed my phone to check my tracker. "Shit."

"What's wrong?" Owen asked.

Eli cleared his throat. "She's starting her period."

Owen made a face. "Oh. Do you need anything?"

"Painkillers. Of course a heating pad. Snacks, and maybe blankets."

Owen looked at Eli. "I'll get the heating pad and painkillers."

"Snacks and blankets," Eli said as he casually made his way into the kitchen. However, Owen was frantically searching for things.

"You're not half werewolf, right?" I asked.

"Nope, all ghost," he said. He brought the stuff over.

I took the painkillers first.

I disappeared into the bathroom next to insert my disc. Once that was taken care of, I came out and looked at both of them. "I'm ready for snacks and blankets. And that heating pad." I grabbed the things from them and settled onto the couch with everything a girl could need.

But I never did use the heating pad because the painkillers set in quickly and I felt great the rest of the day. However I did need my snacks and blankets.

It wasn't that bad this cycle, which was good. But I needed to learn how to be able to fight without all the added comfort. If I didn't learn, I'd crumble the second they targeted me when I wasn't at my best. And that was the last thing I needed to do.

I knew that my emotions were amplified this time around, meaning that any little thing could set me off. I could use that to my advantage. But I had to be careful at the same time because if I wasn't, I'd also cry the second things didn't go my way. It was a never-ending battle with myself.

Owen sat beside me but kept his distance; I guess in case I wasn't feeling all that social.

"Have you never considered birth control?" Eli replied to my earlier comment.

I looked up at him and pulled a knee to my chest. "I certainly have. But there are multiple options. IUD, which was too painful. The shot, which I had tried once. Too much weight gain. The pill, which worked for a bit but it's still not natural and I didn't want unnatural. I'd say being a girl sucks but you already know that."

"What are you two talking about?" Owen asked.

I shrugged. "When I have to fight whoever I need to fight for this war, I need to be able to handle it even on my period." But that didn't mean right now. I wasn't ready now.

Eli grabbed his laptop. "Then we figure out who is behind controlling the shadows. We have three brains so let's put them together and use them. Which kind of creature do you think would be behind controlling them?"

"A shadow king," Owen said. "Don't shadows have those?"

Eli gave him a look. "No. The royalty was mostly a

vampire thing and even that died down. Shadows don't have kings or queens or any of that, and as far as I know, they never have."

"Okay so then we need to ask who would be powerful enough to be in charge of the shadows," he said.

I chewed my lips as I faced them. "What about werewolves or vampires? Or ghosts?"

Eli shook his head. "Vampires have nothing against shadows and even then, certainly not enough knowledge or power to take over."

Owen nodded, rubbing his chin. "Same with werewolves. And ghosts really aren't all that powerful. We're like the weakest of the Kaofi."

"What about fallen angels? Lucas certainly seems capable. And he hates you, and me." I pointed to Eli.

Owen sighed from my right. "No. Fallen angels are powerful and full of hatred and revenge. But they are not that powerful. Maybe but I doubt it."

We named a few other creatures but none of them sounded right, which had me circling back to Lucas and Lucy. They made the most sense. "Just hear me out, okay? It's a possibility and we have to face the facts. The puppeteer hates my guts. Lucas hates my guts. They'd kill Eli in a heartbeat and use him against me, just for their gain. We can't rule it out and I think we should also just really expect it. No surprises. If we plan for it to be them, we're one step closer."

The two of them grumbled but agreed. Maybe they didn't like being wrong or admitting I had figured it out first. But they'd get over it eventually because Hanti were allowed to be the ones with the accurate answers, too.

Lucas was the best answer we had. He had to be the puppeteer. He'd be the one we'd take down, the one we stole control from. We just needed to figure out how to do that. And if that failed, we could lure all the shadows into the ocean instead so they'd never be seen again.

That was the best backup plan I had, and Eli must have wanted to disagree with me but he didn't say anything about it. He just scrunched his face as if my thoughts were full of shit.

"They are, but we don't have anything better," he said.

Owen wanted to ask what the hell he meant by that but Eli made it clear he wasn't about to explain. Owen would have to get used to being out of the loop.

And me? I'd have to get used to having Eli in the loop at all times. Which meant I needed to keep my secretive thoughts buried deep down or Eli would eventually join the army of shadows. We couldn't have that, no. I needed him on my side.

045 Tuesday, September 11th

"It's all wrong." Amari shook her head as she rubbed her temples. "You're doing it all wrong."

I frowned and faced her. "In what way is this wrong? I'm doing the course exactly as you want it."

She sighed. "And that's the problem. If you do everything the way you're supposed to, how can you expect the unexpected? How can you be prepared for whatever is coming? You have to do new and different things. Trying the same failed methods and hoping for a new result is insanity, Mya. Yes, dodge the trees. Yes, you need to get your dagger to hit the target on the mark. And you need to make sure you also avoid all obstacles along the way because what if you miss a branch? What if you happen to miss a root? Then you've fallen and they're going to be on top of you before you can react and you're dead. Shadows are quick. They can skip through shadows as a means to get around. You have to be smarter and think more out of the box."

"Like go near water?"

She grabbed my dagger from the target and handed it to

me. "What do you mean?"

I lifted my chin out of pride. "Eli told me shadows can't go near natural bodies of water. It sucks shadows to the center like quicksand and they can never climb back out." I assessed all my branches and roots, keeping an eye to make sure they couldn't catch me off guard. "I believe Lucas is controlling the shadows. Shadows are like puppets who crave a master. And he's become that master."

As Amari pointed to the target, she asked, "You're proposing we steal control from him?"

"Indeed."

Without another word, I took off running. I started at low speed, dodging trees, but instead of just dodging them and hitting the target, I began to find new routes.

I grabbed onto branches and swung myself up into the trees, climbing up to another branch that led me to a new tree. When a clearing opened up, I jumped down and broke into a sprint. I dodged another tree by twirling around it. I had misjudged my roots and my toe caught onto one, but instead of kissing the dirt, I rolled along with it and jumped back to my feet.

I wrapped my fingers around the metal hilt of my dagger as I embedded it right into the center of the target.

Amari shouted, "That is how it's done!" She came running over. "That is all I asked of you. You have to use your surroundings to guide you and aid you in your fight. Don't look at it as obstacles. Look at the trees as ladders. They help you to the top."

They'd also help me get to the top of the shadows. Maybe even Eli could control them, if that was what he wanted. But someone would need to take the reins and force those shadows somewhere they could never harm another soul.

Footsteps sounded behind us, cut off early by the number of trees that blocked them from echoing. “Well, well, well… Isn’t it a little dangerous for Hunters to be out and about in this area?”

Amari and I whipped around, daggers ready.

Lucas.

Amari snickered. “You? I expected someone with actual scare-tactics.”

He growled and took a step closer. “Watch your damn mouth.”

She didn’t allow him to corner her, so she stepped even closer. “Make me.”

As his nostrils flared, his wings emerged. Black feathers displayed behind him as he spread his wings at full width.

Before things could go south, I stepped between them and pointed my dagger at his chest. “We know about your stupid little plan.”

“Plan?” Amari and Lucas both asked.

“Yes. Plan. You’ve been controlling the shadows. You’re the one who planned to kill Eli, to hurt us both. You’re not going to get away with it.”

Amari nudged me from behind, scowling. “What are you doing?”

But Lucas, he was the one who shook his head. “I don’t know what you’re talking about.”

I scoffed. “Don’t act naïve. Eli and I figured it out. Loud and clear. Shadows require a master. They don’t know how to live or make their own choices all that much, and thus you came along to fix their problem. Much like werewolves need alphas to lead them, shadows need puppeteers—you are that. It explains perfectly why they keep targeting the two of us. You’ve always hated me, and you’ve really got it out for Eli.

I'm not dead, Lucas, and you can't kill me."

Except he still didn't seem to understand my words. Clever boy, pretending to be clueless.

Right on cue, a few shadows popped out of the shadows of trees and sprinted for us. Amari and I stood back-to-back, wielding our weapons in every direction. However, they never made any contact with the shadows because shadows were not weakened by a Hanti's cursed blade. We needed to find nature's cursed waters instead.

Shadows hissed and clawed at us, but we avoided most attempts. They vanished into smoke on instinct and when we turned to scan the area, Lucas had disappeared along with them.

Damnit.

I blew our cover. The only cover we had. We could have used it to our leverage, had I not told him we knew, and now he probably knew that we knew how to trap shadows. Control them—that we weren't sure of. But he knew that we knew he was the one behind it all.

"Mya, what the hell was that?" Amari faced me with the sharpest glare.

I shook my head as I sheathed my dagger. "I should not be allowed to run my mouth, you know. Someone should really do something about that."

Amari internally screamed before stomping her way back to the cabin. This couldn't be any good.

I hurried to follow her, but I retreated just a bit when we entered the cabin and she headed straight for the punching bag in the back room.

"What the hell did you do?" Hunter asked from the couch, magazine in his hand.

"What makes you think I did it?"

His eyes met mine and he tilted his head slightly forward to the right, eyebrows raised.

Swallowing as I rocked on my heels, I nodded. "Okay, so it is my fault. Lucas showed up. You know, the fallen angel." I didn't want to say that he was the same guy who killed Ryan. They knew that, and Hunter didn't need a punch to the gut. Some might have called me considerate.

Clara exited the kitchen. "So, you ran into Lucas and that pissed off Amari?"

I looked down at my fingers, twiddling. "I may have told him that we know he's controlling the shadows."

Hunter sat up and groaned. "Are you stupid? Don't answer that." He rubbed his face. "Nice to know we are back at the bottom. Just continue to knock us down a few more pegs."

Clara shook her head as she sat in the chair. "I'm sure Mya didn't mean it."

But I did. I just wouldn't tell them that.

Hunter stood. "Now we're screwed. Thanks."

"Hey, he doesn't know that I know about their weakness. You know, water." I gestured.

He shot me a look. "Eli knows. Eli knows you know. He'll be the one who tells them you know. You seem to still be under the impression this guy is to be trusted but I don't trust your judgment. I certainly don't trust his."

And here I thought Hunter had been warming up to me.

"Eli also knows I just told you," I said with a shrug.

Clara didn't say a word, but she certainly paid attention to every detail carved on our faces.

Hunter stopped me before I could make it to the kitchen for water. "Whoa. What do you mean he knows?"

"He knows. He's in my head."

Hunter shot Clara a look and this time she decided to join the conversation. “Why is he in your head? Look, I’m always trying to allow you to make your own decisions, Mya, but this decision sounds a little barbaric. Allowing any shadow or Kaofi in for that matter is highly risky.”

I spun around and faced her, planting my feet together. “I didn’t have much of a choice.”

“What?”

“Our trip. We took a trip up to his mansion in the mountains, and Eli was helping me train. But things took a turn, and somehow the shadows got inside my head. They couldn’t physically get *to* me, so they got inside me and Eli was the only one there to stop them. He had to block my mind from them, but that came at a cost... Now, he’s able to hear all my thoughts. And since I think of what I say before I say things, he can hear those thoughts.”

“Are you fucking kidding me right now?” Amari yelled from the hall.

Clara winced. “You might want to run.”

Hunter stepped towards me. “Damn right, if I don’t get to you first.”

Yet, I was tired of running. I was tired of being the girl everyone pushed around. I was sick of being the girl everyone could control. I wanted to make my own decisions. One day I’d be a fashion designer. I’d be a Hunter, too. I could have it all and I would fight like hell for this future.

“What was the other option?” I pulled my dagger out, for my own protection. I couldn’t trust these two not to attack out of spite. “Allow the shadows to raid my mind and torture me? You saw what happened the last time. You were there! Don’t preach to me the dangers of shadows because I’ve experienced it far more than you ever will. But right now,

I've made a choice to trust the lesser of two evils to keep myself stable. It's my head. It's my body. It's my choice.

"And yeah, I effing understand that he hears our plans. If you want to exclude me, fine. But I'm the one bringing home all the answers. So whether you include me or not, he'll still have an idea. And I don't need your help to defeat Lucas or the shadows. I'll do it myself if I have to. I don't care what it takes."

"I—"

"And let me remind you that you are the ones who told me I'm not special. You told me that there's no way I'm special, and I believed you for a split second. But you're wrong. I play a bigger part in this than you want to believe. Eli and I are the targets. If I left you, they'd come after me and me alone. They could care less about you. So yeah, you can be pissed about the fact that I had to let Eli into my head all you want. At the end of the night, nothing changes. You're wrong about us. You don't have the answers. You don't have the plan. So stop effing dismissing everything I do like I'm a child. I was thrown into this world so suddenly last year and I'm doing the best I can with what I have."

What I kept to myself was that I was farther in the loop than they'd ever be. They could kick me out, but they'd never hear from me again if they did. They needed me more than I needed them.

Someone knocked on the door and Hunter looked over. "Who's here? Nobody else knows we stay here."

Except Eli.

Clara went to the door and slowly opened it and I stepped closer to see who it was.

Eli met her gaze first before looking past her and meeting mine. Blood covered him from head to toe, and he stumbled into the doorframe. "I didn't know where else to go..."

046 Wednesday, September 12th

Even as the moon lit up the sky as the stars twinkled, the night weighed heavy on our shoulders.

Eli had fallen asleep on the couch by now, and nobody else dared to tell him to leave. For good reason. After he showed up bleeding and asking for help the way he did yesterday, they didn't have the heart to tell me no. The shadows would stop at nothing.

Lucas would have it coming to him.

Nothing had squeezed the life out of my heart faster than reliving one of my worst memories.

"I didn't know where else to go..."

I rushed over to him and pulled him into the room. "Who the hell did this?" I sat him on the couch before anyone else could even get a word in. They'd have a threat looming over them if they even thought about it.

Eli leaned back and closed his eyes. "They said it was supposed to be a warning..."

"Shadows aren't supposed to be able to get hurt. You're supposed to be untouchable."

Clara brought me some supplies. "Vampires are not untouchable. Sure, he can't die, but that doesn't mean he can't be tortured. There's always a downside to immortality. That's why Hanti exist."

I cursed under my breath before grabbing the kit from her hand. "Clothes off. Hunter, bring me something to put him in."

He didn't argue; he brought fresh clothes.

I pulled the bloody and torn clothes off of Eli's sticky body, throwing them into a bag that Clara had given me. "This isn't going to be very pleasant, and I'm sorry." With the wet rag, I first cleaned up excess blood before switching to rubbing alcohol to clean his wounds.

Eli hissed through his teeth, but he never opened his eyes.

Once his wounds were cleaned, I peered up at Hunter. "How long does it take vampires to heal?"

He handed me the gauze. "In his case, maybe a few more hours."

I patched each and every wound, and I managed to get the shirt over his head, but Hunter had to help me get his sweats on.

I put the garbage in with his clothes before attempting to stand. His fingers wrapped around my wrist as he laid back on the couch. "Please, stay."

I couldn't leave him like this.

So I stayed.

"How long will he sleep? Vampires aren't supposed to sleep. It's like everything I thought I knew is crashing down on me. I don't understand anymore," I said as I continued to stare out the window.

Clara brought me some water. "Hard to say. Torture does a number on anyone, dead or alive. Mortal or immortal.

How long had it been since you'd seen him before he showed up here, covered in blood?"

I closed my eyes as I folded my arms across my chest. "Half a day. He left to go do something and I came here to train. Like we always do."

Was it my fault? I shouldn't have trusted him to by himself after our attack. I should have known better than to leave him alone. They'd gotten their revenge on him now that they knew he was taking my side.

It made me sick to my stomach.

"What do we do?" Hunter gestured to Eli.

Clara released a sigh as she drank the water she brought me. "Let him sleep."

I was thankful that she had said something because I had no more energy. All I had left in me was to stand here and let whatever happen, happen. I knew Eli needed more, but at this moment, I couldn't provide that.

Maybe that made me a terrible enemy.

Or maybe it made me the *perfect* kind.

Amari decided it was time to let me back into her circle, because she approached me with some objects in hand. What looked to be some kind of needle and something else. Art?

"What is this?" I asked.

She nodded her head towards a sleeping Eli. "You can't do much for him right now and there's no use in standing around, moping, and possibly beating yourself up. I know you. I know you like to blame yourself for everything. But we don't need any of that, so here I offer you an opportunity. All of us here have tattoos of this very symbol. If you want to officially claim your Hanti title, you can."

When I looked at the art again, I noticed it looked more like a sharp H, where one of the sides was hanging lower than the rest of the letter. *Like a dagger strapped to a thigh.*

"You want me to be a part of your circle after yesterday? What happened to the fact that Eli can read my thoughts? What happened to the fact that you guys think I'm nothing more than a body to fight? You don't accept my ideas. You don't treat me like part of the group all that much. You made it clear I play a specific role and that role is to shut up and listen, to provide you answers. But it's never to take the lead or make the plans. It's only to make your lives easier." And less about making *our* lives better.

Amari reeled her shoulders back. "Yes. But Clara made me realize I was being an idiot. She does that sometimes. She makes me see things for what they really are." She put the tools down. "We have no right to continue to treat you like you're only here to help us. It's about your life too and you should get a voice in the matter. Even if we don't agree, you're still your own person and we don't get to try to make you fit our mold of what a Hanti should be." Her eyes darted behind me, towards Clara. Then she whispered, "I'm sorry."

Clara came forward. "Exactly. I've never had to experience the grief you have. To love someone and watch them die. We judged you too harshly without fully trying to understand your situation."

Now Hunter decided it was his turn, so he flipped his wrist over to the lighter side, showing off the tattoo. "Are you ready to join us?"

If I said yes, this meant I'd be part of their group forever. Could I still be a fashion designer? I'd make it happen. One way or another, I would.

But deep down, I also wanted this. I hadn't chosen to be born this way, but after the shitstorm we'd been thrown into, this was *my* world now. I wanted to be a part of it, and I knew I couldn't go back to pretending it wasn't part of me.

"Where do I put the tattoo?"

Amari's grin grew as she picked up the supplies. "You get to pick."

They brought up a chair and I sat back in it. After carefully considering, I pushed the hem of my shorts lower and pulled my shirt just under my boobs. I'd always wanted a hip tattoo and this made sense.

Hunter assured me that the needle was sterile and everything was done carefully. I asked them why they couldn't just go to a tattoo artist themselves, but they said it was too risky to expose our group to anyone. That explained the hidden cabin.

He handed me a pop-it to fidget with as Amari tattooed the symbol right into my skin. The pain was horrendous, and that was mostly put on me for choosing a spot right on bone. A mix between burning and stabbing, and all right under the surface of my skin. It'd look dope when it was all said and done though. Eli would wake up to find that I'd officially pledged myself to this life. I was a Hanti, and it wasn't going to end.

Not until I died.

A Hanti still hopelessly in love with a version of a man who'd died long ago. Humiliating—sure. But we didn't get to choose how we went out of this world.

When the tattoo was done, Amari took her tools while Clara gave me a basic rundown of how to care for it. Wash it day and night with non-scented body wash, and no submerging myself in water for long. How long would I listen to that rule though?

I got up, but Clara grabbed my wrist. "Whoa. Not yet." She grabbed something. Similar to a bandage, but not quite.

It'd been transparent. Saniderm—she called it.

She placed it over the tattoo. "That last thing that needs is rubbing against fabric the entire time, especially when you train. It's like an open wound at this point."

That explained all the pain.

"Then what do I do now?" I asked.

You can't do much when your hand is just curses and douches.

Hunter gave Clara a look that I couldn't read all that well. I supposed that was the point though.

Before any words came out of her open mouth, Amari piped in, "We wanted to talk about where we're headed next."

That sounded bad. Very bad.

Next? As in, we would be migrating somewhere else and leaving Eli behind? Owen? Did they make me get the tattoo just to tell me they were going to drag me away from my one and only home? Screw that. I had something to say.

"—and then hopefully that leads us to a few Hanti," Amari said.

I shook my head and looked at her. "Wait, come again?"

"We're going camping. To search for Hanti. Hanti on average hide in odd places. Cabins. Underground caves. Office buildings where you won't come across many Kaofi." She shrugged.

If we were the threats to Kaofi and they feared us, why were we always the ones hiding?

Duh. Predator stalking its prey.

And it was generally easy to hide from one. All we had to do was pretend we didn't see or hear them. Or smell them in my case.

We looked like any other human when we wanted to. But

our safe base, our home... That would always be hidden from Kaofi in case of emergencies. Or in case of training.

"So, we're going camping? The four of us?"

"Five," she said as her eyes moved to Eli. "Can't trust this one to be alone again. If the shadows really did torture him for siding with you, we can trust him. That's only assuming the torture isn't just a ploy to make us trust Eli and then spill all our secrets. But given that he also has access to your thoughts, I don't think they needed to use that to make us trust him. You already do, and he already has access to our secrets whether we like it or not."

I slowly approached him, watching him sleep. I itched to reach out and run my fingers through his curls. What I'd give just to touch him again.

Clearing my throat, I looked at them. "And you think he'll be okay with that? He doesn't strike me as the camping type. You know. Fancy clothes, fast cars, big houses. The last place you'd find Eli is in the woods, sleeping in a tent."

Hunter gave me a look, eyebrows raised. Although I wasn't sure what he was trying to tell me...

"Would other Hanti even trust us, or approach us with Eli at our site? They'll know right away he's Kaofi and they'll attack. It sounds like we'd be taking him right to them. It's not the best idea." I crossed my arms.

Amari scoffed. "What's our other option? Leave him here and hope the shadows don't find and torture him again? His only options are to go with us and risk being targeted by Hanti or stay here and risk being tortured by shadows. Take your pick, Mya. I think he's already made his decision of who he trusts more and where he wants to be."

Where he wants to be.

Was that true? Did Eli really trust me that much and want

to be in my presence? I sounded like a pathetic schoolgirl thinking about it, but I couldn't help myself. Maybe I had been saving him all over again. Maybe the old Eli was still alive, deep down in there somewhere.

Maybe he cared more about me than he wanted to admit after all.

047 Thursday, September 13th

"I don't understand. Why can't you just do it?" I tilted my head as I looked at the poles that were meant to go in the tent.

"Because what if you have to live off the land someday? You should learn." Hunter ripped the poles from my hand. "Now watch." He slid it through the little loops. "It gives the tent shape."

I snickered. "That's assuming I'll be living off the land someday, and that I'll have a tent with me. I'm definitely not going to have these exact poles on hand and there won't be little loops sewn into the tarp, either."

Eli released a sigh. I turned around to face him, only to find him sitting back on a tree branch and relaxing like he was the billionaire around here. "I am." He leaned forward. "Besides, if that's your way of asking if you can have my apartment when I move to the mountains, I can't offer that. You have to learn how to be an adult, Little Hanti."

Hunter scrunched his nose. "Hate that nickname."

I threw my arm at Eli as I turned to look at Hunter. "Why

doesn't he have to help?"

"Because he's a rich vampire-shadow who never has to worry about being forced out of his home. He has the money for another. We don't have that comfort. Not now, not with shadows looming over us," Amari said as she grabbed stakes and hammered them into the ground.

I gave Eli a glare. "What, so shadows aren't after him, too? That's why he's out here with us, isn't it?"

Hunter groaned. "Mya, shut the hell up."

"Love you, too," I mumbled.

"Money, Little Hanti," he whispered. "It gets you everywhere, even if you're forced out of your home for a short while. You always have financial stability to come back to. I can afford to fall out of a lease, or to lose a house without selling it."

"I have to pee." I looked at everyone. "So if you'll excuse me, I'll be behind a bush for a few minutes." I grabbed the roll of toilet paper. "By the way, nobody has *this* when they live off the land." I waved the roll in the air. "There goes your argument." I walked through the trees until I came across some bushes that were high enough. When I finished my business, I winced as I fixed my shorts. The tattoo sure was taking its time.

"Tattoo?" Eli appeared behind me.

I jumped a bit, cursing under my breath. "Don't sneak up on me like that."

"Kaofi do that. You need to be alert at all times including at times like this. I'm only helping you train." He shrugged. "Now what is this tattoo?"

Rolling my eyes, I pulled my shorts down from my hip. "It's healing."

He eyed it, shoving his hands into his pockets. Maybe it

was to keep himself from reaching out and touching me. Although I wish he would.

"You seem to wish I'd do a lot of things to you," he said as he met my eyes. "But what is the tattoo for?"

I pushed away whatever thoughts were forming from his first statement. "It's from the Kaofi Hunters. It's just a tattoo that says I'm officially part of this life and I've made the active choice to *stay* part of it."

"Can I get a closer look?" He stepped forward.

It took everything in me to keep my heart and breathing stable. "It might not look all that pretty. It's barely been a day." I peeled my shorts down a bit, showing the tattoo. It was red, a little swollen, but it was still easy to make out. For now. It wasn't all that clean as the ink began to bleed a little into the saniderm. I hoped it looked clean later on.

This time, Eli did reach forward. His fingers brushed over the area, but I'd never believe it for myself if I hadn't experienced it. His touch had been gentler than ever before. It threw me off guard.

"I like it," his voice came out in a whisper.

My heart definitely skipped a beat that time.

"You like it? It essentially means I'm supposed to kill you." I tried to step away from his touch to gain control of my body.

Eli stepped even closer, and I then learned a tree was behind me when my back pressed against the bark. "But you haven't killed me. It wasn't you who did. It was my own kind. And even if you tried, you could never kill me now." He leaned in so close that I memorized how cold his breath was. Well, when you were two halves of the dead...

"No, I certainly couldn't kill you now." I didn't make any moves to push him away. I wasn't so sure I *wanted* him to step back.

His hand came up, knuckles running down my jaw and neck. Seconds later, his thumb was rubbing over my bottom lip. Whatever control I had over my heart and my breathing earlier had now vanished.

Just as Eli leaned closer—millimeters away—Amari's voice cut through, "I know you're done peeing. Get your ass back over here."

Eli dropped his hand from my skin and took too many steps back. I rolled myself around the trunk of the tree, giving Amari a look, which she understood very clearly. "Did I interrupt something? Too damn bad. We aren't here to make googly eyes. Let's go."

Without sending Eli another glance, I followed Amari, mentally apologizing for her behavior. Only I never heard a response back because this wasn't a telepathic connection we had.

"What if I interrupted you and Clara?" I asked her.

She sent me a look—one of certainty. "Then you'd be dead."

"So why can't I interrupt you but you can interrupt me? Doesn't seem fair." I grabbed my dagger out of instinct, and maybe for comfort. Like a child and her teddy bear.

Amari laughed. She actually laughed at me. *That bitch.* Eli snorted at that comment. "Because it's different."

"Different? What, because your love isn't forbidden but mine is? Because you're Hanti and he's immortal? Right. I forget that I'm not allowed to be happy. You know more than anyone that you don't help who you fall for." I faced forward.

She narrowed her eyes. I could feel the piercing gaze. "You know damn well that wasn't what I meant." She spun her body one-eighty, confident in walking backwards. "So what, are you falling for him now?"

My lips twitched. "No. Never. My brain is just tricked by his looks. He looks like Eli. That's all."

Amari snickered but she didn't say anything. We left it at that.

"What did you need help with?" I asked.

She didn't say anything to that either. Instead, she led me down to a little stream. She ran her fingers through it, before looking around the trees. For what, or who, I didn't know.

Then the words escaped her. Hanti, and their history.

She told me in depth detail all about how we had come to be. I didn't tell her I already knew. She was on edge enough as it was. Hanti had to come about because of the things Kaofi had done to humanity. Someone had to save the poor humans. It wouldn't be themselves.

Hanti were the ones who'd taken on that role with promise. Some days I wondered if it was worth it.

To be with a Kaofi was to go against everything Hanti stood for. Everything we were created for. In her words, my parents didn't have me just so I could fall for a man like Eli. But that was where I had to correct her. My parents didn't want me to be part of this life, and that included allowing me to fall for whoever without having to live up to this ridiculous title 24/7.

Sure, I'd accepted being a Hanti. And Eli had died. Maybe those were the signs that it had never been meant to be. They were simply lessons for me to learn.

When I called her out on reprimanding me for my choices, she stepped back. She continued on her little rant about how maybe we were supposed to take this as a guide and learn how to make peace with people. We'd finally come to learn that Kaofi we're like everyone else. There would be good and bad seeds everywhere.

Judge based on actions, not DNA.

Maybe we could use this war with the shadows to bring two sides together. Maybe this could be the start of a new alliance.

I just needed to figure out how to make that happen. Maybe a Hanti needed to be in charge of the shadows. They craved a puppeteer, and we'd be the ones who could keep them in line so humans wouldn't be eradicated.

I couldn't tell that to the Hanti just yet though. They'd tell me that shadows weren't worth the risk and we needed to send them into the ocean like I originally planned. But if that was true, what about Eli? Where would he go?

He was a shadow, and like the rest of them, half of him craved that leader. He'd eventually find it in the wrong person if we weren't careful, and if the other Hanti realized this, they'd go against Eli next. They'd have no problem sending him to his eternity in the vast ocean just for the humans.

And maybe it was a horrid thought to have, but was his one eternity really worth less than all those humans?

I couldn't allow any of these possible scenarios to play out. So while the Hanti aimed for the plan to stop the shadows and take control just to send them into the ocean, I'd find my own plan. I'd find a way to take control of them myself. I'd save the shadows. I'd save humanity.

I'd save Eli.

I turned and sat up when something snapped outside the

tent. "Eli." I turned to shake him, knowing he'd be awake. But he wasn't there. His spot was empty.

I crawled out and found the clearing empty. Our fire has died out and I craved a midnight snack so desperately. The outdoors was not a life for me. I would much rather live in a big mansion. Too bad Eli claimed that all for himself.

And he heard me say that.

Bastard.

I got to my feet and searched the area. "Where did you go?" I yelled out in a whisper.

After walking a few more yards through the woods, I decided to give up on looking for him. Maybe it was terrible, but I assumed he didn't want to be found. Right?

Or maybe, he had been taken and tortured again.

No. I couldn't think like that. Those thoughts would only lead me to more danger. If I assumed he'd been taken, I'd have to wake the others for backup.

Yeah, like they'd want to go search in the dark, going up against a whole army of shadows they couldn't kill just for one man—who only I seemed to really care about. Nobody else thought he mattered as much as I did.

In a fleeting thought, I realized Eli had nobody to put him first. Not the shadows. Not the Kaofi. Not the Hanti. Not even parents. He only had me.

And as much as he hated to admit it, he needed me. He didn't want to be alone.

I saw through all the remarks and the darkness. I saw through *him.*

I walked along the forest and ignored all the little sounds. None of them could scare me at this time. Eli was probably out there somewhere, no doubt. Wherever he went to keep to himself. Maybe he needed to get away from me and my intrusive thoughts for a while.

Not that I blamed him.

I didn't find Eli. What I did find was a beautiful lake that shimmered under the moonlight. It reminded me of all the things I couldn't have but wanted. Love. A family. It reminded me of all the beautiful things in life that were close enough to grasp, yet these things would so quickly slip away. I'd be left in the dark, hoping one day everything would fall back into place. I refused to be the spectacle any longer.

After discarding my clothes and taking a dip in the refreshing water, I swam towards the middle of the lake and looked up at the stars. Floating like this at this hour had been a whole other experience. But much like the movies, I imagined something large and evil swimming beneath me in a flash.

I turned to face it, afraid maybe something did lurk beneath these waters. Thankfully, I was wrong. It was quiet. The surface of the water laid still, not a ripple in sight.

I'd just be paranoid. Typical me.

As I faced the stars again, every muscle in my body released every ounce of tension. I could fall asleep out here if I didn't drown in the process. Maybe a waterbed would be something to look into, with a star projector for my ceiling.

Conjuring my paranoia to come to life, something grabbed hold of my ankle and dragged me down.

I flailed my arms but it meant nothing to anyone on land. I was too far below the surface to be seen.

I twisted my body in every direction, ripping my ankle free and swimming back to the top. I took gulps of air until I heard someone shouting my name. Eli.

He stood over on the rocks with his hand extended, and I swam closer. Until it happened *again.*

Under I went, twisting and fighting with nobody to save me. Eli couldn't touch the water. I couldn't breathe it in. I was the one with the lower hand.

My hair flew around my face, blocking my view of what little moonlight had been hitting the water. I reached out for the air, but all I met was water. I was pulled further down where the light ceased to exist and water threatened to seep into my lungs.

The creature disappeared and I pushed myself upward until I broke free of the water. I hurried to the rocks and the moment I was close enough, Eli grabbed my wrist and pulled me out and far from the lake. "Are you okay?"

What a stupid ass question. I wasn't okay.

"I was trying to be polite," he said.

Mission failed. Polite would be shutting up and just letting me catch my breath.

Eli shot me a look but took my advice after that, and I laid back on the rocks with only one question running through my head.

What the hell *was* that?

048 Thursday, September 13th

Frigid blue eyes appeared from the center of the lake, cutting into my soul like a razor.

"Siren," Eli whispered in my ear. "Beautiful but deadly. Nocturnal. They're always out for blood. Hanti say they're born of sharks, only the empathy was never present."

Right—because sharks only attacked when they smelled blood, not just for fun.

"She attacked because sirens are in good with the shadows." He leaned closer, his nose brushing against my hair as if he was attempting to comfort me. Well, my heartbeat *was* pounding out of control. It did that when I came inches from death.

As if I needed another enemy.

"Hunters will always have enemies, Little Hanti." He pointed at the siren wading through the water. "But sirens can't do much damage during the day or on land. If I keep an eye on you, we're safe."

"We?" I glanced back at him with an eyebrow cocked. Bold of him to assume he was in danger. And he couldn't save me anyway, given he couldn't jump in the very habitat where sirens thrived. I'd be a dead man if I wasn't careful.

"We. We keep each other safe." He brushed hair from my temple. "No matter what I have to do, I'll do it. Maybe I can't get in to save you, but I'll do it regardless."

"You'd put yourself on the line just because I'm too eager for a swim at night? You're a different kind of man, Kay."

A powerful voice sliced through, "A suicidal one it seems." It came out like a song, one the darkest depths of the lake would sing. The siren watched me, tilting her head. "Shadows are not able to touch water, and that's why we make the perfect ally." She laid her forearms across a rock in front of her.

Pulling my knees up to my chest, I scowled at her.

"Don't flatter yourself. I want you dead an equal amount. It's not personal." Her eyes fluttered as she swam back under.

A subtle snicker escaped Eli. "Sirens like easy targets, and with me here, you'll be anything but easy. Remember, I'm an ally too. What I say to her, she'll obey."

Would she hear his word over the others?

"Of course. Sirens are loyal to whoever provides the information they crave. I tell her that the shadows serve one master and she'll fall putty into my hands."

I could work with that.

He added, "And if we're lucky, they'll pick our side over the puppeteer's."

049 Friday, September 14th

Eli sat beside me as I swung my legs, debating if I should go for a swim without him. "I've been thinking," he said. "I've been thinking that Lucas possibly was telling the truth when he confronted you."

"What?"

"I don't think he knows what's going on. I don't think he's controlling them. Whenever you guess the person behind it, it's never the easy answer."

I shook my head. "But it would make so much sense."

Eli nodded. "It would. And that's why I don't think it's him. I think he's just the easy suspect. Whoever is really behind this wouldn't want to be found out or guessed. They wouldn't want to lose all that power they have."

Now I was beginning to question if it was someone we knew. Owen? Lucy? Maybe even Juliet or Cole, or someone we never saw coming. Ryan? Was he still alive? No, it wouldn't make sense for a Hanti to always have control. I wanted it, sure. But it couldn't be that easy.

"It is way too damn hot out here." I stood.

Welcome to Arizona.

As if I hadn't lived here my whole life. I always seemed to be surprised every year when the temperature got way up there. As if I didn't know it was coming. As if I didn't expect it.

Eli pulled one knee up to his chest, resting an arm over it. "Go swim in the lake then."

"But you'll be all alone." I closed my eyes as soon as the words left my mouth. Why the hell was that my biggest concern?

His foot nudged mine. "So be it. A little loneliness never killed me. Trust me, I'm fine. I won't die from the heat. You, however, can. Heat exhaustion is no joke."

I mumbled, "Tell me about it."

I faced the water. "All right." I pulled my shirt off first, hearing a small squeak followed by someone clearing their throat. When I looked down at Eli, he wasn't even looking in my general vicinity. Clever.

My shorts came off next along with my dagger. "I'll be in the water if you need me." I climbed down the rocks and dived in. I came back to the surface and pushed my hair back, wiping water from my face. "You have no idea how nice this feels!"

Part of me felt bad for him because he could never fully enjoy something like this. Being Kaofi was not all it was cracked up to be.

"Don't feel bad for me, Little Hanti. I've got plenty of other things that keep me occupied. Besides, if I'm so desperate to swim, I'll swim in the pool at my mansion." He shrugged.

"But it's not the same, and you know it. Not the same

as a massive lake. Not the same as natural water. Not the same as…" I scanned the trees above to find the rope swing. "That." I pointed. His eyes moved over to it, but he still shrugged again anyway.

I got out and climbed back up the rocks. "Now we're going to take advantage." But again Eli wasn't staring at me.

I smirked to myself, knowing exactly why he couldn't look in my direction. The man was still straight even if he had died and came back. And as hard as it was for him to admit it, he was definitely fighting a boner.

He shook his head. "No, I'm fine. Really. You must understand that I'm really fine. Really fine."

I lifted an eyebrow. "Uh huh, and is that why you keep repeating yourself?"

His brows furrowed. "Huh? No, I'm not repeating myself. I'm not. I'm not fine. Wait, I'm fine." But the truth was already out and he couldn't take that back now.

I laughed as I walked over to the rope swing. "You know what blows about this whole you being inside my head situation? The fact that I couldn't masturbate without you listening in. I've lost some of my own choices." Not that I've ever masturbated before. At least not about Eli.

Yet.

"You could. It's your body. Nobody is stopping you, and please, don't let me be the one who does. If you want to masturbate and think about me, I can't stop you. You should care less about what I think and more about what you want. You seem to do that a lot, Mya. You care too much about what others think. You know what I've discovered? You're a bit of a people pleaser." He leaned back.

I clenched my jaw at the words. "I am not a people pleaser."

"No, not always. You're learning to finally get out of that. But it still shows a lot of times. You want to make everyone happy. You want to do what makes me content, because you wouldn't want to inconvenience me in any way. And you train hard to try and impress your friends, even if they don't see it that way. You act like you don't crave their approval, but you desperately do. There's nothing to be ashamed of." He shook his head. "Now go."

I didn't have a response to that. It was the downside of someone having access to your thoughts at all times. Maybe he was right, and that's why I officially became a part of the group. Sure, I had my mom. But I'd always been an only child and I craved more people around my age. Siblings. And the Hanti provided me with that. And the way they always chastised me felt much like what siblings did.

Without another word, I grabbed the stick on both ends and ran forward, pulling my legs up into my chest. I let go when I was at the peak of the swing, and the water engulfed me like all the grief I'd experienced over the year.

When I came up, Clara and Amari stood at the top. "We came to join you. It only seemed fair. Since this one can't keep you company," Amari said as she jabbed her thumb down at Eli who then scowled at her in return.

Clara and Amari both stripped down to their bras and underwear before jumping from the rock. Eli didn't look at them the way he looked at me though. And I noticed that. And he now knew I noticed that, by the look of humiliation on his face as he tried to avoid my gaze altogether.

They both came up, but they were a little too focused on each other at the moment. Of course. Being half-naked and wet definitely did something to the hormones.

I swam closer to the rock where Eli was. "Before you

became a shadow, did you ever like swimming?"

He shrugged. "Not all that much. This outdoor stuff really isn't my thing."

"You ever try it?"

This time, he didn't respond right away. It squeezed my heart. He never had the opportunity and now he couldn't even do it if he wanted. If he tried, he'd be spending his eternity stuck in mud at the bottom of a lake.

"Well now you have to," Clara said.

Amari and I turned to look at her. That was absurd. If Eli tried, he'd literally be gone.

Clara shook her head and swam closer. "Hear me out. Your shadow side can't swim in water. But your vampire side can, correct?"

"I'm both. I can't just shut one off." He scoffed at her suggestion.

But Clara wasn't backing down. "What if you can? Not many in this world end up being both. Have you ever tried? It's a gene. You can certainly try to shut it off, right? Kaofi are not normal creatures and you can do things that nobody ever thought would be imaginable. So, let's see you try."

I moved in front of her. "And what if it goes wrong? What if he is sucked away forever? You want to risk that?"

"We'll be here to save him if we need to."

Part of me questioned if she'd put on a front this entire time. Maybe under that pretty face she was a lot more like Hunter and Amari and she was looking for a way to get rid of him.

But it was also Clara. I trusted her. She'd never doubted me much and she always was one of the calm ones. She didn't let emotions get the best of her. And maybe, if we could shut off his shadow side, we could keep him safe that way. He'd never be their puppet again.

Amari cleared her throat. "How does one shut off half of who they are? If he were a full shadow, he couldn't shut it off. So what makes you think he can because he's half?"

Clara never looked in her direction. "Because he wasn't born a shadow. He was turned."

Eli dropped his leg off the rock, dangling beside the other. "I want to try. Allow me to try. It's worth a shot, and if I can shut it off, then we'd all be good."

Nobody argued with him. Nobody stopped him as he closed his eyes and did everything in his power to shut off the shadow side. When he opened his eyes, he climbed down the rocks, slipping into the water. The three of us were there to stop him if needed be, but he seemed to be doing fine.

Seemed to be.

Until *they* swarmed my mind and I grabbed the rock for support.

"Mya?"

I wanted to say I was fine. I wanted to tell them it was okay, but it wasn't okay and I couldn't even get the words out. I tangled my fingers in my hair trying to claw them out of my head. I wanted them gone.

They felt like spiders crawling on my brain just beneath my skull. But it was worse than that. They were black widows—venomous and toxic. It started with the sinking of fangs. One bite, then two. Then they were all tearing into my thoughts and I started screaming for them to stop.

They vanished.

Eli started to grab hold of the rocks but the water had a mind of its own, attempting to drag his body to the bottom.

I wrapped my arms around his waist as Clara and Amari climbed out and grabbed his hands, dragging him while I pushed. When he was laying back on the dirt, Amari met my eyes. "What the hell was that?"

I let go of Eli and leaned forward onto my hands, dropping my head. What did I even tell her?

Eli sat up and rubbed his hand over his face. "You told me to shut off the shadow side, but that meant I also couldn't keep the block up in Mya's mind. The shadows had free reign to raid her thoughts like parasites."

Spiders.

They felt so much more like spiders. Eight legs. Eight eyes to see into every inch of my thoughts. Fangs. Too much like a vampire.

"Mya!" Amari reached forward but Eli caught me as I collapsed.

His arms wrapped over mine and my entire body relished in his safety net. I never wanted to leave.

"I feel so tired. Please, let's never try that again," I said quietly.

Eli tightened his arms, whispering into my hair, "Never. We'll never try that again."

I lost track of time after that. I wasn't sure how long we stayed there, like that, in that position. Even the sun was setting before we let go. And as the moon revealed itself high in the sky once the sun had gone to bed, we still didn't move.

I think Amari and Clara eventually disappeared but I couldn't be sure as to when they did.

Twisting my body a little, I now laid in his lap as I stared up at him. "I'm sorry. I really wish we could let you swim." I felt entirely responsible for the fact that he couldn't. If the shadows weren't trying to get into my head, he wouldn't need to have the block up. He could switch it off. He could *swim* far away from their terror.

His fingers trailed along my jaw, then my cheek before slipping through the strands of my hair. "It's not your fault. There's just one reason as to why they're after you and I. When we figure it out, we can stop them. Maybe then I can swim. I can shut off that side of me without you waiting for them to attack your mental state."

"Does that mean...you plan to stay when this war is over?" I swallowed.

As if trying to occupy the minds of his fingers, they slid from my hair and danced their way down my stomach. It was becoming extremely difficult to keep all the thoughts under control.

Eli shrugged as he glanced up at the stars. "I'm not sure yet."

Like clockwork, he brought his hand back to my hair and tilted my chin with his other hand.

The energy to keep everything under control just vanished like a *ghost*, and all I could hear inside my head was: *kiss me, kiss me, kiss me.*

But Eli didn't do that even if he heard the thoughts himself.

"Because I can't do that to you, Little Hanti." He brushed his knuckles over my temple. "Kissing you is a dangerous slope, and we have far too much to lose now. You and I both know if I kiss you, it'll be like the stars kissing the moon. All that will do is blind everyone in this world when our egos merge into cosmic fuse. It makes us an easier target, and that I can't have." His veiled eyes met mine, and immediately I knew mine had lightened almost pure white from the terror rushing through me like a river. "I can't *have* you."

050 Saturday, September 15th

I tried as hard as I might have to forget about Eli and what he told me. He couldn't come rafting with us, and maybe for good reason. How was I expected to wrap my head around it?

"Mya?" Clara put her hand on my arm and I shook her off. I was fine. Couldn't she see that?

I put on my life vest and looked at them. "Let's go."

Amari cheered as Hunter helped us into the raft. We sat back and paddled towards the center of the river, a cool mist hitting our skin. Clara reached over and wrapped her fingers around Amari's, who then smiled at her.

I watched the rapids as we bobbed through, none of the waves too tall just yet. But as we went farther, the river rolled almost white—like my eyes. And white rivers meant faster currents and heavier movements.

Hunter poked me from the back. "You all right?"

I nodded a little. "I'm good."

"She was attacked yesterday," Amari said. "By the shadows. Eli tried to shut off that side of him and...well."

She gestured to me.

Sure, I was a little upset about that. It was horrifying. But what really had me on edge today was what Eli said. All this time he'd been looking at me in a way he wasn't supposed to. And how desperately I wanted him to look at me that way. Now that he did, my heart ached because we couldn't make this work. Not like before.

"She's thinking about Eli," Clara interrupted my thoughts. "What exactly happened between the two of you?"

Amari smirked. "Is it what we think it is? I mean you were all wet and half-naked and in need of his touch so we can only imagine. Clara and I had a little fun ourselves."

Clara squinted. "No, something's not right. If something happened, she'd be flustered. She'd be glowing. But she's dulled like a light burnt out. He turned you down, didn't he?"

I couldn't even say the words. It all sounded so harsh and I didn't want it to be more real than it was. Eli made it *surreal.*

And that kind of thing killed me.

"Am I mentally screwed up?" I whispered. Nobody heard me over the rushing water. It didn't matter. I got my answer.

I helped Hunter steer the boat towards the center more as we hit a few tiny waterfalls. They were small enough that you could barely call them that, but also big enough you could feel it when you went down and hit the water again.

It splashed right at us, drenching us. The water was freezing but under the Arizona sun, it felt wonderful.

"Hunter, hurry!" Amari was paddling like her life depending on it and Hunter joined her. When I looked at the threat, it was too late. The rock hit our boat and we wrapped around it, flipping under the water.

I was grabbed by my hair and dragged across the rough

concrete. My breath had been ripped away as they shoved my head underwater. I grabbed the edge of the tub, throwing myself against the ceramic to get a gulp of air. My protests didn't work.

Choking on the water entering my lungs, my head was pulled from the tub. I coughed, lungs burning as I fell against the side. Wet hair clung to my skin as I welcomed oxygen.

A squeak escaped me as someone wrapped their fingers around my neck, picking me up and pushing my head back under the water. The further they pushed, the deeper my body slipped into the tub until every piece of me was submerged.

I clawed at their arm, fighting for just a single breath. A single heartbeat. Mine was quickly disappearing.

Fear clung to every inch of me as I feared the end of my life. I'd hardly experienced anything worth living for. I'd barely lived at all. This couldn't be it, could it?

In seconds, my senses began to vanish. First smell, then the taste of the salty water. The rippling surface of the water faded as my hands went limp and sunk beneath the surface. My hearing was the last to say goodbye.

I thought maybe I'd heard my name, but there was no way that was possible. Right...?

"...Mya!" It sounded muffled, covered by a pillow. No, there were no pillows. A cloud? Was I in heaven now? Dead?

"Mya, bloody hell, wake up already!"

Fingers grabbed the back of my vest and ripped me back into the boat. I looked back while Hunter held on tight, like he didn't despise my every gut. "You're okay. We're fine. That's what the vests are for," he joked. "You almost scared us. Damn."

Amari and Clara rowed us to the edge and helped us out,

pulling our raft up the shore.

"Are you guys okay?" a man yelled as he hurried down the bank. As if we needed anymore attention. Embarrassing.

Hunter put a hand up. "We're great. Just a little adventure."

Yeah, adventure. Almost drowning.

What was that memory? I knew Eli had experienced it. It must have been the first time we met, the one we couldn't remember anymore. It didn't make any sense.

"Are you okay?" the man asked as he looked at me.

I blinked a few times, nodding. "Just fine. Thanks. A little scare, but nothing worth doing is without risk."

A woman ran up from around him and stopped almost immediately. "Hunters."

Amari stepped in front of Clara, ready to attack if she needed. Not that she would. They couldn't be Kaofi, or we would have known right away. They didn't have a smell.

"How do you know we're Hanti?" Hunter stepped forward.

The woman looked at the man beside her and she nodded. "Vera has the ability to tell who's a Hanti, human, and Kaofi."

Ability. They were Hanti.

Hunter nodded. "I'm Hunter. This is Amari, Clara, and Mya. You guys live out here?"

Vera nodded. "Safest place from Kaofi."

"You heard about the war from the shadows?" Amari asked.

The man nodded. "We heard." He put his hand out. "I'm Keith by the way. Vera is my partner." Hunter shook it.

We tried to decipher if partner meant romantically or just partner in crime. Nobody really made any moves. Maybe for the best. We were all on edge.

"We should talk, then," Hunter said. "About teaming up."

Vera looked at all of us. "This you?"

"Yes. Do you have any more Hanti with you?"

She shook her head. "Just us."

I climbed up the bank and wrung out my hair. Vera followed me up, watching me. "You sure you're okay? You guys look like you took a nasty dunk."

I simply nodded.

Amari climbed up first and grabbed Clara's hand, helping her up.

Hunter and Keith exchanged a few more words and in the end, we all headed back to our camp. This way we could change into dry clothes.

Eli rushed over to me as soon as I came into view. He grabbed my face and checked for injuries. I wish he'd stop doing that. "I can never stop worrying," he whispered.

In seconds, a knife was pressed into his throat. "Why the hell are you harboring a Kaofi?" Vera spat.

"Vera, you can't kill him," Keith said.

"Why not?"

"He's a shadow. Although not entirely." He tilted his head. "Vampire. And shadow."

Vera hissed as she pushed the blade into his neck, but it didn't do much. "You led us into a trap! What kind of sick hunters are you?" She whipped around to face Hunter.

He simply raised his hands in surrender. "It's more complicated than that, but I promise we're not the enemies. We're on your side of this war." He pointed at Eli. "And he's with us, too."

"Impossible. No Kaofi goes against his own."

"Eli does," I whispered as I stared into his eyes.

Still, his hands never wavered from my face. Even after the cruel words he said last night. He refused to let go, even if it only hurt us in the end. We did a lot of thinking about the present and less about our future. At least for now.

Clara grabbed Vera's wrist and lowered it. "Eli is different. He was murdered by his own kind and that's why he's half-and-half. They killed him for their gain. You'd be surprised at how much they ripped from him. I don't blame him for going against the shadows the way he is."

Keith didn't fully understand, but he seemed more accepting than Vera. She was the one who wouldn't take her eyes off Eli.

Hunter scoffed. "Trust me, we didn't like him either. But we don't get much of a choice in the matter. He's our key to taking the shadows down. He knows more than we do."

Keith stepped forward. "Like what?"

"Shadows are weakened by water. It sucks them into the depths for eternity," I said.

This time, Vera licked the blood from her dagger. "Yes. And shadows require a leader, someone to guide them through life and give them a purpose."

"Puppeteer," I told her. "We think we know who it is."

"Who?"

"Lucas. Well, maybe. Could be anyone at this point." My eyes never met hers. Instead, I watched Eli as if I was afraid she could kill him; and if I didn't look away, maybe he'd be safe in my arms.

Vera noticed the looks in our eyes. "You're wrong. On every level. We know who's behind it. And they've had control for far longer than we ever anticipated. It'll be difficult taking it from them. They're skilled."

"They," Amari said. "They're a team. Who the hell is controlling the shadows? Who's trying to kill us?"

Keith finally decided to fully join the conversation as he came around and looked us in the eyes. "The last people you'd ever expect. You might not recognize their names, but you also might. Emily and David Morgan."

My knees buckled and Eli caught me.

Everyone gave me a look, but Amari knew. "That's impossible. They're dead. I've researched them."

They were supposed to be dead. They were supposed to be Hanti. Why would they take control of the shadows? Why would they be the ones who gave me up? Why would they send the shadows after *me*?

"Mya?" Eli sat down with me, not caring whether Vera stabbed him or not. Not that it would make a mark.

I pushed my hair back and shook my head. "You're lying."

Vera let out a soft laugh. "Why would we lie? It's true."

Hunter looked between the two of us. "Who are they?"

"Hunters," Keith said.

"My parents," I whispered. "My biological parents." The ones who discarded me.

I'd once thought maybe they gave me up to protect me but now I wasn't so sure. They'd sent the shadows after me. They'd killed Eli and destroyed my life, even after they didn't even want me. Was I never going to be enough? And was it not enough for them to just let me suffer without them? They desired to be the cause of all the pain.

"Parents?" Vera squatted. "That doesn't sound right. They never had a child."

"They did," Amari said loudly. "Mya is their daughter. They gave her up for adoption. Supposed to be dead, even. But now it makes sense. They faked their death so they could gain what, control of the shadows? And why the hell are the shadows trying to attack Mya? You'd think she'd be the one who's protected in all of this."

You'd think.

As their daughter, I shouldn't have been the target.

"I effing told you. I was the chosen one in this. I was at the center of this bullshit, and you didn't listen. They're targeting me, because my parents are telling them to." I was physically shaking by now. Rage, fear, sorrow. Every monstrous emotion swirled inside my mind. My eyes lightened until they couldn't anymore. "My parents want me dead."

051 Thursday, June 13th

the summer before Eli Kay

Looking into the mirror, I admired my appearance. My hair was brushed through, my makeup done lightly.

I smoothed my hands over the dress, smiling at my own reflection. Tonight was meant to be a summer dance before the school year started back up for me to finish off senior year, and I was going to make the most of it.

The gown flowed to my feet, as white as a dove's feathers. The sleeves hung off the shoulders and exposed the tan I'd worked hard to achieve. Whether I met my prince or not, I was going to find someone to get me going.

It had been a long time since I'd had a good time and I wanted to begin the new school year off right.

As I stepped out of my room, I dodged my mother before she could ask questions. I was a grown woman and the last thing I needed was her pestering me.

I got in my car and drove to the place. I parked but I never left my car.

I chewed my lip, debating if I should be here. But I needed

it. I craved the escape for just a moment.

People stood, gathering with friends or groups. Everyone was dressed for the occasion and some were even pushing to move to the next step of the night.

A lovely scene to put myself into.

Someone knocked on my window and I rolled it down. I didn't get the chance to ask her what she wanted because she asked first, "Are you Mya?" She even knew my name.

I gave her a hesitant nod.

Blood covered her front. "You have to help me. I tried but I couldn't do it myself. Someone over in the forest needs help and I'm scared they won't make it until the police arrive."

How could I trust this woman? I'd seen those ruses used before. I didn't want someone to die but I wasn't obligated to venture off alone into a dark forest. I was obligated to call the police, but that was as far as my help extended.

"Please. He said he had a little brother. He wanted to make it to his graduation, and I don't want to let him down." Tears flowed down her cheeks as they puffed out, her eyes stained a soft crimson.

I took a deep breath and stepped out of my car. "All right. Where is he?" Damn me and my compassion. Why couldn't I have been *heartless*?

Following this woman, she pointed into the forest, but her shaking figure told me she wasn't willing to go back in. I knew I was on my own, so I told her I'd go in and check it myself. I'd be the hero tonight.

Lucky me.

As I stood on the edge of the forest, distinct laughter echoed from within. If they were hurt, why would they be laughing? My gut told me to go inside. I took a step forward, then a few more until I was walking into something I didn't know of, but she told me they were in trouble. I couldn't ignore that. My heart would never allow it.

The laughter grew and it became clear that it came from males. When I approached, they turned to look at me. "Who the bloody hell are you?" The man with black hair asked.

"Mya. I heard laughing."

The second man, one with brown hair, stretched his arm in front of the other. "Don't. She's a Kaofi Hunter."

"I'm not a hunter. Do hunters dress in gowns? No, they dress in camouflage to hide. I'm not out here to kill animals." I shook my head and looked back at the edge of the trees. "I wanted to check on you. Someone said you guys needed help."

"Help? We don't need help." He laughed and stepped forward.

I crossed my arms. "I can see that now. What are your names?" I turned slightly, ready to head back.

"I'll never tell you my name." He walked over and grabbed my wrist. "You can't fool me."

His nails dug into my skin. "Hey, what the hell? You're hurting me!" I yanked my arm away from him before I stumbled back into a tree.

"Josh, stop," the curly, black-haired man said, coming closer. "She's telling the truth. She has no idea."

"What?" I grabbed my shoes, throwing them at them. "Don't you dare touch me!"

"I'm Eli." He put his hand out. "Josh is an arse sometimes. I apologize on his behalf." He chuckled and glanced at Josh.

I shook my head. "Fuck you both. You're sick." I turned around and headed the way I came. I was not going to get myself killed or worse. Those guys couldn't be trusted and if they didn't need help, I wasn't about to stick around for it.

"Mya, don't go." Eli wasn't ready to say goodbye. That didn't stop me. "Who sent you?" he shouted.

I stopped in my tracks. Who sent me? I spun around to face him, but a word never left my lips. A woman with blonde hair and dark eyes, almost black was who'd sent me. Why did he care?

Eli swallowed, his eyes darting to Josh's. "Lucy is back."

Minutes passed. These two were having a whole conversation with their eyes, and I kept trying to sneak away. Being alone with two men in the forest was not my idea of fun. Part of me screamed: *kill them*. The other part told me they posed no real threats. But it was my safety being compromised. However, it was they who seemed to hate me for some reason I couldn't name. Maybe they sensed my conscience telling me to take their lives.

"She's a fucking menace to society, Eli. Trusting her is a grave mistake," Josh said.

Eli shot him a firm look.

As I walked over to them both, I traced an X over my heart. "I should be the one who's worried. I'm out here, alone, with two men who could rape and kill me, and yet something inside me tells me that you won't do that."

Eli gave Josh a nod. "She's right."

Josh snickered, throwing a glare in my direction. "I still say we drop her. Leave her here. Lucy sent her our way, so why not take the offer?"

"We aren't Lucy," he replied. After glancing my way, then at the camera on the rock, he asked, "mind if I take a few pictures? I'd love to seize the opportunity, and you're captured by the moonlight just right."

I wasn't sure if that was a good idea, but I agreed anyway. The second part of me had won the battle inside my mind.

They hadn't been the danger women were warned of.

Eli had me pose a few different places, telling me what to do the entire time. It eased the anxiety and made me feel like a real model, although I was too short for industry standards.

After some more photos, an owl hooted up from the trees but we never caught sight of it. They were majestic, yet private. Maybe I should have been, too. Who was I kidding? I wanted all the attention. I was living for this photoshoot.

Eli left to check on something, leaving me with Josh. Josh kept giving me the death glare. I didn't understand why he was so against me. I was the woman. I was in more danger than he was.

I looked back to see Eli emerging from the trees. His eyes went wide as he shouted, "Josh, no!"

I was thrown to the ground and a large wolf hovered above me and saliva dripped from his teeth. The size of this monster was larger than any wolf I'd ever seen, and I knew I was about to get my throat ripped out. Before he could, I let out a scream that echoed into the sky, bouncing between trees.

Eli rushed over and tackled the wolf to the ground. "What the bloody hell?" he yelled at it.

I scrambled to my feet and grabbed the skirt of my dress. "You're effing nuts. I can't..." I couldn't gather my words. My breathing was unsteady as I stumbled towards the trees.

A man came from the trees and ran at Eli with a blade. "You are poisonous vermin!" He plunged the knife into Eli's back, and I screamed once again. Eli threw him off, and the man landed on the floor.

The wolf stood in front of Eli, growling and baring his teeth. The man pulled something else from his belt, something that appeared to be a dagger. He barely turned towards Eli before Eli came and tripped him, knocking him to the ground. I took a step back, but just as I had, Eli took the man's knife and used it against him, plunging it right into his neck. His blood would forever stain my memories.

Blood tainted the white of my dress as my screams echoed into the sky. As I lifted my eyes to meet the face behind the murder, almond-colored eyes burned into my soul.

"Run!" Eli yelled.

Taking his advice, I sprinted into the woods. Everything moved by in such a blur. I forgot which direction I'd had come from.

Twigs snapped and leaves crunched beneath my bare feet. Everything around me was one giant blur as I sped up my pace, my feet pounding against the ground. My toes caught on a root a little far stretched, sending me to the dirt. Something hard hit my head—or my head hit something hard. The lightbulb of the world had been turned off and everything went pitch black.

The poke in the crook of my elbow, and everything would wash away for the night. Memories. Cognitive function. A grip on reality.

Pain exploded through areas of my body at different intervals. I never caught a break. Things faded in and out, my vision never supporting me for long.

I swore I saw Eli, and Josh, too. Blood coated nearly every inch and their screams rang in my ears for hours on end. I repeatedly told *anyone* listening to just make it stop. That only seemed to worsen my situation.

I'd heard glimpses of the name Alissa, along with phrases like, "You killed her", and "you've betrayed your own kind".

I was grabbed by my hair and dragged across the rough concrete. My breath had been ripped away as they shoved my head underwater. I grabbed the edge of the tub, throwing myself against the ceramic to get a gulp of air. My protests didn't work.

Choking on the water entering my lungs, my head was pulled from the tub. I coughed, lungs burning as I fell against the side. Wet hair clung to my skin as I welcomed oxygen.

A squeak escaped me as someone wrapped their fingers around my neck, picking me up and pushing my head back under the water. The further they pushed, the deeper my body slipped into the tub until every piece of me was submerged.

I clawed at their arm, fighting for just a single breath. A single heartbeat. Mine was quickly disappearing.

Fear clung to every inch of me as I feared the end of my life. I'd hardly experienced anything worth living for. I'd barely lived at all. This couldn't be it, could it?

In seconds, my senses began to vanish. First smell, then the taste of the salty water. The rippling surface of the water faded as my hands went limp and sunk beneath the surface. My hearing was the last to say goodbye.

I thought maybe I'd heard my name, but there was no way that was possible. Right...?

"...Mya!" It sounded muffled, covered by a pillow. No, there were no pillows. A cloud? Was I in heaven now? Dead?

"Mya, bloody hell, wake up already!"

No, definitely not heaven.

I heard a crack as my chest caved in. No, my ribs snapped. Water spurted from my mouth and someone pushed me onto my side as I spit it all up and gasped for air. The cold hurried under my skin and I began to shake.

Fingers gripped my arm, pulling me upright. "Look at me," Eli said. "You're going to run. Now. Don't look back."

"What..." My words came out in breathless whispers.

What about you?

"I'll be fine. You need to get out. Escape. Josh and I will be fine but they are out for your blood. They killed you and they'll do it again if they return and realize you're alive." He scrambled to his feet and yanked me up, leading me to the door. "Go. Now."

I grabbed onto the frame, wiping the hair from my forehead. I had another chance at life, and I took it. I found the door and slipped out of the building, stumbling through the forest. I'd almost tripped over my dress a few times but I grabbed the skirt and lifted it to keep it from weighing me down.

No. I tore it off my body until I was no longer constricted, until I could take full breaths again.

My bare feet hit pavement, and I saw headlights in the distance, coming closer. I let out a cry, falling to my knees and collapsing onto the road. Tires screeched and a car door slammed. However, I never saw my hero's face before the trauma enveloped me whole.

052 Sunday, September 16th

"You remember," he whispered. "I don't quite remember but I was in that memory so it must be true. But at least one of us remembers."

I didn't look at Eli, but I knew a million thoughts ran through his mind the same way it did mine. The memories. My parents. All of it.

Without seeing his eyes, I knew he had questions. I had them, too.

"I need to cool off before I faint," I said.

I hurried to the lake and stripped down to just my bra and underwear before climbing down into the water. The sun had already set for the night but I wasn't going to let that stop me. The heat here didn't let up no matter the time of day.

Once I was in the lake, my worries slipped away like I'd been wearing a second skin. I was left alone, in the dusk. That was my cue to try something I'd always wanted to. Maybe it sounded ridiculous and maybe it was. But I did a lot of ridiculous things with confidence these days. So, I removed what clothing was left on my body and threw it back up onto the rocks.

"Well, that's an invitation if I've ever seen one," Eli said with a chuckle as he appeared on the rock, sitting down.

My cheeks heated as I lowered myself further under the water. "I didn't realize you followed me." I assumed he would have stayed at camp to do his own thing.

"Your friends don't trust me all that much so it would have been stupid to stick around them. You're more fun, and now I can see why." I might have seen a sly smile but I couldn't be sure. It was too gloomy.

Eli could see me better than I could see him.

"Don't forget it, Little Hanti. I'd love to see more but we've entailed that's not the best idea. And besides, I can't get in the water without one of us being put in danger." His feet dangled just a little above me.

Brows furrowed, I lowered my eyes to the surface of the lake. Something hadn't quite added up. Why would my parents give me up just to take control of the shadows instead?

What did they gain?

Almost as if...

No, it couldn't be.

But was it?

"Spill," Eli growled.

What if the shadows in some form had been my parents' proudest design? A family of their own making. I would have gotten in the way, certainly.

"Then you'll be the perfect one to take them out," he said.

Take out my own parents—how marvelous for me. All because they loved their enemies more than the child they refused to form a parental bond with.

As if I wasn't enough to carry out their legacy. They discarded me for great power, and that was why they needed to snuff me out before I pulled the rug from under them.

Silence weighed down. The water rippled. Hearts snapped.

The words tumbled out before I could even stop them, or think about what I was saying, "We were in love."

Eli didn't move a muscle from that. Familiarity swirled around his irises, like he'd suspected it. Maybe he had. And I was certain the questions were brewing, and rightfully so. I dropped a bomb that I never planned to. Before, he might have laughed or killed me for it. Now, I wasn't sure. I trusted him enough to know the full truth though.

"Before you died, we were...dating. But things went south so quickly between Lucy and Lucas always targeting us and the shadows killing you and..." He had a right to know. I could have kept it a secret and changed our fate. But nothing would erase what happened. My cheating had nothing to do with the Kaofi or the shadows killing him and I had to accept that. "I cheated on you a few days before you were killed. I almost kissed Owen in a desperate attempt to make him stay and when I told you, you sent me elsewhere for a short time." I looked at my reflection in the water.

"You got me killed in more ways than one." His voice sounded so battered and broken. What I feared.

I swam closer to the rocks. "Yes, and I take full responsibility for it. But we made up. And I'm not trying to tell you how to feel or that you should react exactly as you did before. That Eli died and I deserve what's coming. But before we were attacked by Kaofi, you came by to tell me that you made up your mind. You wanted to give us another chance—something about how I was honest from the start. We trained in the woods shortly after and that was when we were attacked. "

He leaned forward. "I knew something was up. I knew there was more to it than you were letting on. Here we are, and now I find out you had cheated on me, and you decided you had the audacity to sleep in my bed, wear my clothes, and live in my apartment. You hurt me, I died, and you get to keep everything?"

My heart cracked. "Now when you put it like that, I sound even worse."

Eli didn't say a word. He didn't need to. I drowned in them myself.

I'd beaten myself up ever since that day. I'd always blamed myself for what I did. Knowing that he had died even, thinking I was never his. I had caused him great pain before his death and I only had myself to blame for this. He was truly a wonderful person, but I was the one who tore him down.

I'd ripped him apart.

I'd created a monster.

And maybe I hadn't been the one holding the dagger that went into his neck, but I might as well have been.

I slowly climbed up the rocks but I stayed low, poking just my head above the rock Eli sat on. "Hey, can I do anything at all to make it up to you? I know I can't bring back your life. I can't change things. And if it makes you feel any better, I don't have those feelings for Owen anymore. I did, once. But they weren't love. Not true love. Just simply infatuation. I'll help you win this war and then we'll go our separate ways. I won't stay at your apartment and I realize now I should have left the second you died."

"Just, please, be quiet for a second," he said quietly, shooing me.

I closed my mouth and grabbed my clothes, pulling myself up onto the rock. I gave him one last look before turning the other way so I could make myself decent.

"So you never loved him?" he said through the empty air.

I wrung out my hair. "I don't think I did, and it took *way* too long to realize that. He was meant to be just a fling for the summer. He died, and it broke me because I was lonely. Not because I loved him."

I'd turned to alcohol to make the bad thoughts go away because they were only ever there due to loneliness. When Eli died, I turned to training. I worked hard to better myself because that's what he would have wanted. Because I loved him so much that even in death, his opinion meant the world to me.

I gasped when fingers slid around my wrist and spun me around until I faced Eli. What was he going to do, kill me? Tell me off? It was a double wound. Having to relive that kind of pain all over again. He never deserved it in the first place.

"Just stop thinking for a moment," he snapped.

I did as he said.

His fingers jumped from my wrist to my hips, trailing up. It was safe to say my body was on fire from the simple movement alone.

Up they traced, brushing the skin of my neck up he tilted my chin towards him. "You've only ever loved me," he whispered.

"Only you," I replied.

He stepped as close as he could get without touching me, twirling a strand of my hair around his finger. I couldn't say or do anything. It was impossible to move a muscle.

I choose you.

I'd intentionally never said the words aloud, but he deserved to know now I would never choose Owen.

Anxiety rose in my veins from the questions. Why wasn't he making moves? What was he doing?

From that, I chewed my lip to keep myself under control, but I'd torn too much skin and then some blood was seeping through. I could almost see his irises from this close and they seemed to darken until they were no longer visible to me.

With his thumb, he pulled my bottom lip down before running his tongue over the blood. My eyes widened and I almost took a step back but this time, Eli didn't let me.

He took me hostage with his kiss.

He poured every desire, every craving, and all the heartaches into me through our lips.

And I returned nothing less than what he gave.

He slipped his fingers into my hair, tangling them as his other hand wrapped around my waist. I was still wet, but that only amplified the heat radiating between us.

Oh how I wished to feel his skin against mine all over again.

His kisses were desperate yet filled with such yearning. It was everything I'd dreamed of for months since his death. He had lost himself and forgotten me, but this kiss had rekindled something buried deep within.

It reminded me I couldn't escape love. I could not pretend. All I could do was accept that I was wholly in love with Eli and I'd die for him in a heartbeat.

He growled as he kissed down my jaw. "Which I'd never allow."

But that was how I knew it was love. I didn't care if it

meant I couldn't see him. The only thing I cared about was making sure he'd been safe. Happy. Tucked in the comfort of his own home.

Eli's lips found mine again as our breaths coincided. "I am happy in your arms. Right here. Right now," he whispered. "Maybe not so safe, but who said danger wouldn't be part of the game?" His nails dug into my lower back and I made a bold move undoing buttons to his shirt. In my favor, he accepted.

Grabbing my chin, he dug his fingers into my jaw, before moving the hand from my hair further south.

"Eli," I pulled away. "Your fingers," I grabbed his hand from my jaw and we both saw a little blood lining the edges of his nails. His face fell.

"Mya, I'm so sorry. I don't know what got into me." He conveyed his apology through his eyes, and I understood all too well. I'd never thought about what loving a shadow meant.

I reached forward, rubbing my thumbs over the insides of his wrists. "It's okay. You got a little too excited. Too much emotion." And it had been so long since he'd touched me. I could only imagine how much his body ached for something like that. I made it pretty hard for him to bring any woman home when I always slept in his bed.

He brushed his fingers over the small cuts in my jaw. "It won't happen again." There was something else behind that promise.

"You mean that's it? You kiss me like I'm the blood in your veins and then you drop me like an old cellphone? Eli, don't allow a little mishap to ruin this." I shook my head. I didn't make any moves to stop him though. He was determined.

"Mishap implies I accidentally said something I didn't

mean to say. But I physically hurt you. I was too rough. What if I were to do that in bed?"

"You make it sound like you slapped me in a fit of rage."

"I may as well have."

"Stop." I pulled him against me. "Don't do that. You went too hard. You didn't get mad and lose your temper. You just got too excited and squeezed too hard. That's not the same. We can make this work. I'll do absolutely anything to make this work." I rested my forehead against his. "Promise me you're going to help me."

He closed his eyes. "Little Hanti ..."

"Promise me."

Silence ensued. Then the words fell from his lips like petals from a flower, "I wholeheartedly swear on my mother's grave."

Even if he didn't remember the life we once had together or the love he gave me, that never stopped him from wanting me. Maybe what we shared was rooted deeper—like the trees. Maybe our love had been a tree and even if you cut it down, the roots still reached out for any sign of life to keep them grounded.

We would have always found each other in the end. Not a single shadow could stop that.

Marionette

"He's turned against his own, and now he loves my daughter. How ghastly." I crushed the glass in hand, wine washing over the fresh cuts and bleeding into my body.

The shadow before me bowed. "What do you suggest we do?"

What kind of question was that?

They'd not only failed their mission, but now they'd in turn lost every braincell through their breathing.

"I'll ask less of you from here on out." As I stood from my chair, I looked over at my husband who carried in a few snacks from the kitchen. Despicable excuse for a partner. I'd still married him anyway.

The shadow glanced up, still bent over. "Ma'am? Master?"

Meeting the sorry excuse his mother gave birth to, I brought my hand up to examine the crimson beads. "Nothing, shadow. From now on, you follow my lead because I've decided it's time to take things into my own hands. If you want things done, you must do it yourself."

My husband dropped the plate, eyes wide. "Em, are you sure?"

Shadows began quivering in, one by one before appearing in droves. After appearing, I moved in my fingers in quick yet unnatural directions as my shadows fell in line, not a billowing of smoke present. With a snap of my fingers, they bowed in unison.

My children. My puppets. *My fabrications.*

A malevolent smile crept up. I squeezed my hand into a fist. "Let's go meet our daughter."

053 Wednesday, September 26th

Storm clouds rolled in but the temperature hardly dropped at all. Eli stood beside me as I watched the sky, afraid of what was coming next. I could sense the danger hanging thick in the air.

And that wasn't just because a shadow was right in my peripheral vision.

"We should get somewhere safe. For your sake," he said.

After nodding my head, he took my hand and led me back to his apartment. I sat down and looked around the room. He came over, shoving his hands into his pockets. "What's on your mind?"

"I never got the chance to apologize to you."

"Apologize for what?"

"Before you died, there was a period of time when I stopped talking to you. Long story short, I thought you had been stalking me and I even went to the police to turn you in after murdering vampires in front of me—before I knew they were vampires of course. But you weren't, Eli. You had been a victim as much as I was, and I'm sorry that I accused you of anything. Even if you don't remember it now, I'm still sorry."

He leaned down and placed a soft kiss on my lips. "I appreciate the apology."

I returned the kiss and unbuttoned his shirt. My hands roamed the muscles on his chest. Why did he get to forget when I remembered ever detail?

I stopped and looked at him. "You forgot about what happened to us."

"What?" he whispered, confusion lacing his accent.

"About us. When we were kidnapped. When we were drugged. Lucy and Lucas tried to destroy us but you got to forget about it. Now I'm the one left to bury the pieces." I nodded.

He grabbed my shirt. "I can't help that I died, Mya. Don't blame me."

With an exasperated sigh, I threw my head back. "But it is your fault. You stepped in to save me. You shouldn't have done that."

He kissed my neck and sunk his teeth in, calling my blood to him.

I allowed my eyelids to fall closed. "You are such a monster."

"Terrible," he murmured into my ear after pulling his teeth out. He gripped my hips, digging his nails into my skin. I was certain that blood was coating his fingers at the cost of my pain.

"Eli, stop," I grabbed his wrists and shoved them away from me.

He met my eyes before looking down at my hips. He pulled the fabric of my shorts just a little to get a better look. "I apologize. Sometimes I underestimate my strength." Eli stood and grabbed some supplies to clean it up. "I forget that what I crave is not what you crave."

"What? Do you crave hurting me?"

He cleaned the blood first before putting a bandage over it. "I crave pain, yes. And I forget I need to reel in my shadow side when I'm around you."

"You think he's going to be bad, again? Do you think maybe it's going to be a sad ending for us?" I asked.

"Maybe it's not about the happy ending. Maybe it's about the story," he said.

I scoffed. "Don't tell me you believe that. I want a happy ending for us. Don't you? You're going against everything you believe in as a Kaofi just to love me."

With a chuckle, he pulled my shirt down. "I promise you that I am going to see to it that we have a happy ending. I actually think that quote is bullshit."

"You do? How so?"

"I want a happy ending. I haven't lived this long just to see tragedy. I think we both have had enough of that. I don't want to live without you. I am in love with you, and I couldn't ask for anything else. You give me everything I want and need. And yes, the story does matter. Our story matters, but everyone deserves a happy ending. That's what *I* think. We deserve to achieve at least that." He kissed my knuckles.

"Knowing my luck, you'll probably die again."

"I can't die. I'm a shadow now." I knew that. But it was still a fear regardless.

"I suppose that's a plus then... No more heartbreak for me. Unless the shadow king and queen—my parents—decide they want to control you. Or Lucy and Lucas find a way. I need to kill them."

Eli pulled me into his lap as he sat on the bed, resting his chin on my head. "Sounds like a splendid idea. However, Lucy and Lucas are experienced, as well as your parents. Do you think you can take them down?"

His sweet scent of vanilla mixed with the cedar wood calmed me. It also gave me the confidence I needed. "I've been training nonstop. During our *no-talking* debacle, as well as after you died, I trained hard. I've been training to defend myself because I'm sick of being the damsel. You died because you had to save me. Ryan died because he had to save me. My parents supposedly died trying to save me, you know, before we found out they actually want me dead. It's safe to say I've learned my lesson."

He tilted his head, pressing his nose against my hair. "I can help. I have the power to show them what nightmares are made of."

"So, I hear." I laughed. "But no. I appreciate it, but this is one battle I need to fight on my own. I need to make my place known to the Hanti."

"Of course. I'll be here whenever you need me." He pulled us closer to the dark side of the bed.

I released a sigh. "It's scary. I'll admit that much. But it's something I need to do just to make sure that our future is safe. I'm going to fight for what I want."

"That is indeed true..." He left a trail of kisses down my shoulder.

"I'm not ashamed of who I am." A nod. "Even though I can't control how I feel towards you, I'm not ashamed that I love you."

"You're not lying?" He tilted his head up to look at my face more.

A shiver ran down my spine. "It's not something I could lie about, Eli. I know what I feel. I know what I want. I'm happy here and there would be no point in being ashamed. I would purposely be destroying my own happiness."

"Good. Can we just stay here forever? You silence the voice in my head." He brushed my hair behind my shoulders.

A laugh echoed as I shook my head. "We can as soon as things are settled down, after I kill those damn fallen angels, and take control from my parents. I would like to say I accomplished it."

His fingers skimmed over my cheek. "You will. I won't let you give up," he joked.

"Nothing about loving you is shameful." I leaned down, pressing my lips to his.

"I feel the same way." His fingers wrapped around my thighs, or as much as they could.

"We need a plan to change the minds of everyone around. I don't want to live in the dark forever." I meant that literally. "I want to be able to explore our life together without being hunted or killed. I'm the Hanti. I shouldn't be a target. I want to be able to love whoever I please." I let out a sigh.

He laid back on the bed. "Tell me, Mya, if you think we can get out of this alive." He rested an arm behind his head.

"I'm scared. I'll be the first to admit that I don't know if we will." I traced the vertical dip down his chest. "We might die, Eli. Or *I* might. Not many people are accepting of interspecies relationships. It might not be that bad now, but if we get married someday, people will get worse. It could lead to kidnapping us and killing us for our crimes against this world." I leaned closer to him and planted a small kiss on his neck. "Blood drives us both. It's what makes us who we are. It just might not be how we both expect it."

He reached down for the blanket and pulled it over us, as far as it could go without falling down my back. "What do you suggest?"

I grabbed his chin, gazing at his lips. "I suggest I rip Lucas and Lucy apart and use that as our example for why nobody should threaten our relationship. I also need to put my parents in their place. Shows everyone I don't care what side you're on, because if you target me, I fight back. I want your help to plan their demise." I grabbed his bottom lip between my teeth and pulled. "Don't you think it would be a good idea?"

His eyes shut and he nudged his nails into my skin. "It's tempting..."

I flipped my hair out of my face, kissing his neck again. "Then it's settled. We're going to kill four birds with two stones." I traced the other side of his neck with my index finger, stealing a moan from his lips.

I slid myself down his chest. "We just need some motivation before we carry out our destruction."

On my walk, the sun set behind the horizon. I ran off, letting all my worries slip away from me. They peeled from my body the faster I sprinted.

When I came to a stop, I neared a stream. I took off my shoes and soaked my feet, sighing in contentment. The coolness was refreshing from the heat of the day.

Crickets chirped and leaves rustled. The wind flew through the trees, flickering like a ballerina. The babbling of the stream blended with the sounds of nature, and all of it put my anxiety at ease.

Footsteps echoed as twigs snapped. I turned my head, letting out a low laugh. "Yeah, you can't scare me. I'm used to this Eli. You tried this on our first date and now I know what to expect." I pressed my lips together. I felt a breath on the back of my neck, causing a shiver. "I see what you're doing," I whispered. Although, this time my body didn't react the way it usually did near him. The scent of burning flesh filled my nostrils.

I jumped to my feet and spun around, coming face to face with the foul man who had caused me so much pain. "You." I narrowed my eyes on him. Eli wasn't around and I wasn't about to scream for help. I had trained for this moment.

"Yes, me. What is it that has the hunter out here by herself?" He chuckled.

I swung at him, ready to smack the smug look off his face. He caught my wrist. He growled at me, gripping my wrist tightly. "I can kill you. Even Hanti are limited. There is always a way to get rid of every walking organism."

I yanked my wrist away from him and spat in his face. "Perfect. Then that means there is a way to get rid of you, too. Thanks for letting me know." I knew what his weakness was, but this was another game of my own.

"I'm not so worried about you. You're still a newbie and you will never match up to my strength. You are a lost cause." He shrugged off my threats.

It never occurred to him that I was still being trained by Hanti *and* a vampire. He was sorely mistaken. I laughed, but no ounce of humor came with it. "Don't be too sure of yourself. You would be surprised at what I can do. I have been training to fight my own battles, to fight my demons. You are exactly what I've been training to fight."

"That's cute. You think I'm a demon. Do you not know by now I'm a fallen angel? I am *not* a demon. Demons don't exist here, Mya. I am the scariest thing you'll ever face." He closed the gap between us, towering over my petite figure. His blackened eyes burned a hole right through my soul.

Rolling my eyes, not fazed by his terror, I said, “That’s not saying much.” I plucked a hair from his head.

“You will be dead before you even get to marry Eli,” he threatened. He backed away as his wings unfolded. Their size couldn’t be downplayed, and their shade was darker than that of vantablack. They carried him up into the wind as he shot up from the earth.

A black feather drifted downward. Lucas was gone in seconds, and all that was left was a soft *forgive me* floating in the air.

054 Saturday, September 29th

"He dropped this." I showed Eli a black feather that laid between my thumb and forefinger. "And when he was close enough, I took a hair from his head. Two forms of DNA are all I need to make the concoction that kills him. Well, and the book, of course. There's just one problem. I have to make him drink it."

Eli folded his arms over his chest. "How do we make him drink something?"

I nodded along while flipping through the pages of the book Amari had given me. "He's very cocky. I'll use that to my advantage."

Grabbing a bowl, I put the needed ingredients inside. I began grinding. They created a fine powder, glowing a purple shade—a color that Amari saw when she spotted fallen angels.

First he cleared his throat, then he said, "I'm going to help you."

I sent him a '*duh*' look. "I knew that. You can't help yourself, even when you want to watch me wither."

He hissed playfully. "Maybe I wanted to watch you bloom."

"And maybe I wanted you to fight regardless of the outcome." I poured half of the powder into a bottle of water before shaking it until the contents mixed.

He came closer. "How do we lure him out?"

"Easy. Egg him on." I used the last half of powder in a second bottle of water, thoroughly mixing it before packing a few things. Pausing, I looked at him and chewed my lip. "Eli, what you're going to see… I don't want you to assume that's all I am." I didn't want him to see me for only the Hanti in me. I needed him to see *all* of me.

Eli gave me that famous sly smile of his. "I know, Little Hanti. You've seen the utter darkness pouring from every crevice of my being. It's time I get to witness your black heart in return."

I said, "All right, let's get going. We have to hurry. We'll meet the other Hanti there."

Eli packed up our weapons while I clipped the front of the half-jacket around my neck, over the one-piece corset I wore. On top of that, I'd strapped a flowing skirt with two cut-out slits up my legs. I laced up my combat boots and took one last look in the mirror as I threw my hair into a bun. My outfit's dark color scheme would prepare for the funerals of today, mourning casualties, but certainly not the lives of my enemies.

We took the bag and walked into the forest. We weren't walking for very long. We began running once we got out of the public eye, and I smirked as I whipped around trees, staying ahead of Eli.

When we arrived at the curved road aside the railing, I dropped the bag. "This is where Lucas threatened me. I have a sneaking suspicion he'll come back here." I scanned the area for any traps he might have set.

On the opposite side of the road, a mountainside climbed toward the sky. Trees covered every inch on either side, encasing us in a gloomy atmosphere. The forest, too, prepared for all we'd lose—or perhaps *gain*.

The Hanti took their hiding places while Eli and I held our heads high in plain sight.

After creating a ruse to lure them out, I shoved Eli up against a tree, pressing the tip of my dagger into the flesh of his neck.

His Adam's apple bobbed, his eyes darting up to the sky. A thud sounded behind me as I angled my head just forty-five degrees to my right. They were too easy to trap. *Fools.*

Digging deeper into Eli's neck, I asked them, "What's the occasion? I didn't dress up for the event."

"You're a hunter," Lucy said with a scowl.

A scoff. "Last I checked, Eli wasn't your own. You tried to kill me to hurt him, or did you forget that part? It's so woefully pathetic how you've done this a thousand times." I laughed. "Your lies don't deceive me."

Lucy lunged forward, but Lucas held her back by placing his hand on her shoulder. "Let me go at her, Lucas."

"No. Not yet. This is a trap."

"How so?" Her eyes narrowed in on me, digging into my skull for the details.

Letting go of Eli, I spun to face Lucas. "Congratulations—you can spot when I tell a lie, too." I fingered my blade. "It's too bad this little dagger won't be able to hurt you." My gaze never wavered from his.

"Now why would you assume that?" Lucas chuckled, vice oozing from his throat.

I faked a gasp. "You mean to tell me that a little weapon can hurt you? Then you aren't as powerful as I thought."

He growled, running towards me. Before he could attack, my reflexes kicked in and I jumped out of his way.

He turned his head back at me. "I'll take my time as I crush every bone in your body until you are nothing but dust."

Shrug. "Doesn't surprise me. That is a very predictable plan. You're not that unique, Lucas." I released a small sigh.

Before I could say another word, Lucy grabbed me from behind and pinned my arms behind my back. "Have at her."

Lucas approached me. "It's too easy. I like a challenge." He shot a look at Lucy.

As soon as she let go, Lucas' fist came colliding with my jaw. I fell to the ground and rubbed it, moving my jaw around. "That was weak." I got back on my feet. "You're holding back for me. Stop fighting me like a cupcake."

He growled, tackling me and shoving my face into the ground. He wrapped his fingers around my neck and tightened them.

"Hey, oversized bird, has nobody ever taught you not to hit a girl?" Amari yelled as she dropped out of the tree onto Lucas while Hunter threw Lucy to the ground.

Lucy punched Hunter, throwing him off. Lucas sent me a bored expression, knocking Amari into the same tree. "You brought the whole gang? You really are afraid of me." He narrowed his eyes, a sneaky smile displayed.

Taking my dagger, I hopped on his back. I stabbed the blade right into his neck just to watch him bleed, but nothing came out.

He tossed me off and kicked me in my side. "You thought you were so close."

I was getting closer with every second I wore him out.

Eventually, I would take a hit to his ego and he would need to prove himself. I would make him drink his own poison.

Clara leaped up and kicked him in the gut. After flying to the ground, a small groan passed his lips. "That's for touching Amari, prick."

I stood and rubbed my sore abdomen. He wouldn't get to me. Not *this* time. "Eventually, the Kaofi Hunter comes out." I swung my leg around and kicked him in the face while he still was down.

He fixed his crooked nose. "That's why I have to kill you first." He grabbed my leg and spun me until I hit the ground chest first.

I gripped my knife, plunging it into his arm to get a grasp on him. I used it to pull him down with me. "Too little, too late." I rolled on top of him. "You sealed your fate the second you targeted me." After getting up, I kicked him where it hurt the most.

He grabbed hold of his crotch and yelled out. It seemed to be the most sensitive place no matter what species the male was.

Amari threw me a sword and I caught it midair, holding it vertically in front of my vital organs. "If we can't make you drink it, we get it in the only way we can, don't we?" Eli came to me and drenched the blade with one bottle of Lucas' demise.

"It is the only thing that will kill you. And I guarantee, Lucas, that I *will* kill you." I flashed him a venomous grin. The fear in his eyes became much more satisfying as he scooted backwards. Regardless, he got to his feet.

"Don't let me hold you back!" I swung my sword at his side, but he blocked it.

His fist came around and hit my cheek. I stumbled, taken

back by the sudden pain. It soon dissipated. I planted my feet, regaining my posture. I swung the sword once again. I spun around as I hit nothing but air.

After flying into the air to avoid my swing, he landed on the ground, charging at me. He took me down and threw the sword out of reach.

Memories flooded my head.

He had ruined my bones. He'd touched me. He wrecked every part of me, physically and mentally. I'd no longer been the weak woman he assumed I was. Now I was a *Kaofi Hunter*. A Hanti.

I yelled out, sending him flying into a tree. When I got up, I narrowed my eyes, gritted my teeth, and ran towards the iron sword. I slid down, feeling the handle as I stood back on my feet. A few swings and twirls to keep it in my blood—to show them what I was made of. I turned towards Lucas and sprinted.

He shot up from the ground before landing behind me. I faced him once again. My breathing came out shallow.

I needed a move that took him off guard, so I twisted around and began running as fast as I could at a fat tree. I ran up the trunk, flipping myself and then pushing my feet off of it. I soared towards Lucas. As I blocked his exit, he tried to duck. *Tried.*

Because the sword didn't fail me.

I slammed it through his chest, unleashing the fury burning from within.

Lucas screamed, his defeat ascending as black liquid poured from his body. He collapsed. His body twitched, a result of the constant state of agony he was trapped in.

I landed right by his head, standing over him, watching him bleed until death swept him away. His body cracked, fire engulfing his cries, exposing him for his sins. His dark eyes glassed over as they captured the last thing he would ever see. *My face.*

To ash he returned. And to ash he would forever stay.

I dropped the sword just as Hunter stole it from me, using his chance to cut off Lucy's head.

She'd meant nothing to me. Lucas was the real end to my game. But not the only.

A slow clap sounded as a woman emerged from the around the curve of the pavement. "I've never been prouder." Too many transgressions but not enough wrinkles to pay for them.

Mom.

Which meant my father couldn't be that far behind.

"The very woman who birthed me and then took control of the shadows to kill me," I said.

She laughed as she shook her head. "No, no, you got it all wrong. We had control before you were ever conceived."

What a nice thought. "So what was it, mother? You want me dead because you control the shadows? Is that it?" I snickered. "What was the purpose? Why didn't you just abort me in the first place?"

"Oh, honey, we did want you. We just didn't realize at the time you'd be a threat to our power. Foolish of us, and now here we are to finish the job. We must right what was wrong." She stepped forward. "Now."

Shadows emerged from every fracture in the earth and attacked, and Eli attempted to resist the urge to come for me, but he couldn't fight it for long.

"You have to shut off the shadow side," I yelled.

He shook his head, hands ripping his hair. "I can't! They'll attack your mind!"

"And you'll attack me!" I pulled out my dagger as if it would do anything against shadows. I needed to show Eli he couldn't protect me forever. I'd rather my parents not be able to control him, however they were doing that, and I needed to somehow *take* that control from them.

Then kill them to make sure it didn't happen again.

Eli shut off the switch completely. The shadows raided my mind as well as sending nightmares my way.

But at least Eli was able to help us fight them off as much as possible rather than succumb to my parents' loathing.

I was thrown to the ground by one of the shadows as it loomed over me, claws extended. My mother appeared from behind, disappointed. "I already know what you're thinking and you won't be able to take control from us. You don't even know how we have it ourselves."

I didn't. But I needed to figure it out in minutes.

Before the claws sank into my chest, I rolled out of the way and scrambled to my feet. "I might not be able to hurt the shadows but I can sure as hell hurt you." I rushed at her and swung my dagger. She threw herself out of the way and pulled her own blade from the sheath at her hip. My eyes narrowed.

"Mya, go. I got her!" Amari gestured for me to go somewhere else, and I didn't understand at first but eventually it made sense.

I hurried off and climbed into a tree. Squatting on a branch, I closed my eyes and searched my mind as the shadows clawed their way in. It stung, certainly, but I needed to find a way to control them. How did my parents do it?

I yelled out as claws sung into my calf, pulling me to the forest floor. "You little bitch!" I shoved the shadow off of me before scanning the area. I took off running in search of any body of water and spotted a shorter brick wall between the road and the cliffside. Climbing over it, I teetered on the edge of a rushing river hundreds of feet below.

Looking back, I saw some shadows coming at me and I hurled myself out of the way, hoping they'd plummet.

No.

They stopped themselves before turning on me again. My foot skid off the rocks and I fell, grabbing onto the edge of the cliff and attempting to pull myself back up. The shadows surrounded me as whispers slithered from their tongues like snakes.

I couldn't go out like this.

"Mya!" Eli shouted as he sprinted.

The shadows lifted their claws and swiped at me. One hand loosened, but I swiped for the rocks again. My core strength was better than it had been a year ago but fire was set ablaze to my abs as I held myself up.

They clawed again, and I let go, dropping back from the cliff. Eli peered over and wasted no more seconds as he dove.

I reached for anything, grabbing at the air, but it didn't stop the icy water from submerging me. I fought the resistance of the current. Once I forced my way to the surface, my hair succumbed to gravity against my shoulders.

After gasping for air, I looked around for Eli and found him by the rocks, trying to swim his way to me.

"Mya!" He pushed harder, but the current swept me under the water and I reached out for anything to pull myself up. Much to my despair, nothing was nearby.

Taking my time, I closed my eyes as the shadows continued to terrorize my mental state.

Spiders.

Venomous spiders.

And how could you ruin one? Squish them, maybe. But what did little Mya do to bugs and spiders as a kid? She pulled their legs off. I needed to use that to gain control over them.

Legs. Skinny legs, like *strings* attached. Puppets had strings and if I was going to control the shadows I needed to locate those strings. But how exactly did I find those, and where were they hidden? Why had my parents been able to find them but no one else?

Fingers wrapped around my wrist and dragged me up to the surface.

I opened my eyes just as Eli wrapped an arm around my waist and pulled me up onto the rocks. "I've got you," he whispered against my hair.

A fin splashed at us as it disappeared back under the river. A siren. What once threatened me had become my hero.

"Eli, you need to switch it back on."

"Excuse me?"

"Please. If you do, I think I know how to gain control. And I need you to trust me. Switch it on and fight it. But make yourself as vulnerable as you can with me," I peered up at him.

"What, I'm not vulnerable enough?" He snickered.

I cried, "Eli, please! Do it!"

His jokes fell as the seriousness flooded his gaze. He nodded before closing his eyes and switching it on. In a moment, he let go of me, and I used that to push him out towards the cliffs. He squeezed his eyes shut as he grabbed his hair, trying to take control of his own mind.

"Please," I whispered.

He dropped all his walls as he looked at me, his eyes glossing over.

It was faint, but I could see it.

Right in front of me. The string.

I grabbed onto it tightly, pulling until Eli straightened his posture as if he was waiting for a command. What did I tell him? But that was the solution. I had his utter obedience because he had been oh so vulnerable. And now the question was, how did my parents get the other shadows to be so exposed?

That was it.

"Get us back up to the cliff, to the war," I told Eli.

He didn't waste another second as he grabbed me and carried me over his shoulder, running full speed and glitching through dark spots until we made it back to top of the cliff.

As he set me down, I faced my parents, before looking at the other shadows. "I wouldn't be so quick to kill me if I were you," I told them. "Hunters are *not* immortal. Or did my parents fail to mention that?" I narrowed my eyes on my mother. "Someday they will die and you will be left without a leader. Do you truly want that? Do you want to live years without a leader? I don't think you do."

The shadows stood around like lost dolls.

"What are you doing?" my mother asked.

I shot the shadows a glance. "But I'm their flesh and blood. And I can take control if you want me to. I have plenty more years on my life than they do." I twirled my dagger in my fingers. "Make your decision."

My mother raced for me. "Don't listen to her!"

I ducked as she flew over me, rolling onto the road before landing on her feet and facing me. I got into position. "But we all know how this ends."

Someone's blood would be spilled. They had the choice between losing their leaders now and leaving this war with none, watching their leaders win but only getting maybe another thirty years with them, or siding with me and taking on a new leader with around sixty years left.

The choice was theirs.

My mother came at me again and this time I spun to miss her, before slicing her arm. She whipped around and swiped her blade at my cheek, drawing blood.

Make the choice quickly.

I spun again, trying to plunge my dagger into her abdomen but she dodged the attempt and grabbed a fistful of my hair, throwing my face into a tree.

Why did I have to look just like her?

"You're far too amateur," she spat in my ear. She pressed her blade into my neck.

"That was your goal all along, huh? Never let me get more powerful?" A chuckle. "And look at how that turned out for you. Targeting us only pushed me to work harder to take you out of this forsaken world." I elbowed her, causing her to slip the tip of the dagger into my neck.

Right before I closed my eyes, I saw faint strings. Hundreds. Maybe *thousands.*

They'd chosen me over her, and she had no idea.

So I grabbed all of them and yanked.

My mother felt the movement and stumbled. "What?" She looked at the shadows. "What are you doing?" she yelled.

"Attack," I said in a low voice.

The shadows lunged for her, ripping her from me. I turned and faced her, watching them claw into her skin. They dragged their claws through every inch of her body before shoving them into her eyes. Her blood splattered against my face as she became no longer recognizable.

They slid away like balloons, parting for me to face my father who watched with wide eyes.

It became clear in that moment that he was never the one behind the operations. He only went along with whatever his wife wanted of him. She had been the only puppeteer.

What did that mean?

Did I keep him alive?

No. Silence was support in his eyes and he supported his wife murdering her own daughter for power.

"Kill him, too."

The shadows tore him apart and his screams drenched the woods around us.

Nothing was left behind but bones as if they'd been attacked by wild animals. Smart, clean, and careful. The police would never question it much and they would certainly never trace it back to me. As far as I knew, I was adopted and my biological parents were dead.

Now, they really *were*.

The weight lifted off my shoulders. I could breathe, and I could live in peace until the next Kaofi threatened us. I had my whole life ahead of me now. "A hard beginning makes for a good ending," I preached to the remains that now scattered the forest floor.

As I turned to face Clara, Amari, and Hunter, I pushed the wet strands of hair from my face. "Let this be a lesson to anyone who tries to harm anyone I love. I don't play nice. I know exactly who I am." I moved my eyes over to Eli as he kept his glued to the only thing left of Lucas, Lucy, as well as my parents.

"And who is that?" Amari asked as she gathered the sword.

I focused on my stained weapon, observing every drop of crimson.

It wouldn't be long before more Kaofi came after us for our crimes. I intended to take every threat out of this world.

That was exactly why I took on my role as a Kaofi Hunter.

However, it'd never changed how I felt about Eli Kay.

I lifted my chin as I reeled my shoulders. "A Hanti." It was what my parents created me for all along.

The ridiculous hunter took a look around the room, exhaling. What was she thinking about? It'd be simple to slip into her thoughts without the key.

But that had been what the nightmares were for.

I couldn't care less about what was on her infectious mind.

Little Hunter disappeared into the bathroom. The shower started, and I took my time stifling through her things. She carried little with her. Phone. Clothes. Dagger. Useless things. Things only hunters would carry around, implying they never stuck around for long.

They had body counts to raise. Blood to spill. Lives to steal. So, why did a hunter live here? Why a Kaofi's apartment? The questions piled on every second she stayed.

If I were lucky, she wouldn't stay much longer.

Somehow I'd get her out of my apartment. Somehow I'd remove the stench of such rotten morals.

I just needed to send her one more lasting trauma to make her *run.*

A scream came from behind the bathroom door and

glass shattered. I hurried over, although my movements felt smoother—much more like floating since the shadow side of me formed.

I pressed my ear to the door and heard the water shut off. Seconds after that, the smell of blood drifted under the door. And heavenly had been an understatement. Her blood had smelt more wonderful than any dead hunter I'd come across in my vampire days.

The knob turned and I flew back into the corner, blending with the gathering darkness.

Little Hunter emerged in her naked glory, walking right on by and out of the bedroom. When she returned with a broom, she cleaned the glass she'd made a mess of. "You really mess everything up, don't you?" I heard a snicker from her. "No wonder your parents didn't want you. You were a curse from the moment of conception."

Didn't want her? Her parents didn't want her? Useful information, depending on how I used it.

Curse could be figuratively or literally. I hoped for the latter. I'd be a hero for removing such a vile hunter from this earth. We strived for safety. And this hunter just so happened to be a sliver in our palms.

She dropped her towel the moment I peeked in the bathroom. Claw scratches—scars created by other shadows—marked her skin. Front and back. Up and down. Was I supposed to feel sorry for her? Quite the opposite, actually. I encouraged such destruction, such mutilation of her body. I had only wished I'd been the cause of so much ruin.

After leaving the bathroom with the light off, she ventured into my closet and emerged with my boxer briefs and a shirt. Every night that I saw her take what was mine, a little more resentment built up.

Just like that, Little Hunter was asleep in *my* bed.

Approaching, I plucked a nightmare from the air and pressed it into her head. "Let the bed bugs bite," I whispered into her ear.

Once it had been taken care of, I jumped through a few shadows, enroute to the void. Everywhere I turned, a new window popped up. The beast deep within me craved a little terror. Games—as he referred to them. Who would win and who would lose? Well, the answer had always been obvious. We won every round, and we never entered a battle we couldn't take victory over.

As I glanced back at the window to my bedroom, I studied the hunter who shot up from the blankets and pillows. Sweat drenched my clothes that she'd worn, causing her hairline to stick to her skin in sheets. She rubbed her eyes first, then she went for her phone.

Quickly slipping back into the window, I settled myself right in my favourite corner.

Her head lifted and she directed her gaze at me, pulling her blade from under the pillow. She must have seen me, in which case I couldn't hide now. If the nightmare didn't scare her, I would.

She squinted before getting up from the bed.

Not allowing her to gain the upper hand, I jumped from the shadows and tackled her onto the bed. I tore the dagger from her grasp and took comfort in pressing it against her neck. Lowering my head out of the dark, her heartbeat picked up pace and my name left her lips. "Eli."

How did she know my name? That answered my earlier questions. She hadn't just picked a random Kaofi to steal from. She had targeted me. My memories ceased to come forward, but regardless, I was certain she had been in my life and possibly been the cause of my demise. Everything made more sense that way.

Widened eyes. Shock painted her face. Like she hadn't expected me to still be alive. Fitting for her, maybe. I personally luxuriated in the cause of her misery, to wipe the satisfaction from her eyes. My purpose served in taking what made her feel the most secure.

Pressing the dagger into her skin, blood escaped as if it had been screaming to leave the poison that was her soul. But that blood… Oh how wonderful it smelt.

How wonderful it could taste.

Loosening my grip, I brought the weapon closer to my lips, eyeing it before licking along the blade. It'd been perfect. No blood had tasted as perfect as hers before. Alissa's had, or close to it, but not quite.

No. That had been a farce. I refused to believe such disgusting notions.

"Are you okay?" her voice cut through. She attempted to gulp down her fear. Rookie mistake. Mother taught me to always clean up after myself, and thus, I did just that by running my tongue over the wound and removing all traces of blood.

If I let her, she'd wreck me all over again like I was certain she'd done once before.

Not allowing her the time to retaliate, I returned to the smoke I'd become before dissipating altogether. She'd never gain leverage, and I wouldn't allow it.

She always lured me with it, too. Many nights I found her in the bathroom, harming herself in ways most should never do. But from the surprise tonight, it had been evident she never knew I was here with her.

Little Hunter hadn't done any of it to bait me. She'd done it because she'd been hurting, or she'd been a sadist deep down.

Either way, the message became clear. She didn't want me around and I'd reciprocate the feelings. However, I paid the bill and I'd be the one to stay. Stubborn she was. Begging for mercy she'd go out.

ALSO BY MONICA SHANTEL

THE FEATHERS AND FLAMES TRILOGY

Beauty of a Crimson Soul

Beauty of a Burning Flame

Beauty of a Persistent Love

THE TO BELIEVE DUOLOGY

To Believe in Peter Pan

To Believe in the Demon King

STANDALONES

Blissful

37 Nights

The Goddess in the Shadows

Acknowledgements

Thank you to Ashly for always helping me out with my stories when I need it most. Thank you to Taylor for listening to my endless ramblings and helping me brainstorm. Thanks to my mom who has always supported me in my career and never made me hide my dreams.

Thank you to my beta reader for pointing out the flaws and helping this book become the best version it could be..

ABOUT THE AUTHOR

Monica Shantel has always had an interest in artistic and creative hobbies of sorts, including but not limited to: drawing, crafting, graphic design, and painting. Although all she has is a high school diploma under her belt, she is not new to the writing community. At the age of twelve, she began building stories to escape reality and find hope in life once again. Her debut novel is Beauty of a Crimson Soul. Along the same genre, she writes dark tales of mythical romance which only add more to the growing fantasy worlds inside her head.

www.ingramcontent.com/pod-product-compliance
Lightning Source LLC
Chambersburg PA
CBHW020241030826
48979CB00030B/2477/J
* 9 7 8 1 9 6 0 6 9 6 0 5 2 *